MONET'S ANGELS

MONET'S ANGELS

Jennifer Pulling

RedDoor

Published by
RedDoor
www.reddoorpublishing.co.uk
© 2014 Jennifer Pulling

ISBN 978-0-9928520-5-4

A CIP catalogue record for this book is available from
the British Library

Cover design: Brown Media
Typesetting: typesetter.org.uk

 printed on FSC-certified paper

Printed in the UK by Knockout Print Services Ltd
(www.knockoutprint.co.uk)

To another house and garden a long time ago

– ONE –

ROBERT

He saw her before she saw him, indistinct in the smoky atmosphere, and somehow he knew it was the American girl. She was talking to a porter and, as he approached, she raised her voice to compete with the hissing steam.

'How much? How much?'

Robert stepped forward. 'Miss Judith Goldstein?' He lifted his cap. 'Robert Harrison.'

She whirled round, laughing with pleasure. 'Oh Mr Harrison, I'm so relieved to see you. When I got off the train there didn't seem to be anybody waiting for me. I thought perhaps... oh, I don't know... maybe there'd been some mistake about the day.'

'Hopeless places for rendezvous, railroad stations. You'd think they'd find a more twentieth century way of stoking trains,' he grinned.

The blue-smocked porter was hovering.

'What's all this about?' asked Robert, switching easily to the man's patois.

'They are big these baggage,' the man said. 'Very big.'

'That is not the point. There is a set rate, we all know that.'

1

'Well?' demanded the young woman.

'He's trying to get away with charging you extra.'

'Oh don't worry about the money,' she said. 'It wasn't that. It wasn't that at all, it was... well... I just couldn't understand him.'

Her voice was low and well modulated with just a hint of Yankee to it, he thought.

'Don't you fret. Now you're here, you'll be speaking French like a native in no time at all.'

Her dark eyes widened. 'But I do. I do speak French.'

He wanted to say, *yeah, but the French you probably learned in an expensive finishing school is nothing like that spoken in a provincial Normandy town* but instead he instructed the porter to bring the trunk and two travelling bags to the front of the station.

'And do be careful, they are Louis Vuitton,' she tried in her careful French.

Robert translated and the man grunted and pushed her luggage roughly onto his trolley, jostling it against other more modest items. Robert noticed a brown cardboard-looking case and thought how incongruous it seemed cheek by jowl with the trefoil-patterned trunk. The porter trundled his load towards the exit.

'Horrible little man, he hasn't taken the slightest bit of notice. My poor Vuitton.'

'You seem mighty fond of them,' Robert smiled. 'They'll be fine, I assure you.'

'Oh, I hope so. I really do.'

She turned to gaze at him and he was startled by her intensity, the inflection of her voice and expression in her eyes. He had a feeling that this defined her whether it was the fate of her baggage, her inability to make herself

2

understood by the porter or something far more profound. He was intrigued.

'You're staring, Mr Harrison,' she commented.

'I beg your pardon, Miss Goldstein.'

'No, I like people staring at me. In fact, it's one of the things I like most in the world. Is it my hair? This is the very latest cut, don't you know?'

Now that he had been given permission, he did stare. Her hair was bobbed to just below ear level and ended in soft waves. The colour was difficult to define as she wore a simple, narrow-brimmed hat but he judged it to be dark auburn.

'Or my clothes?'

'They are rather wonderful.'

'Guess you've never seen any like this before? Madame Chanel paid me a compliment, don't you know? She said I was just the kind of modern young woman to wear her designs. She hates the way the women dress on vacation and I so agree with her. All those furs and feathers, those silly hobble skirts, how could you dream of playing tennis in them?'

Robert did not remark that he had already seen the long V-necked sweater scandalously made in the same jersey used for men's underclothes. The fluid skirt had also made its appearance in Giverny. Several of the young ladies who dined at Hotel Baudy were discovering Coco's boutiques in Deauville and Biarritz. However, he had to admit they had rarely been worn with the flair of this young woman.

'I couldn't come to Europe and not do a shopping trip in Paris, now could I? I love her designs, don't you? So easy fitting, so delightful to move in.'

To demonstrate, she executed a few steps of the Turkey

3

Trot, hopping sideways with her feet apart, rising on the ball of her foot, then dropping onto the heel. It startled Robert. Vernon station had certainly never seen anything like this before.

'*Magnifique!*' a voice called out. A man wearing a wide-brimmed hat had stopped to watch her. Others joined him, which encouraged her to continue. She hummed some bars of the *Maple Leaf Rag*, raised her elbows in a birdy movement and made turkey-like flourishes with her feet. The appreciative males in her audience were urged away by their tutting companions.

'Disgusting exhibition,' Robert heard a woman in an enormous feathered hat mutter as she swept her husband away.

'Enough of that, young lady,' he called with mock seriousness. 'Come along, this way.'

Laughing, she followed him outside, into the heat of the June day. The sky was cobalt blue, the air sweet after the grey, smoky station. The lugubrious porter leaned against a wall, smoking. The precious Vuitton cargo was already stowed and the carter sat above his horse, waiting for instructions.

'Mademoiselle's baggage was very, very heavy,' the porter growled. 'Too heavy.' He indicated the possibility of a hernia.

'*Desolé*,' murmured Robert and slipped him a twenty franc note. The man brightened.

Judith was staring at the debonair automobile parked by the kerb; its red paint and brasswork gleamed in the sun.

'Swell, isn't it?' Robert said as casually as he could when it came to his pride and joy. 'De Dion-Bouton. Latest model.'

'Oh, Mr Harrison, a beautiful French automobile! I'm driving to Giverny in that? This is just *so* European.'

Her guileless enthusiasm was infectious but she was like a flame burning brightly, too brightly. The thought provoked a startling sense of familiarity and Robert shook his head to clear the unwanted memories.

'Oh come now, it's not that special. Nothing like the vehicles you must go about in in New York.'

'Thank God, it isn't,' she laughed. 'Thank God. I haven't come all this way to live the American life. I want to be completely and utterly French!'

Again he was amazed by her intensity; she seemed almost feverish. Her eyes glittered, her pale skin glowed as if candlelit from within. She looked boyish and yet tenderly female, young, yet knowing. He felt drawn to her but not at the level she might suppose. There was more a sense of connection between them: visitors from an urban New World in love with the light and colour of rural France.

'Well come on, Mr Harrison, what are we waiting for?' Her smile was flirtatious.

He saw her give a last glance at the carter bearing her precious Louis Vuitton away before she let him help her into the two-seater.

'Hang on to your hat,' he yelled into the breeze and they shot out of Vernon and started on the road to Giverny.

Robert had travelled this way so many times in the last twenty-odd years he had almost reached the point of not noticing his surroundings, his concentration set on pushing the V8 engine to its limits, revelling in the speed it could achieve. Almost but not quite: there were occasions when the gold and scarlet of a cornfield scattered with poppies made him yearn to paint it yet again. When snow fell, he would stop the automobile to sit and analyse Monet's technique for *The Magpie*, how the painter had traded his usual palette for icy colours of white, grey and violet. It was, he thought, more about perception than description, and might explain why the 1869 Paris Salon rejected it.

At his side, Judith kept up a running commentary, barely pausing for breath. 'Just look at that rolling landscape, the hedgerows, the lines of poplars. And there's the Seine, isn't it? Oh my God, I can't believe it. It's all so... so impressionist. How I've dreamed of it.'

Robert wondered what had brought her to Giverny. He was aware of her expensive scent, its notes of carnation, iris and vanilla, L'Heure Bleue, he guessed. A cross Atlantic voyage on the *Mauritania*, a Chanel wardrobe, not to mention a lengthy stay at Hotel Baudy must have cost a mint of money. He had read about the Goldstein family in Vogue. The old man was very rich. This girl was what... twenty-three... twenty-four? He would have thought she'd be married by now, not indulged by Papa to run around Europe. There had been speculation in the hotel dining room of the spoilt little rich girl to come amongst them.

'Curse that son of a gun who told her about this place. Which joker was that? Metcalf?' Thomas had demanded.

Robert shook his head. 'I don't think he's in Paris right now.'

'Well, whoever it was, he must have spun her a hell of a yarn. We're to be lumbered with her for three months. Madame Baudy told me.'

'I'll bet she'll be a little monster,' David had laughed. 'Make the most of it before she arrives.'

The wine jugs were passed round the table and everyone refilled their glasses.

Robert glanced across at her as the little car bowled along. She's nothing like that, he told himself, but there is something about her that is disturbing. This girl knows what she wants and she will go all out to get it. He felt a return of the unsettling sense of *déjà vu* and tried to push it from his mind.

The automobile made a smooth left turn.

'Giverny,' Robert said, the pride of ownership in his voice.

Judith let out a long gasp. 'My God, the roses, I've never seen so many and what are those others, those tall ones with the bright flowers?'

'Hollyhocks.'

'Hollyhocks, mmm,' she seemed to savour the word.

Robert saw through her eyes the arbours and covered walls, the flowerbeds, scarlet, cerise and deep cream. There were so many varieties from blowsy apricot roses to neat pink rosettes, swathes and garlands and cascades of them.

'Giverny is a village of roses,' he said. 'Everyone grows them here, they have all copied Monet. Mind you, it took them some time to come round to the idea. When he first arrived, they couldn't understand why he was growing flowers and not vegetables. At least you can eat cabbages. Then they realised there was something in it for them: having a successful man in their midst, even if he was a painter, meant there was work to be had.' They came to a halt outside Hotel Baudy. 'Now it's roses, roses all the way.'

The girl said quite innocently: 'Are you a cynic, Mr Harrison?'

'Do you even know what the word means?'

'Of course I do.'

'No, I'm not, not really, a realist I'd say.'

7

'Like Father.'

Robert laughed at this. 'I don't suppose I'm anything like your father, Miss Goldstein.' He leapt to the ground. 'So here we are then and here is Jacques with your precious baggage.'

She stepped down in a fluid movement of jersey cross cut skirt. If he were not so utterly attached, he told himself… He admired the way it enhanced her suppleness, her sportiness and approved.

While her baggage was being carried inside, Judith stood and stared at the building. 'It looks like a store, not a hotel at all.'

'It was a store,' he agreed. 'A grocery store until we Americans came along. The first guy was way back in 1886. He came here, knocking on the door and asked for lodgings. Madame Baudy sent him away; she said he looked more like a tramp than an artist. Obviously, she changed her mind and they have a fine old business here now.'

She stared at the patterned brickwork as if acquainting herself with Normandy architecture. Again he had this sense of her passionate attention to everything. 'It takes my breath away.'

Robert felt envious of her, of that first impact which can never be repeated. It is an innocent gaze, untainted by memories or comparisons, artless as a fool or baby. It is seeing when you don't yet understand, just the miracle of being alive.

One of his friends called his name. A group of them was sitting on the sun-dappled terrace, still in their tennis whites, glasses of cider on the table. He signalled that he would join them shortly.

His companion turned to look at them, 'Golly, are those the other painters?'

'They are indeed.'

'I must let you go.' She held out her hand in a gracious gesture. It felt small and warm. 'Thank you, Mr Harrison, you are very kind.'

Suddenly she looked tired, like a daisy he thought, surprising himself with this poetic image, ready to fold its petals for the night.

'You've had a long journey,' he said. 'Go and rest. Dinner's at eight-thirty.'

– TWO –

JUDITH

When the precious baggage had been safely negotiated up the narrow staircase and delivered to her room, Judith examined it for damage and was relieved to find it as pristine as when her father bought it for her in Macy's: the stout locks and corners had held fast. Then she took off her shoes and lay on top of the white cotton bedcover. She wanted to sleep but the moment she closed her eyes a string of images flickered through her mind: her first sight of France as the paddle steamer reached Dieppe, the unfamiliar countryside sliding past the train window, Robert Harrison's cheery smile… roses, roses, roses. When she looked at her little travel clock, it showed an hour had passed; she must have dozed off, after all. She wiped a sheet of *papier poudre* over her face, combed her hair and slipped on her shoes.

The dining room door stood half open and Judith peeped inside. The tables were laid with red-checked cloths, a cast iron stove crouched in the grate, unlit, of course and against the far wall there was an upright piano. At this moment the room was silent and empty but in another hour or so the diners would be arriving, that crowd of boisterous, laughing people she had glimpsed on the terrace. There was an ache in her temples; she could still sense the motion of the train. Did she really have to face them all tonight? Judith remembered there was a box of candies in one of her bags, she would go back to her room and make do with them. As she turned away, she collided with a plump, blonde woman who told her she was too early for dinner. This time Judith managed to make herself understood.

The woman patted her cheek. 'Of course, you are tired. You have come from far away. Go to your room and I will bring you a little something.'

Her kind words made Judith feel suddenly a long way from home, alone in a place where she could scarcely make herself understood. How would she ever manage? She blinked away tears.

'Ah *cherie*, don't cry,' the woman pulled her to her bosomy chest and hugged her. 'There is no need to cry. Tonight you sleep and tomorrow wake refreshed.'

Half an hour later there was a tap on the door and Angelina Baudy bustled in with a tray. As she lifted the lid of a terracotta tureen, a delicious scent wafted into the room.

'Onion soup,' explained the woman. 'I think that is sufficient for tonight.'

Judith smiled. Soup! Exactly what she needed. This was not chicken soup with barley, her mother's answer to all sorrows, but it would certainly do. The tureen was set on the table with a jug of wine and there were rolls wrapped in a red-checked napkin.

Madame Baudy filled an earthenware bowl. '*Bon appetit*,' she said and closed the door quietly behind her.

11

Judith took a sip of the savoury liquid, then another and realised how hungry she was. She ate greedily, breaking off chunks of the rolls, dipping them in the soup. A glass of the rough red wine and she was feeling steadily better. Soon she heard the scrape of chairs along the floor, the buzz of conversation from the dining room below. There was laughter, and then someone began to play the piano. She was glad she was up here, on her own. It was wonderfully peaceful, an evening breeze stirring the muslin curtains. Mr Harrison was kind but she had been thrown among strangers since she left New York, inundated by new experiences. Tonight, she needed to stay quiet, go over the events of the past weeks and plan her next move.

Mother hadn't wanted her to come at all. When that other ship, the *Titanic*, had gone down last year, she declared it a sign. Judith's passage was not yet booked, there had been a long delay in finding a chaperone who measured up to her mother's standards: physically strong enough to cope with Judith's energy, not too young but neither too old. Why not forget the whole idea? It was outlandish, anyway, to embark on such a trip when Judith should have her mind focused on her forthcoming marriage. Then Emily Whitaker's application had arrived, accompanied by excellent references. Her placid, round face gazed from the photograph, inspiring confidence. Father had announced the problem solved. Miss Whitaker would be waiting on the quay when the *Mauritania* docked in Southampton and would remain by Judith's side to accompany her on her European tour until the time came for her return home. He saw no reason why his daughter shouldn't have a lark before she embarked on marriage.

Mother was still not convinced. 'You indulge the child

12

too much, pandering to her whims,' Judith overheard her say. 'All this delay over setting the wedding date. If you're not careful the family will call the whole thing off.'

'Good,' Judith had murmured, 'I wish they would.'

'Don't be foolish,' Father had replied. 'Young man's head over heels. He'd never let them do that.'

Her mother sighed. 'Sometimes, Maurice, you are so naïve. There's far more at stake than just love and you know it.'

'Exactly,' he had replied. 'So isn't she entitled to some little reward?'

It wasn't that Judith didn't love Charlie; at least, she thought she did. She enjoyed the wooing, the theatres and dinners, seeing the expression on his face when she came into the room. It was the same as she had seen on Mr Harrison's at first sight of her this afternoon.

'You've inherited my magnetic quality,' her mother told her once. Her tone was grudging. 'It can get a girl into trouble. The sooner you're settled the better.'

But she did not want to get married, not yet. She was only twenty-five and there was so much still to do before she joined other young wives to talk about problems in finding an even-tempered cook, and a good nanny for the children. She had hardly dared hope Father would agree to this trip, not after all the other things he had allowed her to do. There had been the painting lessons, piano, learning to speak French, though much good that seemed to be doing her among these folks. Somehow she had managed to persuade him to send her to London and Paris but nobody, least of all herself, had calculated she would end up staying in a small Normandy village; one she would never have heard of if it hadn't been for Emily developing a sick headache.

13

The relief after she'd said goodbye and turned her back on Mother's tearful face, then seeing those tiny figures far below blur and disappear as the ship moved out into the open sea. Oh, that glorious feeling of escape.

Judith had a second bowl of soup, poured herself another glass of wine and gazed about the room. It seemed familiar already, its cleanliness, the simplicity of the rustic oak wardrobe and night table, a red and blue tufted mat on the wooden floor. And here I am, she told herself. Here I am in my very own room in Giverny and *he* is only a few yards away.

She went to the window and looked out over the garden. It seemed to be constructed on several levels, steps dimly glimpsed leading upward in the dusk. And there were roses again, masses of them, standards, clambering over arches and walls, ghostly in the fading light. It was all so new and different from home; mysterious what lay ahead of her, waiting to be discovered.

The notion came that all this was meant to be, beginning with that glorious afternoon when she had slipped out of the hotel to roam the streets of Paris alone, crossing the Seine with the voice of Emily in her ears: 'Not a very nice area, Miss Judith, it's full of artists and other down and outs.' Then the café where she'd ordered café au lait and smoked a cigarette, marvelling that nobody stared or appeared to think she was being too bold. There were other women seated in the café, though mostly in twos and threes, some of them also smoking cigarettes. They seemed very free and lively and she longed to join them. Then she caught the sound of American voices and glancing to a neighbouring table, saw a group of men deep in conversation. When one of them tried and failed to light his cigarette, she offered him her Ronson. Half an hour later, she was sharing their carafe of red wine. When she finally made her way back to the hotel it was almost eight o'clock.

'Oh, Miss Judith, I've been beside myself with worry. When I came downstairs in the afternoon no-one seemed to know where you were and as time went on...' Emily reached for her handkerchief. Her eyes were red; it was obvious she had been crying. 'I kept thinking about that horrible story I once read, *The Vanishing Lady*, you know where one of the women disappears and the hotel staff swear only the other is on the register.'

Judith took out her compact and was satisfied with what she saw. 'Well I am here now so everything is dandy.'

'But where on earth have you been, Miss Judith?'

'Oh, out and about, exploring this wonderful city.'

Emily's eyes widened. 'I can't believe you just wandered around Paris on your own – anything might have happened. And all because of my silly sick headache. I am so sorry.'

Judith was growing bored. 'Please stop apologising, Emily. Nobody was going to murder me in broad daylight and I had an extremely pleasant time. Now shall we go into dinner before the restaurant closes? I'm starving.'

A hearty serving of veal blanquette accompanied by asparagus and green beans, followed by apple tart seemed to restore Emily. She began to talk of their plans for the following day. 'The Louvre I thought and if there's time we might do the Cluny after luncheon.'

She popped a piece of bread into her mouth. Judith had noticed she never wasted a morsel of any food set before her. 'I'm just relieved that you are safe and we can put all this behind us.'

15

For Judith it had only just begun. Over the next few days, visiting this or that art gallery or museum, walking in the Tuileries Garden, her attention was elsewhere, trying to work out her next move. That conversation in the café with the American artists, their tales of Monet's Giverny and the hilarious life at Hotel Baudy had set her mind racing. She wanted to experience this place for herself. Who knew what might happen if she managed to get herself there? She had to meet the artists again and she had to dispense with Emily.

Somewhere from the depths of the garden a bird began its evening song. From a distance another answered it. She would not think of her time here being limited; in three months she must return to the life set up for her. Something would prevent it. That something was vague at the moment but promising. All would be well. She had got herself here; that had been the major hurdle, managed to wheedle more time and money from her father, why shouldn't the rest of her plan work out? She sat on the wide windowsill, sipping her wine, and let the essence of the June evening pervade her.

Below, the voices grew louder, the pianist was singing a song she recognised. Judith smiled wryly, recalling Charlie. He had taken her to see the show on Broadway not long before she left. Softly she sang along:

> *By the light of the silvery moon,*
> *I want to spoon, to my honey I'll croon love's tune,*
> *Honeymoon keep a-shining in June,*
> *Your silvery beams will bring love dreams,*
> *we'll be cuddling soon,*
> *By the silvery moon.*

16

She struggled to recall the feelings those words had evoked, seated close to Charlie in the darkened stalls, smelling the scent of his macassar hair oil. Already, it seemed a long time ago.

The pianist switched to a French tune Judith also knew. It was the Gaby Glide. Only last November she'd seen her idol dance at the Winter Garden. Wonderful Gaby Deslys! She'd learned the Turkey Trot because of her. Mother was, as always, disapproving of any of these new dances while Father just found her birdy movements comical.

She stayed at the window until the garden merged with the sky and night came then she slipped between the sheets. They smelled deliciously of lavender. The images were there but growing fainter now as sleep gained its hold. She dozed, woke to the sounds below, dozed and woke again. This time the voices and piano were silent; she heard the mournful hoot of an owl.

In the morning after breakfast, Judith sent a letter by the Baudy's boy servant to Le Pressoir.

– THREE –

CLAUDE

The darkness thins, grey light seeps into the room and the shapes of furniture swim up from oblivion: the marquetry desk, the chest of drawers. He is learning to perceive things from memory, knows by heart the subjects of the three paintings that hang on the wall: *Haystacks* by dear Blanche, *Gate Onto Flowering Cherry Trees* by Butler and *Camille on her Death Bed* painted by him.

He shuffles his feet into slippers, drawn, as always, to the window. Here he remains, watching as the sky lightens and changes colour from indigo to lavender to pink before that moment when first light brings another day. He prefers dawn and dusk to any other time and not only because of the shadowy effects of light. These are the hours when he shares his clouded vision with the rest of the world. The garden is coming to life under the sallow sun; soon it will appear to him as an explosion of colour, of orange, yellow and red hues bleeding into each other. He is barely able to discern the detail of trees and plants although he knows them intimately. Like children he has seen them grow into the mature garden it is today. In fact, rather than his eyes it is his mind that sees: a fusion of sensations and memories as if in retrospect, as if he were looking back on a visit to his beloved garden. This, he understands, is also what now drives his painting, memory traces of the paths, the shrubs and the lily pond coming to replace the ever more fragile images of his failing eye.

Cataract. In his head he hears Dr Coutela's voice. Aware of photography's influence on his patient he had likened the eye to a camera. 'Light rays focus through your lens onto the retina, the layer of light sensitive cells at the back of the eye. In a similar way to film, the retina allows the image to be "seen" by the brain. But, *mon vieux*, as we get older, chemical changes occur in the lens that make it cloudy and that prevents light rays from passing clearly through it. *Voila*, a cataract.'

They had viewed photography as a threat, he, Manet, Degas and the others. It captured the moment, seemed to undermine their painterly talent to mirror reality. People were talking about the 'truth' of the camera's eye. It was a challenge and he had taken it up: colour of course, which photography lacked and his perceptions of nature, rather than create exact images of the world. Set an artist beside him, even Blanche, and their expression of the lilies would be very different because their eye was different. This was what you were always trying to capture, to get under the carapace, reach the essence of the thing. He smiles to himself. You could say like cracking a lobster's claws to reach that delectable meat.

He is startled to notice how time has passed. Over these last months he seems to have spent hours in a meditative state. 'Never thought I'd get to this,' he mutters aloud. 'I was always up at the crack of dawn and out without a backward glance.' Suzanne and then Alice: losing them seems to be

19

tilting him into old age. Still he lingers, his thoughts turning to Blanche. How he weighs on her and how she puts up with him. He is sometimes amazed by her patience. The 'blue angel' Georges calls her; a bit of an exaggeration in his opinion. They have their moments, well, what can you expect when there are just the two of you, rattling around in this big house? But she is a good girl. What would he do without her? And it isn't going to get any easier, not with this business of his eyes. At least they agree on that: a cruel streak of nature to one whose life lies in the looking but…

'It's risky, Papa, at your age. Surgery might or might not help.'

They might bicker about Marguerite or rather the lack of her but on this point they are united. Even if he has to give up painting he would not hazard losing what sight he has and therefore not seeing his garden, the people he loves.

In his dressing room, he selects one of the summery white linen suits. *Dieu*, the belt of the trousers is tight! Alice's voice swims into his head: 'You're too fond of cream, Claude.' What's wrong with cream? Marguerite's banana ice cream, marriage of an exotic fruit and cream, was a Noel joy. Thick smooth cream from Normandy cows: he adores it. Palate or palette, someone once teased him, which comes first, Claude? All right, he enjoys his food: it is one of life's pleasures. Thank God that hasn't deserted him. He takes a deep breath and the button fastens. He doesn't often glance in the mirror these days, doesn't want to see an old man looking back.

He moves on to Alice's bedroom as he does every morning. 'Good morning, *cherie*,' he says to the bed with its white cover tightly tucked. As always, he pauses by the

20

fireplace to look at her photograph with Nadar's scrawl on the bottom. Nadar! Dear friend, crazy friend with his dream of flight and that ridiculous giant air balloon. Ah, but if it wasn't for him they'd never have had that first exhibition, so long ago. He'd been a good age but somehow you thought he would go on forever. He passes the silent children's rooms, treading carefully over the boards – a habit that clings – down the stairs and lets himself out into the garden.

Roses fill the air with their fragrance but he walks under their arches, making for the door at the end that leads to the other, now more important, area: the lily pond. No trains at this hour, simple to cross the stretch of tarmac and enter the water garden. Here he strolls among the arrowheads, marsh marigolds and agapanthus, pausing for long moments to admire this peony, that azalea, or simply gaze in the water, shaded by willow and poplar, continuing and then stopping again. The lilies or rather their reflection on the water absorb him, these days. They lead him into another world of mists and transparencies.

Some lines of poetry come into his head.

> *They are not long the days of wine and roses*
> *Out of a misty dream*
> *Our path emerges for a while, then closes*
> *Within a dream.*

Morbid type, Ernest Dowson, always writing about death. Drank but didn't eat. That time at the Café de Paris, he was hardly able to get a word out, and he, a poet. No wonder he'd died so young. Claude moves on but the words stay in his head and with sudden urgency he makes his way back to the house and his studio.

21

Here are his paints waiting for him with their labels in Blanche's neat handwriting. He just prays she's mentioned to that girl, Annette, not to lay a finger on them, never change their precise order. He absolutely relies on this. He knows he is using stronger shades of blue and green; that the reds are beginning to look muddy. Another symptom of cataract, Cautela said, something about the yellowing of the lens. Think of the days when a painter had to grind and mix his own colours. He'd be in a pickle then. His style is changing too from short to much broader brushstrokes, though still the pursuit of sunlight and colour, of impression or snapshot, as Nadar called it.

He takes up his brush. Venice this morning, the exhibition isn't far off, still something to be done to the gondola picture.

Alice was smiling in all the photographs of that trip, happy, she said, seeing him doing 'such beautiful things, something other than those same old water lilies.' He'd moved through the city to the sun's rhythm: early morning, San Giorgio Maggiore, at ten, St Mark's Square, facing San Giorgio. After lunch, the steps of the Palazzo Barbaro, painting the Palazzo da Mula. As the sun set they treated themselves to a gondola ride, but always at the back of his mind how to translate this beauty, express time stopped, an instant of light.

The painting isn't going well, he throws down his brush; it is almost half past eleven, after all. Time for luncheon.

– FOUR –

BLANCHE

In the kitchen Blanche gazed out of the window at a fine show of Reine des Violettes. Such a beautiful rose, it made her think of pastel crayons from pink to lilac and blue to deep magenta, smudged one over the other to achieve a delightful smoky effect. It was doing well this year, in spite of Papa complaining it had been over-pruned in March. It was all very well his saying it bloomed better if left alone but you simply could not allow it to grow unchecked. She wished she could be out there, burying her nose in those large rosettes, sniffing the damask scent.

For the past ten minutes, she had been discussing Yorkshire pudding with the new cook.

'It is unbelievable!' Marie exclaimed. 'This pudding served with meat! I don't understand.'

Reluctantly, Blanche tore her gaze from the garden and turned to face the woman.

'There is no need to understand. The English have a different view of food, I know. The only thing you do have to understand, Marie, is that m'sieur adores Yorkshire pudding. And when he adores something, it has to be prepared to perfection.'

Marie's dark hair had become loosened from its bun and hung round her face. She pounded her fist on the blue table. 'It will not rise. I beat and beat but it remains flat.'

'I believe it is not an easy dish. It took even Marguerite a long time to master it,' Blanche said soothingly.

'Marguerite, always this Marguerite!' She seized one of the copper pans as if it were a weapon. 'She must be a saint!'

'Not exactly…' Blanche remembered some of their former cook's muttered oaths as yet another attempt was sent back to the kitchen. '*Sacré bleu*,' was the least of them. There had been worse problems with Marguerite's attempts to recreate the tarte tatin. In the end, Papa had given up and they all piled into his beloved car and drove to the Hotel Tatin to consume his favourite dessert, '…but she got there, in the end.'

Marie snorted. 'Well!' She twitched at one of the gingham curtains, which hung perfectly straight. 'And then there is the question of the asparagus.'

'It was overcooked. You did fine the second time.'

'It is not good for the digestion to eat asparagus raw.'

'Not raw, Marie, he likes it very lightly done. You'll remember from now on.'

'Oh yes.' Marie wiped the perfectly clean table surface using large, angry movements. 'And as for all these… peppercorns, madame. A little too much, don't you think?'

'Yes, yes I know, he does use them rather a lot.'

'The duck, the salad – when does it not appear? Ah!' Her sarcasm returned. 'Summer pudding. I believe there are no peppercorns in that.'

'Oh, Marie. Please don't upset yourself any further,' Blanche pleaded.

She stared at the wall tiles, concentrating on the blue

against white, asking herself once again exactly how many there were. She mused on the change of design over the oven area, whose idea was that? Maman had pronounced the overall effect bizarre.

What if Marie handed in her notice? There would be all that interviewing again, the need to go through the dishes that delighted his palate, explain the precise way he liked them prepared. If only Marguerite were still here; it was so difficult to find anyone to measure to the esteem Papa had held for her. Blanche felt weary of all this responsibility.

'Have patience,' she pleaded. 'The old are difficult.' She had hit on something they could both agree upon.

Marie's tone changed. 'Yes, madame, my grandmother is the same. She drives my mother to distraction.'

'You see? We must both stay calm and collected.'

'I feel sorry for you,' grunted Marie and turned back to the oven to check on the fish.

Blanche felt relieved but time must be getting on. She took her watch from the breast pocket of her blouse. God, it was practically half-past eleven. There was going to be trouble. The staccato sound of a whistle sent her scurrying away, aware of Marie's pitying look.

Sunlight streamed into the dining room, the glass fronts of the cupboards reflected its beams, and the cutlery sparkled. Blanche thought, as she often did, it was a shame that, by some sleight of hand, the paintwork could not be changed for summer. You needed bright, light colours during a gloomy Normandy winter but she found all this yellow dazzled and confused her when the sun shone into the room.

'Here I am, Papa.'

He was standing with his back to her, examining one of

25

his prints but as she entered whirled round. 'Luncheon is late, Blanche.'

'It is on its way now.'

'Over five minutes late.'

'*Pardon*. I was speaking to Marie.'

He took his place at table and poured a glass of cider. 'Couldn't you have done it at a more convenient time?'

'It was she who broached it. She'd obviously been brooding over it for several days.'

'Brooding over what, Blanche? Can you be more precise?'

Oh dear, Blanche told the porcelain cat that viewed her from the dresser, he's been getting himself into a state about something this morning. But was it his painting or his eyes? He wouldn't tell her. They never discussed anything very serious over meals. Whatever it was making him anxious he would simply take out on her.

At that moment Annette rattled into the room with the trolley and she was spared discussing the Yorkshire pudding again. For a while they ate the salad.

'The green beans are good,' he broke the silence.

'Yes. Jules says there is a bumper crop.'

'So are the broad beans. But the lettuce…'

'Apparently they have suffered in this warm weather.'

He threw his fork down with a clatter. 'They need extra watering then.'

'Papa, of course they are watered but it is very hot. Personally, I am enjoying the summer.'

'You wouldn't if you were a lettuce,' he remarked dryly and they caught each other's eye and burst out laughing.

He resumed eating then halted again. 'There is not enough peppercorn.'

Blanche's eye returned to the porcelain cat, it seemed to

26

gaze at her scornfully. Peppercorns again! She dreaded Marie's reaction if the salad was sent back to the kitchen.

'Didn't you tell the woman?'

'Please be lenient. She's only been with us a fortnight. We don't want to lose her, do we?'

There were days when she found it particularly difficult to cope with his irritability. This was one of them. Early this morning, she had dreamt of her mother, seen her sitting in the garden wearing a white dress, and woken with a dreadful sense of yearning. Thank heaven they were over Papa's initial collapse, those weeks he had scarcely spoken or eaten but just mooned about reading Maman's letters. At least he was back to painting again, although he never seemed satisfied with the results these days; then there was the continuing anxiety about his sight. She had done her best to support him but it left her little space for her own mourning. In the dream, her mother was reading a book but looked up as Blanche approached her and smiled. The image had lingered with her and she had little appetite for the fish.

If only there were someone else to share the burden. Yesterday, she had walked up the road with some roses to lay on the family vault. She saw several other bouquets on the white marble, some of them simple posies of wild flowers; the poppies Maman loved. The warm evening air intensified the scent of the roses and she hesitated, bringing them to her nose before setting them against the latest inscription. How did you cope with him, she asked her mother. All that business over the Japanese bridge, the trips to Lyon for yet more horticultural specimens – you used to say he loved the gardens more than you. You ordered your life around him but why must I sacrifice mine? She had entered the church and prayed to its patron saint: 'Radegonde, take some of this weight off my shoulders. It's too much to bear alone.'

'Blanche?'

She realised he was offering her plum brandy and shaking herself from her reverie, accepted a glass, sniffed the rich aroma and took a sip. The trolley came rattling in once more: Marie had made a passable peach ice cream. Maybe she had peeped into one of the cooking journals. Blanche watched him spoon it eagerly into his mouth and thought how frail he was looking.

He glanced up and met her gaze. 'You are always so good and I must be irritating to everyone.'

The remark made her feel guilty about her earlier impatience, on the other hand, why did she feel she must apologise for her feelings? Was there always this conflict of emotions when you cared for an elderly relative? The compassion, the anger, the jealousy of sisters who were wives and mothers and somehow exempt? His visitors did not see his surly and difficult side; only Georges realised what she had to bear. She reached in the pocket of her skirt for a handkerchief and felt the letter. She drew it out and laid it on the table.

'Papa, I forgot this, it came this morning. Baudy's boy brought it.'

He helped himself to more ice cream. 'Not another one.'

'Shall I read it for you?'

Taking his silence for agreement she unfolded the sheet of paper. The writing reminded her of past calligraphy lessons: an educated hand. She read:

Dear M. Monet,

I am a great admirer of your work and am writing to ask if you would allow me to come to see you. I have just arrived from America and am lodging at Hotel Baudy. I should be much obliged if you could send word of when it would be convenient to call on you.

> Yours sincerely,
> Judith Goldstein

He reached out for the bottle. 'Another wretched American! Hasn't someone told her I need to be left alone to paint?'

'You never used to think that way. We had such fun in the past,' Blanche said. 'Remember those wonderful meals at Hotel Baudy?' Remember John Leslie, she thought. 'It would take you out of yourself to see a new face.'

'I have no time, Blanche. You know how it is.'

'And what of me, do you never imagine I might enjoy company?'

He had lit a cigarette, narrowed his eyes against the smoke. 'You have friends in the village.'

And when did she ever have the time to see them? Blanche felt she could scream with frustration. He put his painting before everything else, what about hers? All those years she had spent working on her technique… She eyed him over the rim of her coffee cup. There was a time when people mistook her work for his.

He picked up the letter and stuffed it back in its envelope. He brought it so close it almost touched his nose, sighed and ran his hands over his face. Her anger dissolved into pity. She knew his fear of following in Degas' footsteps. Since the turn of the century, they had both noticed the coarsening of that painter's once precise detail, the blurring of his careful shading, the lessening of attention to the folds of ballet costumes and towels.

'Papa, are you using the drops?'

'Of course.'

Blanche refilled his cup. 'And they're still helping?'

'I'm not sure. Perhaps I should go to Paris again.'

'Is that necessary?'

'I probably need to have some more tests.' Abruptly, he pushed back his chair. 'Now I must get back to work.'

Blanche remained to savour the last of her coffee. She counted the chairs round the table: ten, fourteen including those that stood against the walls. She looked back over the years spent in Giverny, remembering the time when this room rang with the family's voices and laughter. The table would be adorned with bright floral arrangements from the gardens, set with Monet's yellow and blue Limoges. She seemed to hear Suzanne's chiding as he carefully decanted the Veuve Clicquot. Now the Limoges was imprisoned behind the glass-fronted cupboards and there were only two place settings, Marguerite's lavish menus a thing of the past. The Japanese prints gazed out at the silent room. The geishas' self absorption and devotion to the pleasures of life seemed to mock her. It was hard not to feel bitter about what had happened to her life and her art.

1888

That afternoon she escaped the relentless watering duties in the garden and walked through the fields of golden yellow wheat with Suzanne.

It was her sister's idea. 'Oh come on Blanche I think I'll go mad if I don't get away from all those plants for a while.'

Suzanne stood on a hillock, tall and slender, her pale dress ruffled by the wind. She held a parasol and looked as if she were posing for the picture Monet had painted of her, two years before. 'Isn't this far better on such a lovely day?'

Of course it was but guilt came into it. As a rule she never let him down. 'He'll be furious if the lawn gets parched,' she said.

But Suzanne only laughed at her. 'You're far too much the dutiful daughter, Blanche. All these years of trailing after him like a little packhorse: life is to be enjoyed, not spent stuck in front of an easel all the time. I can't wait to get married and have a husband who takes care of all the boring things.' She looked so pretty, her skin lightly flushed, her eyes sparkling with mischief. 'I'd just like to stay up here and laze in the sun and not go home for dinner.'

'You know we can't do that,' Blanche scolded. 'Monet would be furious.'

'There you go again! So serious! He has you round his little finger.'

It was half-past five before they made their way back through the village. They had almost reached home when they heard laughter and voices speaking in English, which seemed to come from the garden of a pink washed house. As they peered over the wall, they glimpsed a tableau against a setting of green grass: a table spread with a lacy cloth on which were set tea things and a cake stand. Seated round the table were an older woman in a lemon summer frock and two young men who looked strikingly alike.

'Now, now John Leslie, we won't indulge you any more today,' they heard the woman say.

Suzanne whispered, 'I think they are some of those Americans.'

So these were the people Monet grumbled about, saying they were ruining the peace of Giverny; he had warned the girls to

31

have nothing to do with them, even threatened to move away. How clean they are, Blanche thought, and then wondered at her choice of such a word. But it was true, they were, clean and fresh in their light coloured clothes, also their voices, which were quick and merry, filled with laughter. Spotlighted by the sun, they seemed to symbolise another, much younger world. She was charmed.

The young man who had been addressed as John Leslie left the table and began to wander round the garden, stopping now and then to admire this plant, that flower. She felt her heart beat faster as he approached where they were standing. Then she gasped as they saw him peering through foliage like the face of a young Pan. Their eyes met and he whistled and said: 'Holy mackerel! What have we here?'

Suzanne giggled. 'Good afternoon.'

Blanche took command. '*Pardon*. It was very rude of us to spy on you.'

But the young man was opening the garden gate. 'Come in,' he said. 'Come in and get acquainted.'

When they hesitated he smiled, showing even white teeth. 'I won't bite, you know.'

Suzanne had already slipped inside so Blanche had no choice but to follow. By this time, the two seated at the table had noticed what was going on.

John Leslie led them over. 'Just look what I found!' he laughed.

'Shall we be properly introduced?' The woman, who was as tall as Suzanne, rose and held out her hand. 'I'm Mrs Breck and these two scoundrels are my sons, John Leslie and Edward.'

To Blanche's surprise, the men clicked their heels and bowed their heads.

Mrs Breck sighed. 'That's what comes of sending them to study in Germany. They have become perfectly Teutonic.'

32

Blanche caught John Leslie's eye and blushed. He looked so fine in his open-necked white shirt, an exotic species it seemed, in contrast with her noisy brothers. There was something about his gaze, an intentness as if he noted everything with particularity. She was the current focus of it and felt the colour rise into her face. Gazing down at her fingernails, she heard Suzanne make the introduction.

'And do you live around here?'

Suzanne twirled her parasol. 'Certainly we do, at Le Pressoir.'

There was a pause.

"But isn't that the home of Monet?'

Suzanne hesitated.

'Our mother is married to him,' Blanche lied. There was no need, she thought, to explain the exact position of Maman.

'Oh my dears!' said Mrs Breck. 'You have no idea how much we would like to meet him, John especially, of course. He's the painter in the family, you see.'

John Leslie took his disconcerting gaze away from Blanche and turned to Suzanne.

'Could you arrange that, ma'mselle?'

'I don't think so,' Blanche broke in. 'You see for Monet, the world ends at his garden gate. He does not admit just anyone beyond it.'

'Maybe he doesn't like Americans?' The mother suggested.

'It is not so much that, although he does find their presence disturbing. Ever since we arrived here, four years ago, the local people have put obstacles in our way. Once when we were boating and had tied up for a picnic they cut the mooring rope.'

'But why should these people behave like that? It seems mighty unfriendly.'

'They don't consider painting an appropriate occupation for a man.'

33

The Breck family found this very amusing. If that was the case why were so many Americans studying in Paris? The city was swarming with them.

'It is different there; Giverny is an agricultural village. People farm, they grow vegetables not flowers. You cannot eat flowers.'

The mention of flowers conjured a picture of Monet emerging from his studio into the garden to find no watering being done. 'It's time we went,' she said. 'Come along, Suzanne.'

Her sister was obviously fascinated by these people. 'Oh must we?'

'You must call again,' Mrs Breck urged.

'Oh yes do, please,' John Leslie added. He saw them to the gate. 'Until the next time,' he said, keeping his eyes on Blanche's face.

'Well, well,' murmured Suzanne as they walked away. 'He's certainly taken to you.'

'Don't be such an idiot,' Blanche frowned. 'Americans are obviously less formal than we are. He was just being friendly.' But she had a sense of unease about the encounter as if it had not been quite the thing. 'All the same, it's best we don't mention it to Monet.'

– FIVE –

JUDITH

Another clear blue day. Hot sun but a touch of sultriness in the air and no hint of a breeze. Judith sat under the trees on the hotel terrace, sipping lemonade. The afternoon drowsed about her, serene but for the soft thwack of tennis balls, the occasional cry of triumph or dismay from the courts below. It made her want to jump up and do something, anything rather than endure the sense of frustration she felt. She drummed her fingers on the table, sighed and turned her mind onto herself.

She imagined if a painter saw her now he would think what a charming picture she made, the sun coming through the leaves, dappling her new sailor blouse and plain straw hat. She just loved this *garçon* look, especially as it went right against Mother's opulent dressing, all that silk and furs. Whatever Charlie said, and he could be awfully old fashioned, she intended to carry on in the same style over there. That was of course unless a way opened up for her to stay here, which somehow depended on meeting *him*. Now she was back to the nagging anxiety, the lack of power to do anything while her first and then her second letter remained unanswered.

35

A smatter of applause from the courts and, a few moments later, Robert appeared, smiling as he came along the terrace to join her. His face glowed and he looked tired but triumphant as he sank into the opposite seat. Judith felt immediately soothed by his presence. It was only a few days ago he had collected her from the railroad station but already he was an important part of her life here. He understood her sense of not belonging in New York society, the quest for a life that was unbound by social conventions and what other people thought of you. It was all so delightfully bohemian in Giverny; they were already on first name terms.

'You can be yourself here,' he'd told her. 'You don't have to pretend any more.'

She could not make out what he thought of her, whether he found her attractive. He certainly made a point of sitting next to her at dinner and, that morning, had invited her to come to the studio to watch him paint. She didn't mind that he scarcely spoke about himself but seemed content to listen to her, as she talked about London and Paris, the seventy-eight George Apperley watercolours she had seen at the Walker Gallery, the Lady and the Unicorn tapestries at the Cluny, of course, and the hours she had spent in couturier houses. She loved his attention and compliments, his open admiration of how she had engineered her stay in Giverny.

'And all on the strength of what Dodgson told you? That man is always fooling around.'

'He was just so enthusiastic about life here, how free and easy it all was. And when I told him how tired I was of trailing around with Emily he perfectly understood and said he knew you folks would welcome me with open arms.'

Robert had sighed. 'Good old Dodgson, setting the cat among the pigeons.'

What did he mean by that, she wanted to know?

'Nothing, carry on with the story.'

'Well, the thing was I had to rid myself of Emily.'

'Exactly. How did you?'

'I tell you, this was destined, I really believe that, Robert. I was meant to come here.'

Judith recalled how a few days after her conversation with Mr Dodgson she had come across Emily, head bent over a book, weeping quietly. Questioned, she had explained she had left behind a sick mother but had had no alternative, as they needed the money.

'Let me finish,' Robert had interrupted. 'You paid her off and went along with Dodgson's charming suggestion?'

'Something like that. I told her there was no question but that she should be with her mother. I would give her her wages and something more besides. When she asked what I would do, I told her I knew an old schoolfriend of my mother's who lived in a little Normandy village where I should be perfectly safe.'

Robert had raised an eyebrow at this. Judith went on to tell him how she had telegrammed her parents suggesting that, as she had found London and Paris quite tiring and in view of the forthcoming wedding, a relaxing stay in Giverny was just what she required.

There was a pause while he lit a cigarette and appeared to ponder. 'There is one thing that still foxes me: why you found it so appealing to come here. Surely, it must seem like a bit of a backwater to a girl like you.'

'It's where Monet lives,' she had replied.

'And so?'

'I'm not entirely sure but somehow I think Monet holds the key.'

'Key?'

'To my destiny, of course.'

'Hey, that's a bit of a tall order.'

Judith had shrugged, 'It's just a feeling I have.'

They were quiet for a while before Robert spoke again.

'So what's wrong with the little lady, this afternoon?' He was teasing her now. 'You look as if the weight of the whole world is laid on your pretty shoulders.'

She shrugged.

'That's a stylish blouse you're wearing.'

'Thank you.'

'Chanel, I guess.'

'Yes.'

He poured himself a glass of lemonade, lit a cigarette and leaned back in his seat. He glanced up at the leaves above their heads and gave a contented sigh. 'Mmm, what a glorious afternoon. The roses are blooming, the bees are humming and we just beat Gervase and Thomas by three sets. Harry was on top form. What more can you want?'

She had noticed that he often spoke of his tennis partner. Harry was quite a bit younger than he, tall and blond with cornflower-blue eyes. They were often in the studio, painting together. She was somehow reminded of uncle Simon who always brought a young man called Gerald to her mother's dinner parties. 'That pretty boy,' Father called Gerald and her mother would say, 'Please, Maurice, they're just friends,' which made him laugh.

'You're right,' Judith said. 'It is lovely and I'm happy to be here but…'

'But?'

She sniffed. 'I don't know what I'm going to do.' Her sudden change of mood startled him.

'Hey, hey, no need to cry.'

She fumbled for a handkerchief and Robert handed over his. It was large and white, smelling of the same lavender scent as her sheets.

'Now come on,' he said. 'A big blow.'

She obeyed, dabbed at her eyes.

'I guess you didn't get a reply.'

'I'm desperate, Robert. He must get back to me, he must. If he doesn't I think I'll die.'

Robert seemed to find this amusing.

'I mean it.'

She gazed at her hands screwing the handkerchief as if it were a rag. At the same time she was aware of how sweet and innocent she must look, her eyes shining with tears. 'To be here almost on his doorstep and not able to see him…'

She realised his attention had been distracted. He was waving to someone, pointing to his watch, a Cartier model she recognised because Charlie had one, and then holding up six fingers. She turned to see the person was Harry who averted his head and went into the hotel.

'I beg your pardon, Judith, you were saying?'

'He just ignores my letters. Oh, what can I do, Robert? I might as well throw myself in the Seine.'

'I told you it wasn't going to be easy, Judith.' Robert's tone was patient. 'He almost never sees people, these days, especially us Americans. He just shuts himself up in Le Pressoir and paints.'

She tossed the handkerchief on the table. 'But I'm not people, I'm me. I shall send another letter, I'll just go on sending letters until…'

'Whoa. Whoa! You're a very stubborn young lady, I have to say. But that isn't the way to go about it, he can be just as stubborn unless it's something he wants to do himself.'

There was a pause. She took her compact from her bag and inspected her face, put it away again and still he was silent. He didn't really care, no-one here cared, they were just too busy playing tennis, eating and drinking and, of course, talking endlessly about art. She gazed at the half empty jug on the table, the sweep of countryside beyond the terrace. It suddenly felt pointless being here.

But now Robert was smiling. 'Hmm, yes, I think I have an idea. Listen to this...'

Dinner that evening was once again a noisy affair, they were celebrating Thomas's sale of his Normandy Landscape to Monet's art dealer Durand-Riel and the wine jugs emptied rapidly. Madame Baudy had risen to the occasion and prepared a splendid coq au vin. Judith passed her plate for a second helping and nodded to Robert as he poised a jug above her glass.

'Feeling better?' he murmured.

'Oh yes! It's a swell idea.'

'We'll take a stroll in the garden later and discuss it properly.'

'Marvellous.'

They had had to cut their conversation short when Robert realised it was time to catch up with Harry. Judith ordered a cocktail and lingered on the terrace a while longer, she watched the shadows lengthen across the tennis courts, relaxed now and confident the meeting would occur. Later she had spent an hour in her room doing her nails and dressing for dinner. She hung up the sailor blouse, deserting Chanel who had not seemed to offer much in the way of evening frocks and put on a Fortuny. She loved these Delphos models of his, the long clinging sheath that rippled with subtle watery shades, the feel of fine silk against her skin. She gazed at her reflection in the cheval mirror, admired the effect of pale skin and dark hair. What would be the effect on Robert, she'd wondered.

'Pretty dress,' he had said and Harry on his other side agreed but that was all.

Now she sat among the group of noisy diners, silent herself, content to savour Robert's plan. She sipped her wine and gazed at the paintings round the walls, a still life of fruit and flowers, two women in a garden, a poppy field. Most of them as Robert had told her, were accepted by Angelina Baudy in lieu of payment for board and lodgings. They were discussing the painter, Pissarro and she listened eagerly.

'They'd known each other a long time before that, of course,' Thomas was saying. 'They met at the Quai des Orfèvres when he and Monet were studying at the Academie Suisse. He soon turned his back on the traditionalists, far more interested in the way scenes and objects imprint themselves on the mind.'

Robert took it up. 'Particularly conditions of light: Pissarro considered light as inseparable from the things it illuminates. I find it amazing that those paint strokes of his took him beyond just seeing into the realm of emotion.'

'It's comic how the term "impressionist" came about though, isn't it?' said Harry, 'As a criticism of their work.'

'Well, it foxed the Salon, didn't it? They'd been so used to technical detail and photographic accuracy, they simply thought this technique was childish. He had a hard time convincing anybody.'

'He certainly had a profound effect on Monet.'

The wine jug was poised again and she nodded. She was intent on absorbing all this information, committing it to memory; it would come in very useful for what she had in mind.

Richard, the pianist, carried his glass over and played *Silvery Moon* again. Judith went to stand beside him and sang the words; she was feeling pleasantly tipsy.

'I hear you're a swell dancer,' he spoke above the music.

'Who told you that?'

'Robert. He said you entertained the whole of Vernon railroad station with the Turkey Trot.'

'Well, yes, I did.'

'Why don't you give us a demonstration now?'

As he changed the tune to ragtime, Robert rose from the table and came over to them.

'Not now, young lady, we're taking a stroll in the garden, remember?'

Outside, the air was still balmy though pleasantly cooler after the scorching day. They took a small flight of steps that led to the second level of the garden and strolled along paths edged with the ghostly blossom of roses. She could smell their scent, faint and sweet on the night air. Below them the lights were still on in the dining room, the pianist played and sang:

> *Come into the garden, Maud,*
> *For the black bat, night, has flown,*
> *Come into the garden, Maud,*
> *I am here at the gate alone;*

She felt overwhelmed by it all: the shadowy garden,

Robert's presence beside her, the moon silvering the foliage. It seemed impossibly romantic.

'It was fascinating what you said about Pissarro.'

'He was a wonderful man, generous with his gift. But it's their personal lives that really interest me, his relationship with Monet. When you see that wonderful house and the gardens, the fame he has today, it's difficult to imagine how the great man struggled in the early days.'

'Tell me about it.'

'Well for a start, he kept being refused by the Paris Salon when Pissarro and some of the others were accepted. At one time, he hadn't a sou. He was living with this young model, Camille, and they had a hard time of it. Pissarro and another artist, Bazille, kept them going.'

'How romantic.'

'If you call not paying the bills and not being able to afford to eat romantic then I would agree with you. Our friend Monet took it badly and as for Camille, she had to go without the fashionable clothes she loved. There's a marvellous painting of her. She's wearing a green and black striped gown and fur-trimmed jacket all set off by a little feathered hat. The pose is inspired. She has her back to us but her face turned in profile, her hand is raised to adjust the tie of her hat. We wonder what she is doing. Leaving? She was a young, local girl but in that painting he's transformed her into an elegant, mysterious Parisienne.'

'She sounds like a girl after my own heart. What happened to her?'

'She died.'

They went up another level, passed thick shrubbery, retraced their steps and came to a wooden seat.

'Let's sit here,' Robert suggested.

Once again they were enveloped in the scent of roses from the arbour above their heads. The pianist sang.

> *There has fallen a splendid tear*
> *From the passion-flower at the gate.*
> *She is coming, my dove, my dear;*
> *She is coming, my life, my fate.*
> *The red rose cries, 'She is near, she is near;'*
> *And the white rose weeps, 'She is late;'*
> *The larkspur listens, 'I hear, I hear;'*
> *And the lily whispers, 'I wait.'*

She felt like the heroine of a Henry James novel, one of his heiresses come to Europe. Maybe Robert would fall in love with her and the problem be solved; she could stay on in Giverny.

'You look like a moth in this light,' he was saying. 'A beautiful, exotic moth.'

'Why, thank you.'

'It's a wonderful dress,' he continued. 'I was looking at it earlier; the effect of the colours is extraordinary. I'd love to try to paint them.'

'Maybe you'd like to paint me.'

'Maybe,' he said and changed the subject. 'As I said to you, this afternoon, it will be my birthday in ten days' time and I thought… do you know Renoir's *Luncheon of the Boating Party?*'

'No.' She wasn't going to admit she had once spent ten minutes gazing at it in the Phillips Collection museum. She was just disappointed he had switched his attention from her.

'It is a wonderful work of art, beautiful young people

enjoying a day by the river. You can almost hear the voices, the jokes and the laughter. It's such a happy painting, the way the light shines through the awning, the rich colours, the texture…'

She sighed in her breath and Robert paused.

'Sorry, it is such a marvellous painting, you could discuss it for ages but I'll get to the point. The luncheon in the picture took place at the Maison Fournaise, a restaurant by the river. In the seventies and eighties, most of the major impressionists went there and painted nearby, including Claude Monet. He could have been one of the people in the picture. Now, if we create a magnificent picnic luncheon by the Seine in memory of those happy summer days, I'm hopeful Blanche will be able to persuade the old man to come.'

'Who's Blanche?' Judith was alarmed. 'I thought his wife was dead.'

'She's his stepdaughter but as she married his son she is also his daughter-in-law. When I first knew her she was a good painter but I understand she's given it all up and just looks after Monet.'

'How sad.'

'The French have a very strong sense of values, of family loyalty, respect for hard work and financial security. Blanche would have thought it her duty to care for him.'

Judith found this turn in the conversation dull and boring. 'So, what about this picnic?' she said. 'Do you think it will work?'

'We can but try.'

– SIX –

CLAUDE

It is approaching the blue hour, that time between sunset and nightfall when everything seems to be azure tinged. He has longed for this moment, the day too bright, everything seeming too focused, exposed and raw has worn him down. At luncheon, they had been tetchy with each other, like an old married couple. Blanche said the yellow dining room disturbed her, took her appetite away. He complained about Marie's cooking, compared it with Marguerite's, the way she'd had with lobster. They were both feeling the heat.

'You'd better speak to that girl again. I'll swear she moves the paints around on purpose. I'd started with the wrong colour before I realised.'

'You're imagining things, Papa. There is no reason why she should do that.'

'If you only knew what it is like to rely on labels when you paint; I never thought I'd reach that point.'

Usually she would have commiserated, congratulated him for carrying on in spite of his disability but today Blanche merely remarked that at least he had the time and the opportunity to paint. He hadn't known what to say to that and then there was too much peppercorn in the salad.

'Impossible!' Blanche had sighed. 'You can never have too much.'

Now she has gone to the churchyard with flowers once again and he is in his garden. He ambles up and down the straight paths between the flowerbeds, pausing to examine a particular flower that catches his attention, a geranium, salvia, a drift of nepeta and, of course, the misty colours of the Reine des Violettes, that Blanche had remarked on the other day. The evening is bringing out the scents of honeysuckle, the white flowered Graham Thomas, jasmine, and nicotiana, whose fragrance will soon draw moths. As usual, he ends up in the water garden and here he stands on the bridge, gazing down at the reflection of wisteria in the green water. He is remembering when the family first came here, all those years ago, the chain of events that brought him to Giverny: Camille's illness, the birth of their second son, Michel, the household chez Hoschedé, then Alice helping him with the boys after their mother's death. Above all, he recalls the joy of making this house and gardens a work of art. He speaks aloud: 'Remember that afternoon when I had you sitting so long for that painting, *cherie*? You were always restless, scolding me that there were things to be done. "Alice, please, just a few more minutes," I said and you looked up at me and smiled and I felt so much love for you. But you were alarmed about this bridge, weren't you? You said, "you're not going to paint it red are you, Claude?"' He chuckles at the memory.

'M'sieur?'

He starts, dragged back to the present, embarrassed that

47

Breuil has heard him talking to himself again. Old man getting a bit soft in the head, he can imagine him thinking.

'What is it?' he snaps.

'Excuse me, but there has been a delivery from Belgium, the plant you have been waiting for and I thought...'

'The erythrochaete?'

'Yes, m'sieur.'

'Where is it then?'

'In the greenhouse.'

'What are we waiting for?'

'*Pardon*, is it all right with you if Michel comes with us? He is keen to learn.'

He notices the young man standing behind Breuil, dark eyes meet his, then shy away. Something about his stockiness, the way his hair grows reminds him of his dead son at that age, and impulsively he puts aside the notion that he wanted his first sight of the new orchid to be shared only with his head gardener.

'Certainly.'

In the greenhouse there is silence while Breuil unfurls the cocooned plant and hands it to him to examine. For Claude, this moment of encountering a specimen is akin to seeing a newborn child, the same emotions of wonder and respect. A moment later and he has become the botanist.

'Come here, Michel, let me show you. This is the red tufted Dracula as it is commonly called, the scientific name derives from the Latin, little dragon. It refers to the shape of the flower which some think resembles a small monster face.'

Michel gives a nervous giggle, which he quickly stifles.

Claude searches in his mind for what he has read about this variety among his library of horticultural books. 'They have no pseudo bulbs, that is the thickened part of the stem that lies above ground as with many other orchids, and they grow by sending out rhizomes to make thick clusters.'

Aware this is probably going over Michel's head – the boy's been here only a few weeks – he suddenly turns on him. 'What is your family name, young man?'

'Duval, m'sieur.'

'Louis Duval? The farming family? Huh! I've crossed swords with him in the past. All that business over the water lily pond: poisonous plants, I ask you! And you have escaped. What do they think of you, then, tending flowers and shrubs? They look beautiful, smell wonderful, yes, but cannot be eaten.'

'They are not happy, m'sieur, but I have always loved gardening.'

Michel turns his hands palm upward as if to demonstrate his capacity for this work. They are big, square hands, the hands of a Normandy peasant. They please Claude; he has never been afraid of getting his own hands dirty. When even the thickest brush won't achieve his desired effect, he daubs with his fingers. This young man might have the makings of a good gardener.

'Have you indeed? Then tell me which is your favourite flower?'

'Roses.'

'Roses. Well, there are rather a lot in Giverny. It would be hard not to like them, not very original, try again.'

Michel shifts his feet. 'Er... iris.'

'Ah ha! Iris was a Greek goddess, messenger of love, did you know that? The word iris means a rainbow and you certainly find them in many different shades. Yes, and in the language of flowers iris symbolises eloquence.'

49

'Well,' says the head gardener. 'You learn something new, every day.'

Michel reddens.

'Now we've embarrassed the young man, but I like your choice, I share it with you. I've painted them many times, haven't I, Breuil?'

'Yes, m'sieur.'

'And the water lilies, of course.'

He thinks about the two small boats moored on the edge of the pond and the numerous times he and Breuil circulate the lilies, checking their state, making sure they are pristine. If there is a speck of soot from the passing trains, he cannot paint them. He remembers Alice reporting to him something the gardener had said: 'He's painted them once, I don't understand why he has to keep on doing it. And when he's finished, they don't even look like lilies, just a blur in my view.' He is aware that the other's admiration is not for his art but his knowledge of flowers and shrubs, his creation of the gardens.

'How long have you been with us, Michel?'

'Six weeks, m'sieur.'

'And how old are you?'

'Twenty-three, m'sieur.'

'I moved here before you were even born, spotted it on my way to Vernon and knew it was for me. At the beginning, the whole family worked here. I used to dig the ground, plant and hoe up the weeds myself. And at night, the children would water the plants. As the money started to come in, I kept on extending the garden, eh, Breuil?'

'That's right, m'sieur. When was it you built this greenhouse, early nineties?'

'I was becoming famous, you see, young man, I could afford it and the gardeners, of course, seven of them.'

He catches Michel's glance going to Breuil and can well imagine what the older man is thinking: silly old fool, I've heard all this before. He doesn't care, he enjoys the retelling too much; it has become like a fable, that far off joyful era when the sun always shone and he saw colours acutely. If he wants to bore them stiff, he will do so.

– SEVEN –

BLANCHE

The boy brought the invitation when Blanche was sorting the personal laundry. The large wicker baskets were overflowing as usual and they stood at the kitchen table, she and the laundry maid, Lilli, dividing delicate from more robust items: Papa's silk shirts in their pastel colours with the pleats that were such a devil to iron, one of his white linen suits, her own sensible blouses, bloomers, petticoats, camisoles and night gowns. They were almost finished when she came to a folded item at the bottom of a basket.

'Where did you find this?'

'On a shelf in the landing cupboard.'

Blanche shook out the creased cotton and held it against her. 'My old painting smock.'

Lilli eyed her in amazement. 'I never knew you were a painter, madame.'

The remark was innocent but it wounded.

'Of course I am a painter. My stepfather gave me palettes and brushes when he saw I was interested. I used to carry his easel and canvasses on a wheelbarrow out into the countryside and then set up my own easel and paint beside him.'

She thought of the eleven-year-old girl who had taken to him immediately when he and Camille shared the house at Vétheuil with Papa and Maman. The hours she spent sitting in his studio watching him work were bliss; his presence seemed to bathe their surroundings in a clear light and a bond was created between them. There was the year when he was creating his series, Haystacks. She had come utterly under his influence, using the same palette and colours to produce pictures which some said were almost indistinguishable from his.

'Next time you take linen to my stepfather's bedroom look at one of the paintings on the wall: *Haystacks*. It is mine.'

'Well I never.' They usually discussed domestic matters, now Lilli was swimming out of her depth. 'I never dreamed…'

'Oh Lilli, you have no idea of how it felt to be out in the open air with a great painter. He was so much younger then, so lively, we used to laugh such a lot.'

'He never seems to smile, these days,' Lilli remarked. 'What did you paint?'

Blanche gazed at Lilli's corn coloured hair, her large blue eyes but seeing in her mind's eye the collection of canvasses and framed pictures stored away upstairs. She hadn't looked at them for a long time; it was too painful.

'I did landscapes mostly, meadows by the river, the house and gardens here in Giverny, and Rouen too when my husband was alive. My work has been exhibited at the Salon des Indépendants and two years ago, I had paintings in an Artists of Rouen show.'

'Well!' Lilli busied herself, returning the clothes in their layers into the basket. 'And then Madame Alice died?'

'Yes, I couldn't leave him on his own after that, not with these cataracts and him so depressed. I had to come back here, he needed me.' As he has always needed me, she thought and sighed.

'And now there is no time for painting, eh? You are always too busy round the house.'

'Exactly.'

'Difficult?'

Surprised by this perceptive remark, Blanche smiled at the young woman. She liked Lilli, she seemed different from the other servants, intelligent, observant. Blanche felt she could carry on a conversation with her almost as if they were equals. It was good to tell someone her story, the only other person who really sympathised was Georges, of course.

'I find it very difficult. It was what I had always done, you see, what gave me the most satisfaction. I thought I might be able to carry on but... well, you can see all there is to do here. My stepfather needs to know that everything is running like clockwork. In my day, we were brought up to believe duty to the family came first, particularly if you were a woman. Of course now, with all this talk of women's suffrage in England, things are changing. They are fighting to have the right to vote,' she added, seeing Lilli's puzzlement. 'Decide who rules the country.'

'Oh I wouldn't want to do that,' the girl said. 'It's men's work, my father says.'

'Well now, Lilli,' Blanche was curious. 'What is it that you want out of life?'

'I would hope to marry, madame, have a little house of my own in the village.'

'You don't want to leave Giverny?'

54

'Why should I? I was born here.'

'Have you anyone in mind?'

Lilli dumped the basket on the floor and lifted up another. 'Well, there is someone… he came to work in the gardens, a few weeks ago.'

'Ah Michel? Yes he is an attractive young man. Is he courting?'

'I don't think so but I wonder how to make him notice me. I thought… there is a dance in the village next week, all the domestics will be going.'

'Then you should, too. Certainly you should. Have you something nice to wear?'

'There is my blue Sunday frock.'

'Very well, and I have an Indian shawl that will set it off nicely. It has blue and rose in it. I will lend it to you.'

'Oh, madame, would you? Thank you. You are so like Madame Alice, she was always so generous.'

'Yes, she always wanted those around her to be happy. She gave me the shawl one summer over twenty years ago.' Her gaze went as it often did to the pattern of tiles above the oven.

1888

The next time she saw John Leslie was when they almost collided outside a café. As before he bowed his head to her, and politely excused himself. Instead of moving on, he paused and, fixing her with those disconcerting eyes, complimented her on the colour of the frock she was wearing. Blanche felt herself flush.

'May I offer you coffee?'

She hesitated. 'Well I… I have taken it already.'

He laughed. 'Surely another would do no harm.'

To her surprise, she found herself following him into the café, aware of the inquisitive glance of the proprietor.

'Where is your charming sister?' John Leslie wanted to know.

'She is at home, reading in the garden.'

She thought of her sister who loved nothing more than immersing herself in a book. Face hidden by the large sun hat she liked to wear, she would be lounging under the paulownia tree wishing luncheon didn't have to be so early so she might finish a few more chapters.

John Leslie lit a cigarette. 'It must be a swell garden.'

'It is now but it wasn't when we first arrived. There were just a lot of trees and an orchard. Monet has created it all himself though the whole family has been involved with the clearing and weeding. He is devoted to his garden.'

In the pause that followed, she knew he was looking at her but couldn't raise her eyes to look at his face. She felt she must speak, break this silence, but did not find making conversation as easy as her mother who always seemed to know the right thing to say.

She cleared her throat. 'So how are you settling in, you and the family? Does your mother find it easy to be in a strange country?'

'She'd do anything to help me in my career. She and my brother are a wonderful support.'

They seemed to be carrying on the conversation at one level but at another she wasn't thinking what she was saying and felt that neither was he listening.

When he told her they would be staying at least until winter, she felt the tightness of joy under her ribs.

'It will be a chance to get to know you and your sister better,' he continued. 'And even, dare I hope, pay a visit to the house. I understand that Theodore Robinson is already a guest.'

She thought of the shy man who sat in Monet's studio and discussed the theory of impressionism by the hour. Sickly but courageous, Monet had labelled him. 'He has suffered from asthma all his life and yet he travels, he paints. I admire a man like that.'

'They are good friends and fellow artists,' Blanche replied. 'But as I told you the other day Monet does not admit many people into his circle. He spends all his time painting.' She did not add that he would certainly disapprove of her taking coffee with an American.

Again there was a pause. She felt the closeness of his hand resting on the table, of her own lying in her lap. She had an urge to reach out but fear suddenly overcame her happiness. She glanced round the café and caught the proprietor's eye; how they loved to gossip in Giverny.

'Ah well,' he said. 'But of course you never know in this life.'

'You never know.' Blanche met his gaze then glanced away as she picked up her gloves. 'And now I must go. I only came into the village to post a letter. Thank you for the coffee.'

They came out into the bright day where they paused, both it seemed unwilling to say goodbye.

'We are taking our meals at the Baudy family's establishment,' John Leslie said. 'The cooking is excellent. Would you and mademoiselle Suzanne give us the pleasure of coming to luncheon there, one day?' He was looking directly into her eyes. It took her breath away. 'Please.'

The luncheon was the first of several during that summer. Soon they were invited to dances on the terrace and picnics in the countryside – Maman had persuaded Monet there was no harm in the girls enjoying themselves and broadening their narrow circle as long as they stayed together at all times. Robinson had vouched the Americans were reliable young men. When she was with John Leslie, Blanche felt intoxicated with the joy of being alive, seeing everything around her so vividly that it seemed to take on a special meaning.

57

It was during one of these soirees, the terrace hung with Japanese lanterns glowing like exotic fruit among the leaves of the trees and John Leslie playing his guitar, that the fear struck again. This was too good to last. She was Monet's chosen one, his painting companion and he would never allow this to go any further than friendship. Blanche shivered and pulled the Indian shawl closer round her shoulders.

'Are you cold?' John Leslie had taken a break from his playing and come to sit beside her.

'No, not really,' she replied. 'Just… a goose walked over my grave.'

He had taken her hand and gently stroked it. She felt the light touch as if he were kissing it. In this corner of the terrace they were alone together for the first time, out of sight of the others. She could believe that the world extended no further than these, their immediate surroundings. She gave him her other hand. She wanted him to take her in his arms. She looked down at their joined hands and the pattern of rose on the blue silk of her shawl. He said her name. She looked up and saw a query in his expression, one that she was at a loss to answer.

She knew he felt too the sudden need to draw closer together and it came to her that she was falling in love with him. She had never felt like this before and she panicked. What would she do when autumn came and he returned to Paris?

He was looking questioningly at her so that she thought her expression had given her away.

'Blanche? It's lovely to be here, with you.' She felt a knot of happiness and fear of where this might lead. The shawl slipped from her shoulders and fell unnoticed to the ground.

Annette came into the kitchen, holding out an envelope. Blanche took it, turned it over and saw the Hotel Baudy stamp. Oh dear, another note from the American woman, asking yet again for an audience with the great man. There was no point reading this third one to Papa, it would simply irritate him. She opened the envelope and read.

A picnic by the Seine (Déjeuner sur l'Herbe) has been arranged to celebrate the fiftieth birthday of Mr Robert Harrison. You are cordially invited to attend. RSVP.

Reply if you please. Oh it would please her so much to reply: yes, yes, yes to a picnic by the sparkling Seine where John Leslie once rowed them, singing,

> *Row, row, row your boat,*
> *Gently down the stream.*
> *Merrily, merrily, merrily, merrily,*
> *Life is but a dream.*

1888

She sat in the stern of the rowing boat and they glided through the water. She noticed the green reflections, the alteration of light to shadow and then to light again. They came to rest under a canopy of over hanging willow trees and she listened to John Leslie telling her about his life. It seemed to her so romantic, how he was born at sea on a clipper ship in the South Pacific, which might explain, he said, his affinity with water. How he was determined to be a painter and studied in Germany but Paris had always been his goal, where he sits with his friends in cafés for hours and discusses art and politics. And then he tells her of how they couldn't decide where to go to paint for this summer.

'We wanted to find a new location so we consulted the destination board at Gare Saint-Lazare and decided Pont-de-l'Arche was appealing. As we approached Vernon, Metcalf pointed out a little village of white houses and a Norman church and said how lovely it was. At Vernon, we were told the village was Giverny. We agreed that if Pont-de-l'Arche was not to our liking we would return to Giverny, the following morning, which was exactly what we did.'

'Is that true?' she asked.

'It could be.' He laughed. 'Or it could be that we just got out at the wrong station.'

'Well, whichever it was I'm glad you did.'

He brought her hands to his mouth and kissed them. 'And so am I.'

Ahead of them the river sparkled with points of light, inviting them out of the shade, the sun was warm on her face. Blanche felt perfectly happy.

Later, when they met up with the others, Robinson said: 'I have a surprise for you, Breck. Monet has invited you to visit him.'

What could have caused this change of mind, Blanche wondered. Curiosity, perhaps?

How strange the invitation should arrive at this moment, almost as a sign. She caught Lilli's interested eye, realised she had sighed aloud, and stuffed the envelope into her skirt pocket. It was the turn of the household linen but as she counted sheets and pillow cases, her mind was busy wondering when would be a good time to broach this to Papa.

'There is a tear in m'sieur's coverlet, madame.'

She glanced at it, he was clumsy at times but she wouldn't scold, she wanted him to be in a good mood.

'I can mend it so as it won't show,' Lilli was saying.

'Good Lilli, thank you. Can I leave you to finish the rest on your own? There is something…'

Blanche hurried from the kitchen, calling over her shoulder, 'I won't forget about the shawl.' She was impatient to show the invitation to Papa and, of course, she chose the wrong moment.

He was in the garden, supervising the removal of wallflowers, which had now gone over, making ready for a planting of antirrhinum. The new young gardener, his face flushed beneath a straw hat, was trying to obey her stepfather's snapped orders.

'No young man, don't dig them out, pull them out. That's what we do here, the moment they've done their job. No expense spared, no sentiment either.'

Approaching them, Blanche saw an old man with a bushy white beard, a soft hat clapped on his head. She experienced, as she often did these days, the dismay of seeing him growing old.

'Papa, can you spare me a moment?'

Reluctantly, he ordered Michel to carry on with the job and followed her to sit on a garden bench while she read out the invitation.

'Répondez s'il vous plaît.'

In the pause that followed, she stared at a bed of pelargonium, noting the hot pinks and reds, and nearby some small mauve flowers whose name she did not know; she marvelled, as she often did, how in nature there was no clash of colour. Imagine wearing a mauve frock with a red cape. She glanced sideways and saw he was also staring straight ahead, his hands resting on his stick.

'Well?'

'I don't think it is possible,' he said. 'I'm not used to

61

socialising with these Americans any more, Blanche. I wouldn't know what to say, besides I am too busy with the painting.'

She had to speak up, she must. She always bit her tongue, stifled her complaints, but now she must. 'Oh Papa, could you not do this for me? I should so much like to go.'

He laughed. 'You want me to sacrifice my precious time for the frivolous party of a mediocre painter? It is hardly worthy of me, Blanche.'

Anger suffused her. Sacrifice! He didn't know the meaning of the word. Yes, she was going to voice it, why shouldn't she? She had held her tongue on so many occasions; this was too much, it needed to be let out. 'It would be the first time in your life if you did,' she retorted. 'This household has always been ruled by your painting. Nothing must interfere with it: luncheon at eleven-thirty because you need the afternoon light, no guests for dinner because you need to go early to bed. And then there are your moods, the black ones when your work goes badly, the euphoria when it flows, we have all supported those. It is we who have sacrificed… I…'

She reached for her handkerchief. 'I'm sorry, Papa, but sometimes I feel in despair when I think of how fulfilled I was as I sat at my easel and painted. Then… well… I was aware of who I was, Blanche Hoschedé, where my destiny lay. Now, oh the loss, the desolation.'

He did not speak, sighed, laid his hand on her arm but she shook it off.

'Leave me alone and get back to your garden.'

She watched his bent figure walk slowly away and pursed her lips against the inevitable defeat. I will not feel guilty, I will not, she told herself. I will stand firm, hold up my trident

62

to the offending hordes and not be vanquished: Boudica, wonderful warring woman. For once I will think about myself. She felt the old impotence in the face of his unbending will. She was back to that day when he had said, 'I don't want to let you go. I need you here, working with me.'

An image came into her mind: the day of Suzanne's wedding, Butler taking her mother's arm and her sister and Monet leading the way along a sun-bleached path. *Wedding March* Robinson had called the picture he painted more than two weeks after the event, filled with movement: the wind in the bride's veil, the groom's leading leg depicted in mid stride, almost like a photograph. To Blanche, that picture had represented something else, had seemed enigmatic, expressing the fleeting moment, the flux of life. There were also, it had occurred to her, disturbing elements that threatened the joy. Suzanne's gown and her billowing veil were much less white than those elsewhere in the picture: the men's collars, the little girl's hat, Maman's dress, it was somehow a colour of foreboding. As the marchers, all in effect faceless, walk down the dusty path past the overgrown remains of a crumbled cottage, the lower part of Suzanne's white wedding gown, trailing in the dust, takes on a much darker tone. Suzanne's face behind the veil is barely visible, ghostlike. The dust, like the crumbling cottage, hints at mortality, while Suzanne's gown and veil more nearly resemble a shroud.

She remembered how her misgivings had been realised over the next few years. Robinson died in New York from a severe asthmatic attack. Three years later, after a lingering illness, Suzanne was also dead and buried in the churchyard of Sainte-Radegonde. In one way or another, both she and Blanche had been defeated.

63

Dinner that evening was a dismal occasion. Marie had prepared a game dish, which Monet attacked with gusto while Blanche sipped a glass of wine and stared at her plate. She was considering her outburst of that afternoon, her determination to stand firm and fight him on this issue. Now, she told herself, she should have known better. Hadn't she lived by his side long enough to understand the way his mind worked? He might be a great artist but on a personal level, he could be contrary as a child and, as such, one had to be more foxy.

'How is the game?' she asked.

'Surprisingly good, the girl is coming on.'

'I'm glad to hear you say it.'

He glanced up and considered her. 'But you've scarcely touched yours.'

'I haven't much appetite this evening, Papa.'

He helped himself to more of the sauce. 'Or perhaps you are sulking.'

Blanche said nothing.

'Because I wouldn't agree to this picnic.'

She met his gaze and shrugged. 'Maybe you don't recall Mr Harrison? Robert Harrison? He was a friend of Robinson.' And John Leslie, she thought. 'He might not have been the world's greatest painter but he was always a connoisseur. I have an idea this has been arranged to honour your work. It just seems rather ill mannered to snub him, but if that is how you wish to behave…'

The meal ended, coffee was brought in.

'Plum brandy?'

'No thank you, Papa.' She heard the liquid poured into a glass.

'Blanche?'

She glanced up.

His smile was rueful. 'You had better accept the invitation,' he said. 'Or I shall never hear the last of it.'

- EIGHT -

JUDITH

The morning they were to drive into Vernon, to shop for the picnic, Judith was late for breakfast. She had overslept and then spent ages choosing her outfit for the trip. When she finally came downstairs, wearing a two-piece of tunic top and bias cut skirt in Chanel beige, she found the dining room was empty except for Robert and Harry, lingering over their pastries. They looked up as she appeared.

'Good morning, young lady.' Robert leapt to his feet. 'What can I fetch you? The oeufs bénédictine are very good now that we've finally persuaded Madame Baudy to substitute that salt cod and potato for ham, or there are chops or herring.'

She grimaced. 'I'll just take coffee and a brioche, thank you. I've been eating far too much since I came here.' Her regime had slipped and she was anxious she might be putting on weight.

'Please yourself.' Robert poured coffee into the blue and white bowls, added cream to his own and went back to his pain au chocolat.

Harry laughed at him. 'Piggy.'

Robert shrugged. 'Say what you like, I love the way the French enjoy their food, and their wine for that matter. I'm with Monet there, the palate is a God-given pleasure.'

Judith screwed her eyes shut for a moment. 'It's the wine I'm bothered about. It's wonderful while you are drinking it but the next morning, ugh!'

'Then don't drink it,' Harry retorted. 'no-one's forcing you.'

Robert reached over for a chunk of bread, he smeared it with cherry jam and took a bite. 'If you really don't feel like coming into Vernon this morning, Harry can help me.' He smiled at his friend.

'No, I want to come. I've never been to a French market before and you said you'd show me the gargoyles.'

'Okay. Finish your coffee and we can go. You coming with us, Harry?'

Judith was relieved when he said he would prefer to spend the morning in the studio. She wanted to share this excursion with Robert alone.

'You look all geared up for the run,' he was saying. 'But be careful you don't trip over that scarf, it does rather trail all over the place. Maybe choose something more practical?'

She was horrified. Change her Knossos scarf! 'Oh no, I paid enough for it, it's meant to be worn, to be seen.'

She did a few steps of the Turkey Trot in defiance and even Harry laughed.

'Let's go then.'

'Drive carefully,' Harry called after them.

They stepped out into the sunshine where the scarlet automobile waited, gleaming as it always did from Robert's loving care. As they rushed through the country roads, lined with poplars, under the high blue skies, Judith felt a surge of joy at being alive. What could equal this bright June morning in rural France and the prospect of meeting the great man only hours away? When the boy brought the reply from Le Pressoir to the terrace table where she sat with Robert, they had ordered champagne.

'This is a triumph,' he exclaimed. 'I wasn't at all sure we'd pull it off. Obviously, Madame Blanche has some influence.'

Once more the mention of that name made Judith feel uneasy without understanding the reason why. On the other hand, maybe she had reason to be grateful to the unknown woman.

Vernon was crowded this Saturday morning. Robert cautiously parked his vehicle near the Notre Dame Collegiate and they stepped out of the blinding sun into its cool interior. Light shone through the stained glass windows, illuminating St Jacques and St Genevieve in their glowing reds and greens, the more sombre Stations of the Cross. The ornate organ, set against its backdrop of the rose window, seemed poised to pour out majestic chords.

Judith was enthralled. She stood in the central aisle and threw out her arms. 'This is the most beautiful thing I have ever seen in my life.'

'What about the Notre Dame in Paris?' Robert questioned dryly.

'Oh, I didn't have time to visit. I was too taken up with the couturier houses… and museums, of course.'

'Of course.'

Outside, Robert clapped on his panama and they walked round the building while he pointed out the grotesque stone figures jutting from the façade, their sad and twisted faces gazing out, trapped in stone. 'In medieval times, the

68

church was seen as powerful enough to turn evil around to work for its own good. So, gargoyles are the wicked fire-breathing demons that have been converted by the power of the church, which they now protect, spilling only water from the heavens out of their mouths.'

'You know so much about this country,' Judith said as they made their way down rue Potard.

'I'm fascinated by the history, Judith. America is young and go getting but France is ancient, its houses and monuments have witnessed so much, everywhere is stamped with the past. I'm in love with its culture, its food and its language.'

'Do you plan on ever going back home?'

'Not if I can help it.'

'You're so lucky, Robert.'

'I don't think it's a question of luck, more knowing what it is you need and going all out to make sure you have it.'

'I meant you don't have anyone expecting great things of you. My father's parents were émigré German Jews, they came to New York with nothing and gradually made their way. It was a struggle and Father never forgot what it was like when he was a child. He set out to make a lot of money.'

'And succeeded by all accounts.'

'Yes, but he always has the fear of losing it all, slipping back to the kind of lives my grandparents lived. Mother tells him to ease off but he won't, I don't think he can. He loves the power of money and position. And I'm supposed to carry it further by making this marriage with a rich Harvard boy.'

Robert halted outside one of the half-timbered houses. 'My, that's a great deal to lay on a young lady's shoulders. Do you love the gentleman in question?'

'I really don't know. He's charming to me, generous, always buying me nice presents. But maybe I don't understand what being in love is. I've never met anyone else to compare him with. Tell me something, Robert, have you ever been deliriously in love?'

'I hardly think this is a conversation for a carefree summer morning,' Robert said abruptly. 'Let's talk about it some other time. Look at this building, Judith, the Hotel des Fleurs. See the carved heads, how striking they are; each one is unique.'

Judith stared at the inscrutable expression on the nearest carving's face, the hooded eyes, long nose and wry mouth. She thought of how long it had been there... centuries. While tourists came and went it endured, gazing sightlessly ahead. It dawned on her how singled out she was to be here in Vernon on this particular Saturday morning, seeing these marvels in the company of an intelligent, sensitive man; so far life was on her side, guiding her into this fresh, new world. She would give herself up to it, go where it led her. How really very easy it was. She told herself: I will not marry Charlie.

In the centre of Vernon, the market was in full swing. Judith delighted in the colour and sound, the calls to look and buy from the fishmongers, the morning's catch of fish laid out to the customers' view, the dull rhythmic beat of the butcher's knife. The fruit and vegetable stalls made a magnificent display: fennel, scarlet tomatoes and olives, green and black. There were great heaps of glistening cherries, tiny, wild strawberries nestled in white tissue, purple plums.

'You just ache to paint it all, don't you?' Robert remarked. 'It's one huge still life.'

They shopped for cheeses, Roquefort, creamy Camembert and Brie; they chose plump tomatoes, cucumbers and heads of lettuce. There was Normandy cream for the strawberries, olive oil from Provençe to dress the salads. A pillowy woman sliced ham to the precise thickness of Robert's command.

'We'll buy the bread tomorrow morning so it's fresh,' he said. 'And I've ordered tarts and pies from Madame Baudy, especially a tarte tatin, it's Monet's favourite. Harry and I will pick up the wine later on. We know an excellent cellar. It will be a feast.'

Later they sat in a pavement café watching the passers-by. A woman in a black dress crossed the road bearing a pannier on her back loaded with bread, some children ran along bowling hoops. There was a man on a penny-farthing. Judith ordered their coffee and pain au raisin, her pleasure complete when the waiter apparently understood her French.

'I want this to be the picnic supreme,' Robert was saying. 'A replica of those paintings they did in the early days when the Industrial Revolution set people free for leisure, you know, all those river scenes and boating parties. I want to recreate that marvellous sense of freshness and light, of celebration, people interacting.'

Judith had little idea what he meant and wondered what she would reply if he continued. She smiled and nodded but there was something she needed to ask him: she wanted to know whether Blanche would like her.

He shrugged. 'How could she help it? Pretty young lady like you?'

'You said she was a painter?'

'Yes and a very good one; she came to Giverny before she

was twenty but already Monet had taken her under his wing when he saw she was talented. Like him, she has painted the gardens and the lily pond but one of my favourites is the view of Giverny from the hilltops. It looks like a little jewel.'

'But what is she like as a person?'

'That I wouldn't know any more. You don't see her around the village much these days, but she was the life and soul of the party at one time. She was head over heels with a Yank.'

'Maybe she just wanted to escape?'

'Possibly. Possibly it was just true love.'

They were back to that again.

'I don't think it's like that with Charlie and me. We've just known each other since we were children. Mother made sure of that.'

'Then don't marry him.'

'Oh Robert that's just what I've been thinking.'

'You should go where your heart leads you, that's my motto. Charlie isn't the only man on this earth.'

What was he suggesting? She could never tell with him, he often seemed on the verge of saying something and then shied away. She wondered how she would feel if he wanted to kiss her. There had been nothing more than hand holding with Charlie and she was curious. On the other hand, he was rather old; it would be more like kissing your father.

'What do you advise, Robert?'

'I'm not advising anything just pointing out that if you really don't want to marry this man, you'll have to find a way out of it.'

'But how?'

'That you'll have to work out for yourself.'

Back in Giverny they parted. He was lunching with Harry and did not suggest she join them. Judith was grateful to step into the cool vestibule where the girl behind the desk handed her her key and also a letter. It bore an American stamp. She carried it up to her room and set it on the night table. She washed her hands and face and powdered her nose. From the corner of her eye she could see the letter lying there but picked up a book and tried to read it. The envelope was addressed in her mother's hand, which should have pleased her, but the only feeling she had was one of annoyance that it had intruded into her life here. Finally, she laid down the book and read the letter. Mother wrote of plans for the wedding going ahead, one or two society magazines wanted to feature it. Charlie's mother was being an absolute brick, organising all the catering details that she found so tiresome. She hoped Judith was enjoying this unplanned time away but she would have to pull her weight on her return.

Judith laid down the letter and gazed out of the window down to where Madame Baudy was feeding the hens. She tried to picture Charlie but he swam indistinct in her mind, instead she saw Robert standing outside the Hotel des Fleurs, pointing to the carved head. He had seemed so at home, happy in his skin. Judith tore the letter into small pieces and threw them in the wastebasket. She dabbed on some L'Heure Bleue and went to join the others on the terrace.

– NINE –

BLANCHE

If there had been more time, she might have taken the trap into Vernon and bought a new frock. But there was the trouble over Annette who had handed in her notice after Papa shouted at her yet again about touching his paints. Blanche had an inkling that if indeed anyone had disturbed their order it was more probably Lilli with her jackdaw curiosity. Fortunately, she had managed to persuade Annette to retract, with the offer of three extra half days to be taken over the next year. Annette was too valuable, too versatile to lose even if she did clump around the house in that boot of hers. And anyway, a new frock would be an unnecessary extravagance. When would she ever wear it again?

Blanche lifted her chosen hat from its box, quite a jaunty little boater, and placed it on her head at a slant, tilted towards her right eyebrow. It was decorated with tulle bows made to look like butterflies. She stepped back from the mirror to examine her overall appearance. It was said women were dispensing with their corsets, opting for a more fluid line; well she would certainly never be able to do that, especially now with the menopause nudging. She hated the pink satin thing and sometimes threw it across the room, when in the evening, she was finally released from the lacing to relax in a shift. On the positive side, her hair remained as thick as ever with hardly a streak of grey, as dark as any of those soulful demoiselles of Dante Rossetti's fevered imagination, she thought. Doomed love was all very well but you had to expire early or it simply became mawkish.

1888

As Blanche had guessed, Robinson had managed to bypass Monet's suspicion of the Americans and alert his curiosity about John Leslie.

On the day of the visit he was all smiles and enquiry. 'Mr Breck, delighted to make your acquaintance. How do you find Giverny? I understand you paint. What are your subjects?'

He gave a tour of the garden, pointing out the various combinations: shasta daisies, sweet rocket peppered with orange wall flowers; the purple tulip negrita rising up from a bed of white violas; and, of course, his favourite, iris: variegated, the purple and yellow making a bold contrast. As usual, Robinson was taking photographs. Blanche watched John Leslie, his sharp eye darting about as he absorbed everything. He was the only one of the party who appeared not to be simply enjoying the sunny afternoon, the air filled with fragrance; there was something else on his mind. As soon as he had the opportunity he began to ask questions. What brush strokes did Monet use? Which colours?

'The point is to know how to use the colours,' Monet replied. 'The choice of which is, when all is said and done, a matter of habit.'

'Okay, and how does one become an impressionist?'

'I didn't become an impressionist, Mr Breck. As long as I can remember I always have been one is the answer to your question.'

Blanche could see that this was irritating Monet. She wished John Leslie wouldn't persist but he did.

'Is it true, sir, that all of your paintings are done in situ?'

'Whether my cathedral views, my views of London and other canvasses are painted from life or not is nobody's business and of no importance whatsoever.'

And with that, it seemed, John Leslie must be satisfied. Monet turned away and addressed Robinson. 'That's enough, my friend. You have strolled about far too much. Let us go back to the house.'

Although the slender man, whose head always seemed slightly too large for his body, protested he was fine, it was obvious he had begun to wheeze.

While the others turned back towards the house where Maman would be waiting to serve tea on the balcony, John Leslie nudged Blanche and indicated they should slip away into the garden. There was something lawless about him, she realised, an obstinacy, which reminded her of Monet. She had glimpsed it as John Leslie confronted him and continued to ask questions. She felt as she might feel, standing at the edge of a high cliff, looking down onto a sea running between rocks, a mixture of awe and fascination. She knew what she ought to do, join the tea party, yet instead she found herself hurrying away down one of the side paths with this man.

After a moment he paused and glanced back towards the house. 'They won't see us now.' Taking her hand he urged her on until they reached the seat under the paulownia tree.

She was aware of how what she was doing was laden with complexities. Only a short space away the family was taking tea and soon they would be wondering where she was. Someone

76

might be sent to look for her. But there was another part of her that yearned to be alone with John Leslie, to have his full attention. They sat for a while, his arm about her, her head resting on his shoulder. The only sound was that of bees in the bright lilies, fumbling their stamens.

Then John Leslie spoke. 'You know, I love it here: this garden, Giverny, I love the Normandy countryside, the food...'

He turned to look at her. He leaned closer and she saw the shape of his face, his mouth. She felt a pulse beat in her throat. He lifted his hand to cup her chin, looking into her eyes as though to read her thoughts. He leant further forward and his mouth touched her forehead and her closed eyes; he kissed her mouth and her lips curved upwards under his. He drew her closer so that her body curved backward as he kissed her; they embraced each other, acknowledging their desire at last, in silence. She forgot the family waiting for her beyond this place under the paulownia tree. There was no-one but John Leslie. Her mouth opened under his and the roughness of his kiss surprised her. He lifted his mouth from hers and looked into her eyes again. He said her name and the kiss was gentle now, gradually they moved apart but their hands came together again. Beyond him she saw scarlet climbing roses, the flare of orange lilies as she became aware once more of her surroundings. They were here together for such a brief moment. What would come after? Her joy was now mixed with pain and uncertainty. He was watching her face and she knew he was reading her thoughts.

'I know, we haven't done this in the correct way, have we? Getting acquainted with your family, the chaperone. We've bypassed all that.'

Blanche frowned. 'Maybe this is how you do it in America?'

'Not at all. I don't understand it any more than you do, how we have moved on so quickly from that first meeting. All I know

77

is it has happened and we can't guess how your family is going to react.' He raised her chin so that she had to look at him.

She realised he too was nervous and susceptible.

He said: 'you do know that I love you?'

In the following silence, Blanche felt a flutter of happiness.

'I just wanted to tell you, that's all. And I want you to think about it.'

'That's all I shall think about!'

'Blanche, when shall we meet again, like this, I mean?'

'We will, somehow, but it will have to be in secret. Please don't mention it to your family either, or it is sure to get out. This place is a devil for gossip and then it would reach Monet and heaven knows how he would react.'

'Okay, okay. Don't worry, Blanche, please.'

They went into each other's arms again and she leant her head against his shoulder, happiness driving out all other feelings. With his mouth against her hair, he murmured they should rejoin the others.

'Let's go separately,' she said. 'And appear from different parts of the garden.' She moved first, feeling if she didn't she never would, walking up the path towards the balcony.

There was a cry of 'Oh here she is! We thought you'd got lost.'

Blanche sat down and her mother handed her a cup of tea. 'Where is Mr Breck?' she asked.

'I don't know,' lied Blanche. 'The last I saw of him he was talking to the gardener.'

Blanche gave herself a mental shake, enough of this melancholy.

When had she last worn this two piece? It must have been at least ten years ago, the short bolero effect jacket might be a little passé but the colour made up for it. She had always liked herself in pink. The reflection in the mirror smiled; she would do.

From the floor below, there came a burst of laughter, Blanche snatched up her handbag and hurried down the stairs. As she opened the door of Papa's room, Lilli struggled to get up from the laundry basket where she was sprawled like a starfish while Annette hid her giggles.

'We was just changing m'sieur's linen, madame,' Lilli straightened her pinafore and looked down at her feet.

'So I see.'

'A little cat dashed in with a mouse and tripped me up.'

'Very well.'

'Beg pardon, madame,' this from Annette.

She was forever apologising, Blanche thought absently, as if for her disability though God knew who had taught her to behave like that. These local people were so superstitious, they believed the cause of a clubfoot was because the mother stood on a cross in the churchyard before the child was born, so evil came in. No wonder Papa had never had much to do with them but stuck to his Parisian friends. She was too concerned with his absence to be inclined to scold. Instead she peeped into his dressing room, which was also empty and was told he had not been seen since breakfast.

She swallowed hard, feeling tears well up. Was he going to sabotage her one outing? How could he when he knew it meant so much to her? She turned away from the young women's curious gaze and rushed down the second flight of stairs, out into the garden. Where was he? She hurried along the central path, dimly aware of the parades of brilliant colour, the palettes of scarlet, pink and purple, calling his name. Her hair was coming down, after all that careful pinning, she held on to her hat and dared not look up to the house where she felt sure Lilli and Annette were watching her spectacle from the bedroom window.

The problem, which had engrossed Papa, wiping out all notion of preparing himself for the picnic, was rose rust. Blanche found him with Breuil and Michel in a solemn group by one of the arches. They were discussing the efficacy of baking soda.

'My father swears by sulphur,' Michel was saying.

'Listen to the young man,' she heard her stepfather comment. 'He's a farmer's son. He should know what he's talking about.'

'There are several new products on the market,' Breuil ventured.

'Nothing like the old remedies.'

'Then maybe mixed with a little oil to adhere the mixture to the leaves? And, of course, we will get rid of the infected ones. Michel, you can make a start on that right away.'

'Papa?'

He glanced across at her with that veiled stare which, these days, she found difficult to interpret. Was it disinterest or merely that she appeared to him in a blur?

'It is time we left. The driver is waiting.'

He grunted. 'We are trying to resolve this rose rust, Blanche.'

'Very well, but the rose rust will be with us tomorrow, the picnic will not.'

'And if they die, that will be the tragedy.'

The two gardeners murmured their assent. The fate of these roses was paramount.

Blanche stepped forward. 'Excuse me,' she said loudly, 'but there are people waiting for you, Papa, artists, men of letters. Some of them have come especially from Paris to

80

meet you. On this occasion you cannot,' she waved her arms about, oblivious of her precarious hat, 'simply cannot put these plants first.'

He sighed and exchanged glances with the men, he stared at the diseased roses, even reached up and tore off a leaf. He shrugged. 'Ah well, you win for now, Blanche.'

'Excellent, then shall we go?'

'A moment.' He turned back to Michel. 'You will go to Vernon and buy a quantity of whatever M. Breuil demands. This afternoon you will start to apply it. By the time I return, I want to see work in progress.'

She was all anxiety, seizing his arm and hurrying him away. On the terrace he halted and gazed at a nearby standard rose.

'That, too.'

'Papa, please, I beg you.'

He followed her inside.

For his picnic location, Robert had chosen a particular bend in the Eure river with its splendid view of willows and poplars. Beyond, there stretched cornfields studded with poppies. Huge white tablecloths were spread on the ground surrounded by piles of cushions, with chairs for the less agile. Blanche caught her breath at Mr Harrison's talent in recreating *The Picnic*, as an homage to Papa's painting, completed in the year she was born.

'Mr Harrison, you have created a true tableau vivant,' she exclaimed as she handed him her gift. '*Bon Anniversaire*.'

'You are intelligent also in choosing the perfect day for it,' added Monet.

'Maitre, thank you but that was the Lord's doing not mine. Now let me fetch you some champagne.'

They had been almost the last to arrive, delayed further

by the automobile developing a flat tyre. Blanche gazed round, aware she searched for familiar faces among the guests: Manet, Degas, Renoir… none was here. How could she expect them to be? The years had passed and with them Manet while age crippled the other two. Someone waved, for a moment she didn't recognise him then realised it was Richard. The last time she had seen him, he was terribly young, a precocious painter. He'd grown a moustache, which made him seem older, but perhaps it was also assumed responsibility for his wife Harriet and the solemn faced child he introduced.

'Maitre!' He made a little bow, 'it is an honour to see you again.'

'I don't think I know you,' her stepfather replied, his hand still firmly grasped by the young man.

'Of course you do, Papa, it's Mr Miller, you remember, Richard Emil Miller. You always admired his paintings of lovely, young women… Miller,' she enunciated the syllables.

'Ah yes, yes now I do. They were always in their dressing gowns and kimonos, doing very little of any practical value; they sewed, or gazed into mirrors or merely meditated. You had this way of suggesting they were enjoying a wonderful secret life without male company, as they probably were.'

Harriet laughed. 'You bet they were.'

'And children,' the little girl put in. 'Daddy paints children, too. He's just done one of me and Mummy, looking at some goldfish.'

'*Voila*, so you are famous, *ma petite*.'

You always had a way with children, Blanche thought ruefully. You certainly had with me from that first moment I saw you, the great artist with your long hair. And now, as

82

much as you sometimes annoy me and in spite of what you have done to me in the past, I still love you.

She turned to Robert who was standing respectfully by, listening to this conversation.

'And you, Mr Harrison, how is your painting going?'

'Okay, I suppose. It's always difficult to judge your own work, madame.'

He was behaving so formally towards her and yet she was certain he must remember her, recall a summer's afternoon when Sargent had painted Papa at his easel, and Robert lurked among the trees to watch, turning to smile as she and John Leslie walked into the woods. It stuck in her mind because it had been that day the remark was made. Sargent had said he needed black paint.

'I never use it,' Papa said.

And Sargent: 'I don't understand how you do without it.'

'No shadow is black, it always has a colour, white and black are not colours.'

There lay the difference in their work, she had thought.

'I'm sure you must have come along by leaps and bounds,' she said. 'You've been in Giverny for some time, haven't you?' And John Leslie was one of your friends, she added, silently.

'Over twenty years, yes, I've seen some changes.'

'Robert?'

A young woman had approached them and now stood at his side. Blanche frowned, resenting the interruption, but he turned, drawing her into the circle.

'Hey, let me introduce you. Madame Blanche, this is Mademoiselle Judith.'

What Blanche saw, startled her. The girl was young but there was an assurance about her, an air of being accustomed to such social occasions. She proffered her hand in the most gracious way and murmured '*enchanté*' with the American accent Blanche always found charming.

She noted the bobbed hair, the summery dress with its simple collar, the blue and white birds eye spot silk cravat. She held herself well and obviously had no need of corsets. Blanche watched every eye including Papa's drawn to this freshness, this youthfulness.

It was his turn to murmur '*enchanté*' and bend his head over her hand. 'Well, mademoiselle, you look as if you have stepped straight out of a painting.'

Those nearest to him laughed. The young woman joined in, making a little bow to her left and right. She had the air of seeming poised, ready to dance. Blanche immediately scolded herself for being fanciful.

'Why, thank you sir for the compliment and I guess that's quite something coming from you!' She addressed him as an equal, there was no deference in her tone.

Robert filled their flutes and she clinked hers against Monet's. '*Santé.*'

'*Santé*, dear mademoiselle.'

It occurred to Blanche she was witnessing an extraordinary scene as her stepfather now turned his full attention on the American girl and she to him. He took her arm and led her about, pointing out the line of poplars, indicating the poppy fields, while she listened, apparently rapt. Blanche wasn't near enough to hear what they were saying but guessed he was talking about painting, the inspiration of these landscapes, his way of seizing on a moment and making of it something. There was nothing sexual about it, nor in the least flirtatious. 'The master and his acolyte', the title swam into her mind as if she were observing a painting. For Judith with her short hair and slight figure was androgynous, might almost have been a boy at the feet of this bearded, esteemed old man. They were seated now, he indicating a chocolate gateau, she shaking her head. He laughed and the sound was strong and joyful.

Judith said loudly, 'I've dreamed of this moment for so long.'

Everyone agreed the picnic had been an enormous success, the company, the food and drink, the general ambiance. It would be an afternoon to be talked about for many months to come. For Blanche, the experience had been something quite other. While she had, of course, accepted the plates heaped with food and several glasses of champagne, her attention was directed onto Judith, how she looked, what she did, what she said. The thing that struck her most of all was the girl's insouciance. She knocked a glass of wine over Robert and mopped him with her handkerchief, laughing as she did so. She had three bowls of strawberries, emptying the cream jug over her final portion with no concern for anyone else. Blanche watched her, feeling a mixture of envy and curiosity. Was this the way American women behaved, uncaring of their effect on those around them? Giving Papa a playful little cuff over something he said, seizing another young lady's parasol and calling out: 'Has anyone got a camera?' Oh, to be twenty again or whatever age this child was, twenty and permitted to behave like that, uncaring, concerned only with self… what dreams she might have fulfilled. What was I doing in my twenties? Carting Papa's canvasses behind him, always prepared to produce the next that would correspond to a particular moment in the day. Locked in his world of art, his expectations of me, so much to lay on the shoulders of a young girl.

1888

After that brief time with John Leslie her whole world changed. She might have thought that going back to her normal surroundings, it would all seem the same but of course it didn't. She forgot to post her mother's letters, sat dreaming in the hen house when she should have been collecting the eggs. She felt life at Le Pressoir was surreal and the true one was with John Leslie.

'Are you feeling all right?' Maman asked. 'You're not sickening for something?'

'Perfectly all right, Maman.'

'Well, I am worried about you. You haven't seemed yourself for the past few days.'

It was true. She had lost her normally healthy appetite, her impatience to be out painting with Monet, her thoughts were obsessed with John Leslie. That evening, she made an attempt to clear her plate, fearful that her mother would send for the doctor, but when pressed to more she had to refuse.

Monet was talking about a walk he had taken the day before, his interest in a haystack's reaction with light, both absorbing and giving off refracted colour. An idea was growing in his mind, something to do with registering these effects with passing time, she could scarcely be bothered to listen.

'So Blanche, up and off very early tomorrow morning!' his loud tone jerked her out of her reverie. 'I want to make a start.'

With a sense of surprise, she realised that, for the first time in years, she could not care less about painting. Neither did she want to get out of bed at the crack of dawn. Suzanne was right, she thought, remembering that conversation on the day they had first met the Brecks. There is life beyond sitting before a canvas. Immediately she felt guilty that she was having these mutinous thoughts, she who had always been Monet's willing assistant, his 'pack horse' as her sister called her, trundling behind him with the wheelbarrow loaded with canvasses.

'Not necessarily haystacks, it could be anything,' he was saying, 'another kind of structure, a wall even. That is not the point... the point is...'

Impossible, she thought. Was she thinking it was impossible to change her life or impossible to go on as it was?

On Saturday, they celebrated Jean's birthday. Maman had asked her to help prepare the table, knowing he was her favourite stepbrother. They brought in greenery from the garden and laid a rose by each plate. Sunlight streamed into the yellow dining room and she felt dazzled and disorientated,

'Salmon mousse to begin with and then a saddle of lamb with new potatoes and garden peas,' her mother was saying. 'Marguerite has made a surprise dessert, she refuses to tell me what it is but I think it might be banana ice cream.'

Blanche heard herself laugh but the sound seemed to come from someone outside herself.

When everyone was crowded round the table, Suzanne laughing at Monet as he solemnly decanted the champagne, she tried to join in but felt adrift and separate from all of them.

'Do you remember that year when Jean was twelve and we asked him what he wanted for his birthday and he said a chemistry set?' Maman was saying.

'Oh yes,' said Monet, 'and he mixed hydrogen sulfide with ammonia and filled the place with such a stink!'

'And what about the time when he singed his hair on the Bunsen burner?' put in Michel.

Jean laughed. 'Ah well, ten years on and I'm still here.'

Blanche watched them all, talking and joking and they seemed remote even Monet. She had a strange feeling of their being strangers and the only person who was familiar was John Leslie. As she sat there, her plate untouched before her, she thought about him and was sure he was thinking about her. She remembered his kisses and longed for him so desperately she clenched her fists and felt her nails digging into her palms. She seemed to be watching this scene as if from a great distance. Her mother leaned across and asked her once again whether she was all right. How could she explain this feeling that nothing was real except John Leslie? She thought back over of her life with Monet since he had arrived at her parents' chateau, the excitement of having an artist among them, this exotic creature with long hair and a beard. She had taken to him straight away and he to her. She remembered the joy when he had praised her painting, the years they had worked side by side. He had been her lodestar and she had worshipped him, wanting only to please. Life here, at Giverny had been filled with company and laughter. How had this happened… in a day, an hour, and what could she do about it? Monet would expect her to be out with him all day tomorrow painting and for days after that. There would be no opportunity of meeting John Leslie. She felt weak and helpless, sick with longing. As the week progressed so did her feeling of apartness grow, her yearning to be with John Leslie again.

'You look thoughtful, madame.' The gamine had arrived beside her. Close to, she was even more astonishing, the marble complexion against the dark auburn hair.

'Oh just observing it all, mademoiselle, I am something of a spectator.'

'I guess a painter has to be, especially a painter of your

skills. Why there is difficulty to tell the difference between some of your work and M'sieur Monet's.'

'Oh! Where have you seen my paintings?'

'I haven't actually seen them but they are famous, of course. I've heard them spoken about in New York by the most respected artists and at lectures, of course, in the museums and art galleries.'

'So, you are a serious student, mademoiselle?'

'Yes, I am and of impressionism in particular. The moment I saw the exhibition in New York, I fell in love with that vision, the happy, carefree lives they must have led, you know, drinking wine in cafés, having long earnest discussions about art. My family have everything mapped out for me, you see but I…'

She looked so earnest Blanche was forced to smile. 'I think that is an over romantic view. Yes, they discussed art but also there were all the arguments and jealousies as there always are with a group of creative people.'

Judith seemed not to hear or want to hear. 'Oh, if only I'd been alive then… the fashion, the bohemian life of artists. It would have been my era.' She hesitated. 'Madame Blanche, I said my dreams had come true today but the final dream would be to visit the house.'

There was something about her hunger for life, her preoccupation with self that reminded Blanche of her stepfather. Like him, she appeared to see no reason why she should not have what she wanted from life. She felt a grudging admiration for Judith who behaved as she had once dreamed of behaving. It would be intriguing to study her further.

'Well then, I will make sure he invites you.'

– TEN –

ROBERT

At this hour of night, he cherished his solitude; he needed this time before sleep to settle his mind. He liked to go over the events of the day, remembering moments that pleased him: the smell of coffee, sunlight through leaves, a sparrow pecking crumbs, before putting them to rest. He had gone through this ritual for as long as he had lived in Giverny but tonight, somehow, was different. This young woman with her energy and demands had unsettled him. Her urgency to achieve her goal at whatever cost, her irresponsibility had stirred up the past, summoning to his mind images he had believed laid to rest.

He saw himself sitting by the creek with his dog. Cautiously, he pursued the memory further. There he was with his arm round Rusty's neck, the animal leaning slightly against him as he watched the play of light on the water beyond the willow trees. He felt the peace around him and his reluctance to leave it. He saw them walking, that other Robert and his dog, back along the path through the trees, a path beaten hard by the children coming down to swim in the creek.

As he pushed open the back door he saw his mother standing at the sink. She turned and gave him a wry smile. 'Good to see you, son. Maybe you can help quiet Florrie a little. She's a mite overexcited.'

There he was in the dining room where his father and Florence were already sitting at the table. Now he remembered back to those family meals when his sister was wilful and funny, making them laugh in spite of themselves. These were that other Robert's memories: the house in small town America and his life there, the boy he had been. There was a loaf on the table and a jug of water. He sat down and poured himself a glass. Florence was giggling as she told his father something and he was pretending to scold her. Then he saw Robert and gave him a quick grin. His mother came into the room, carrying a casserole of meat and dumplings and sat herself down at the table.

'Hey, Annie!' his father said. 'Just listen to what Florrie has been up to today. Tell your mother, Florrie, go on.'

He saw his little sister's blonde curls, her wide blue eyes. He watched his parents' patient gaze as she told how she and Elsie had jumped from a low garden wall onto the walnuts Elsie's father had laid out to dry before he stored them in his attic.

'And cracked them all?' His mother shook her head. 'Every man jack of them! You naughty little girl, what am I going to do with you?'

She turned to Robert as if for support and he shrugged. Florrie had a will of her own, even at six years old.

There was a chocolate pudding made with tapioca. They were always eating tapioca, it was supposed to be good for you. He found his mother's cooking heavy. He preferred to nibble apples and nuts from the trees when he was out in the country. Aunt Mattie had an old English cook book and she sometimes made him a crème brûlée, which was light and tasty and which he loved. He never told anyone where he went on those jaunts with Rusty, roaming the fields or just sitting by the creek. He could be himself then, a nine-year-old boy let loose from watching over Florrie. He sensed his father's gaze on him and wondered what he was thinking.

'Are you going fishing on Sunday, Father?' Robert asked for something to say.

'That's right, are you coming?'

'Oh Frank don't be silly, you know he isn't,' his mother said. 'He'll be taking Florrie to Sunday School.'

Robert met his mother's gaze, *and making sure she behaves herself,* her expression implied.

His father was exploring the chocolate pudding again and saw none of this.

Robert stirred himself and gazed at the garden sinking into the night but he was wide-awake, sniffing the scents of drowsing flowers, hearing the hoot of an owl. After a while, he rose and wandered along the path, eased open the studio door and stepped inside. There was a full moon, which shone through the window directly onto the easel where a painting was propped, the one he knew Harry had worked on over the past three days. He was far more single minded. In fact, he came out with it the other day: 'she's a disruptive influence, Robert. Do as you want but I am not going to allow her to distract me from my work.'

The picture was almost finished, it gleamed in the silver light, the paint not yet dry. It showed a local woman washing clothes in the river, a subject Robert wouldn't touch. He never had any figures in his paintings, preferred landscapes, fields of corn and poppies, willows by the river. Harry had a gift for capturing movement; his figures looked robust, planted fair and square in their setting, although he found it strange that Harry never painted men. But then, he needed people as Judith did, they were both physical, he with his tennis and rowing, she ready to break out in dance, and they were both much younger than he.

This place had been his home far longer and he had memories they couldn't share. For them it was a quite affluent place where people had transformed their cottages with flowers, roses in particular. Giverny's inhabitants felt themselves superior to the other surrounding villages, which did not have an artist in their midst. But he recalled a time when he had held his breath as he passed the hen yards with their terrible smell and watched the local people rise with the sun and go to bed with it. They had been wary and kept themselves apart but, in his view, it was much more authentic. He was one of that first small colony; now youthful Americans journeyed here because it had become known as the place to visit. One saw them everywhere, lounging in cafés, cycling to Vernon and painting, of course.

In those days, the community had centred on the Hotel Baudy where Lucien made himself responsible for the guests after the secret police had watched them for six months. He smiled as he remembered how cheap it was, all that free red wine. He cherished Giverny as his sanctuary from that awful event he had left behind. He stayed on the outside, observing the couples who came and went, the very young man who arrived with his tutor from Paris. There had been a group of pretty young women, the Hoschedé and the Perry sisters. They seemed to be having a fine old time with the Americans. 'Don't tell Monet,' one of them had pleaded. Her name was Blanche Hoschedé who joined them sometimes to paint, whose easel was set up near to John Leslie's and he knew they were falling in love.

Fine looking man, John Leslie, high cheekbones and an aquiline nose, but it was his eyes that drew one, his penetrating, enquiring gaze. He was a master of composition and, for a time, he had seemed close to Monet but then…

– ELEVEN –

CLAUDE

He takes a turn around the garden, pauses by each rose arch to satisfy himself that the work has been done. He gazes upward and the sun dazzles his eyes so much he has the sensation of blindness. It never used to be like that but then Doctor Coutela says it is another of the symptoms and to be expected. He pulls the brim of his hat down over his eyes and pokes at the ground with his shoe, pleased to find the soil is damp. He sees Michel with the hose, directing it towards the nasturtiums. Thirsty plants, nasturtiums, but they grow like wildfire and give you such a show with their pretty plate-like leaves that catch the dew, their jolly reds and oranges and yellows. That's what he loves about his garden, this cheek by jowl arrangement of classic varieties and so called humble plants. He has no time for manicured lawns and clipped privet; there is lushness here, a combined energy of thrusting growth and flowering.

'*Bonjour*, Michel.'

The young man is grinning, his shirtsleeves and the bottoms of his trousers are damp. He is like a boy with a water pistol.

'How are you enjoying working for us?'

'It's good, m'sieur. I am learning a lot.'

'Better than working on the land, eh?'

Michel gives an expressive shrug.

'Be good and maybe you will take over M'sieur Breuil's job when he retires.'

They laugh at this. Breuil has said he will work until he drops.

He stays a moment longer, watching Michel watering the roses. The boy has wide shoulders and powerful arms though his legs are short and if he is anything like his father, he'll have a belly on him in a few years' time. But this morning, with the sun glinting on his black hair, arm thrown back to direct the spray, and backed by hollyhocks, rose, white and yellow, he becomes abstract.

'One could paint that,' he murmurs and Michel looks across in question.

'Nothing, nothing, I'll leave you to your work.'

In the studio he is still thinking about the garden and why he created it. From the very beginning, from those days when they were all out here working, he had in his mind what this store of flowers would offer to impressionism, the use of colour without resorting to line. Light, colour and detail: his forte. What was it Cézanne said of him? 'Only an eye but what an eye.' The important thing is to know how to use the colours. That came with practice, was a matter of habit. He'd soon moved away from dark colours and never used pure black, rather obtained an appearance of black with a combination of blues, greens and reds. It is wonderful what shades you can achieve with a limited choice. Even when his palette became much lighter and brighter, he stuck with white lead, cadmium yellow, vermilion, madder, cobalt blue and chrome green. That was all.

But now this invasion of reds and yellows, distortion of colour in his work as his vision deteriorates, details fade, shapes blur, he sees everything through a mist. Even so, he finds it beautiful and paints it because he is accustomed to paint what he sees. Others have said this is artistic development; he knows it is because of his sight. That is why the ordering of his paints is crucial, their labels trigger memory, call up colours in his mind's eye. This morning, no doubt about it, they have been disturbed. He calls, 'Blanche, Blanche!' No reply.

Lilli passes with an armful of linen. 'Madame is in one of the children's rooms, m'sieur.'

'What on earth is she doing there? Blanche!' he bellows up the stairs.

'Oh dear, is something wrong?' She comes hurrying down. 'What is it, Papa?'

'I can't paint. Everything is disturbed. That girl…'

'Hush. We'll soon put it right.'

He watches her deft sorting of the paints and marvels at her patience with him. His irritation ebbs away, she has always been a calming influence. He sees her in a pinafore, what would she be, about eleven years old? She trails behind him with the wheelbarrow, they set up their easels. Every time the light changes and he calls out: number five or seven or thirteen, she selects the right canvas with the same surety as now. And she paints, adapting his style to her own palette, her brush marks, though often they are very much the same as his.

She looks up and meets his eye. 'Remember how we said we shouldn't work together, that I was becoming too influenced by you?'

'You were good in your own right, my dear.'

'Yes. It would be easier if I weren't.'

'You should still be painting now.'

'How can I when I am taking care of you, making sure you carry on?'

' I'm sorry. I'm a nuisance, I'll have the operation and then it will be easier for you.'

'We have discussed all that and come to the conclusion you're too old.'

'I feel so helpless.'

Blanche sighs. They stare at the names of the paints: vermilion, cobalt blue.

'I can't tell you to give it up, can I? It is life itself for you.'

There is a pause. His thoughts go to yesterday's picnic, of how, for a short time, he had felt like his old self.

'What was the name of that vivacious American girl? I took to her.'

'Judith Goldstein.'

'That's it.'

'She'd like to come and visit you here.' Blanche's tone is casual.

'Why not? Perhaps it would cheer me up.'

'You could certainly do with that.'

'Take the strain off you a little. Very well, invite her please.'

For the rest of the morning he paints and by lunchtime is satisfied with what he has produced. There is another, unfamiliar feeling: he has something to look forward to.

– TWELVE –

ROBERT

There was to be no getting out of it, Robert told Judith. The painting trip was arranged and she was coming with them. 'It will take you out of yourself, keep you from moping about, waiting for news.'

When she protested she really didn't feel like painting, he put his hands over his ears.

'I can't hear you, Judith.'

This was his opportunity to resolve something that was bothering him and he was determined to take it.

They set out immediately after breakfast, he, Harry, Judith and a young couple, Rupert and Hattie, who were staying at Hotel Baudy for a few weeks. He planned to take a favourite route that led across fields, through woodland until they arrived at an expanse of cornfield. It was a marvellous day of blue sky and breeze blown cloud, the poplar leaves gently shaken. They were all in high spirits, striding through the countryside, walking among trees, along sun-dappled paths. Rupert whistled *When It's Apple Blossom Time In Normandy* and they all joined in, laughing when they failed to hit the higher notes. After a while, Judith seemed to catch their mood and brighten.

Robert fell into step beside her. 'See those hedges, they're a special feature of this area. They're made up of such a wide variety of trees and shrubs: oak, ash, sweet chestnut and cherry. Most of the ones you see here date from the middle of the eighteenth century through to the last when they went in for enclosure in a grand way. They were planted largely for firewood and known as the Peasant's Forest. Oh look…'

He broke off and stooped to peer at a small purple orchid. 'No, don't pick it,' he snapped as she made to do so.

'It's just so pretty.'

'That's no reason to have it. This is where it belongs.' Robert felt a stab of annoyance. This girl was used to having her every whim satisfied. He was unreasonably delighted she had not been granted this one.

'Okay.' Judith shrugged and changed the subject, 'I was thinking of what you told me, the other day, about Camille. Was she very pretty?'

'If the paintings of her are anything to go by she was beautiful. She had a magic about her, a gift for striking a pose. There's a picture of her sitting on the grass, wearing the purest of white dresses, spread out grandly around her. Her little boy, Jean, has thrown himself down beside her and she holds a red fan. Both Monet and Renoir painted her in the same pose but Renoir makes her features more vivid. What a time it must have been for her with these great artists wanting to paint her.'

'So the family had some money by then?'

'Oh yes, Monet was selling well, they had a lovely house and garden in Argenteuil. The Camille in that painting must have felt life was perfect.'

'But you said she died.'

'Yes, in her thirties, I believe. It was very sad.'

'I'd say it was romantic, to have led that glamorous life and then to die before she started to get old and ugly. All the heroines in the books I read die young.'

He caught a flash of the extraordinary intensity about her, the glittering eyes and earnest expression. Once again she provoked that sense of *déjà vu*, disconcerted him. Robert wondered what was behind this studied interest in Monet's first wife.

He shaded his eyes and gazed around, the others had walked on and almost reached the cornfield. They must hurry to join them. As they arrived, the breeze ruffled the full ears of corn and ran through the trees, crows rose up complaining and for a moment all seemed to dance with life. He was reminded of the painting of Van Gogh, his use of intense colour, impassioned brushstroke, the movement and vibration of form and line. Poor tormented Vincent, trying to interpret what he saw beyond the veil. The thought reinforced his own delight in the world around him, his ability to paint it.

There was good-natured teasing as everyone set up their easels. Judith moved a distance away from the group. They opened their paint boxes and then there was silence.

Using a broad bristle brush, Robert applied himself; this was what he enjoyed about painting landscapes as opposed to the figurative genre Harry used. Large areas of sky, fields and wide horizons allowed loose broad brushstrokes, ladling the pigment onto the canvas, working with a limited palette. It meant the work could be completed in one sitting. First, he killed the whiteness of the canvas, priming it with permanent rose and cadmium yellow. While he waited for it to dry a little, he took the opportunity to watch

Judith. She wore the pretty summer frock he had seen the other day and the plain straw hat, but beneath it her expression was grave. She dabbed with her brush then sighed and paused, then dabbed again. After a while, she sat back from the canvas, reached for her handbag and powdered her nose. She looked out of place among the absorbed painters yet she'd told him how much she had enjoyed her painting lessons in New York.

Robert turned back to his work. He made a sketchy composition with a soft pencil and began on the palest colour of the sky. Then he added a little burnt sienna and ultramarine to the mix and dabbed it onto the darker areas of the clouds. He lit a cigarette.

This time he caught Judith's eye and she made a little grimace then turned away. She seemed to be using her brush like a knife, slashing it across the canvas. He wondered how she was seeing the scene before them. Was she giving it that special attention it required? He always wondered about perception and marvelled how there could be so many interpretations of the same subject. He knew he would never paint like Van Gogh though he continued to strive for Monet's style. Judith's mind seemed elsewhere.

He went back to the clouds; he had given them a rippled effect, which would echo the texture of the corn. He added a little blue and sketched the sky using a few brush strokes to add cumulus clouds, then sat back to examine his work.

Judith was gazing off into the distance, the picture of someone who wanted to be anywhere else but here.

Robert mixed again, adding burnt sienna and viridian. He took up a sable brush to sketch in detail around the cypress trees, moving the brush in the direction of the trees' growth. He glanced up and noticed that Judith was attempting to paint again. A part of him felt guilty he had pushed her into this situation, she was very young, after all. On the other hand, he was doing it for her own good.

Now the corn itself: going back to the bristle brush, he dabbed around the distant area, allowing the paint to skid across the canvas. For the foreground he returned to permanent rose mixed with a little burnt umber. It only remained to knit the areas of colour and tone with a clean soft brush and, *voila*, the painting was complete.

Time had passed unnoticed and his stomach rumbled. He looked across to where Judith sat frowning at her canvas, her hands idle.

'How are you doing?' Robert stood up, stretched and strolled over to look. There was a pause. 'The purple shades are interesting. Was that how you saw the cornfield?'

'Don't be silly, Robert, you can see with your own eyes what it looks like. My painting isn't anything like it.'

'Painters see subjects in all kinds of colours.'

'Oh, stop humouring me.'

'Judith, please.'

'It's a terrible painting. I'm useless at it, can't you see?'

She flung down her brush, jumped up and hurried away in the direction of a small wood.

Robert sighed and followed her. 'What was that all about?'

'I'm not a painter,' she said. 'I don't know why you invited me to come with you, today.'

'Oh Judith, it was just meant to be a bit of fun, painting in the open air together. Not a competition.'

'I envy you all, your talent. You are artists, you have a reason to be here. I envy you, don't you know? This life you all share.'

Robert steered her to a fallen tree trunk and they sat down. 'So that's what it's all about.'

He lit a cigarette, recognising the opportunity to say what he had planned. 'Listen, maybe you're making yourself unhappy with this notion of staying on here. If you could treat it as a long vacation and not take everything so seriously…?'

Judith turned on him. 'You've lived here for years and years. You told me you could never go back.'

'But it's completely different for me, Judith.'

'How is it different?'

Above their heads a blackbird sang, melodious and flute-like, unhurried in its delivery. Robert caught sight of a butterfly with rich brown wings, its yellow dappling a perfect match with the lightly shaded wood. There was harmony here, the myriad pieces fitting so beautifully together, the whole a great artist's creation. The only note that jarred was Judith's persistence.

He sighed. 'I had to leave America. I'll tell you about it some time. It just wasn't possible to go on living there. But you have a loving family who wants the best for you.'

Judith had been staring ahead, now she turned to glare at him. 'Is that what you think?'

'I know it may not seem like that, at the moment. But they sound like good parents to me. Look how they are supporting you here, three whole months in Giverny. But I can't imagine they would go on doing that indefinitely. Then where would you be without money? Judith, I don't think you have much choice.'

'Of course I do. Everyone has the right to decide her own destiny. If my parents won't support me I have other ideas.'

She leaned down and picked a dandelion; once again the action annoyed him.

'Okay,' he said. 'Tell me how you intend to go about it.'

'The other day at the picnic, Monet was very taken with me. He said I reminded him of his first wife. My hair is dark like hers was, he said, and he liked the way I dress. He told me I knew how to wear clothes, just as she did. I made him laugh, you saw that, unlike that frump, his stepdaughter. He needs a new interest in his life, someone to make him feel young again. Maybe I can be his new muse.'

'And what about Blanche?'

'What about her?'

'That woman is a saint. Remember what I told you? She sacrifices her life to him.'

'Then she is very stupid.' Judith tore the dandelion into pieces and scattered them on the ground. 'She should employ a nurse. That's what my mother did when grandmother went batty.'

'It would bring shame on the family here. People would see it as disrespectful.'

'Well it certainly didn't bring shame on my mother, but it allowed her to carry on enjoying her life. Grandmother doesn't seem to mind but then she's hardly compos mentis. Golly, I never ever want to get old like her.' Judith kicked at the undergrowth with her foot. 'I don't understand what it is about these folks in Giverny. Why do they care what others think? They all seem mighty interested in each other's business.'

'It is a close knit society here,' he said, weary of the subject, 'that's why I like it.'

'But to sacrifice everything the way this Blanche is doing!

Women are changing, Robert. Look what's happened in America, the demonstrations in England. I just adore Emily Pankhurst, I'd chain myself to railings if I were there. No, I would never dream of devoting my life to old relatives.'

Robert grunted. 'It is called being accountable for your actions, Judith, of being aware of their repercussion on others. That is why you would never fit in.'

There was a pause, from the corner of his eye he saw her purse her lips.

Then she said: 'I'll wager Camille didn't think that way.'

He did not care to answer. After a long silence, he cleared his throat. 'Anyway, it's time for luncheon. Let's go and open the picnic basket.'

Judith muttered she was not hungry. In the end he left her sitting on the tree trunk and went to join the party, to fall on the quiche, the juicy tomatoes and little sweet apples Angelina Baudy had packed for them.

'Isn't the young lady joining us?' Rupert asked.

Robert shook his head.

Hattie sipped her wine. 'Sulking, is she? I cannot imagine anyone who possesses such wonderful clothes feeling any need to sulk.'

They laughed and Rupert remarked that happiness was more than having nice frocks.

'Sure,' replied his wife. 'But they go an awful long way.'

While he ate, Robert thought of their conversation. Far from putting his mind at rest, it had made him more anxious. He hadn't meant to be harsh but there was something about Judith, an egoism he felt he wanted to crush. It was more than that. The sense he had had on their first meeting that she would stop at nothing to get what she wanted, had intensified. Just what was she capable of doing?

'How did the painting go?' Harry asked him.

His friend was watching him. Dear Harry with his self-contained take on life. He'd stated already he wanted to have nothing to do with Judith, didn't like the girl.

'Well, I think. I never tire of painting cornfields. There is something about them that is so joyful.'

'You and your landscapes,' the other teased. He clinked his glass to Robert's. '*À ta santé.*'

They smiled at each other.

After the picnic, they made a tour of the canvasses, commenting upon each other's work. When they came to Judith's, there was silence, no-one seemed to know what to say.

Then Hattie remarked: 'What an awful daub.'

Robert eyed it again; there was something about those muddy colours and the angry brushwork he found disturbing. He turned and saw Judith had come out of the wood and was standing a short distance from the group. Had she heard Hattie's comment, he wondered.

The party that returned to Giverny was much quieter. The heat of the day had tired them and they had all worked hard. Judith trailed behind, seeming in a world of her own. Robert's thoughts turned to a bath, a change of clothes and a cocktail on the terrace, preferably with Harry. As they stepped into the cool entrance hall, Lucien Baudy passed through and said there was a letter for Judith.

She seized the cream envelope, tore it open and read, then turned to Robert with a triumphant smile. 'I win this round!'

THIRTEEN

BLANCHE

On these summer days, when it was too hot to be outside, Blanche had taken to spending some quiet time in her room after luncheon. The house was still, there were only the subdued sounds of Annette washing up in the kitchen. Lilli would be ironing, Marie putting her feet up before she started preparing supper. Papa, of course, was working.

As she stole up the stairs, for some reason not wanting anyone to know where she was, and closed the bedroom door behind her she felt she was keeping a clandestine appointment.

There was a velvet padded seat by the window and here she sat and gazed out over the garden, though not really seeing it. She concentrated on Maman, her illness, her death and the funeral. Sometimes she cried as she had not been able to do in the weeks of supporting Papa, now and then she spoke aloud of love and yearning, even anger that Alice could leave them. Over the past week, she had started to examine their lives together. Today, she looked back to that time when they were living in the chateau at Montgeron. In her mind's eye, she saw the expanse of parkland, the rose garden, the pond; giant white turkeys with drooping red wattles roamed over the grassy hill and beyond, the red brick building could be glimpsed through trees. She thought of her sister Marthe, of the two of them wheeling their dolls' prams along the paths, always together, fussing over Josephine and Isabelle, making sure their porcelain faces were protected from the sun; but there always seemed to be another real life baby in the family. She smelled the crisp autumnal air, heard the crack of rifle shot, saw dead pheasants and rabbits lying on a leafy forest carpet.

Always there was Maman: kind hearted, eager to please, the perfect mother, inventing games and outings for them all during the long summer days in the country. She found it difficult to conjure up her father, a shadowy presence who came and went. If she thought of him, it was with a sense of the unease he brought into the house when he returned from his trips to Paris. There would be anxious conversations and her mother went about the place looking strained until more guests arrived, as they always did, and once again, she became the delightful hostess.

'How brave you were, Maman,' she murmured. 'I would come to your room to watch you dress for dinner. I'd watch while you arranged your hair and put on your jewellery. You'd be wearing one of your beautiful gowns, the rose silk was my favourite. When you'd finished, you'd stand up and say, "Well how do I look, Blanchefleur?" All smiles, all worries gone and I'd feel so proud you were my mother.'

Down in the garden she saw Michel come from the greenhouse with a box of plants under each arm. He knelt by one of the lozenge flowerbeds and began to plant them. He was wearing a straw hat, you needed one in this heat; it must be tiring working under that sun, it was warm enough here in the room. She took up a fan and moved the still air.

She was seeing the train that brought Monet to the chateau, arriving along the tracks Papa had had put down through the parkland. Though how they could afford to commission an artist was a mystery to her, Maman had said. After a while they became used to seeing the man with long hair and a dark beard at his easel, painting every day. When they were curious, he didn't shoo them away as their father would have done, instead he explained patiently how this colour mixed with that made this. They watched the paintings grow and were fascinated, Blanche especially. He noticed this and singled her out and she became his slave. There was something about him so expansive and grand, the way he slapped the paint onto the canvas with a hand that never faltered. She also noted that, when her father was away and it was just her mother and Monet in the chateau, the atmosphere altered and there was laughter and fun. She heard her mother singing in her room on the day they all made an excursion to Bois de la Grande for a picnic. They walked along the avenue of trees with their leafy branches lacing over ahead and Monet said it was better than going to church, any day.

'Oh Maman, you didn't scold him as you might have done anyone else, devout as you were. Instead we all took hands and strode along singing *Frère Jacques*, singing and singing until we tired of it.'

Blanche laid her fan in her lap. And then there was the surprise of being told yet another baby was on the way. Could it be that Monet was the father of Jean Pierre? no-one had ever said anything but as things had turned out...

One afternoon, she stood on a chair to open an upper

cupboard and fetch down some of her paintings. She had tried to put them out of her mind but the conversation with that American girl, Judith, resonated, the remark that she, Blanche, was spoken about in New York. She carried them over to the light: *Monet's House*, *The Pond at Giverny* and two or three others, and examined them critically. They were good, no doubt about that, she had a fine eye for colour and the atmosphere was tangible, of a garden heavy with foliage, waiting for its summer flowering. She surprised herself by not feeling upset or angry, the reactions she would have expected; it was as if she were examining with a dispassionate eye, admiring what she saw. They stirred memories of other, happier days.

1888

On Tuesday of the following week Monet had announced his intention of going into Rouen and she had managed to slip away, unnoticed. She hurried along the street towards the pink washed house, praying he would be there but preparing herself in case he wasn't. With her heart beating fast, she peered through the foliage into the garden and there he was, seated at his easel, intent on his work. There was no sign of anyone else. She called softly to him and he looked up, grinned and came quickly to the garden gate.

'John Leslie!'

'Blanche!' his eyes shone. 'You're here.'

'I had to see you,' she whispered. 'I couldn't bear it any longer.'

'No need to whisper, there is nobody here. Come in.'

She stepped into the garden and they stood for a moment gazing at each other then he took hold of her hands.

'I was praying you'd come,' he said. 'It's been such a long time.'

'A week.'

She looked at him, the sun on his dark hair, the sharp curve of his cheekbones, his mouth, the truth of his presence made her catch her breath. Her sense of separateness vanished and she was just Blanche, heart pounding, mouth dry with a mixture of delight and anxiety.

'It has seemed like forever,' he said and she saw the longing in his expression.

Maybe people could see what was happening? She felt it was written as clearly on her face as it was on his. Thank God, no-one had said anything at home, not yet...

'I'm sorry I couldn't come before, I have had to go out painting with Monet, every day,' she told him. 'Listen to him going on about haystacks.'

'Haystacks!'

'It is what he is painting at the moment. You have no idea how difficult it has been for me, out in the fields with him each day, talking about atmosphere and changing light and reflection when all I wanted to speak about was you. And at home, I have to behave as if everything is as usual when the truth is everything is utterly changed.'

He brought her hands to his lips. 'It is, isn't it? Everything is changed. I find it hard with my family, too.'

Why should it be a secret? she wondered. Why can't I share this happiness?

'I cannot understand his loathing of us Americans, it seems out of all proportion,' John Leslie said. 'What have we ever done to him?'

'It is what you represent,' she replied. 'As interlopers in his precious domain. He will tolerate you as painters but apart from Robinson he sees you as a threat to the way things are done at Le Pressoir.'

She looked up and met his gaze. He caressed her face and

112

kissed her gently. 'The others have gone to Vernon to the market. They went early and I'm not sure how soon they'll be back.'

Over his shoulder she gazed at the easel. 'Won't you show me your painting?'

It was a simple subject of orchard grass and the beauty of apple trees in snowy blossom, the candid promise that spring offers, every year.

'A Normandy orchard: I came across it a couple of months ago. I thought I'd finished it but when I fetched it out today, I saw there was still work to be done.' He indicated areas on the canvas. 'I love that time of year, don't you, with everything coming to life again.'

Blanche, gazing, wondered but will the promise be fulfilled? What is to happen to us? Spring has gone and summer is passing, when the autumn comes he will be gone. The uncertainty returned.

He put his hands on her shoulders and turned her to face him. He looked into her eyes then, it seemed, into her mind. 'Blanche, don't worry. I am planning to come back here next summer, only then I'll stay with the Baudy family. I am trying to persuade them to transform their property into a small hotel. Somewhere where we can create a colony of painters, maybe even build some studios.'

'Really?'

'You always ask me that. Yes, really. I am attracted to this style of painting. Since I've been here my work and my palette have changed radically. Never mind what anyone says, I intend to become an impressionist.'

And you want to be with me? She asked him silently.

As they spoke they were aware of the two levels of dialogue starting again. They avoided the topic of Monet although he was as close as if he were beside them, the threat to their happiness.

'I don't want you to go ever,' she murmured.

113

'I will have to for a while, there are my studies to follow.'

She felt a stab of panic. 'I'm afraid something will happen to prevent your coming back and I won't ever see you again.'

It was all right while they were here and now and she could feel his solid presence, hear his voice. But she knew, when the moment came to say goodbye, the wrench would be so terrible she didn't know how she would bear it.

'Oh darling Blanche, of course you'll see me again and I'll write to you, often. Don't worry it will all turn out just fine. We'll overcome the problem with Monet, I'm sure.'

They moved into each other's arms and she clung to him, her face wet with tears, closing her eyes as if to shut out the world.

'Promise me,' she whispered. 'Promise you'll come back. I think I'd die if you didn't.'

'I promise,' he said.

After a while, Blanche mounted the chair again and stowed her work back in its hiding place. There was no time for painting these days but perhaps she would try a little sketching.

With a start she remembered she had arranged to see Lilli today. She glanced at her watch. At four o'clock, she had said, we will have a dress rehearsal for the dance, it was nearly half past. She hurried across to the door only to find the young woman hovering outside in the corridor.

'Oh Lilli, forgive me. I must have dozed off in this heat.'

'Beg pardon, madame? I don't want to disturb you, if you're feeling unwell.'

Blanche became brisk. 'Nonsense I am feeling perfectly fine, and we must try everything today with the dance on Thursday. Now have you brought the frock and the shoes?'

'Yes, madame. I hope they will be nice enough.'

'I'm sure they will and the shawl to set it off.' She opened the door wider. 'Come in then.'

Lilli followed her into the room where she stood clutching her package.

'Shall we begin? I need to see the frock on you first.' Realising the girl's shyness, she added, 'You can go behind the screen to change.'

After a moment, Lilli emerged. She wore a close fitting dress, blue with white spots, and edged with white at the neck and cuffs, buttons ran down the front. It was a country dress, Blanche saw that at a glance, but the girl looked fresh and charming in it. The shoes were a surprise, pretty and pointed with a low heel.

'My father has a friend who is a shoemaker,' Lilli explained when she commented on them.

'So far so good,' Blanche smiled. 'But we are going to do something rather special with your hair. If you'll sit before the mirror and take out your pins?' She smiled at the girl's surprise. 'I promise you'll be pleased with the result.'

Lilli released her hair from its neat bun and shook it out. It fell down her back like a rich golden wave. She touched it protectively. 'You're not going to cut it, are you, madame?'

'Cut hair like that? It would be a sin!'

Blanche busied herself, assembling the items she needed, the Marcel curling iron, comb and pins. There was also a horsehair rat to give extra fullness but, fingering the texture of Lilli's hair, she decided she probably wouldn't need it. They waited for the iron to heat. How grateful she was that Papa had had electricity installed a few years ago. You never knew where you were with those awful old tongs that were either too cold or too hot. There was nothing as unpleasant as the smell of burning hair.

115

She brushed out the tangles, grateful that Lilli had washed her hair recently; it crackled with electricity. Annette was inclined to be lazy about personal hygiene, sometimes unpleasantly obvious when she served at table. She divided the hair and pinned the top section out of the way. The iron was ready and she set to work taking up strands of hair, not too little, not too much, and making soft curls all round the girl's head.

While she worked, she talked. 'Did you know curly hair is meant to indicate a sweeter temperament? Straight haired girls are considered reserved, even awkward. Silly old wives' tales, of course, but I do think waves look romantic.'

Lilli was charmed. 'I've always wanted curly hair.'

'I'm afraid it won't last, though. You'd have to do this every day.' Blanche ran her fingers through the curls, turning them into soft waves. 'There, prettier still.'

'Oh thank you, madame.'

'We haven't finished yet.'

She pinned back each wavy strand to form a full bun, leaving a few soft curls at the nape of Lilli's neck. Next she curled the front section before pinning it back but left more tendrils to frame the face. Blanche felt a flutter of satisfaction as the style took shape, its effect to make Lilli's face look rounder, softer. It was almost like creating a painting, she thought, as she tucked a stray strand into place, smoothed over with a comb. Finally she stepped back and fetched a hand mirror so that the girl could see the back of her head.

'There, not exactly the Gibson girl look but on those lines.'

Lilli gave a squeak of delight. 'That's never me!'

'It most certainly is. Now let's try the shawl.'

116

She pulled open a drawer and lifted out the silk shawl, pastel blue and rose silk with self coloured embroidery. She arranged it round Lilli's shoulders.

The effect was impressive. From a pretty country girl, Lilli had become an elegant woman, one who held herself proudly, whose clear blue eyes surveyed herself solemnly in the mirror, whose mouth curved in a secret smile. She seemed unable to tear herself away.

'You're pleased?' Blanche asked at last.

'I am enchanted, madame. Thank you for taking this trouble to help me.' Her expression changed. 'How will I manage for Thursday?'

Blanche smiled. 'Don't worry, I'll do it all again for you then.'

'Oh thank you! I'll be the belle of the ball.'

She looked so young and excited, so full of expectation of what the evening might bring.

Blanche laughed. 'You will and I hope that Michel appreciates it, too.'

Let her have her heart's desire, she thought. Don't let Lilli be disappointed.

1889

John Leslie sent her a letter from Paris where he was spending the Christmas holidays with his friends. At first she had been despondent that they would not be able to stay in contact; Monet opened any correspondence that arrived at the house.

'Poste Restante,' John Leslie had announced. 'That is the answer. Go to the post office in Vernon and set it up before I leave.'

It was a simple matter to say she was going to do some shopping in town and then pass by the post office to pick up letters, although she always felt a guilty twinge as she did so, glancing back over her shoulder as if someone was watching her.

His letter spoke of how much he missed her and that she was always in his thoughts, then went on to describe his lodgings and the concierge whose blanched face and pale hair 'reminds me of a plant that has been kept in the dark too long.'

'Her meanness is legendary and even now in the depths of winter my room is unheated although there is a chimney piece. I'll tell you something: there is nothing like the damp chill of a house that is never heated. It penetrates to your very marrow. When I and some of the other tenants got up a petition to complain, she produced a charcoal stove, the kind that can be wheeled from room to room. However, there is such competition for it that often one has to rely on a good circulation to keep warm. I do a great deal of jumping up and down and flapping my arms. In particular, there is a French lady who 'borrows' the stove and 'forgets' to bring it back. In spite of all this, Paris is still a wonderful place to be. I wish you could see the snow on the streets, the branches of the trees in the Luxembourg Gardens bowed down under its weight and, of course the great church of Notre Dame which, at the moment, looks like a strange iceberg. Enough, I must get to the point of this letter. Darling Blanche, I have some news to tell you which I know will gladden your heart...'

She hid the letter in the drawer of her night table and, during preparations for the festivities, often stole upstairs to read it once again. On Christmas Eve and after Midnight Mass, the family attended a party held at a friend's house. Amid the jugs of cider and almond cakes, the laughter and conversation, she had something momentous to celebrate. Monet had sent an invitation to John Leslie and some of the other American painters to join him at Giverny – and spend a few months there. I won't give you lessons, but we'll wander about the fields and woods and paint together, he had said. A few months, she thought. A lot can happen in a few months, my darling.

Suzanne came to find her where she sat apart from the others, savouring this news. 'What is it, Blanche? Are you unwell?'

'Oh, not you too. Maman is forever asking me that.'

Her sister eyed her closely. 'There is something, isn't there? You can't deny it. You seem so distant and sometimes when I speak to you, you don't seem to be listening.'

In that moment the weight of keeping this secret to herself seemed too much to bear. It was terrible not to be able to speak of John Leslie when it was really all she wanted to do, She longed to confide but at the same time was afraid.

'Come on,' urged Suzanne. 'You can trust me, you know.' She smiled so that dimples showed. 'Are you in love?'

Blanche said nothing.

'You are, aren't you?'

Finally she nodded. 'How did you guess?'

'Oh, that's easy. You are behaving exactly like all the heroines in the books I read.'

Blanche was dismayed. Was it so obvious? If Suzanne had realised why not everyone else? 'I will tell you,' she said. 'But promise me you will keep it to yourself.'

That year the village was changing, American voices were heard increasingly along the street. Some of the villagers shook their heads and clicked their tongues at the sight of these young people who apparently did not work. Others sized up the situation and opened bars and cafés. Angelina and Lucien Baudy were the most enterprising. John Leslie's persuasion had prevailed and with surprising speed six rooms were built in the courtyard of their property and then, with Angelina's shrewd perception, they started on a studio. The young people needed to have amusement too; workmen arrived to construct tennis courts.

'When will that noise cease?' demanded Monet. 'What are they trying to do? Force me out of my home?'

In the midst of all this activity there came another letter from John Leslie. He would be arriving the following week. Blanche felt she would faint with joy.

'Let's go for a walk,' she suggested to Suzanne. Her sister had a book in her hand and was obviously all set for a quiet session under her favourite tree. 'Please?'

They took the path by the river. It was a dull overcast day and the water was dark, showing no reflection but catkin buds were breaking through and celandine shone among the trees.

'He is coming back,' she said.

'Oh Blanche, you must be so happy.'

'Of course I am but afraid too. What if Maman guesses? She's always watching me, these days. She'd be sure to tell Monet and then where would we be?'

Suzanne laughed. 'Oh don't be such a misery! It will all come right in the end. True love always finds a way.'

'You've been reading too many books,' Blanche said. 'Real life isn't always like that.'

But her sister tucked her hand under Blanche's arm and urged her along the riverbank. 'Remember what I said to you not so very long ago? We should each of us meet a wonderful man and marry and have lots of children. We'd bring them all to the house to visit and Monet would dote on them? A fairy story with a happy ending.'

Yes Blanche remembered and how moved she had been by Suzanne's innocence and hopes for the future. Now as then, she felt an urge to protect her from harm. She shivered. 'You're just an incurable romantic,' she said. 'Come on let's go back, it's turning cold.'

120

On Thursday morning of the following week, the day of John Leslie's expected arrival, she and Suzanne walked to the Baudy establishment, which was now proclaiming itself an hotel with obvious pride. On their enquiry, Madame Baudy told them that John Leslie would not arrive until later in the evening.

Blanche sat with the family at supper, imagining the taxi drawing up, the welcoming voices as someone appeared to carry in his valise, and the figure of John Leslie following, marvelling at the changes he had provoked. She wondered if he would dine sitting at one of those red-check-clothed tables, or would he too have no appetite, only the longing for the next day?

Maman's voice broke in on her thoughts. 'I met Madame Baudy in the village today. She tells me the Americans are returning for the season.'

Monet gave a short laugh. 'Hmm, surprised they can tear themselves away from the pleasures of Paris.' He lit a cigarette. 'When I think of myself at their age, oh, delicious!'

Maman clucked her tongue. 'Enough of that!'

At once, Blanche's joy was suffused with fear. John Leslie had told her of the cafés he frequented, his circle of friends and their discussions of art and politics. Now, to that scenario, she added young women: sophisticated, vivacious Parisiennes, maybe some without virtue. They laughed, they flirted, lovable charmers without a care in the world. Yes, he had sent her loving letters saying he missed her but when he saw her again, might she seem provincial and dull in comparison with what the capital had to offer?

Monet was speaking of his forthcoming trip to Paris. He would be away from the following morning and would remain so for several days. He was going to see the World Fair where Eiffel held court atop his one thousand foot tower and a host of artists and personalities, Buffalo Bill, Annie Oakley, Gauguin, Whistler and Edison travelled to Paris to mingle and make their mark. But while others queued to mount to the second level, Monet's goal was water lilies.

'This man, this Latour-Marliac is a genius. I cannot wait to see the colours of these new hybrids. White, yes we all know white water lilies, but apparently these are pink and yellow and heaven knows what other shades.'

'Very nice,' murmured Maman.

'Nice! Nice! They are wonders, Alice, possibly one of the wonders of the world. Listen, if ever I have enough money I'll buy a piece of that grazing land and build a pond, and I'll stock it with those Latour-Marliac water lilies.'

What do I care about water lilies, Blanche thought.

Next morning, she lurked in the library until she heard Monet's valise being dragged down the stairs, he following, barking last minute instructions to Alice. There was a final '*au revoir*' from her mother and the brisk trot of the horse as the trap bore him away. Blanche rose, took a last glance in her pocket mirror and stole out of the house. She felt her heart race as she hurried along the road, hoping he would think her pretty in the frock she had chosen for this occasion. Or was it too naïve after the fashions he must have seen in Paris? She didn't know, in fact, she felt at that moment, she knew nothing about this business of wooing, which Suzanne appeared to have learned from the books she read. Blanche took a deep breath. One thing was constant: she loved John Leslie with her heart and soul.

'Blanche!'

He was standing outside the hotel in his shirt sleeves and she remembered their first meeting, her first impression of him: the contrast of tanned skin and dark hair against the open necked white shirt. But there was something in his expression that mirrored her earlier thoughts.

'Am I dreaming or are we really together again?'

Had he too feared the danger of their separation?

'John Leslie! Oh, John Leslie!'

They were in each other's arms uncaring of curious stares, oblivious of everything except coming together until his hand raised her face and they kissed, a long, sweet kiss.

After a while, they drew apart and he smiled at her. 'I cannot tell you how happy I am to see you again. Sometimes, I thought, I don't know, that you might have changed your mind, gone back to your life with the family and I couldn't bear it.'

'Really?'

He laughed.' Sweetheart, why do you always ask me that?'

'Because I can never hear enough times it is true.'

'True, true, true... a thousand times true.' He kissed her forehead, her cheeks, her closed eyes and returned to her mouth again. 'I love you, Blanche,' he murmured. 'More than ever. Love, love, love you.'

She raised her arms to him and his encircled her waist. The sun blazed and spotlighted them in its glare. After some time, Madame Baudy appeared.

'My children, I do not want to interfere but perhaps it would be more discreet if you either came inside or went for a walk by the river.' And to Blanche in French, she added: 'You know how they talk in Giverny.'

'I know,' said John Leslie, who understood. 'We are going.' He took Blanche's hand and hurried her away.

'A pond!' he smiled when they were sitting together by the river. 'Well, that should keep him out of mischief.'

'If only,' breathed Blanche.

'Perhaps tonight?' he said. 'What do you think? If I came to the house, could you slip out into the garden?'

'Yes, of course,' she said. 'Come tonight. I'll let you in by the gate at the back. With Monet away it should be easy.'

123

'Well hello, look who's here!' A voice interrupted them, a female voice with an American accent. Blanche saw a young woman with blonde hair had arrived beside them. She was dressed in blue voile and wore a shady hat. 'When did you get back then?'

'Oh hello, Veronica.'

The woman was looking questioningly at Blanche.

John Leslie said quickly, 'This is Mademoiselle Hoschedé. A friend of mine.'

'Pleased to meet you.' The other smiled but it was obvious it was John Leslie who held her interest. 'How long are you staying this time?' she asked him. 'Isn't the Baudy marvellous? They've built tennis courts, did you know that? Maybe we can have a game sometime?' she lowered her eyes flirtatiously.

He seemed at a loss as to what to say. Her presence had clearly unnerved him. Blanche felt him tremble.

The woman turned her blue gaze onto Blanche and something like realisation came into her expression. 'Gee, I'm sorry if I butted in?'

To her astonishment Blanche found she was jealous, jealous of the free and easy way this woman spoke, the assumption that she and John Leslie were friends. She was bewildered as she felt this jealousy mount within her. It was irrational, she knew, but uncontrollable and she had to get away.

'It's perfectly all right,' she said. 'I really must go.'

With the sound of John Leslie's protest in her ears, she rose and walked away and did not look back. She heard Veronica's whining tone: 'What have I done?' and John Leslie's curt reply: 'Did anyone ever tell you it's rude to interrupt a conversation?'

Blanche hurried back to the house, feeling she wanted to cry. Her emotions were all jumbled up, love and pain, anger and sadness, like a great knot inside her. She longed to go to her mother and tell her all that was troubling her, as she had done when she was a child. She would love the indulgence of crying and being comforted and then to be told that, yes, there was nothing to worry about, yes, of course she could marry John Leslie. But she knew she had to keep quiet. That was the problem, she found it difficult to say very much at all to Maman these days, in case it veered onto this dangerous topic. It was the same with Monet, if she came near to the truth with him, her defences would break down and all the guilty happiness come spilling out. So over the past months they had worked in silence, painting side by side but, at least for her, with the sense of a great distance between them.

In the garden that night, the moon only a sliver in the sky so that they were hidden in shadow, John Leslie took her hands in his and kissed the knuckles. 'I wanted to come to tell you I love you.'

'I know,' she said feeling helpless. 'And I love you.'

She had spoken the words that up until then had been only in her head; they were out in the open now. Deception and lies that was what her joy had made her do. Just to hear his voice and the reassurance they had given each other made her unbearably happy. But the same happiness stung her as she gazed about seeing ghostly roses clambering over an arch, the dark mass of foliage, realising this was Monet's domain, which he guarded jealously, and she was part of it; he relied on her and would never agree to her going very far away. She felt trapped here by the sediment of her life. She turned to John Leslie and he drew in his breath and with his thumb wiped away the tears streaming down her face.

'Blanche what's wrong? Oh my love, my love.'

Somewhere in the house a light appeared, shining through a window.

'I had better go,' he said. His hands slipped out of hers and they hurried down to the gate.

'Goodnight, Blanche.' He kissed her swiftly and was gone.

In her bedroom, Blanche undressed and lay between the unfriendly sheets. She thought: What shall I do? What shall I do?

– FOURTEEN –

CLAUDE

Breuil says Michel's work and dedication please him. 'You know me, m'sieur, I'm not one to enthuse but I must admit the boy has gone beyond my expectations.'

Aware of his head gardener's critical eye, his perfectionism, Claude is surprised. Just what exactly has Michel been doing to gain such praise? To illustrate, Breuil takes him on a tour of the roses whose leaves now gleam dark green and perfectly formed without a trace of rust.

'He went over them so carefully I'll swear he didn't miss a diseased leaf,' Breuil says. 'Took him hours. It's surprising to find such patience in a young man.'

'Excellent. I was really worried.'

'Me, too but not any more, he won't allow it to return.'

It appears that the admirable Michel has since busied himself finding other jobs to do.

'Young rascal even suggested we were behind on the seed collection,' Breuil chuckles, obviously delighted with his pupil. 'He's already taken cuttings from fuchsia and penstemon, got them in cutting compost over here, in this shady spot, ready to pot up.'

As he speaks, they walk slowly from bed to bed where

each variety, zinnias, salvias, gladiolus and cosmos speak to Claude of some memory. Year in, year out, when their season comes around, they bloom again while the voices of those guests who walked among them are now silent: Pissarro, Cézanne and Berthe Morisot. Nasturtiums overspill the pathway where Mallarmé once spoke of the sound rather than meaning of words in his poetry.

This garden, he thinks, was planted with regard to paintings not yet painted and the paintings were a response to a garden where the elements of colour and array are also a work of art.

They arrive at the circle of grass where Alice once sat in the shade of the paulownia on such a day as this, doing her needlework. And here they find Michel sprawled, drinking from a bottle of lemonade.

He springs to his feet. '*Pardon*. It has only been a few minutes.'

'Stay where you are,' commands Claude. 'It seems to me you deserve a rest now and then after all the work I hear you've been doing.'

The young man flushes.

'What gave you the idea to take cuttings, I'd like to know?'

'M'sieur Breuil lent me some gardening books, I've been reading those.'

'Ah.'

'There is so much to do at this time of year, what with the lack of rain. I plan to mulch tomorrow.'

'Well done, that should help to keep the ground moist, eh Breuil?'

He catches Breuil grinning like a proud father.

'Your parents should be happy that you have such an excellent teacher. I had to start from scratch and learn as I went along. When I first started painting, I tried to go my own way and my father threatened to cut off my allowance.' He chuckles. 'He told me to get it into my head that I was going to work seriously. He wanted to see me in a studio under the discipline of a reputable master.'

He feels at peace with the world, this morning. He woke with a delicious sense of anticipation. When he said his habitual good morning to Alice, he added, 'well, *cherie*, not long to go now. I am sure you are happy for me.'

With Breuil's permission, he cuts some roses and when Annette serves him breakfast he asks her to lay them by Blanche's plate at luncheon. He drinks his café au lait, dipping a pain au chocolat into it. The taste is intense as it used to be. It seems to him that all his senses have come alive except, of course, his sight but at this moment he feels the others compensate for it. It is the imminent arrival of this American girl that is responsible. He always liked an attractive woman.

Light floods into his studio, bird song comes through the open window. He takes up his brush and paints with firm, confident strokes.

It is as if a cloud has lifted.

At luncheon, Blanche gives a little cry of delight when she finds the flowers.

He shrugs. 'Bit of an apology for my awful moods.'

'Ah well.' She brings the flowers to her nose. 'Which are these?'

'Duchesse d'Angouleme and another gallica, I forget the name... Tuscany something.'

'The petals look like velvet.'

'Yes, the texture, the fragrance, makes you want to paint them.'

He is enjoying his luncheon today without fault finding. The pike has come from the lily pond, caught this morning. It is always a favourite of his, the flesh lean and firm, but you have to look out for the bones. Marie has prepared it simply, grilled with a sauce of parsley, oil, garlic, salt and plenty of black pepper. Half way through, he sips a digestive glass of Calvados. Blanche also appears to have a good appetite.

'How did your work go this morning?' she asks.

'Well. I was looking at the abundance of blues in the garden at the moment, how the shades vary under the effects of the movement of a stem. I was trying to capture that certain colour in the folds of an iris. They come into flower so swiftly.'

Blanche accepts a glass of Calvados and smiles at him.

'At what time does Mademoiselle Judith arrive, tomorrow?'

'I said early morning, to give you a good afternoon's painting.'

He sighs. 'I can't wait.'

Blanche teases, 'Anyone would think you were in love.'

'There is something about her I find energising, an intensity, a zest for life. I had it myself, when I was her age. The world is your oyster. I remember those early days in Paris when I had a furnished room in rue Pigalle. There was this famous beer house where all the important artists and writers met. Of course, I was an unknown, then, and could not mingle but I could watch. I saw Baudelaire, even Courbet. I was living the bohemian life and everything seemed possible.' He lights a cigarette, draws, coughs, draws.

Blanche says: 'I meant to tell you, Francois Brun is dying of cancer. Dr Du Pont says cigarettes are the cause.'

'To hell with Dr Du Pont, what do you expect me to do, change the habits of a lifetime? Besides I wouldn't paint without a cigarette.'

'Well maybe you could modify, cut it down a little?'

'Don't nag me.'

'I am not nagging, I am only saying if you want to live long enough to finish your projects you need to look after your health.'

'They will be finished.'

There is a pause while they resume eating then Blanche asks: 'Explain this to me, I can never understand the pleasure of putting a little white stick into your mouth and puffing away.'

He laughs. 'You don't know the half of it. I love smoking, it is my friend. It heaps pleasure upon pleasures like eating, reading, sitting in the garden. It makes every other form of enjoyment that bit more satisfactory.'

'Ah well.'

Now that he has begun, the joys of smoking crowd into his head. 'When I am pleased with how a painting is going, I congratulate myself with a cigarette. When I am finding it difficult to concentrate, smoking gives me a point of attention and shuts out distractions.'

Blanche shakes her head. 'I find that prayer does much the same thing. I just ask for help and it often comes.'

'Prayer! Your mother was the same. I don't need a god to help me paint. The richness I achieve comes from nature, that's the source of my inspiration.'

He stubs out his cigarette and picks up his fork but he has not finished with the subject of smoking.

'Then there are the special cigarettes, the first after breakfast when I know I have work to do but indulge

131

myself in a little extra pause before I begin. The last before going to bed rounds off the day. And you know, it's a fascinating thing to watch the smoke, like clouds it can form different shapes. I like to sit back and blow rings and then blow another ring through the first. One is perfectly relaxed.'

At this moment, the door bangs open and Annette trundles in the dessert trolley: Cherries yet again; there has been a glut of them, this year, this time swathed in the batter of a clafoutis.

'Odd,' observes Claude as he pours cream liberally from its jug, 'that Marie has mastered this dish but still struggles with the Yorkshire pudding.'

'I think it is the name that foxes her,' Blanche suggests. 'She finds it absurd.'

'Then she is a fool.'

While they eat, his mind returns to the subject of smoking. He thinks of those evenings after Alice had died, how lonely he felt. Then he would light a cigarette, see the glow in the darkness as if it came to life and was his companion. He lights another cigarette.

'Plus ça change…' Blanche comments.

'Exactly my thoughts, you can't change history. Ah well,' he uses her phrase. 'A glass of plum brandy?'

'Certainly.'

They meet each other's gaze like old combatants who always call a truce in the end. He laughs and so does she and he is suddenly overwhelmed by affection for her, she was always his favourite.

'*À ta santé, Blanchefleur.*'

'Oh Papa, it is a long time since you called me that.'

– FIFTEEN –

JUDITH

The dining room was empty when Judith came down that morning, the red-checked napkins still folded, the settings undisturbed. There had been an entertainment on the terrace the night before when Gervase gave a concert on his banjo and people from the village joined the artists for dancing by lamplight. There was the most astonishing array of recreations here, she thought. You could go cycling to Vernon or join Thomas on an outing to photograph the landscape; people went sailing on the Eure, even built a boat and there was always tennis. Some of them were so occupied they seemed to forget they were painters.

Yesterday evening, she had slipped away early to her room. Her visit to Le Pressoir was much more important and she wanted to look fresh and rested for it. She could hear the music and laughter but distantly and it had not prevented her sleeping soundly.

She helped herself to rolls and coffee from the buffet, grateful there was no sign of Robert. The last thing she wanted this morning, was to see the expression of disapproval on his face. Since the day of the painting trip he seemed to have avoided her, spending all his time with

Harry. He was polite at dinner or on the terrace, but that was all. Not that she cared or gave him much thought, her mind was set on what the meeting with Monet might yield. A remark of Mr Dodgson's came into her mind, one she had not reported to Robert: 'We can't get anywhere near the old man, these days, but a lovely young woman like you... with your looks he might well want to paint you. And then you'd never look back.'

Madame Baudy put her head round the door to enquire if there was anything Judith needed. She seemed surprised to find her up so early, everyone else was still in bed.

'What chic!' she added, her gaze going to the green silk two piece Judith wore. 'But then you are always chic, mademoiselle. Another model, I suppose.'

Judith knew she was longing to ask its price. She had soon realised the importance of money to Madame Baudy. She sold artists' supplies in the hotel as agent for a Parisian supplier, Robert told her. The place was always full of people coming and going, eating and drinking and she was ready to please her American guests. If they wanted Boston baked beans or a Thanksgiving dinner then apparently Madame Baudy had learned how to prepare them. Father's success in the world of commerce had taught Judith to admire good business sense.

Outside, a slight haze lingered across the rooftops. The road was empty and silent except for the hum of bees among the hollyhocks and roses. She walked slowly, savouring the sun on her skin, the blueness of the sky and brilliant flowers. She thought of Robert's reaction when she had told him of her plans. Perhaps it would have been better to keep quiet but she had imagined him a friend. She wondered whether it was because he was jealous of her. She was young, he was middle aged and, although a good painter, had not achieved great success. For me, it's all just waiting to happen, the thought instilled a sense of power. Her future was in her hands, everything was possible.

For the first time in days, she turned her mind to Charlie and realised she had scarcely given him a thought. The time had passed swiftly, filled with all the new experiences Giverny had to offer. Now she remembered the conversation they had had just before she was due to leave New York. Charlie had taken her for dinner at Delmonico's, suggesting they dine in a private dining room, but she was in far too high spirits to want to be out of sight of the other diners. Anyway, she wore a new oyster satin frock she wanted to show off. They had eaten steak and Caesar salad and Charlie ordered a bottle of Bollinger Blanc. Not only the wine but also the excitement of her forthcoming journey had gone to her head. She chattered on about the *Mauritania*, the museums she would visit, and the clothes she planned to buy. She asked him whether he was envious of her seeing, actually seeing the landscapes impressionists had painted. Finally, she had realised how gloomy he looked, scarcely speaking a word, and asked him what was wrong.

'I don't want you to go,' he said.

She had laughed and replied: 'Oh Charlie, the time will soon pass and I'll be back again.'

'If you want the truth, I am frightened of losing you.'

This was not like Charlie at all, he was usually so cheerful and optimistic about life. What nonsense! She had tossed down her champagne and suggested they order another bottle. She was annoyed with him for spoiling the evening when she had felt so good as heads turned when they entered the restaurant and walked between the crowded tables.

'Maybe you'll meet some handsome Frenchman,' Charlie said.

At that, she had laid down her fork and extended her left hand to him. 'Look, your ring is on my finger and it's going to stay there. no-one is going to be interested in an engaged woman, now are they?'

Of course, the ring had not stayed there. The day the liner pulled out to sea and she was unpacking in her cabin, she had slipped it off and put it safely in her jewellery case.

She wondered what he was doing at this moment; mooning about not knowing what to do with himself without her, probably. He was very unimaginative, left it to Judith to suggest this outing, that party or dance. He had probably buried his head in work, she told herself, counting the days until she returned. Several of his letters had arrived at the hotel. With a flash of guilt, she thought that maybe she should open them and reply. But at this moment, she didn't want to think about Charlie, nor what the ring represented.

In her invitation to Le Pressoir, Blanche had written: 'I will meet you outside La Musardiere at nine.' But as Judith arrived and saw there was no-one there, she felt a wave of panic. Had she mistaken the time? Surely not, she had read the note enough times. Then a door in the wall opened and Blanche was there.

'Ah, excellent, you are very punctual. If you will follow me.'

Judith stepped inside and the door closed behind them. She had arrived.

'I thought I would give you a little tour of the house first. Then I will present you to my stepfather.'

Judith felt a stab of disappointment that the meeting was to be delayed, if only for a short while. She followed the stout figure into the house. The tour began with a small sitting room where everything, the walls and the furniture, was painted in tones of blue. She gazed at the tall clock, noting how its features were cleverly emphasised by a different shade.

Blanche said, 'it seems very modern, doesn't it? When we first arrived here, all the furniture in Normandy was heavy and dark. But my stepfather loves colours and he chose all of them in the house. Do you like the tiles on the floor? Back in the eighties, they were considered very avant-garde.' She ran her hand over the back of a sofa. 'When my mother was alive and we were young, we all used to sit in here. Imagine how noisy it could be with eight children.'

Judith wasn't listening. Her eye had been caught by some pictures hanging on the walls, several of women in beautiful flowing kimonos. She longed to move nearer, to pause and examine them but Blanche urged her on. There was a brief look at the pantry with its bamboo style furniture and buffet which, Blanche demonstrated, was firmly locked.

'Food is expensive,' she said. 'Though we keep hens and grow our own fruit and vegetables, which is a great saving. My stepfather is particular about the quality of what he eats.'

They moved on to the dining room where Judith saw the walls were nearly masked with many more of the pictures.

'Golly! What an amazing colour!'

'You like it?'

'Oh yes, it… it is incredible!'

'Exactly.' Blanche's tone was disapproving.

'Don't you?' Judith enquired.

'It is too yellow for my taste but then I had nothing to do with the choice.'

They would not go into the kitchen, she said, as Marie would have begun to prepare luncheon and disliked being disturbed.

In the pause that followed, Judith seized her opportunity. 'Would you tell me something about these pictures?'

'They are Japanese woodblock prints known as Ukiyo-e. The translation, I understand, is "pictures of the floating world." It also refers to the changing world of fleeting pleasures, moments in people's lives, the seasons' changes. They have been a huge influence on impressionist painters, especially my stepfather.'

Judith stared at the painting of a great wave; there were three boats in the turbulent water. Tiny humans were being tossed around in the slough of the wave with what looked like a hill in the distance. The tension of the scene startled her; it gave a feeling of something about to happen in the breaking of that wave.

She moved on, drawn by the paintings of women, their white inscrutable faces and glorious kimonos. They were arranging flowers, drinking tea, dressing their hair, surprised in their daily activities, to speak a secret language to her, of an intimate pleasure-seeking world. These women seemed to be absorbed in themselves and how they might appear to onlookers as they enjoyed their leisure. There was one of the back view of a young woman she particularly liked. She was applying white powder to her neck while watching her reflection in a hand mirror. Somehow, Judith was reminded of herself.

'Mademoiselle Judith?'

Judith continued to stare, fascinated by these beautiful, uncaring women.

'Before I take you to the studio, there is something I need to tell you. My stepfather has very bad eyesight. Cataracts.'

Judith tore her gaze away. 'How terrible, a painter who cannot see! It is unthinkable.'

Blanche shrugged. 'Wait till you arrive at his age. No, wait till you arrive at mine. Life diminishes.'

'I don't ever want to get old,' Judith said. 'I want to be like a candle that flames brightly and then is extinguished, like Daisy Miller.'

'What a romantic view!' Blanche laughed. 'And we know what happens to romantics. No, I think you'll find one clings on, even if things go wrong. Somehow you survive.'

'I couldn't bear not to be able to dance, stay up all night.'

'Are all women in America like you?'

'What do you mean?'

'Well, aren't you free? You seem so to me, your hair, your clothes, a liberated woman.'

'You should see my mother. She looks exactly like a fashion plate. She was the first woman in her set to crop her hair. She's a real beauty, far more than I am.'

'One is always beautiful when young.' Blanche sounded wistful. 'Don't throw it away, don't let other people define you. Define yourself.'

Judith laughed. 'Oh, I thoroughly intend to do that.'

'Good. Come, my stepfather will be waiting.'

An idea had come into Judith's head, one that startled her with its inspiration. She seemed to come to her senses, realised Blanche was eyeing her questioningly. 'Of course, madame.'

'I'll show you to his studio.'

As they entered the room, the sun's glare through the large windows blinded her and she could barely distinguish him. Bearing in mind Blanche's warning about his failing sight, she thought she must appear much the same to him. The room seemed to swim in a dazzling light, obliterating detail; there was an unclear impression of furniture and objects. She hesitated while her eyes grew accustomed to it.

Blanche spoke. 'Papa, the young American lady, Mademoiselle Judith, is here.' Her voice was loud as if he were also hard of hearing.

Judith made out a man with a beard, seated on a sofa under the window who rose with the help of a stick and came towards her. Although they had already met on the day of the picnic, seeing him in this new setting, lit from behind in a halo of light, he seemed like a glorious stranger, though one of average height and assured, sturdy build. It was a peculiar sensation. He appeared not to recognise her either until he was close, then his narrowed eyes relaxed and he smiled. His large hand stretched out from a pleated shirt cuff and engulfed hers, his remembered voice was firm and resonant.

'Dear mademoiselle, how good it is to see you again. Come, sit down over here.'

When she was placed with her back to the light, she was able to view the room. The wooden floor was varnished and scattered with rugs. The walls were panelled and there were sofas and rattan chairs. She admired a beautiful writing desk. Rosewood, was it? Her mother owned a similar one. The photographs and the familiar objects lent an intimate and comfortable atmosphere.

Blanche, who had been hovering near the door, said: 'I'll

leave you for a while then. By the way, we've done a tour of the house, Papa, so you won't have to waste time on that.'

'Don't fuss, Blanche,' he said.

'I am not fussing. It is you who is always thinking about your painting time.'

'And there are days when I don't paint, you know that.'

'Very well, ring the bell when you need me.' The door banged behind her.

Monet clicked his tongue. In the moment of silence that followed, Judith watched his face and was struck by the enormity of sitting here alone with the great man. A thrill ran through her. She had proved them all wrong: Mother and Father, Charlie, Robert, all of them scoffing at her dream of coming to France. Monet smiled, commending her presence here. As on that day when he had taken her arm and drawn her away from the others, there was a sense of complicity between them. He had talked to her about the elusive landscapes and his constant striving to capture light but never being quite content he had done so. Then, as now, he had grown so enthusiastic, seemed delighted by her presence. It occurred to her that she would sacrifice everything, go to any lengths to continue on this path, no matter who she had to overcome. The realisation made her tremble.

'So what do you think of my house?' he asked.

'I have never seen anything like it before, it is beautiful, wonderful.'

He laughed. 'And what is it you like best?'

This was her moment of opportunity. She paused as if in contemplation before letting out a long sigh. 'Oh the Japanese prints, of course.'

'Really?' He seemed surprised. 'I expected you to say the

colours or maybe the furnishings. The prints, eh? You are a discerning young lady.'

She recalled what Blanche had just told her.' I like them because they seem to speak to me of all those little moments in life, not the great big ones but small pleasures, the fleeting seasons, women surprised in their daily life. I love the women's kimonos and how they wear them, they're so elegant, so sure of themselves.'

'Well well, you certainly have an eye. I would never have thought it in a young woman like you. Are you an artist?'

'I do paint,' she said, hoping she gave the impression of being modest about her gift.

'Then you will understand why they're very dear to me. I have been greatly influenced by the techniques of some of those painters, particularly Hokusi, Hiroshige and Utamaro. You'll recognise Utamaro because he painted some of those geishas and courtesans you have just admired.' He chuckled. 'He also seems to have had an eye for women. It will amuse you how I came by them in the first place.'

Judith was all attention. If this were his passion then she would show him how interested she was, coax every detail from him. 'Oh, do tell.'

'I had the good fortune to discover a batch of prints at a Dutch merchant's, it was in Amsterdam in a shop of Delft porcelain – I am also fond of Delft – where I was haggling over an object without any success. Suddenly I saw a dish on a lower shelf, filled with images. I stepped forward. Japanese woodblocks! I couldn't believe my eyes. The merchant appeared unaware of the value of those prints. He let me have them with the china jar. There! What do you think of that?'

She joined in his laughter. 'Oh my golly, my golly!'

His eyes were twinkling, he suddenly looked youthful, mischievous.

'I suppose it was naughty of me but his ignorance was really to blame. This must have been in the seventies. Of course you are too young to remember, but back then, there was a craze for Japanese art and design. There was even an opera about a Dutch girl who becomes jealous of her artist friend's fixation on woodblock prints. *The Yellow Princess* I seem to remember it was called.'

But why, then, she wanted to know.

'Trade with Japan had been closed since about the fifteenth century. Suddenly it was opened up again to the West. It swept France and someone came up with the name Japonisme. I saw an exhibition in Paris and was carried away by it. I appreciated the focus on simplicity but, at the same time, how such a simple print reveals new details the more you observe it. I love their use of vibrant colour and light, the off centre arrangement and snapshot quality, as my old friend Nadar would have called it. They freed me from the old conventions. Those prints set up a resonance for me and I became impassioned, so Judith – I may call you Judith mayn't I? You are young enough to be my grand daughter – I continued to collect them.' He took a deep breath. 'Excuse me, I'm probably boring you.'

'Not at all,' she smiled at him. 'I find it fascinating.'

While she listened, she had been looking at the display of paintings arranged in three rows on the walls, formulating further questions to include them.

'How many do you have now?'

'At the last count it must have been over two hundred. It's a kind of addiction, you see. You just can't stop.'

'Why should you?' Judith shrugged.

He caught her eye and laughed. 'Exactly, why should I? You understand me, little one.'

Oh yes, she thought, I can understand the pressure, the determination to have something. Again, she felt the sense of involvement between them.

'There is something else,' he was saying, 'If you will pardon me, your appearance... well... it is extraordinary. That hair, those eyes, the way you wear your clothes, you could be a French woman.'

She met his gaze, wondering how clearly he could really see.

'Well I do believe there may be some Gallic blood on my mother's side.'

'There you are, you see.' After a pause he added. 'As you know, I remarked on this the other day when we first met. You remind me so much of Camille.'

This was another opportunity and Judith seized it. 'Camille?'

'My first wife, Camille Doncieux. Let me tell you a little about her.'

It was all going wonderfully to plan. Judith leant back against the cushions of the sofa and prepared herself to be patient.

* * *

It is one of those indefinable days in Paris: a little warmer and it might hold the beginnings of summer, but a nagging wind reminds him it is still only April. He walks through the Luxembourg Gardens where couples stroll arm in arm. An elderly man sits on a bench in muffler and overcoat, reading a newspaper. He admires the carefully tended flowerbeds, the new Medici fountain, and lake where children sail their boats. He walks on through rue de l'Odeon where books are stacked from floor to ceiling in the little shops. He can smell the horse manure on the road, daffodils as he passes a flower stall; he notices the flaking bark on the trunks of plane trees, the sun coming through their leaves to lay dappled shadow on the pavements. He is twenty-three and feels he is seeing the world for the first time and in a way he is: this view of the city where he has only recently arrived. He is making his way to Batignolles where he will buy some artists' supplies. Afterwards, he will sit in the Café Guerbois where he always goes on Fridays to what has become something of a salon. He loves these meetings with the other artists, and the stock of enthusiasm it generates, the urge to paint and keep on painting to achieve his dream. What he does not know on this particular Friday is that he will catch his first glimpse of the slender, dark-haired Camille. She will pass by on an errand and catch his eye. On this day, their future together will begin to be mapped out. He will ask her to model for him when he decides to break away from his predecessors, reject the studio settings, references to the past or mythology, and paint in the open air. He will capture a moment, create a picture of young people enjoying a picnic in the countryside just as he would like to imagine himself. He will believe this painting will attract the critic's eye and be put on view for all Paris to see. Because Camille has quickly become very important in his life, he wants to keep her to himself. He is an impoverished painter, uncertain whether his father will continue to send an allowance. He cannot afford to employ many models, so out of the five

145

women in the picture, Camille poses for the three brunettes. He paints two of them with their backs to the viewer and the third with her arms raised to adjust her hat, therefore concealing her face, the face he doesn't want to share with anyone. Camille brings a sense of style and elegance to his work. She introduces him to fashion plates and tells him of her devotion to Le Printemps. This recently opened department store allows every woman to aspire to an upper class look; it is something that hasn't happened before. She uses it like a museum, coming and going, admiring the displays and dreaming. He remembers a white dress she wore for that painting, fashioned in a modern design with a magnificent trailing skirt at the back. This exploit of painting out of doors dictated a new palette. He used mostly grey pigment for that dress so that she seemed to be standing in the shadow cast by the tree above. He concentrated on the idea of being modern and thought to make his reputation with this painting, but the Paris Salon turned him down.

He remembers her wonderful eyes, her excitement at embarking on this new life. She was eighteen years old. He remembers the rented green dress, the beauty she brought to his chilly little studio, her warmth and love. The idea of depicting her as the woman seen in the latest fashion magazines, a window display of Le Printemps appealed to them both. This time he did not entirely hide her face.

She was his jewel with magical properties, his muse and he was ready to declare his adoration to the world when he entitled the picture *Camille*. The public loved her.

Then there is the painting of Camille in a sparsely furnished London flat after their flight from the Prussian war. He shows her face for the first time, eyes downcast, lips tightly clasped, all her spirit and elegance gone. She looks vulnerable, wears a dark dress with long sleeves and white cuffs; in her lap is a closed book with a red cover. The transparent curtain conceals her view of the street, a place she found lonely and uninviting.

He remembers the happy summer days of their return to France. He paints Camille and Jean in the garden at Argenteuil. Now she is a woman in her own right, his wife, not just a model for his imagined world. For her their wedding day was one of intense joy. The season's bounty of flowers surrounds her; she wears not a chic Parisian gown but a simple figure-hugging country dress. She raises both arms high to adjust the red ribbon in her hair and looks back at him, her expression straightforward, direct and open. What is she saying? 'You adore your son but do you love me? No matter, we are your family, you have no other. You may come and go but now we are bound together, you will not abandon us.'

A decade later he is in desperate need of a big sale. He thinks back to his first success *Camille*. It is the height of the craze for things Japanese in Paris. He borrows a fantastic red Japanese kimono and sets up the scene in a friend's studio. Camille tries one pose after another and eventually they decide her body shall be in profile, her face turned towards her husband. He doesn't remember how it came about but they go out and buy her a blonde wig. He chuckles to himself even now as he recalls the Japanese fans stuck on the wall behind his wife. On one of them is painted the head and shoulders of an elegant geisha who looks apparently astonished by this strange French rival.

He seems suddenly aware of the American girl who has sat quietly on the sofa and listened to all this reminiscence.

147

'*La Japonaise*, I called that picture. It dazzled the Parisian art world when I exhibited it at the second impressionist exhibition in 1876. I painted it for money, it wasn't a genre I liked but it fetched two thousand francs.

'Ah Judith, I wish you could have met her, such a marvellous woman. We loved working together. Camille delighted in choosing costumes, trying out poses, acting out the roles I chose for her. I took enormous pleasure in her gifts. That picture was full of laughter and allure. I'd never seen her look more stunning.'

His voice died away. Judith's first reaction had been to envy Camille, beautiful, elegant Camille admired by Monet, the fashionable Parisian public. The way had opened up for her when she was only eighteen years old to change her destiny. She had lived the bohemian life Judith dreamt of with no parents trying to control her.

'How lucky she was,' she said.

'Lucky?'

'Of course, to have met you and become a model, to have worn those wonderful clothes. I'd love to have been Camille.'

His laugh was rueful. 'I wonder if you would, really. It wasn't always fun and laughter, you know. We had difficult times, especially at the beginning when the money wasn't coming in.'

'But you were able to live as you wanted.'

'With certain constraints.'

Judith didn't want to hear him qualify the strength of the fairy tale he had told her. 'Did you always want to live like that?' she asked.

'I wanted to be free, yes. As a boy at school I didn't want to study. I drew cartoons all over my lesson books. I rebelled

148

against my father who wanted me to have a safe job. If you have a dream, Judith, you have to go all out to realise it.'

'Even if you tread on people along the way?'

'Well yes, even that.'

'That was what she wanted to hear. 'I'd like…' she began.

There was a tap on the door and Blanche came into the room. 'I thought perhaps it was time for Mademoiselle Judith to leave, Papa.'

He frowned at her. 'Not yet, Blanche, first we are going to take a turn round the garden.'

'Oh, very well, it's just…'

'Don't worry, I'll see her out when we're finished.'

As they stepped outside and he led her to stand in front of the house, she felt another thrill of excitement. She was here, actually here in Monet's garden. He was telling her about his choice of pink on the walls, how shutters in this area were traditionally painted grey but he had changed these to green.

'Then I added the gallery and pergola to create a canopy of roses. I wanted the house to blend with the garden.'

She nodded and smiled while the voice in her head continued: you have won!

They walked down the main path, flanked by a series of small oblong beds, she saw a mass of oranges and reds.

'Day lilies,' he said. 'And these are phlox.'

He was listing so many flowers: stock, alliums, salvia, geraniums, petunias, foxgloves, hollyhocks, and Canterbury bells. Her eye caught flashes of pink, white and yellow while other voices came into her mind of those who would foil her attempts to escape, to forge a new existence.

There was Mother's, 'Why not forget the whole idea? It is outlandish, anyway, to travel all that way just because of a caprice! All this delay over setting the wedding date! If we're not careful the family will call the whole thing off and there's far more at stake than just love.'

There was Robert's: 'Treat it as a long vacation, don't take everything so seriously. You have a loving family who want the best for you. Look how they are supporting you here, three whole months in Giverny. But I can't imagine they would go on doing that indefinitely. Then where would you be without money? It is called being accountable for your actions, Judith, of being aware of their repercussion on others. That is why you would never fit in.'

Finally, there was Charlie at Delmonico: 'I don't want you to go. I'm frightened of losing you. Maybe you'll meet some handsome Frenchman.'

Judith switched her attention to the elderly man, pointing out this and that with his stick. He was obviously enjoying telling her about his garden, although she had scarcely listened. Monet had taken to her, she had made him laugh. And he had told her that if she wanted something, she had to go all out to get it. She wanted this way of life, she wanted it so much.

She realised they had reached the bottom of the garden but now he opened a door and they stepped through, crossed a section of rail track and entered through a door on the other side. He led the way round a stretch of greenish water, listing the plants – agapanthus, pampas grass, astilbe and more Canterbury bells – as they strolled. They came to a curved bridge and here he leaned, gazing down at what she at least knew to be water lilies.

'Mark this, Judith, mark this well, for here is the heart of my work. See how the sun passes beneath the bridge and lights up the area where the lilies lie in the shade.'

She gazed without knowing what it was she was supposed to be seeing.

'See the light and shade effect that creates. I have painted this scene again and again, in many different lights, at different times of the day. I am possessed by them. It began years ago when this water garden became my main source of inspiration. I sat here for hours trying to capture the colours, the reflection and movement of these lilies, waiting for the perfect light, to convey it to the canvas. I used to grow them but never realised I could paint them. It takes time to become immersed into a landscape. And then suddenly, the utter beauty of my pond came as a revelation. I took my palette and since that day, I have hardly ever had another model.'

Two figures had appeared on the other side of the bridge, one was pointing out something on a stretch of water to the other. Monet called out to them and they turned their heads. Judith saw a man with grey hair but the other was young. His hair glinted blue black in the sun, he narrowed his eyes against the light. He was staring at her with a startled expression as if he couldn't believe what he saw.

'My gardeners,' Monet said. 'I'll introduce you.'

They walked on over the bridge.

'This is M'sieur Breuil and this, Michel.'

Judith smiled and nodded, murmuring '*enchanté*.' The young man was very handsome, she thought, definitely more handsome than Charlie. As if he realised her thoughts Michel lowered his gaze.

– SIXTEEN –

BLANCHE

Blanche had gone to bed but she couldn't sleep, the room was stifling, her body burned under the thin sheet. The evening had been oppressive with the sense of a storm brooding but no rain had arrived to freshen the still air. As she lay there, staring through the darkness, her thoughts turned to Suzanne, to a night over twenty years ago sullen with thunder, at first growling from a distance then moving closer. Forked lightning streaked the sky. There had been a tap on the door and her sister came into the room.

'Oh Blanche, can I sit with you for a while?'

She looked so pretty standing there in her white nightgown, the gaslight haloing her hair.

Blanche made room for her in the bed. 'It's only a storm,' she said. 'Just hot air rising quickly and... but I've told you all that so many times before.'

'Yes, I know you have, but they still terrify me. I hate the noise and oh!' White light briefly illuminated the room. 'The lightning, too, it seems like a wild monster out there and one cannot escape it.'

Blanche knew her sister too well to laugh at this image.

Suzanne's vivid nightmares had often resulted in the midnight tap on the door. The storm was now raging overhead, the thunder and lightning almost simultaneous. To take her mind off it, Blanche had asked her what she planned to do with her life and Suzanne told her she wished to marry, of course, she wasn't clever like Blanche and couldn't paint. Blanche had laughed and replied that that didn't exclude falling in love.

Suzanne hugged her. 'Of course not and it will all turn out well, I'm sure of that. We shall each of us meet a wonderful man and marry and have lots of children like Maman. We'll bring them all here to visit and Papa will be a doting grand father. It will be like a fairy story.'

Blanche remembered how moved she was by Suzanne's innocence and hope for the future. She had felt an urge to protect her from harm, almost as if, she thought now, she had had a presentiment of how matters would turn out. She remembered how happy and blooming her sister had looked on her wedding day but then the pain she had suffered before and after the birth of her first child, the brace she had worn, the crutches she used. Later paralysis in her legs had set in and she could not walk. The doctor's expression had been grave as he spoke of 'pressure on the crural nerve.' Poor Suzanne, she had had to spend so much time in bed and the baby girl brought in to visit her. There had been the tears when she was forced to give up Lily's little brother, Jim, to be cared for by Marthe, her weakness, and her beauty withering over those years until the final decline. They had all been drawn into that suffering and death except perhaps Papa who found consolation and escape in his painting... Who knew with him, however? Maman had been inconsolable, backwards and forwards to the cemetery, those dreadful dawn visits, until Papa bought the automobile and they began on their jaunts.

But was that the only reason she couldn't sleep? Wasn't she also wondering how Lilli was getting on, investing in her the hope of happiness and fulfillment that had eluded both herself and Suzanne? Even her name was curiously close to that of her niece.

Earlier that evening, she had kept her word and arranged Lilli's hair in the style she had created before, tweaked her dress into place, helped arrange the shawl. The girl was as excited as a child going to her first party, chattering away, hardly able to sit still.

'*Bon chance*,' Blanche had murmured to herself as she watched the slight figure walking away from the house.

About half past ten, she heard the door to the servant's entrance open and close. Half an hour late: it seemed like a good omen.

1889

True to his word, Monet included John Leslie and several other young Americans on trips to the fields and woods where they set up easels and painted together. Blanche went along too although she found it difficult to sit so near to John Leslie and not be able to touch him. She was constantly aware of him and found it difficult to concentrate on her work. Sometimes, she would glance across, hoping to catch his eye and share a secret smile but he seemed capable of concentrating wholeheartedly, applying himself to the canvas so that she felt shut out.

He continued to demand answers from Monet. 'How do you achieve this effect? Why did you use vermilion there? How can I produce a similar result?'

'Young man, I have no answers. As the painter I am only concerned with giving my impression, my view, which I cannot pass on to you. Just be yourself. Look with your own eyes, paint what you see.'

He refused to teach, Blanche knew that, but still John Leslie persisted.

Meanwhile Suzanne spent the summer days in the garden sewing or reading, absorbed in her world of romance and fairytale endings. Ironic, Blanche thought, when, at the end of her nose, a real life drama was being played out. Her sister bent her head to her activity with a certain self-consciousness, arranging her skirts so that they might be seen to their best advantage. Monet had painted her so many times, Suzanne it appeared found it difficult not to pose.

One afternoon, John Leslie forsook his landscapes and asked her to sit for him. He painted her in profile, her face shaded by the usual large hat so that the eye was drawn to the piece of sewing between her fingers. There was a contrast between the firmness of the hat and the soft wrap of blouse and skirt around Suzanne's body, which seemed to comment on the wearer's docility. The effect was to make it appear not as much a portrait as an archetype of domesticity, of a young woman at ease with the natural world where no shadow clouded the future.

Blanche was surprised by the competence of John Leslie's brushwork, the brighter palette he was now using, the casual almost snapshot pose. How far he had progressed in so short a time. As he had vowed to her last year, he was achieving his aim of becoming an impressionist. She tried to analyse the unsettling effect this aroused in her, at odds with her feelings for him. Might it be jealousy?

'I am not there yet,' he said when she remarked on the painting, 'but I am much taken with capturing the changing effects of light on a solid figure and the surrounding landscape. It is elusive and challenging.'

'John Leslie is so serious,' Suzanne said when she and Blanche were alone. 'So single minded. He reminds me of Monet, the way he paints as if it were the most important thing in the world.'

Whatever she had thought on this topic, Blanche sprang to his defence. 'Of course it is important, it gives shape and meaning to one's existence.'

'More than loving another human being?' Suzanne gave her a wry smile. 'Surely there is nothing more important than that? If being an artist means withholding a part of oneself from your beloved then I am happy I do not paint.'

And there was where the difference between them lay. Blanche thought of Monet's painting *Blanche Hoschedé at her easel, Suzanne Hoschedé reading*.' Her sister's skirt flecked with white, pink, yellow and blue seemed to melt into her surroundings, making her seem acquiescent, while he had depicted her upright and resolute, focused intently on her work. Her gaze beneath the red-brimmed bonnet was alert, her arm upraised as brush touched canvas at the instant of creation. In his painting, Monet appeared to compare them: pretty, passive Suzanne and enterprising, active Blanche. He seemed to her to say: 'this is her vocation and no other, this we share with no other and let no-one else encroach.' Her sister might read and dream on these outings but, for she and Monet, the landscape offered the opportunity to work swiftly, transcribing its shapes, colours and moods. It was their testing ground.

'You wouldn't understand,' said Blanche.

Nevertheless, Suzanne had a point, she mused. Artists cannot give all of themselves, there comes the moment when they need to withdraw and go away to the studio or writing desk to battle out the creation.

Summer was long and hot that year. As August neared its end, the branches of the fruit trees were bowed under the weight of apples, pears, damsons and quince. Then came a week of rain.

'Time to go hunting for mushrooms!' Monet announced. 'Chanterelles, Alice, how does that take your fancy?' They exchanged an intimate smile.

Mushroom hunting was an annual ritual but no-one knew why it seemed to cause amusement between Monet and Maman. The chauffeur was summoned to prepare the car. Very early in the morning, they donned their capes, veils and goggles and off they went, driving to the forest of Andaine. The undergrowth was warm and damp and mushrooms were pushing up through the wet grasses. The air was chill, fresh and lovely. When the sun broke through, the dying bracken blazed and then it was all golden and beautiful on this autumn morning. The family entered the forest, eyes firmly fixed on its floor, following trails specified by Monet. It was not long before the silence was broken by the shrieks of a happy picker. Soon everyone was absorbed, walking quietly, staring at the ground then pouncing with glee. Chanterelles blended into the autumn bracken; spy one and suddenly a dozen more came into focus. Hedgehog mushrooms flashed white at the foot of trees, identified by the spines underneath. Now and again, someone would run back to Monet who assumed the role of official identifier.

'No you can't eat that one, throw it away. No, that's a sulphur cap not a cow bolete. It wouldn't kill you but it's not nice to eat. Yes, that's a chanterelle, you can tell it by the dimple on top. Wonderful chanterelles,' he commented.

There came the sound of rain pitter-pattering on the canopy of leaves above their heads. Soon it will percolate through and we'll all get wet, Blanche thought miserably.

But Monet was jubilant. 'Good weather for mushrooms,' he

crowed. He made them all stand in a circle round him while he ran through his 'rules', ones they had heard many times before. 'Don't pick the very small mushrooms. If you don't allow them to reach a reasonable size they will not have released their spores. Use your knife to cut the mushroom at the base. Don't just rip it out or you will damage the underground part.'

And, of course, they all carry wicker baskets so that the gathered mushrooms can drop their spores through the holes and, *voila*, propagation will occur again.

Damn his rules, thought Blanche. She felt the now familiar sense of separation from all of them and asked herself: what do I really want to do with my life?

She listened to Monet's voice delivering orders: 'Germaine, take that way, Michel you go this. Alice and I will take the other path to the left.' Suddenly she hated him with a passionate anger; she hated this man she had always adored but who now seemed a tyrant, undermining her happiness. What was wrong with her? She used to enjoy these pursuits of family life but now she felt the structure was falling apart. Her basket was empty, she lifted her face to see the sun reappearing through the leaves. She didn't want to grub about searching for stupid mushrooms.

Monet was there. 'What is the matter, Blanche, you look moon struck. I used to be able to rely on you to find the best mushrooms. You seem to have taken leave of your senses.'

'Don't be so hard on her,' Alice put in. 'Maybe she's not feeling well. Are you Blanche?'

'Don't fuss, Maman.' She felt she wanted to lash out at everything, Monet, the family, to send those baskets of mushrooms flying and see the look on their faces.

Impatiently, Monet turned away and Alice followed him. Blanche hated the world and her part in it, everything except John Leslie. She stayed where she was, hearing the family's voices calling to each other at yet another find. Then this anger evaporated and left her weak and trembling. She thought, I can't stay here. I have to leave everything and go with him. The decision left her feeling strangely calm and after that she picked mushrooms, uncaring what they were, dropping them mechanically into her basket.

On her way to the dining room, next morning, she almost collided with Lilli, rushing from the bedrooms with a pile of laundry in her arms.

'Oh madame, it was wonderful!'

Blanche gave her a warning look. She did not want anyone else to know about her part in all this. 'Wait till we are doing the laundry.'

Over the shirts and drawers, the chemises and nightgowns, Lilli related the evening. Sometimes, she moved around the kitchen to demonstrate.

'At first he didn't seem to notice me. He was dancing with that so and so Marianne. Hmm, the airs and graces she puts on, you'd think she was a princess although she could do with losing a bit of weight, disgusting I thought, bursting out of her dress. Well, I wasn't going to dance with anyone else so I went to take some refreshment and suddenly there he was beside me. You could have knocked me down with a feather, madame. We danced the valse musette and the polka and the mazurka. Of course he went off to dance with other partners but he always returned to me.'

Blanche could feel her cheeks go pink with pleasure. 'I'm so happy for you, Lilli.' It all came back to her, those evenings with John Leslie, those times before the first words of love were spoken, the first kiss, a breathless feeling of hoping and praying it might come true.

'Oh then we did the Cakewalk. Have you ever heard of it, madame? The maids from Hotel Baudy showed us, they said the Americans had taught them.'

Lilli was sashaying round the kitchen, humming a Scott Joplin tune. Blanche heard the clump of Annette's boot from the scullery and the girl came scowling into the room.

'What's all this?' she asked suspiciously.

'Lilli was telling me…' Blanche began and then stopped short, remembering the girl's clubfoot. There would be no dancing for her. 'Oh, never mind,' she finished. 'It's time to get on. If you'll carry on here, Lilli, please.'

The girl shot her a beseeching look, one that Blanche read of the story unfinished, that there was more and she was dying to tell someone. She halted in the kitchen door way. 'I've just remembered there is a tear in my bedroom curtain. Will you come and see what you can do, Lilli?'

Outside, she put her finger to her lips and drew the girl into the dining room.

'Oh thank you, madame.'

'Come on then, Lilli, tell me. I can see you can't wait.'

The girl was grinning. 'Michel has asked me to go for a walk on my next afternoon off.'

'Well, that is quite something. Remind me when it is?'

'Sunday madame, a whole week away, so long to wait!'

Yes, Blanche thought, I remember that. I remember when I couldn't sleep for thinking of John Leslie and the next time I would see him, how you tell yourself not to be too eager but you simply cannot help yourself. 'It will pass, Lilli, it will pass.'

'Yes, madame.' She looked unconvinced.

Life seemed to be arranging itself, Blanche thought, going into the garden to see how the hens had laid,

160

imperceptibly but definitely. Papa's meeting with Mademoiselle Judith had set him up no end; Lilli was on cloud nine, while she was being given the opportunity to sketch without feeling guilty. It was like one of those shakes of a kaleidoscope, where the pattern magically changes. But her mind went back to the Japanese prints, the floating world of small pleasures and fleeting moments. 'Please God,' she prayed. 'Let it remain so, at least for some time.'

– SEVENTEEN –

ROBERT

It was half past two in the morning and Robert told himself he had never felt less like sleep. He knew it was pointless going to bed so continued to sit at his bedroom window and smoke a cigarette. The moon was in its first quarter and the night dark and silent. Unusually, he was finding it difficult to pick out the pleasant moments of his day, its scents and sounds, a flavour he enjoyed. Even if he did, they were soon banished by thoughts of Judith and how she continued to unsettle his life. He was recognising how this compunction to protect her sprang from those old feelings of guilt that until now he thought he had overcome. Now as Giverny slept, the images returned.

He saw himself seated in the trap, looking over the sturdy back of the piebald pony. The reins were loose in his hand. What was her name? He closed his eyes. Lucy, that was it, a docile creature, you could almost let her make her own way apart from a light pulling on the reins when, now and again, she was wayward and tried to turn left or right instead of keeping straight ahead. This was the first time he had been allowed to take the trap into town. He had wanted to enjoy his new freedom alone but Florence pleaded to go with her big brother.

She was lifted up into the trap and sat beside him, dressed in a pink smocked pinafore and a sunhat. She looked demure and pretty as a picture. 'Now you'll stay quiet, won't you, Florrie?' his mother said. And to Robert: 'Take good care of her, son.'

He felt the familiar weight of responsibility.

Suddenly the atmosphere seemed filled with sound. Robert closed his eyes again, concentrating on the memory. The middle of the street was lined with market stalls and crowded with people. He walked among them and never let go of Florence's hand. There was a farmer selling cabbages and housewives with their wicker baskets buying cheese and preserves. His sister tugged him to a stall selling stuffed toys and he bought her a small brown monkey. Then they made their way to a haberdashery stall where he found the gloves his mother had asked him to bring back for her. He saw that other Robert picking through the piles, searching for her size; Mother had very small hands. He saw them sitting in a bar where he had taken Florence to have a sarsaparilla as a reward for behaving herself.

On the way home, she kept on asking to take a turn at the reins. After a while, she began to cry and to pacify his sister he moved over and let her take the reins. At once she gave them a savage jerk and the animal, unused to this, broke into a running trot. They bowled along the road.

Now Florence was crowing with delight. 'You see I'm cleverer than you.'

He felt the panic rise, heard his voice: 'Florrie no, stop it, Florrie.'

She jerked the reins again. That other Robert knew the

road well, knew they would soon be coming to an uneven stretch. He felt a thrill of fear.

'Do you want to kill us?' he shouted. 'Give those reins to me.'

He moved back and snatched them from her hands. The pony responded to his touch. 'You promised you'd stay quiet,' he said. 'Please Florrie, you scare me the way you go on. How do you think Mother and Father would feel if you got hurt?'

'Sorry.'

She looked so pretty and innocent with her tear stained face beneath the pink sunhat, he wanted to hug her, protect her from all harm.

'So were you my good little girl?' his mother asked Florence.

Robert was silent.

'I was naughty on the way home,' murmured his sister.

'Oh Robert, what did she do?'

His parents' faces were concerned. 'It was nothing,' he lied. 'She was tired, that was all.'

'Well, that's all right then.' His mother was smiling now. 'It's early bed for you tonight, my girl. You've had enough excitement for one day.'

As Florrie began to protest she wasn't tired at all, Robert whistled for Rusty and with an urge to escape, took him off for his walk.

Out of the darkness came the eerie drawn out cry of a vixen calling for a mate. Robert looked back to that first meeting at Vernon railroad station. It seemed a long time ago. How fresh and innocent she had seemed, a pleasure to the eye and ear. He had loved her carelessness of what people thought when she danced the Turkey Trot. Might he have been like her if his boyhood had been different, not afflicted with an unfair liability he had tried so hard to undertake, a father who judged and found him lacking?

He recalled the day of the painting outing, his annoyance when Judith picked the dandelions only to tear them apart; how he had attempted to point out she was not financially independent. It gave her no choice but to do what her parents had mapped out for her.

'Everyone has the right to decide their own destiny. I'm sorry Robert but I'm determined to stay here. If my parents won't support me I have other ideas.' she had said.

And what were they? To make capital out of the old man's admiration of her, to ride roughshod over poor Blanche? The arrogance of the girl, imagining she could transplant New World behaviour to this Normandy village, likening herself to Camille. How pointless it had been to suggest she should be responsible for her actions and their repercussions on others when it was obvious she thought her goal justified any means to achieve it.

Nevertheless, he continued to be fascinated by her, her will to achieve her aim; she seemed to him like some blind force of nature that cannot be tamed. He was fearful for her as he had been fearful for Florence.

'I wonder how she is getting on with Monet,' he had remarked to Harry, that morning at breakfast when Madame Baudy told them the young lady had already departed for Le Pressoir.

Harry lit a cigarette. 'Does it matter?'

'No, of course not.' Robert busied himself with spreading cherry jam on his bread. 'I only wondered.'

'You're always wondering, Robert,' the other's tone was sharp. 'Where is she? What is she doing? Is she eating enough? Does she drink too much? You give far too much thought to that girl.'

'Nonsense.'

'It's becoming rather a bore, I have to say.'

Detecting a warning note in his friend's voice, Robert met his gaze and sighed. 'I'm sorry if you think that. The thing is, I can't help myself. I feel drawn to her almost like a moth to a flame.'

'Oh really?'

'Not like that, you idiot, but there is a quality about her, surely you must have noticed? An intensity of purpose that is absorbing.'

Harry rose and moved to the buffet, willowy and graceful in his movement as he was on the tennis courts. He considered the oeufs bénédictine then settled for another rasher of bacon and sausage. 'I'll grant you there is something about her that catches the eye. She's very stylish and quite pretty but it doesn't impress me. I just think she is selfish and self absorbed, only ever thinking about how she looks or the effect she is having on other people.'

Robert, watching his friend's pose by the buffet, smiled to himself. Wasn't this a case of the pot calling the kettle black? He would not pursue the subject, would not remark that perhaps the metaphor he had used of the moth more likely applied to Judith and his interest in her was a sense of trying to save her from the flame. How far had she gone already? How had she been received? He had seen the closed expression on her face when she returned from Le Pressoir and needed to know.

Two days later he had the opportunity of asking her when she appeared in the dining room just as they were finishing their breakfast.

At the sight of her, Harry rose from the table and left, calling over his shoulder: 'I'm going to the studio, are you coming?'

'I won't be a moment.'

He was pouring coffee and asked her if she wanted some. She replied that she would. He remarked on how lovely the day was and she agreed.

'If you would like more pastries I can ring for them.'

'Swell.'

He sighed. 'Oh Judith, please…'

She gave him a questioning glance. 'I thought you didn't want to talk to me any more. You seemed so disapproving.'

'Not so much disapproving, more anxious that you don't seem to understand what you are doing.'

Judith laughed. 'Oh, I understand very well, Robert. There is no need to worry about me.'

He sat opposite her and dunked a brioche in his coffee. 'You're engaged to be married, you know that. You are here for a vacation but you are expected home afterwards. Your life is in America, not here.'

'You're like all the others, you think you know what's best for me. But you don't.' She dabbed her mouth with her napkin then flung it down. She drained her coffee cup and banged it onto its saucer.

Robert saw this was no way forward. He waited until the girl had brought more pastries then tried another tack. 'Judith, I don't want to argue with you, you're young, you're pretty, you've got so much going for you. Come on, can't you see that?'

She had smiled when he said she was pretty, patted her shoulders: 'What do you think of this outfit?'

'Very nice.'

'Only nice?'

'Chic then... yes, very chic.'

She poured herself another cup of coffee and sipped it, looking dreamily ahead.

After another pause, Robert tried again. 'So how did it go?'

'How did what go?'

'You know what I'm talking about, your visit to Le Pressoir.'

She shrugged as if to say what a foolish question. 'Very well, of course, Madame Blanche likes me. Monet does too. I spent a long time with him. We had a conversation about his Japanese prints.'

'You did?'

'I'm not a complete nincompoop.'

'I never said you were.'

'Then he took me round the gardens and showed me the flowers, told me about his lily pond.' She paused.

'And?'

'Nothing.' She rose and helped herself to another pain au chocolat. She appeared to have forgotten her regime this morning. With her back to him she said. 'I'm invited there again.'

'You are?'

'Oh Robert!' She whirled round on him. 'Is it all so surprising that people might actually like me? It certainly isn't to me. Why shouldn't they invite me back? You are just so... so conservative.'

He smiled to himself. Conservative, he? If only she knew. There was a pause.

'I am not a child, Robert.'

No, he thought, in spite of your youth you have been

brought up in an atmosphere of sophistication, taught from a young age how to dress and behave; you have been groomed for the role of wealthy matriarch. And what you haven't been told, you have made it your business to find out. He had an image of a small creature opening letters, listening at doors, attentive to any change of nuance in her parents' conversation. He remembered that first impression he had had of her, young yet knowing, paradox of new woman and atavistic wiles.

He felt he couldn't deal with this any more and anyway he dared not keep Harry waiting any longer. He rose from the table. 'I just don't want you to get hurt,' he said.

Her scornful laughter followed him out of the room.

– EIGHTEEN –

JUDITH

As the door closed behind Robert, Judith sprang up from the table. Damn him and his anxious face, poking his nose into her business. She knew exactly what she was doing and needed none of his middle-aged caution. He had made her so angry she couldn't finish her breakfast nor stay in the hotel a moment longer; she would go for a walk by the river, sit and gaze at the landscape, Monet's landscape, and calm down. But as she stepped outside, she realised it was already scorching hot and chose instead a seat on the terrace, under the trees.

A woman sitting nearby caught her eye and smiled. Judith gave a quick nod and turned her attention to the tennis players already darting about the courts. She wondered whether one of them was Harry, then remembered he was tucked away in the studio with Robert. She disliked Harry as much as, she suspected, he did her. Everything about him was neat; he reminded her of a tailor's dummy. At the thought of him, she tugged out her compact and inspected her face.

'Do you mind if I join you?' the woman had left her table and come over. 'I'm waiting for my husband,' she explained, taking a seat without waiting to be invited. 'I never know when he will turn up. He goes off to do something or other and forgets all about the time. The artistic temperament they call it,' she laughed.

She was somewhat older than Judith with a pleasant freckled face and merry eyes. She wore a simple tucked blouse and blue cotton skirt, her hair in a rather untidy knot.

'He is a painter, you see.'

At that moment, the serving girl arrived and the woman ordered citron pressé, insisting Judith should join her.

'It's good to meet you. I've seen you about in the village and thought, I'd really like to talk to that person.' She spoke with a drawling Southern accent, which Judith found soothing. 'You always look so fresh and pretty.'

'I can't remember seeing you,' Judith smiled, pleased with the compliment.

'Well, I'm often busy round the house and garden. These cottages may not be very big but they sure take some looking after. I'm quite a gardener, too, and there is always so much to do.'

'Do you live here?' Judith was interested now. 'Oh, how wonderful, to live in Giverny.'

'It is rather. We first came here back in the nineties when Paul had finished studying in Paris. He was doing such good work and we were so happy here then, I can't remember why, we decided to go back to the States. But this place had got under our skin and we had to return.' She paused for breath and sipped her pressé.

Judith gazed at her and felt a stab of envy. 'How lucky you are, it would be my absolute dream come true.'

The woman made a little grimace. 'Nothing's perfect you

know, not even Giverny. It is a beautiful place and I am always telling myself I'm lucky to be here but I tell you, I get lonesome sometimes. Oh, Paul has his work, it takes him up and he doesn't choose to mix much with the locals. He's right in a way, one gets so tired of gossip about some relative or other, feuds about inheritance and so on.'

Judith smiled. 'I guess so. But it goes on everywhere, doesn't it, even in New York?' Especially in New York, she thought. She remembered the conversations at her mother's tea parties, the marriages that were examined, the husbands put under scrutiny.

'But it's just so provincial here. I mean look at you,' her companion turned her gaze onto Judith. 'Your wonderful clothes, they're so thoroughly modern and your hair, well! Tell me something, what does it feel like to have such short hair?'

Judith ran her fingers through the waves. 'Free and easy, there is none of that boring time it used to take to dry. I'd never grow it again.'

The woman gazed at her for a moment as if she had finally run out of things to say. A change came over her expression. She seemed to consider before giving a quick glance round as if to check they were alone. When she spoke again, her voice was low. 'Tell me something, what do you think of French men?'

'Well, they seem very pleasant, I have to say.'

'Pleasant! Pleasant!' The woman went into peals of laughter, showing large teeth. She leaned forward and spoke even more softly. 'Let me tell you something, they are far more than pleasant when you've got them into bed.'

It was Judith's turn to glance round for fear they might be overheard. 'I thought you said you were married?'

Somehow she was shocked, although she'd heard such things about her mother's friends.

The woman laughed again. 'What has that got to do with it? Oh sorry dear, you are rather young, you may not have come across these things. You see, Paul and I have a very open marriage, we like it that way.'

The players had come together at the net to shake hands, now they went to sit in the shade. Judith imagined how very hot it must be down there, running about under that sun; she was grateful of the trees' shade, imagined how cool she must appear. She could feel the woman considering her.

'I wonder you haven't thought about it,' she said at last. 'You're pretty enough and not married, by the look of things.'

'I do have a fiancé.'

'And where is he?'

'America.'

'Ah well, you know what they say? What the eye doesn't see. Listen, I've had a couple of friends who've died of tuberculosis. It makes you realise how short life is and how one has to take advantage of whatever it offers.' She glanced around furtively. 'I'll give you a tip, treat them like Americans, be bold, they like that.'

'Oh here you are.' A man had arrived at their table, a rather ugly man, Judith noticed, wearing a straw hat. He didn't sit down.

'Darling, I've been having a delightful conversation with this young lady but we never introduced ourselves.'

'Judith Goldstein,' she supplied.

'Goldstein, eh?' She thought his tone was sneering.

'That's right. I'm Maurice Goldstein's daughter.'

'Yes, I've heard all about you. Staying at Hotel Baudy, eh?

173

Seems you've been to Le Pressoir, spent some time with Monet.'

'My, my,' Judith mimicked their Southern drawl. 'How news travels round here.'

'Glory me!' her new acquaintance pouted. 'Why didn't you tell me?'

'I don't think we've had time to get round to that,' Judith replied.

'Well that's a bit of a scoop,' Paul said. 'An audience with the Master, I wonder how you managed that. He's been avoiding us Yanks like the plague. You must tell us your secret.'

His nose was bulbous and he had a scrappy moustache, his lips were very red. Judith decided she didn't like him one bit.

'Now Paul, don't provoke the girl. It's easy to see how she does it; she is such a charming young lady, who could resist her? Oh my dear, what is he like? We haven't seen him for years. Did he show you the gardens? I'm dying to know.'

'But not now,' her husband interrupted, 'we are going into Vernon, remember?'

'Oh very well.' She rose and put up her parasol. She held out her hand. 'I'm Dorothy, by the way, Dorothy Young. See you again soon, I hope. I'll look out for you in the village. Now don't forget what I told you.'

Judith watched them go: the thin woman with red hair, the short man in a straw hat. She wasn't surprised Dorothy looked at other men. How could she have married a toad like Paul? And yet off they went, arm in arm, sharing some joke and seeming perfectly happy together. She ordered another pressé and considered their conversation.

A few hours later, she was loitering near the door that

led to the water garden. She had taken into account Normandy habits and supposed the gardeners would be back at work after luncheon. The sun was as hot as ever and a sharp smell rose from the tarmac, pleasing in an odd sort of way. She strolled up and down, trying to find a patch of shade and, although she wore her hat, mused that Dorothy's parasol was a superior idea. Then there was the scrape of a bolt and the door on the other side of the track swung open. She had no idea what she would say if the older gardener appeared and was relieved to see it was Michel. His eyes widened when he saw her and he glanced around as if looking for a means of escape.

'Michel,' Judith stepped forward. 'Judith, the friend of Monet, remember?'

His gaze darted over her and away. He nodded. 'Ah, yes.'

'When I was here the other day, I believe I dropped an earring, a pearl one. It is rather precious to me and I wondered if you would help me search for it.'

'I am busy, there is much work to do.' He made to move away but Judith held up her hand.

'I'm sure there is. Please, this is very important. It belonged to my mother you see.' She contrived a catch in her voice. 'Those earrings were the last thing she gave me before she died.'

'*Ta mère?*' He seemed to straighten up as if her absent mother were present in the garden.

'Please,' she urged again.

In reply he shrugged and beckoned to her: 'come. 'They crossed the tarmac and entered through the green door into the water garden. As it closed behind them, she felt a frisson of delight that she was alone with the young French man. There was no sign of Breuil.

175

'Oh, you are so lucky to be working here in this beautiful place!' she breathed.

He had no time for pleasantries. 'Where do you think it was lost?' he asked.

She was amused by the way he kept his distance, almost as if he were afraid she might pounce on him.

'I'm not sure. We walked all the way along that path and then stood on the bridge before returning on the other side.'

'Difficult,' he grunted, 'when it is something so small.'

He started along the path and she followed, noting his broad shoulders under the linen shirt, his powerful stride. Perhaps he was not as tall as Charlie but then Charlie was rather skinny, with the beginnings of a stoop from so much sitting at his desk. This man had such a physical presence about him, like a beautiful creature in his natural habitat.

He was searching with such deliberation that she began to feel guilty about her lie. She joined in, lifting leaves, peering about. Now and again, she pointed out a plant or a flower and said it was pretty, but he did not respond. He kept on repeating how difficult it was. He grumbled it was like looking for a needle in a haystack; maybe she would have to resign herself to the loss. It was obvious he wanted to be rid of her.

They had crossed the bridge and were gradually making their way across the other side, moving towards the door again. Judith racked her brains as to what else she could say or do to persuade him to talk to her. He was silent to the point of being morose.

Suddenly she stopped by a tree covered in a wild clamber of roses and put her hand to her head. 'Oh, dear.'

He glanced round, frowning at her.

176

'It's this sun, it's made me feel faint. I really must sit down for a moment.'

In answer, he led her to a green painted bench where she sank down. From somewhere, he produced a bottle and drew out the stopper.

'I have no water but here is some lemonade.'

She brought the bottle to her lips then gave a deep sigh. 'That's better.' She smiled up at him. 'How old are you, Michel?'

He shrugged.

'You are young like me but so serious.'

He gave a faint smile. 'That's what my mother tells me.'

'Are you serious all the time, even when you are not working?' She imitated his expression, which forced him to laugh. It encouraged her to pat the seat beside her. 'Sit down for a moment, it is very hot. I won't bite, you know.'

He hesitated then sat beside her. 'I have to be serious here,' he explained. 'It is a great responsibility to work in these gardens and M'sieur Breuil is a tough man to work for.'

'Well, he isn't here at the moment so you can relax.'

His mood seemed to change and he looked at her inquisitively. 'You are American, aren't you? There are so many Americans in Giverny now. They speak French in a strange way.'

Judith laughed. 'Strange? Do I?'

'Well, yes, I suppose you do but it sounds pretty when you speak.'

Judith smiled to herself. They were getting somewhere. 'I like the language,' she continued. 'I like France and I love Giverny.'

'It is fine for you,' he replied. 'You don't have to work.'

'Oh work!' she laughed. 'Such a horrible word. My father is always talking about it and Mother is always telling him to relax and enjoy life, sometimes.'

She realised he was watching her intently as if amazed by what she was saying. She must seem very different to the folks he usually mixed with. 'What do you do to relax, Michel?'

He spread his hands. 'I don't know. Sleep.'

'Oh! Oh my goodness, what a waste! We'll have to do something about that.' This was her opportunity. 'I know, oh yes, why don't you come to Hotel Baudy, one evening after work. We can sit on the terrace and have a cocktail. What do you say?'

His expression was wary. 'A cocktail! What is that?'

She clicked her tongue. 'Oh really, you're missing out if you've never had a cocktail. It's, you know, liquor.'

Ah, but that is medicinal: anise, brandy. Whenever my father thinks a cold is coming he drinks a small glass of whiskey.'

Judith laughed. 'Medicinal, well I suppose you could call it that. I have to say a cocktail sets me up no end. A classy champagne cocktail, mmm!'

But Michel had stopped listening. He rose from the bench. 'We must go, M'sieur Breuil will be asking himself where I am.'

'Oh, just when I was enjoying myself.'

They walked to the door and he made to shoot back the bolt.

Judith put out her hand to check him. 'So you'll come to Hotel Baudy?'

'I don't know, I usually go straight home after work. My parents expect...'

'Oh come on, Michel, don't be such a baby. What are you, six years old?'

He frowned. 'Very well, I will come. Tomorrow evening.'

'Oh that's swell. Seven o'clock, then? I'll be waiting.'

– NINETEEN –

JUDITH

He was late in arriving but it never crossed her mind he wouldn't come. She had enjoyed arousing his curiosity that afternoon, teasing him and gradually drawing him in. It had been a heady feeling as she took control. The serving girl came to take her empty glass away and she ordered another cocktail, leaned back in her chair and closed her eyes. It was a beautiful evening, warm and still, and she was enjoying this moment alone, listening to the sound of starlings gathering for the night. Then she saw Michel coming along the terrace but for a moment hardly recognised him. Standing on the bridge above the lily pond, he had looked self-assured, comfortable in his role of gardener, now he kept his head down and seemed ill at ease. He wore a suit, which she guessed was probably the only one he possessed and, as he approached her table, she saw the jacket was rather tight, the trouser legs too long so that they dragged on the ground. But his dark hair shone with brushing. His nails were scrubbed clean. In this different setting, he seemed a stranger.

'Michel!' She jumped up from the table and pulled out a chair for him. 'It's so good to see you. Do sit down.'

He did so, looking about him and murmuring: 'well, well, so this is Hotel Baudy.'

'Like it?' She so much wanted to please him. 'It's lovely here, isn't it, especially on an evening like this? Now, let me order for you.'

She caught the eye of the serving girl and ordered a second Champagne Charlie. Michel queried the name and she told him the story behind it: the music hall song that had been so popular back in the last century, its singer who had been paid in money and in kind by Moet and Chandon. She sang a few bars.

'Pretty,' he said. 'Very pretty.' He seemed to be lost for words, embarrassed by these unfamiliar surroundings, his gaze darting about.

Judith was struck again by the animal quality about him, his very physical presence. She eyed the large hands holding the flute, so different from Charlie's hands. What would they feel like, hard and rough if he touched her? She raised her glass to him. '*À ta santé.*'

He took a sip and an expression of wonderment came over his face.

'Don't you like it?' she asked. 'If you don't, I can order something else.'

Michel shook his head. 'But no, it is delicious.' He took another sip. 'Mmm, delicious.'

She laughed and he joined in. What was in this wondrous drink he wanted to know.

'It's made with a shot of apricot brandy and champagne. You pour the apricot brandy into a flute glass and top up with chilled champagne. If you're feeling romantic, you serve it garnished with a pale pink rose petal.'

'Ooh, la la!'

181

They were away after that, coasting through the next hour or so, any barrier between them of language or background vanished as they talked and joked and Judith ordered more cocktails.

'So this is what you do while I'm working hard in the gardens,' he teased her. 'Sit on this terrace and drink champagne.'

'Oh, I do other things as well. I watch the artists paint. I read and now, of course, I've made the acquaintance of Monet so I'll probably be up at the house more often.'

'What a beautiful life!'

'Sure, but it's nice to have some company of my own age.'

The other tables were filling up and Judith noticed several people turn to stare at them, attracted by their laughter. Then she caught Robert's disapproving gaze. He sat alone, a glass of beer on the table before him, observing her. Damn him, what right did he have to be so critical, telling her what to do, behaving like her mother? She was relieved when Harry appeared from the tennis courts and distracted his attention. When the two men rose and went into the hotel, presumably for dinner, an idea came into her head.

'Say, Michel, you like gardens. Why don't we take a stroll round the one here?'

He hesitated. 'What is the time?'

'Oh, it's early yet. Come on, just a little stroll. There are some marvellous roses.'

She led him along the same route she had taken with Robert, away from the hotel, up the uneven flights of steps to the higher levels. Michel remarked on how different this garden was from those of Le Pressoir. Apart from the roses, which had obviously been intentionally planted, it seemed to him that the rest had been left to nature, self-seeding and rustic, filling every available gap.

'I suppose it has,' Judith said without much interest. She eyed the vines snaking their way up the tree trunks and walls. 'It's the kind of place you dream of as a child, where you can play hide and seek and get lost.'

'You play that also in America?'

'Why yes, of course, the children are the same as anywhere else.'

Michel sighed. 'I would like to go to America.'

She laughed. 'I wouldn't bother if I were you. It's much nicer here.'

'All those beautiful American limousines.'

'Noise and dirt.'

'Money.'

'Yes, there is that,' she agreed as they started down the little steps again. 'Money is useful.'

The scent of the roses was powerful and she thought of the secluded bench where she and Robert had sat. She wondered what Michel would say if she suggested they sit there now, hidden from view. Would he think her awfully forward? This was something she had never done in her life before: be alone with a stranger, because he was a stranger, really. A shiver ran through her body at the realisation of what she had done. It was her turn to fall silent, wondering what to say. Michel, too, said nothing but she could feel his eyes on her. Did he imagine she wanted him to kiss her? Did she want him to? Now that the effects of the alcohol were subsiding, she felt suddenly nervous, at a loss as to what should be her next move.

There came into her mind an image of Charlie in his

tweed plus fours and pullover, on his way to play golf at the Buffalo; tall, lanky Charlie with an anxious expression on his face. He had stopped off at the house in Madison Square after her telephone call to tell him her little dog Daisy had died. The scent of his cologne as he held her close to him, the sound of his voice were so known to her. The catch phrase he always used, 'cheer up Cully, you'll soon be dead,' had made her smile through her tears.

'Oh kitten, I just can't bear to see you sad.'

Charlie adored her, she was certain of that; he always said he would give her the moon if he could. Why was she behaving like this? Judith felt a jolt of fear. Supposing he had read into this European trip a lack of commitment and found another girl? So they passed the bench and approached the hotel again.

Michel looked away. 'I must leave now. I begin work very early in the morning.'

'Oh, well…'

They reached the door and here he paused, gazing at her. She thought she must look rather lovely in her pale frock, standing there in the dusky light. What was he thinking? He had probably never been in the company of someone like her in his life. But then he was unknown to her too. Where did one go from here?

He was smiling. 'It has been very pleasant, may I come again?'

She pushed thoughts of Charlie from her mind. 'Sure. Of course you may.'

'Sunday… er… no, I have something to do on Sunday. Monday?'

'Monday it is!'

'*Au revoir*, Judith.'

184

The moment he had gone, she went into the hotel and ordered a bottle of champagne to be served at the table under the wisteria. She would sit there and drink it while she thought over the day and how she was progressing very nicely. It was then Robert appeared, he might have been spying on her, his timing so perfect.

'What are you doing here?' she demanded. 'Can't a girl have a quiet drink without you popping up?'

'Stop being so angry with me.'

'Then will you stop following me about, criticising me? Leave me alone.'

She turned away from him, staring out over the garden, the roses shining ghostly pale; a night bird called. The only presence that was spoiling things was his.

Robert said: 'Do you realise what you are doing, Judith? Tonight, for example, who was that young man?'

'A gardener from Le Pressoir, if you want to know.'

'A gardener from Le Pressoir sitting on the terrace with you, drinking champagne, and you have a perfectly decent fiancé in America.'

'Oh, stop keep reminding me, Robert.'

'Well it's the truth and you need to consider what I'm saying. I'll bet he's waiting patiently for you to return not dreaming...'

Judith drained her glass and reached for the bottle. 'I said stop it.'

'How would you like it if he did something like that?'

'He wouldn't,' she said, certain of that now.

'Okay.' Robert paused to light a cigarette. 'How did this come about?'

She shrugged. It was none of his business but it only made her more determined to see Michel again.

'Tell me something, Judith,' Robert persisted. 'Was it a pick up?'

She turned on him. 'What do you take me for? A tramp?'

'It was, wasn't it? You picked up a gardener and invited him here. I'm sure no-one else at Le Pressoir knows about this. Didn't you see all those people staring at you? And there you sat, plying the young man with drink. I told you before, the culture is different here and you must understand it. Women just don't behave like that.'

For some reason, she found this amusing: he so earnest, she knocking back the champagne. 'You're jealous.'

'No, I'm not.'

'You are, because I'm young and enjoying myself.'

'If it were only that, but it isn't, you worry me. There is something about you that is reckless, impervious to danger. It's attractive in a way, this *joie de vivre* of yours. I'm not against you, Judith, I guess I want to protect you.'

'I don't need protecting. I am twenty-five years old, Robert.'

'Well you don't behave like it.'

He was making her feel uncomfortable again. Judith stood up and thumped her glass on the table.

'Know something? I was having a lovely evening until you stuck your nose in. I don't care what people do or don't do here. I shall carry on behaving exactly as I choose and to hell with the consequences.'

She went into the hotel and left him sitting there.

TWENTY

ROBERT

He felt his present self dissolving, his mind changing again. He saw the family kitchen, his childhood home. Florence was standing on the pine table while his mother put the final touches to her gown. It was made of sprigged muslin printed with a green leaf motif, the bodice low cut with puff sleeves. His sister was so excited she couldn't keep still. 'I'll never have this finished if you jiggle about all the time, child.'

His father came into the kitchen and put the back of his hand across his eyes, pretending to be blinded. 'Who's this vision? It can't be Florrie Harrison.'

'Oh Father, you know it's me.'

'Well I'll be darned. I tell you, young lady, you'll be the belle of the ball.'

Tonight his aunt was ill and his parents were taking the trap to visit her. They couldn't disappoint Florence who had set such store by going to the dance. He was to accompany her on his own.

His mother uttered the familiar words, 'Take care of her, Robert.'

In the church hall he saw the trestle tables laid with

white cloths and decorated with sheaves of corn and stacks of apples and pears, in honour of the harvest supper. Each table was crowded with dishes of food: there were jerky and cured hams, pies, puddings and tarts; set at regular intervals were jugs of lemonade. All the congregation was there, laughing and joking with the minister, eating and drinking, their faces flushed in the light of the lanterns strung across the hall. He saw Florence in the midst of them and saw himself in his best striped waistcoat cross to join her.

'You don't need to stick by me all the time, Robert,' she said. 'I'm sixteen, remember. I can take care of myself.'

But could she? He was filled with a nameless fear of where her recklessness might lead her.

Then the black fiddler arrived and struck up a reel and Florence was pulled away from him to join in. Throughout the evening, he caught glimpses of her, flushed and excited, oblivious of him and he envied her. Envied her popularity, her capacity for throwing herself into the moment without a care or a thought, while he remained on the outskirts, unnoticed and alone. But there was something else, a quality about her, which made him afraid. She was like a flame burning brightly, too brightly, he thought. At ten o' clock he went in search of her for it was time to go home. She was sitting on one of the chairs ranged around the hall and there was a young man with her. They were deep in conversation and at one point, rocking with laughter, Florence laid her hand on the young man's hand.

'What would Father and Mother say?' she mimicked him as they walked home. 'Don't you dare tell them.'

He wouldn't, of course, not admit that, in spite of his best endeavours, he had failed their trust in him. He remembered his powerlessness and his fear.

– TWENTY-ONE –

CLAUDE

It has rained during the night and when he takes his morning walk in the gardens, he is delighted to see how everything has responded. There is a scent of refreshed earth, the poppies and marguerites; the satiny peonies hold their heads high. The delphiniums have taken a bit of a beating and he is glad to see Michel is busy reinforcing their stakes. He pauses, smiles down at the crown of the young man's hat, and moves on. You can water a garden as much as you like but nothing revives it like a heavy shower of rain.

Mealtimes have lifted his spirits even more. Finally, it seems, Marie is coming to understand his palate and his standards. Last night, she had produced a passable Yorkshire pudding and there was enough peppercorn seasoning in the duck. A sense of contentment seems to have settled over the household, Blanche is not bickering with him, even the little blonde laundry maid seems happy.

Now he sits in his studio, the blinds drawn against the sun, sketching. His hand moves quickly and surely over the paper as he falls into the old familiar rhythm, simple and direct. It is a long time since he did any figurative drawing, the garden and now, of course, the lily pond have so absorbed him.

But Judith has impressed him with her liveliness and audacity. The meeting of a few days ago continues to resonate. He searches in his mind for the poses she takes, her self-absorption; there is a bird-like quality about her. She is undoubtedly chic which is something he had never expected in an American; maybe not as beautiful as Camille was beautiful, but she has that *je ne sais quoi* quality which magnetises the eye. With a stick of vine charcoal, he sketches in the shape of her head, its angle tilted slightly sideways, quizzical, the long lean contours of her body. Then he will move on to compressed charcoal for texture and detail.

You have to be watchful with charcoal, he reminds himself, it is capable of going a rich, dark black. There need to be areas of white and shades of grey in the composition to lift and give it drama. While he works, he muses on how the artist, be he painter or writer, lives on two levels. There is the one of everyday experiences, sometimes good or not so good, and the other that selects from these and transmutes them into art. Even as he recounted a part of his life to Judith, flattered by her attention, there was that detached part of him looking on, measuring with his eye, taking note.

Drawing has always gone hand in hand with his painting. You must begin by drawing, above all observing the contours because you can never be too sure of holding on to them once you start to paint. He understands there were many who believed he painted directly onto the canvas. They knew nothing of his preparatory studies, his draughtsmanship, and he had never publicly acknowledged the gift.

He chuckles to himself, picturing the eleven year old strolling the streets of Le Havre, drawing caricatures of anyone who would sit to him. It was the money he was interested in, the ten or twenty francs he would charge but, unconsciously, he was developing his drawing skills and powers of observation even then.

The thing one noticed about that girl was the contrast between the dark hair and pale skin. It is remarkable skin; white and translucent, alabaster comes to mind. He discards the charcoal and takes up a graphite pencil. He scribbles onto the paper then blends with a piece of soft cloth. *Voila*, flawless looking skin!

Always there has been this dialogue between line and colour. The time he spent drawing and preparation for *Déjeuner sur l'Herbe*, and look where that ended up. But he couldn't do it any other way.

He takes another sheet of paper and sketches Judith's body curving away, almost in profile, head tilted towards the viewer, it is a pose he likes, the view which gives a picture a sense of informality, of movement and an instant in time. Camille in the green dress was just such a pose, her look of inwardness as she makes her graceful movement. Claude remembers the broad strokes he used, focusing on the sweep of the dress, its multiple folds of rich fabric. He makes a further sketch of the American girl, this time with her head averted, gazing at his paintings. Did she understand what she was looking at? She certainly made an intelligent remark about the Japanese prints. It had surprised him.

Direct and simple, simple and direct, that's what he likes about the language of line, it can be so easily communicated. Now of course, there are the lily pond sketchbooks, the numerous studies he is making, the notion that is forming in his mind for a massive series of paintings, great panels of light and shade.

While he works, there is a part of him that feels guilty and he knows his occupation this afternoon should be kept a secret. What if Blanche came suddenly into the room? He would thrust the sketchbook into the open drawer he has waiting, reach for his cigarette case, which is never far away. He is unsure of her reaction, but thinks she would probably not approve, would consider he was wasting his time when he should be working. He wants nothing to disturb this *détente*, the wonderful relaxation of the tension that has reigned over them since Alice's death.

Later he goes for his stroll in the garden. Michel it seems is working late. Claude moves up and down the paths, noticing how, as the month passes, the flowers of June have started to give way to those of July. The wallflowers and azaleas are beginning to look past their best while there is a hint of orange and yellow among the nasturtiums, which will soon snake over the path in all their glory. Yesterday, he glimpsed one of the water lilies in bud. It occurs to him how swiftly this year seems to be advancing in the gardens. Why it seems only a few days ago the place fluttered with waves of daffodils and narcissi. One needs to be constantly alert to these changes. It is probably a sign of age, he tells himself, that things seem to move on more quickly and you find yourself looking more attentively, or wish you had, wish you had taken note of this day to day progression, in case this should be the last season you saw them.

'M'sieur?' Michel is dead heading and cutting back spent flower shoots. He has a bag into which he is dropping seeds

192

according to Breuil's instruction. 'It's sad,' he comments. 'One day there is a beautiful rose and soon it is dead.'

The boy has noticed too, even at his young age.

The lines of that wretched poem come once more into Claude's head. *They are not long the days of wine and roses.* He is overwhelmed by the melancholy of time passing. It is time Judith came again. He will ask Blanche to send an invitation for this coming week.

– TWENTY-TWO –

BLANCHE

'Something light this evening, Marie, wouldn't you say after that splendid duck?' Blanche enquired.

'Certainly madame, soup and an omelette, perhaps?'

'Good idea, the hens are laying particularly well.'

Blanche's attention had strayed to the kitchen window to gaze out at the Reine des Violettes. There was one velvety purple bloom left, a particularly fine bloom to be sure but only one. Its flowering appeared to be almost over. There might be a repeat in the autumn as there had been last year, but she did not want to think that far ahead, to the passing of these summer days. With the newfound sense of peace in the house, she was enjoying them. There was the feeling of a weight lifted from her shoulders, one that had settled after Maman's death. Sometimes, she could almost believe it had not happened, that she would walk down the garden and find her mother sewing or reading under the tree. Some mornings, Papa had even been heard singing snatches of opera.

'Tomato and basil,' Marie was saying as Blanche gave a last look at the rose, noticing it was already ageing to violet, before she turned back to the room.

'Pardon?'

'Jules says we have a glut of tomatoes at the moment, and there is plenty of basil.'

'Excellent. I'm sure that will satisfy even my stepfather.'

They smiled at one another. Blanche had noticed that Marie's hair was often a barometer of her state of mind and today it looked sleek in its dark bun. Her sometimes flushed face had only a pinkish hue. The sight was reassuring. She did not look like a servant about to give in her notice.

'Marie, I just wanted to say how very pleased I am with the way you have settled into the household.'

'Don't mention it, madame.'

'I realise how hard you have worked and the results prove it,' Blanche continued. 'It hasn't been easy, I know, to cater to my father's tastes but you have persevered. Take the Yorkshire pudding last night, it was quite light and open textured, such an improvement. Why, I believe even Marguerite would have praised it.'

An expression passed over the cook's face, one of slight annoyance at the mention of her predecessor but swiftly replaced by a smile. 'I am happy you are satisfied, madame,' she said.

'More than satisfied, Marie. I am happy and relieved that we seem to have overcome initial misunderstandings, that you have accepted my stepfather's views on cuisine.'

Marie, as she often did when she felt she was being undermined, wiped the blue table with savage movements; a strand of hair escaped the bun. 'Hmm, you mean the peppercorns.'

'Not particularly but yes, you have certainly recognised my stepfather's liking for them.'

Blanche thought back to luncheon and Papa's childlike

195

delight that the duck was seasoned as he demanded it. She had wished she could be as easily pleased, put such store by food and wine. She was at once envious and irritated by him. Life in this household revolved around him, tailored to his needs and rigid timetable and she had the responsibility of making it so.

'He is not easy to please, Marie,' she said now. 'And you have been very patient.'

In the pause that followed, they listened to the grandfather clock in the library strike the hour. Blanche's gaze went from the terracotta tiled floor to tiles on the walls, from the walls to the floor. The reds of the terracotta with its tomette pattern enhanced the cool blue and white geometric patterns on the walls. Papa had taken for his inspiration such patterned floors and wall tiles that decorated homes in Spain and Italy and bought tiles from Rouen. But Papa being Papa, he had invested it with a *je ne sais quoi* touch, turning pattern making into an art form.

Marie was folding her apron in preparation for an hour or two of repose before she began to prepare supper. 'Thank you, madame.' Several times she had cast glances towards the dresser and it was obvious she couldn't wait to pick up the novel lying there.

Curious about what her cook read, Blanche had examined one of the books, expecting it to be a tale of love and romance. However, it seemed Marie had darker tastes and had been seized by the latest craze for Fantômas. Blanche's interest had grown as she flicked through the pages, reading of an arch criminal who was ruthless, and loyal to no-one. It seemed he was a master of disguises, always appearing under an assumed identity, often that of a person whom he had murdered. Fantômas made use of bizarre techniques for his crimes such as plague infested rats, giant snakes and rooms that filled up with sand.

At this point, Blanche had laid the book down. It wouldn't do to get on the wrong side of a woman who read such literature, she had told herself.

'Will that be all, madame?' Marie was losing her patience.

'Certainly, and I must be getting on.'

Blanche left the kitchen. She had spent enough time on mundane matters. A slight breeze stirred the curtains as she stepped into her room and closed the door. The easel stood where she had left it, the painting she had begun a few days previously propped on it. She glanced at her watch, calculated she had three hours at her disposal. Gone were the days when she could paint undisturbed, now it was time snatched from domestic duties. But at least she was working again. The subject she had chosen was an oblique view towards the house with the Reine des Violettes to one side of it. During this month while it was flowering abundantly, she had made a number of sketches, following her father's method of preparation for a canvas. Simple and direct, he had said to her. Drawing is fundamental to a good painting. Capture the contours, Blanche, or you may lose them when you take up your brush. Yes, she had captured them at their most beautiful and made notes of their pastel smudgy colours. Now she was recreating that vision she had had several weeks ago. She settled herself, using the broad strokes she loved, laying the paint confidently onto the canvas, mixing and painting, painting and mixing. As the rhythm took hold of her, she had a feeling of such calm, the brush an extension of her mind recording the roses in all their beauty.

It was like defying time, she thought, capturing a moment. How she loved this process, how it rendered up to her that real and true self. And as she painted and the image grew, she regretted she had left it so long, had been unfaithful to what meant most to her in her life. She forgot the minutiae of the household, its irritations and entered this other world. They had the American girl to thank for this, Mademoiselle Judith who had somehow rescued them all from sinking under the weight of grief and disappointment. Blanche felt young again, with all the hope she had once had of becoming a great painter.

1889

Two days after the expedition to Andaine forest, Alice developed a temperature and aching limbs. Monet sent her to bed with firm instructions not to get out of it until she was well.

'How can I?' she protested, 'with this house to look after.' She gave him a wry look. 'Not to mention you.'

'That's easy. Blanche can take over. She's perfectly capable.'

no-one suggested that Suzanne as the elder should be mobilised. She was considered too fragile and whimsical. Whereas I... thought Blanche... the dutiful daughter.

In fact she welcomed the routine, the meals to plan, laundry to check, the supervision of the servants. Dull as it might be, it took up her day and her thoughts and gave her some respite from mooning over John Leslie and when it might be possible to see him again. It also kept her out of Monet's way. Since the day of the mushroom hunt the atmosphere between them had been tense.

He had lost his temper with her again when he collected the baskets of mushrooms and saw what was in hers. 'What's this, a bitter bolete and this and this? God in heaven, girl, do you want to poison us all?'

198

She knew it was a rhetorical question. Anything that did not pass the scrutiny of his eye would never have found its way onto the dining table. Nevertheless, he made her feel like a criminal.

'I'm sorry, Monet, I wasn't thinking straight.'

He met her gaze. 'No, and you haven't been for some time, have you? Your painting is all over the place.'

She bit her lip as the remark seared her. He knew her weakest point and had unkindly probed it.

Blanche glared at him. 'Maybe I haven't been concentrating as I should... maybe...' She longed to tell him the reason, instead she said: '...there is always so much going on in the house, these days.'

He shook his head. 'That is no excuse. You disappoint me, Blanche.'

For the next few days, Alice stayed in bed and Blanche ran the household. She made sure she was never alone with Monet although she could feel him watching her. Then one evening, as she was stowing the eggs she had collected into the little pantry, he came up behind her.

'Blanche?'

'Oh!' She started, almost dropping an egg.

'I need to talk to you.'

'Not now, Monet, please. I have to go to the kitchen, Marguerite wants to show me a dish she has been experimenting with.'

'It can wait.' His face was stern. 'I want to talk to you now.'

She followed him into the studio and sat with her back to the garden, gazing at his paintings, which lined the walls.

Monet also sat and lit a cigarette. 'You know what this is about, don't you?'

She shrugged.

'Of course you do. There is no use in pretending you don't.'

Blanche said nothing.

'I am tired of your behaviour, Blanche. I want to know what is wrong with you. You show a complete lack of interest in everything around you, the family, even your work. You put a dampener on the mushroom expedition and your long face is enough to put me off painting, too.'

She made herself look up to meet his gaze. 'That is simply not true.'

'Isn't it? I think it is.' He stubbed out the cigarette. 'I ask you again: what is behind all this?'

Once more she was silent. The last of the sun streamed through the window, burning the back of her neck. She longed to be anywhere but here, had a sudden yearning for John Leslie.

'Is it John Leslie?' he asked. It was as if he had read her mind.

She felt the blood rise into her face, her heart thudded. For a moment she thought: tell him. Tell him now. Bring it all out in the open. She looked down at her hands and muttered, 'No.'

There was a pause and when she finally looked up, his expression had altered. She realised what an effort it had taken him to ask the question, and what a relief to hear her reply.

'Forgive me,' he said. 'I was so worried, that's all. You know my opinion of those young men. It is all very well to take an interest in their painting but we know nothing about their backgrounds – or their morals. You must realise they are not husband material.'

Blanche thought of John Leslie's passionate kisses, his eager hands. If only Monet knew. She might have smiled if it hadn't been so tragic.

'You see, Blanchefleur,' Monet was saying. 'Your presence in this house is so important to me, your understanding of how an artist thinks and feels. no-one else comprehends so well, not even Alice.'

His voice trailed off and he smiled at her, she held his gaze with a sense of horror of his expectations of her, his attachment.

'I don't want to be without you. I admire and respect you as a painter. Perhaps, for that reason, I ask so much of you.'

She sighed. 'You have taught me all I know. I owe a lot to you.'

He spoke quietly. 'Don't ever leave me, please.'

At that moment the bell rang for supper and they rose and went to join the others.

The following day they went out early into the fields together. He wanted to demonstrate to her the effects of light he had noted on those quaint structures the Normandy farmers built to store and protect their grain until it could be threshed. It was by now late September and, although the days were still warm, the mornings had an autumnal chill. Blanche drew her jacket closer round her, folded her arms and tried to concentrate on what Monet was saying.

'I think I have stumbled on a wonderful subject... the alteration in atmosphere from moment to moment, its effect on colour.'

Her mind kept drifting off, not onto John Leslie as much as into a dreamlike state so that in this grey dawn light she was unsure if she were asleep or awake.

'Need to buy some more canvasses,' his voice came to her, 'other paints... go to the dealers on Thursday.'

Immediately, her mind became crystal clear and filled with joy. On Thursday she could go to John Leslie.

Blanche glanced at her watch and sighed. It was always the same if you were a woman. Her father could carry on working, knowing the house ran smoothly around him, but for her there were things to attend to. She went down to the kitchen and found Lilli with the laundry baskets and, as she approached, heard the girl humming under her breath. A broad smile spread over her face when she saw Blanche.

'You sound very happy, Lilli.' Blanche tugged the clothes roughly from the basket and began to sort them. 'Let me guess. It is because you are soon to see your young man again.'

'Oh madame, not my young man, well not yet.'

'Very well, but he has asked you out for a walk. That's a good start.'

The camisoles, the drawers and the nightgowns… it only seemed like yesterday they had worked on this task. Oh the tedium of domestic life, Papa's shirts, the ironing they demanded.

'My grey skirt and I've a new blouse which is prettily tucked,' Lilli was saying. 'It will be quite suitable if the sun shines but what if it rains?'

Blanche gazed at the girl's anxious face and laughed. 'I shouldn't worry about that. If it rains, well then that is the perfect excuse to take shelter somewhere. And while you are waiting for the shower to pass, you can talk, make each other's acquaintance.'

Lilli's expression softened. 'Do you think so?'

'I speak from experience, Lilli. You remind me of myself when I was about your age. I was in love with a young man but it was early days and I was unsure what he thought about me. One day, we went for a walk and like you I'd planned my outfit. Although it was summer there had been quite a lot of rain. We hadn't gone very far before we felt the first drops.' She smiled, recalling how they had turned to each other and then laughing, hurried for shelter. 'There was a little stone building, we sheltered inside and he kissed me.'

'Oh madame, really?'

'Yes, really.' Blanche laughed at the girl's wondering face. 'I was young once even if you find it hard to believe. I wanted the rain to last forever. I wanted to stay in that moment with his arms round me and feel his heart beating so close to mine. Don't worry about the rain.'

'Let's go for a walk,' he said.

'Where?'

'Anywhere... the moon even. I just want to be alone with you, to kiss you and hold you in my arms, to hear the sound of your voice. It's been terrible these weeks sitting together painting, feeling you so near and yet so far.'

She laughed. 'You seemed so occupied with your work. I thought it was only I who couldn't think of anything else.'

He shook his head. 'Not true. Maybe I am better at hiding it and Monet keeps a sharp eye on us Americans.'

They decided to walk through the fields in the direction of Vernon. Once there, they would have tea in one of the cafés near the street of the Old Clock. They set off, talking and laughing with the sheer joy of being together once more. But the day, which had begun clear and bright, clouded over and it began to rain, only a light shower to begin with but steadily becoming heavier.

'We'll get soaked. What shall we do?' moaned Blanche.

'Find shelter.' He seized her hand. 'Come on, run.'

To their relief they had not gone far before they saw ahead of them an old stone building. Breathless and laughing, they flung themselves inside.

'Look at you!' gasped Blanche, 'with your hair plastered to your head.'

'You look a little bedraggled yourself,' he teased.

'Oh dear,' she looked down at her wet clothes.

'And perfectly beautiful,' he added.

She lifted her head and he cupped her face between his hands. He bent to kiss her throat and her mouth. He stroked her breast and her mouth opened under his, she forgot everything except her need for him. There had been such an ache of separation, what mattered was they were together again. He whispered with his mouth against her hair, 'my love, my love.' She murmured 'I love you.'

'I want to marry you,' he said. 'Take you to America or Paris or wherever you want to come with me.'

'I should say I can't, she thought, can't leave Giverny, Monet and the family but I can't be without you. She felt as if she were being torn apart.

She pulled away and looked up at him. 'We must take care not to hurt Monet.'

'Of course, I understand that but we will be together. We must, Blanche.'

They came together again, hungrily reaching out for each other, Blanche knew such an intensity of physical longing she had never imagined existed. She longed for him to touch her and, understanding this, he undid the buttons of her blouse, bent his head to kiss the curve of her breast as the material fell away. She closed her eyes as she felt his fingers stroke her nipple and buried her face in his hair. This time it was he who moved away. 'Not here,' he said quietly.

With their arms around each other they gazed out beyond the entrance of the building and noticed with a sense of surprise the rain had stopped. He took her hand and they stepped outside and began to walk back the way they had come. With every step she felt herself being carried nearer to the house and Monet and the complexity this represented. Somehow she must overcome it because she couldn't bear to lose John Leslie.

'It won't be easy,' she said. 'He will put every obstacle in the way.'

He paused, turned to her and took her hands. 'I know,' he said. 'But we belong to one another.'

A while later, as Giverny came into sight, they halted, both reluctant to take the steps that would separate them.

'I don't want to leave you,' she said.

'How long is Monet away?'

'He won't return until tomorrow evening.'

They looked at one another and laughed as school children laugh when there is nothing really to laugh about.

'Tomorrow? Can you get away so that we can spend the day together? We could meet in Vernon.'

She smiled at him. 'Yes.

* * *

When she arrived back at Le Pressoir she found her mother, Suzanne and Marthe having tea on the balcony.

'Oh dear!' exclaimed Suzanne. 'Someone got caught in the rain.'

To Blanche's relief no-one asked her where she had been nor noticed there was a button missing from her blouse. She laughed and turned the attention onto her mother.

Maman, what are you doing out of bed?'

'I couldn't stay there a moment longer. Monet fusses so but I am feeling much better.' She reached for another almond biscuit, seeming restored to her usual self.

Blanche longed to slip away to her room, to savour what had happened that afternoon but her mother patted a chair and poured her a cup of tea.

'Anyway, poor Blanche has done enough. It's time I took up the reins again.'

Suzanne caught her sister's eye. 'So you'll be able to get back to your painting tomorrow?'

Blanche helped herself to two almond biscuits. She was ravenous. With glance averted she said: 'In fact, I thought I would go to Vernon tomorrow, I need one or two skirts for winter. There should be a fabric sale about now. I'll take them to Madame Renée to make up.' She returned Suzanne's gaze. 'There are several other things I need so it might take some time.' She hoped her voice didn't sound forced or her colour give her away.

'Excellent idea,' agreed her mother. 'It will do you good to have a day out. You've worked hard over this past week. You might pick up some gloves for me, you know the ones I like, suede, in grey I think.'

'Would you like me to come with you?' Suzanne gave her a sly smile, 'to help you choose the fabrics?'

Blanche took a sip of tea, controlling the urge to shout 'No!'

'I think I can manage alone, thank you.'

They seemed to be satisfied and the conversation turned to a friend of their mother's who was leaving her husband: far more interesting. Blanche was grateful Monet wasn't present, he would probably have seen right through her.

The following morning she waited until everybody had disappeared for their various activities, Marthe and Germaine to visit some friends, Suzanne to read in the library, and then went to her room. She stood in front of her wardrobe, choosing and discarding until finally she settled for a pale grey flannel skirt and flower sprigged blouse. She brushed and brushed her hair until it gleamed and crackled with electricity then arranged it into a loose bun so that tendrils escaped and framed her face. She seemed to see the face of a stranger in the mirror, one about to do something dangerous. She panicked. What was she thinking of, setting out to meet this man, defying Monet? She was

206

behaving in a way young women in her position should never behave. She thought, I could stay here and somehow let him know I can't come, after all. But he would be waiting for her and she could not let him down. When she came downstairs the trap was waiting for her and took her into Vernon.

He was sitting in the café they had chosen, smoking a cigarette, and in the moment before he saw her, he looked like a formidable stranger and she had the urge to turn and run away. But then he glanced up and the light came into his eyes.

'Blanche, you've come.'

All her fear was dispelled. She sat down at the table. 'I said I would.'

'I know but I wondered… maybe something would stop you.'

All the longing and apprehension was in their gaze.

'What will you take?' he broke the silence. 'I know nothing about your tastes, how you like your coffee or whether you prefer tea or even whether today you would prefer an aperitif before I take you to lunch.'

Her hands were shaking, she felt slightly out of breath. 'An aperitif, I think. Something fresh.'

'Martini?' he suggested. 'Let's have a dry Martini.'

'Is that what you Americans drink?'

'I guess so.'

When they arrived she took a tentative sip.

'What do you think of it?' he asked.

'It's fascinating but difficult to define… herby, a bit tangy, what's in it?'

'Vermouth and gin.'

She laughed, 'You'll have me drunk.' But she began to feel steadier.

It was easier away from Giverny where the weight of family seemed to pin her down; here she felt this thing between them

207

could be possible. He put his hand over hers and she gazed at him, seeing the eyes, the mouth she now knew so well. She yearned for him to kiss her.

'Come on,' he said. 'Let's go and have lunch.'

He led and she followed through the streets of Vernon. They passed the market and she saw the stalls heaped with fruit and vegetables, seeming so bright and shining and she was filled with a simple joy. They walked along rue Potard and she thought she had never fully realised how the buildings were so imbued with history and how singled out she was to be here, now, living in this moment.

The little bistro where he took her was quiet, it was still early for lunch, and the smiling waiter said they could have any of the blue clothed tables. They chose one set back in an alcove and John Leslie ordered a bottle of white Bordeaux. The sole she chose was beautifully cooked in a white sauce studded with grapes, it fell off the bone; the wine was dry but fragrant.

'It is to your liking, madame?' the waiter enquired.

'Oh very much!' she laughed.

She felt her skin was glowing and that her eyes shone; she was beautiful and amusing. Everything that was good and important came together as it usually only did in a dream. She seemed to step outside her ordinary self and become a woman in love. Nothing could go wrong. Around them people arrived and left and still they sat on. They were only dimly aware of time passing, sometimes speaking, sometimes silent, holding hands across the table until the last petit four was eaten, the last cup of coffee drunk.

John Leslie paid the bill then looked at her. 'Shall we go?'

She followed him out of the bistro not knowing where they were going and not caring. She had surrendered herself and would go wherever he led.

The hours had passed while they sat in the bistro and the shadows were falling across the square. The earlier warmth of the day was fading and she pulled on her jacket.

John Leslie drew her arm through his and they walked like this for a while. It felt so right as if they had done this many times before.

'What shall we do now?' she asked.

His expression was nervous and vulnerable. 'Would you... that is, shall we go to a hotel?'

She hesitated.

'Only if you would like to,' he said quickly. 'Otherwise we could...'

She raised her head to kiss his cheek. 'I think it is a wonderful idea,' she said.

* * *

In the bedroom with its rose strewn wall paper, light streaked through the slatted shutters and lay on the wooden floor. There was utter silence as if they were the only two people in the hotel. They paused and Blanche felt the sweetness of being alone together, invisible to the outside world. They turned to each other and smiled then their mouths met, tenderly at first but then more urgently, filled with longing. 'I love you,' she said. Their bodies moved in and out of the dim light as they undressed each other. She watched his face as he looked at her and, although she had always envied Suzanne her slight figure and tiny waist, she knew by the expression in his eyes she was beautiful to him. She reached up to stroke the fine skin of his shoulders and chest then they drew closer, their bodies fitting as if already known to each other.

It surprised her how simple and easy it was as if she instinctively knew what to do. She touched him, tentatively at first and then with more insistence. He drew in his breath and guided her towards the bed. Here he laid her down and she felt the softness of his touch between her legs. She looked up and met John Leslie's gaze while his hand continued to caress her. Then he lent forward and kissed her, but gently this time. His mouth was firm and strong and she responded, opening her mouth to him while his hands moved upwards and touched her, delicately, tantalisingly. She heard her voice whisper, 'yes,' and her body softened, yielding to him, while his tongue flickered against hers. She felt herself opening, opening to him, wanting him to go on touching her, not to stop this pleasure he gave her. His fingers slipped inside her, still gently and she saw he felt the moisture welling up. She moaned, felt herself swelling, budding, blooming in an explosion of joy.

He took her hand and guided her, helping her fingers to move up and down, regulating the tempo if she went too fast but soon she understood what to do, as if she had always known how to give this delight. There came the moment when she reached up her arms to him and he came into her, joining them together.

She opened her eyes and raised herself to gaze round the room almost surprised to find herself here. His arm tightened round her and she turned back to him, her hair covering her face as she bent to kiss him and they came together again. Later, as the light changed and the room grew shadowy they lay looking into one another's eyes until they fell asleep.

When she woke, her first thought was: what a waste of their short time to sleep. He stirred and opened his eyes and she saw in them an instant of bewilderment as to where they were.

'What's the time?' She remembered she had asked the trap to return at six.

'I don't know.'

She got out of bed and looked at her watch. 'Five o'clock, I must go soon.'

'Not yet,' he said. 'Not quite yet. Come back to bed.'

She hesitated; she knew she dare not be late.

'Please.'

She looked back at him, propped on his elbow, watching her. She smiled and moved towards him and they made love again. The light was going from the day, the room was shadowy and had become somehow familiar. She could believe that they had overcome their difficulties and were truly never to be parted again.

She stirred. 'I…'

'I know, you must go.'

She washed, admiring the pretty flower sprigged jug and bowl, and put up her hair, trying to rearrange it into the bun she had made so carefully earlier in the day. She stood at the window for a moment, gazing out over the rooftops to the darkening sky. There were trees where starlings were gathering in preparation for the night. She opened the window to listen to their scolding chatter. John Leslie came up behind her and put his arms round her waist, resting his chin on her shoulder.

'Don't go, Blanche.'

She sighed deeply. 'I must, you know I must. They will be waiting for me and Monet returns tonight.'

'Can we meet like this again?'

'As soon as I am able.'

He turned her round to face him. 'I can't live without you.'

His expression reflected her love amid the pain of separation. For a moment they gazed at one another, lost for words.

Then John Leslie said, 'Come on, let's go.'

The trap set her down in the road before the house and she went quietly in, hoping to go straight to her room. But as she passed the library, her mother called out: 'Is that you, Blanche?'

As she entered, she saw to her dismay that Monet was there. They were both staring at her and it seemed as if they must know. She felt her mouth was swollen and her hair wild.

'Good evening, Blanche,' Monet said. 'I hear you have been doing some shopping.'

'Where are your packages?' Maman asked. 'Did you leave them in the trap? I'll get someone to bring them in. You did remember the gloves, I hope?'

Blanche said quietly: 'I'm afraid I didn't.'

'Oh Blanche, I was relying on you!'

'I didn't buy anything at all.'

Monet lit a cigarette. 'I see.'

In that moment she realised he did see, he had seen for some time, while she had pretended to herself she had deceived him. Maman was looking from one to the other with an expression of bewilderment on her face.

Blanche turned away from their searching gaze and rushed out of the room, up the stairs to her bedroom where she lay on her bed staring at the ceiling. She heard the voices of her sisters as they went to their rooms, and the bell rung for supper. She heard everyone going downstairs and their voices and laughter in the dining room. There was the rattle of the trolley as the courses were taken in and out. She lay there in the dark for what seemed like hours and hours until she fell into an exhausted sleep.

In the morning she was up very early and was sitting in the dining room when Monet appeared for his breakfast. He muttered a greeting and then settled to his food, turning the pages of *Le Matin*.

Blanche spread a croissant with apricot jam and eagerly sipped her café au lait. In spite of everything she was hungry. She kept glancing across to Monet but he appeared engrossed in the

212

newspaper. The silence between them grew and became charged with tension. At last she could bear it no longer, she cleared her throat. He continued to read.

'Monet, we need to talk.'

Silence.

'Please,' she urged. 'I want to explain, try to make you understand.'

At that he stubbed out his cigarette, folded the newspaper and pushed back his chair, 'I have work to do,' he said.

She shrank from his cold stare.

Blanche dumped the folded clothes back into their basket. 'When you're in love the weather isn't important.' She turned away and gazed once more at the last bloom on the Reine des Violettes, it seemed more faded since last she looked, its petals loosening ready to fall. She had tried so hard to capture its beauty but one could not stop time passing. 'Seize life with both hands, Lilli,' she sighed. 'It goes so quickly.'

As she had predicted, her stepfather enjoyed the soup and filled his bowl again. Marie had made an effort, adding a sprinkling of chopped basil and serving it with a dollop of cream. Annette clumped in to replace the soup bowls with the omelette, which was not such a success, being rather leathery. To Blanche's surprise, he ate it without comment, then dabbed his mouth with his napkin, poured wine into his glass and met her eye.

'Remind me, Blanche. When is the day we have invited Judith to visit again? I enjoyed talking to her immensely. It will cheer me up to see her, you know?'

You, always you and what gives you pleasure, she thought. What if I told you I have stolen some moments of delight up there in my room, at my easel; that I have spent several hours without worrying about you and the state of your soul? I wonder what you would say.

'I suggested the day after tomorrow,' was all she said.

– TWENTY-THREE –

JUDITH

On the morning of Judith's second visit to Le Pressoir, Madame Baudy came into the dining room and handed her two letters with American stamps on the envelopes. They reminded her of her own long overdue letters to be written home, of those she had opened and merely glanced at. Feeling a stab of guilt, she went out into the garden and sat under the wisteria to read them.

The first was from her mother, describing how she had opened her copy of *Photoplay* to find a photograph of 'darling Mary' pictured in her latest movie, *Friends*.

Oh Judith, she was wearing such a pretty gown with huge puffed sleeves that showed off her tiny waist. And those ringlets and curls, I declare that when her hair is loose it must fall in waves about her face like a princess. It made me so sad when I thought how lovely your hair was once until you chose to wear it in that bob. I can hear you protest it is fashionable and I know how much you like to be à la mode, but to my mind there is nothing so feminine as long hair. Men adore it. Remember how upset Charlie was when you had it all cut off? But darling, that photograph has given me some great ideas for the wedding. We'll have Mrs Gibbons copy Mary's dress and we can use some hair extensions to create a lovely effect, then a circlet of flowers, rosebuds I thought, to hold your wedding veil. Write me soon and tell me what you think of the idea.

As you can imagine, summer has well and truly arrived and it is very warm in the city. We had dinner at Dora and Bobbie's house the other evening, and the room was delightfully cool. They told us they had just had this new air conditioning installed. I am trying to persuade your father to do the same here. That reminds me: Judith, please remember to stay out of the sun. We don't want you ruining that lovely complexion of yours. Why only the other day I was reading about its dangers in *The Word*. Mr Harold Waldwin Percival says that only the legendary salamander can withstand the fiery heat of the sun. I miss you, sweetheart, and am so looking forward to the fall when you'll be home with us again. I'm sure I'm not the only one.

Judith sighed and tucked the letter back in its envelope then she turned to Charlie's. She expected it to be like the others, full of longing and sleepless nights thinking about her, etc etc. But he wrote describing his golfing successes, a trip to Long Island. 'Remember Scott, the man I went to Harvard with? Well, he looked me up and we have started going around town together. Of course I miss you, darling, but I am certain you will be glad I am not just mooning about at home.'

For some reason this angered her. While she was having a great time, she had not imagined he would do the same, and if he dared to go dancing she really would have something to say. As for her mother's suggestion about the gown, she could not imagine anything more awful than to be dressed up like a doll. If, and she didn't want to contemplate it, but if she had to go through with this marriage she had very different ideas of what she would wear. Judith shook her head from side to side feeling the bob flick against her cheeks, the way it so beautifully settled back into place. She smoothed her hair with her hands. If anything, she would have it cut even shorter.

She roamed the garden as if by movement she could escape the idea of America and returning there, but the silence broken only by the hum of bees did nothing to calm her. She decided to go for a walk through Giverny. There were still several hours before her appointment with Monet and it would fill in some time. She was delighted therefore when she saw Dorothy and her parasol coming towards her. It would be amusing to have another conversation with her. Dorothy had on a frock in a rather odd shade of green this time, but she certainly appeared a deal smarter; a large hat perched on her sandy hair. It looked precarious, however, as Dorothy hurried along, for a moment pretending not to see Judith.

'Good morning, Dorothy,' she said. 'May I offer you a pressé?'

'Oh Judith, pardon I was miles away. How lovely to see you again, my dear, but no I cannot stop. We are invited to lunch with some friends of Paul's.' She put up her hand to straighten her hat. 'They're artists too so they'll all talk shop, I'll be bound. I should far rather have a little chat with you.' She laughed. 'You'll have to forgive me, I must hurry away like the White Rabbit. I do want to hear about your escapades at Le Pressoir, however. Why don't you come to tea one afternoon and you can tell me all about it.'

Judith, who thought escapades an odd word to choose, smiled. 'Of course, when would you like me to come?'

'Oh, I am sorry. This life out of society is making me forget my manners.'

217

The Wednesday of the following week was decided upon and Dorothy hurried on her way. There was nothing left to do but return to the hotel, sit on the terrace and order lunch. She chose an *omelette aux fines herbes* and slowly sipped wine, whiling away the time until she could go to her room to freshen up before she made her way along the street to Le Pressoir.

Blanche was already waiting by the door in the wall but this time took her arm and drew her quickly through the house to stand on the balcony overlooking the garden. 'Look at that,' she said. 'Will you look at that? I thought they were all gone over.'

She seemed extraordinarily delighted by a rose but, as they approached it, Judith struggled to understand her excitement. She had never seen one that colour and did not much like it. Charlie bought her red roses and those in the drawing room at home were always yellow and cream to go with the decor. This one seemed not to have made up its mind what colour it was, but Blanche was ecstatic.

'I felt so sad yesterday, thinking their season had passed,' she cried. 'But I came down this morning to find this new bloom. It has really raised my spirits. Don't you love the way the colours shade into one another, just asking to be painted?'

While she spoke, Judith caught sight of Michel making his way up the garden. He wore a hat and was carrying a spade and some other tools. He looked as if he was finishing work for the day. As he approached, he seemed to realise it was she and stared. Blanche was still gazing at the rose, so Judith was able to catch his eye briefly. He closed one eye in a wink, which surprised her.

'Ah well, I can't stand here looking at it all day.'

Blanche turned back to her. As they moved to go into

the house, Judith could feel Michel watching her and she basked in the sense of power it gave. She made up her mind to be more forthright at their next meeting.

Now they were in the studio and Blanche raised her voice.

'Papa, *voila!* Mademoiselle Judith.'

He rose eagerly from the sofa, smiling as he came towards her. The large hand stretched out from the pleated shirt cuff.

'Dear mademoiselle, I am so pleased to see you again.'

As before, she was seated with her back to the light and this time Blanche made no mention of a limit to their time together. In fact, she seemed eager to be gone.

'I'll see you in the garden afterwards, mademoiselle,' was all she said.

As the door closed behind her, softly this time, Judith felt again the thrill of being in Monet's presence. Her mother and Charlie could write all the letters they wished, trying to draw her back into the world they considered was where she belonged. This was what was real to her, the panelled walls, and the rugs on the floor and paintings on the walls. This was what made her feel she was truly living, the great artist giving her all his attention, the sense of shared pleasure in each other's company, of involvement.

'So how have you been amusing yourself since we last met?' he asked.

'Oh this and that. There is always something going on at Hotel Baudy.'

'The food is excellent, isn't it? We've had some magnificent luncheons there.'

'The food is very good, but I'm not a big eater.' She smoothed her skirt. 'One has to keep in shape.'

219

He laughed at this. 'Oh, I never let that bother me; food is one of the pleasures of life. Enjoy it, palate and palette, that's my motto. By the way, have you done any painting?'

It felt like a challenge. 'Why yes, of course.'

'You must show me some of your work. I'd be interested to see your style.'

Judith laughed. 'Golly, I'd be terrified to show you anything of mine.'

'If they are as elegant as you are, I'm sure they are delightful. Meanwhile, may I show you something?' He rose and pulled open a drawer, took out a sketchbook. 'I hope you will excuse the liberty.'

Curious, she took the sketchbook and found she was looking at images of herself. How well he had captured her in a few sparse lines: the shape of her head, the way she used her hands when she talked, even the dress she had worn. She remarked on how clever it was to remember so much.

'The artist always observes,' he said.

'Gosh, they're wonderful. I'm flattered.'

'I've told you how you remind me of Camille. I used to love the way she dressed, the poses she took. You have the same natural gift for showing yourself to the best advantage.'

She was silent, staring at them, thinking, Monet has sketched me, Judith Goldstein. Maybe, one day soon he'll paint me and then I shall be famous: *Judith* or *Young Woman in a Blue Dress*.

'I don't know what to say.'

'Then say nothing,' he laughed and, taking the sketchbook, stowed it away again in the drawer.

There was a pause.

Judith said, 'The last time I was here you told me about

your life with Camille. I found it fascinating. Won't you tell me some more?'

'Ah yes, dear Camille…' he lapsed into silence.

'You described the painting you did of her wearing the gorgeous kimono,' she prompted, 'how successful it was, what fun you had.'

'After a long struggle. The life of a painter is hard, Judith. At times I despaired, you see…'

She settled down like a child waiting for the next part of the story.

Summer in Normandy: the sun is warm on his face but the boats bob in the choppy water of the harbour and the wind tries to take his hat when he walks along the beach. Each morning he paints, boats, buildings, incidental figures and the pebble beach, attempting to record the impression, that momentary vision of what is seen rather than known, with vitality and movement. He is absorbed with trying to convey the sense of light. He paints the sun as having the same luminosity as that of the sky, the varying effects of the weather. Using an almost sketchy technique and complementary colours, he takes up the struggle of trying to convey the ever-changing atmosphere.

While he paints, his eye and mind are focused on transmitting to his hand what is seen. At other times of the day, taking coffee, walking on the beach, at dinner with the family his mind is in turmoil.

He considers the events of the past months that have brought him here to the family home… lack of money, the intensity of his work on *Women in the Garden*, only to have it rejected by the jury of the Salon. To cap it all, there was the news that Camille was pregnant. He loves her, of course, and almost more, he loves her belief in his work, her

221

understanding of what he is trying to achieve. What would he do without his muse? But if he goes against the family's wishes, he'll be cut off without a franc. The dilemma haunts him.

In the early morning, he stands to watch the mistiness over the sea, the waves tipped with rosy light. He thinks of her alone in Paris in the room he found for her, awaiting the birth. How must she feel, worrying about the lack of money, wondering when he will return? She is being very good about it, reasonable, but how can he think of supporting mother and baby? Bazille, dear friend that he is, thinks only of Claude. In his opinion, the child should be placed in a foundling hospital. Sensible of course but how does he feel about separating a mother from her child?

Judith, who had been sitting quietly, let out a sigh. 'That is so sad.'

'So you see, my child, it wasn't always roses. We struggled for years.'

Judith was having difficulty with the lack of chronology in his story telling. Last time, he seemed to have moved to a much later event when he told her about the kimono. Her imagination was captured by the image of Camille alone in Paris, how lonely she must have felt, of Monet commuting between the city and Le Havre. He wanted to hold on to everything, just as she did, seize life and live it to the full.

'What happened?' she asked. 'I know you and Camille stayed together but what about the baby?'

'I was coming to that.'

August arrives, the lion sun beating down at midday, erasing shadows. Sometimes, it is too hot to paint outside. He sits in the shade, sipping a glass of cider and thinks how stifling it must be in Paris, with no sea breeze to stir the air.

He pictures Camille's awkward figure walking through the Batignolles district to the market, among all that noise and dust. He knows she is near her time and he wants to be with her for the birth.

His father watches him closely, compliments him on his painting, hints of forthcoming money. 'As long as you continue to behave yourself.'

By the time he manages to slip away to Paris, the baby has been born, Jean Armand, his beautiful big son. In spite of everything, he feels a surge of love. The decision is made, he cannot part with the boy.

They go to the city hall and register him as 'the legitimate son of Claude Monet and of Camille Leonie Doncieux, his wife, born on Sunday, eleventh of August.' The date is altered to conceal the fact Claude had not been present at the birth. One of the witnesses knows the document is false but because he was illegitimate himself he turns a blind eye.

Camille is very emotional, she weeps. 'How shall we manage, Claude? We have no money.'

He strokes her dark hair, he kisses her mouth and beautiful eyes. 'I will work and I will succeed,' he tells her.

The day after, he rushes back to the coast, fearful of upsetting the family and also because he has insufficient money to stay in Paris. Camille is left with the new baby, without two francs to rub together. However, he feels he has reassured her by creating the fiction of a marriage ceremony that never took place.

He remembers how, during the autumn and winter that followed, he divided his time between his family in Le Havre and Camille and Jean in Paris. On New Year's Day, he cannot afford to pay for heating and the baby has a cold.

223

'We were so poor, Judith, you cannot imagine. I was forced to write to friends asking for money. But nothing destroyed my joy in becoming a father. I did a painting of Jean, snuggled in his cradle with his nurse watching him.'

'I thought you said you had no money,' Judith couldn't help remarking.

'Ah well you see, Camille could not feed the child, so a dear friend hired and paid for a wonderful nurse. She did excellent work and the little doll became a beautiful baby. It is an astonishing thing to watch a child develop. No doubt you will have that pleasure, one day.'

'I guess so,' said Judith. 'One day.'

He laughed. 'I like it when you do that.'

'Do what?'

'Lean back, fold your arms and scowl. I'd like to paint you, one day. If I don't go blind before that.'

'Blind!'

'That's what happens eventually when you have cataracts. Even now, things are blurred, colours look different.' He picked up a tube of paint. 'Blues, for example. Fortunately I have a good memory for colour, at least I have that.'

'How awful! You could have them operated on, though.'

'I know, but I am afraid in case it wasn't a success.'

'But they're doing some wonderful things with surgery, these days,' she protested. 'A friend of my father's had cataracts and now he can see perfectly well. You shouldn't be afraid.'

'You think not? Well, it's good to hear someone being positive about it instead of trying to discourage me like...'

'There was a tap on the door and Blanche came into the room. 'I am sorry to disturb you, but supper is in half an

224

hour and I am sure Mademoiselle Judith will need to return to the hotel for her meal.'

Monet's gaze sharpened at the mention of food. 'And what delight is Marie preparing tonight?'

'Asparagus braised in thyme.'

'*Mon dieu*, she is doing well.'

'She is trying her best, Papa,' said Blanche. 'I think you should go and change and I will offer the young lady an aperitif. You would accept one, mademoiselle?'

Another triumph, Judith told herself, the mistress of the house extending an invitation! 'I'd be enchanted,' she replied.

She went to sit with Blanche on the balcony, and an ugly girl wearing a surgical boot carried out a tray with glasses of Dubonnet and a bowl of olives on it.

'What a beautiful evening,' Blanche said. 'I am beginning to appreciate this fine weather after several months of mourning.'

'Oh my God, who?'

'My mother,' Blanche said simply. 'There is nothing so dreadful as to lose your mother. You suddenly feel like an orphan.'

Judith found this an odd comparison. Blanche's mother must have been the same age as her grandmother. She had a vision of the old woman who could not remember anything, of a remark an uncle had made of its being 'better for her if she died.' The idea of her own mother, her youthful, ambitious mother, dying just wouldn't cross her mind.

'Maybe she was suffering?' she suggested.

Blanche glanced over to her and laughed. 'Oh dear, I forget how young you are. You think that being old adds

225

up to suffering. You're like my laundry maid, Lilli, who cannot, however hard she tries, imagine I was once young… younger than she is now.'

Judith disliked the spotlight being put on another young woman, although Lilli was only a servant.

'She is a very pretty and intelligent young woman who has her sights set on a certain young man. I will tell you something, Judith, I would dearly love to see them married.'

Judith smiled. 'That's all they seem to do round here. They don't want to achieve anything, just get married and have children.'

Blanche nodded. 'Achieve, yes, that is something you and I have in common, the desire to make something of our lives. You are a woman after my own heart.' She hesitated then continued, 'I've been wondering, Mademoiselle Judith, my father enjoys your company so much, would you visit us regularly while you are in Giverny?'

– TWENTY-FOUR –

JUDITH

Dorothy and Paul Young lived in a pretty cottage, a few streets away from Le Pressoir. The hollyhocks and roses Judith was now accustomed to seeing everywhere in Giverny crowded the front garden; smaller red roses trailed against the white walls and above the green painted door. She raised the heavy doorknocker shaped like a lion's head and let it drop with a thud. Footsteps came hurrying to answer it.

'Judith, honey, come right in.'

She was startled to see that Dorothy was wearing a tea gown, something she had not glimpsed since she left New York. This one was in shell pink silk, the skirt elaborately flounced and trimmed with a plain bodice of the same material. Over it, she wore a loose coat made of lace, transparent enough to show that, in spite of her full figure, she wasn't wearing a corset. The delicate shade of the silk showing through the lace work gave a charming effect.

Dorothy led the way into a parlour whose walls were hung with pictures.

'Mostly Paul's,' she explained, 'though there are one or two by his impressionist friends.'

The flowery patterned curtains and sofa, the vases of lilies, carnations, and yet more roses, seemed to echo the intense bouquet of the perfume she wore. Judith, well schooled by her mother, identified it as Quelques Fleurs. Set between two rosewood chairs, again with flower-patterned seats, was a small table covered with a lacy cloth and on it a cake stand and a tea set.

'Now sit yourself down,' said Dorothy. 'Let me pour the tea and then we can talk.' She indicated a lavish looking cake on the stand. 'Strawberry short cake; I made it this morning just for us. We can devour the lot without anyone judging us.'

Judith wondered what it was about this place that made everyone want to eat so much. Mother and her friends were always moaning about their weight and talking about dieting. From time to time, her mother followed the Horace Fletcher regime. She became an annoyingly slow eater, chewing every morsel thirty-two times – one for each tooth – she told Judith, then spitting out the remains.

'Don't be so foolish, Maurice!' she scolded her husband when he protested. 'This way the body absorbs the nutrients it needs without swallowing extra calories.'

'Ridiculous,' he had replied, 'and very off putting, my dear, to those in your company. As for that foolish woman, that Dolly Kendall, what about her and her leech diet?'

'It seems to work,' her mother had declared. 'She has lost a lot of weight.'

Judith found the idea of attaching a blood-sucking creature to her arm disgusting and neither did she have the patience to do all that masticating. In her view, it was simpler to restrict what one ate.

Dorothy poured the Earl Grey tea and, in spite of

Judith's protests that she did not as a rule eat sweet things, took up a cake knife and cut her a generous slice of the concoction, laden with strawberries and oozing cream.

'Afternoon tea,' she sighed. 'I think it is probably my favourite meal. I do have such a sweet tooth. I'm reminded of our own Henry James and what he wrote about tea. "There are few hours in life more agreeable than the hour dedicated to the ceremony known as afternoon tea." I couldn't agree more.' She licked some cream from her lips and giggled, 'and of course, you know what the French call this time? *La fif o'clock*, the four to five when a lady may entertain her lover.'

Judith gazed at her. 'Really? Is that what happens here?'

'Don't look so surprised, young lady. It's probably also the time when her husband has an assignation. That's what I like about the French, they are so open minded about these things, open and honest, not to mention they adore their food.'

And don't care how fat they get, Judith mused. She thought of Monet's remark about food being a gift from God.

As if Dorothy read her thoughts, she said, 'Come on, young lady, eat up. I hope you're not affected by this dieting nonsense. You're far too skinny, men like something to cuddle.'

Judith forked up a sliver of cake. The union of ripe juicy fruit and thick Normandy cream was divine. It was just a pity that something so nice should be bad for one.

'Now come on, tell all, I've been dying to hear,' urged Dorothy.

The recounting of her visits to Le Pressoir allowed her to ignore the cake on her plate while Dorothy, an eager audience, finished her slice and cut herself another. She was a good listener only murmuring, 'oh my' now and again and 'well I never' when Judith told her about the sketches Monet had made of her.

'And now his daughter Blanche has invited me to be a regular visitor,' she finished.

'It sure seems you have made a hit,' Dorothy declared. 'Pass me your cup and I'll top you up.'

Judith watched her pour. 'It's true, we get on so well.' She hesitated for a moment and then decided to plunge in. 'Dorothy, you remember our conversation on the terrace when you spoke of French men?'

Dorothy laughed, showing her big teeth. 'I surely do.'

'Well the fact is I've met one myself.'

'You naughty little thing! Oh, don't get me wrong. I thoroughly approve. Who is he? Someone from Giverny?'

'He works in Monet's garden.'

'Not M'sieur Breuil, he's quite old.'

'No, an under gardener, his name is Michel and he's very attractive. I invited him to have a drink on the hotel terrace and he came and afterwards, we walked in the garden. But then… oh, Dorothy, it was all so romantic just him and me, and I thought he might kiss me but he didn't. The truth is I didn't know how I was supposed to behave.'

Dorothy set down her cup. 'I thought you told me you had a fiancé. Don't you know how to behave with him?'

'Yes, but that's different. We've known each other since we were children.'

'I see.' She seemed to suggest 'how boring.' 'Well, you know what you must do? You must flirt. I'm surprised you haven't tried it, a pretty girl like you.'

'I wouldn't know where to begin.'

'You know what they say? Practice makes perfect.'
Dorothy rose from her chair and moved around the room,
gesturing with her arms so that the lacy sleeves fell away,
revealing pale, plump flesh. 'Alrighty, first of all eye contact,
that's essential when flirting, but don't overdo it or you'll
put him off. Ask questions and listen. It's flattering to have
someone show a genuine interest in your opinions, what
you like and don't like and your experiences. Don't tense up
and cross your arms, or hunch over like you're enduring a
blast of cold air. Lean toward the person you're flirting with
and imitate their body language in a subtle kind of way.
Then compliments: everyone loves to get compliments, and
that's a great way to flirt.'

She returned to her seat and leaning forward, cut a third
slice of the cake. 'And finally, smile, it is the most powerful
flirting tool you can use. Everyone loves to see a pleasant,
happy face, and a smile sends all the right messages.'

Judith laughed. 'My golly, there seems to be an awful lot
to it.'

'Not really,' said Dorothy 'You already have a lovely smile,
you may well be a natural flirt.'

She had been so fascinated by what Dorothy was telling
her, she found she had eaten the cake and Dorothy, seeing
her plate empty, had swiftly cut and given her another slice.

'Alcohol always helps to loosen them up,' she remarked
in a casual manner. 'Why not have champagne, served in
the garden?'

Judith was startled by the genteel outward appearance of
Dorothy and these suggestions of what lay within. She
found her intriguing, a woman after her own heart, not
caring a fig for convention. How she ever became married
to that funny little man, she could not imagine.

231

Dorothy laughed. 'I just love the expression on your face, honey. You make me feel quite wicked, suggesting such a thing.' She sighed and reached for the teapot. 'Oh to be young and innocent, to have everything before you! I'll tell you something, if I had my time again I'd...' she paused as if fearing an eavesdropper then continued, lowering her voice, 'I'd never have married Paul, free thinking though he is.'

'What would you have done?' Judith was curious.

Dorothy appeared thoughtful. 'Well, it is lovely here and I do have my fun, but I think I would have stayed in America. I was having such a wonderful time in St. Louis, all those balls and parties. I had my share of gentlemen callers, I can tell you.'

'Then why...?'

'It's hard to tell. Paul came along and he was so very different from the men I knew, a painter who was going to study in Paris, *la vie bohème* and all that.' She finally seemed to have finished with her plate and set it down on the table. 'I remember a party he came to. I was actually with someone else, but he came over and introduced himself and after that we couldn't stop talking. We ended up sitting in the conservatory and my partner of the evening gave up and went home. Paul was the kind of person I had never met before, you see, Judith, and I was fascinated by his life. He dressed like a painter; I remember a red scarf he wore round his neck and he had a moustache. My parents had someone else in mind for me to marry but in the end they gave in and I married Paul.'

Judith sipped the last of her tea. 'But that's wonderful. You did what you wanted to do. You went where your heart led you. Isn't that swell?'

232

'It seemed like it at the time, but looking back I think my parents knew me better than I did. I love elegance and beauty, you see, and those things cost money. Paul sells but not enough to provide that, we have a struggle at times. He would do so much better in America, but he won't think about going back. This frock, for example, it's very old.'

'It's still lovely,' Judith put in.

'Well thank you, honey. But you know what I mean, its so passé. Look at you so divinely à la mode; you radiate ease and money. I would love to have a bob, but I couldn't maintain it.'

In the silence that followed, Judith gazed round the room. She saw details she hadn't noticed before: the carpet was worn and threadbare in places, the flowery fabric was cheap; she suspected the mahogany console table was a copy. The furniture in her parents' house was always the genuine article. She could see the difference. But did that matter?

'Does it matter?' she asked Dorothy. 'I'd give anything to be living the life you have here in Giverny.'

The other shook her head. 'Then you are wrong. A long vacation as you are having is pleasant. A summer flirtation is the icing on the cake. But live here for some time and the attraction wanes. You realise the differences in culture, the fact that the locals don't accept you, will never accept you. I had felt so rootless, Judith, so alone until I decided to take lovers, as Paul does, I know. I realise I have gained a reputation here but I don't much care. They are a provincial lot and have nothing better to do than talk about each other. They probably think I am a jezebel.'

As if she realised she had said too much, her expression changed and she smiled. 'Ah well young Judith, it has been swell to have you here.'

'I've really enjoyed it,' Judith replied, realising the correct time for taking tea had passed. 'Thank you and for the cake, it was delicious.'

'Well, I actually got you to eat some.'

They laughed and Dorothy saw her to the door.

'Come again, it's been lovely to talk.'

'I will,' Judith said but she was not sure she meant it.

The afternoon had unsettled her and she stepped out into the heat, which had now become oppressive, feeling disorientated. At the end of Dorothy's street she paused, glancing from right to left, left to right, wondering where to go from here. She glanced at her watch, it was five o' clock and for once she felt disinclined to sit alone with a cocktail on the hotel terrace and gaze down at the tennis players. There was nowhere else she could go. She had tried sitting in one of the cafés and felt out of place, conscious of the local people's stare. She thought she would walk a little by the river and set off, briskly. As she went, images of New York came into her mind: she and her mother, moving through the rooms of the Met, taking in the latest exhibition… always the slight shock when one left that hushed atmosphere and paused for a moment, standing at the top of the steps, gazing down, to be greeted by the noise of Fifth Avenue; tea at the Waldorf where women, smartly dressed like themselves, chatted and laughed; her bedroom, she sitting at her dressing table in her petticoat, wondering what to wear for dinner that night. The expression on Charlie's face as she entered the drawing room, hearing him exclaim how pretty she looked. Judith felt herself caught up in a wave of nostalgia so that she scarcely saw the village church, the slate roofs of the low houses, the road that now ran by the banks of the river.

Dorothy's words had depressed her and for the first time since her arrival the idea of dining at Hotel Baudy did not appeal. She walked for a while then sat and gazed at the river, its surface sparkling in the sun. A boat went by, crowded with young people singing a French song, all seeming to be having a wonderful time. Judith watched them until they disappeared round a bend in the river. Then she felt something in her stir and she rose and walked briskly back in the direction she had come, shaking off the gloomy feeling that had come over her. She would put Dorothy's words out of her mind. The woman was middle aged, in an entirely different situation to her own. Maybe she was even jealous that she, Judith, had the attraction, the flair to get what she wanted; that was probably it. By the time she reached the hotel, all her determination had returned. Michel was coming again tomorrow evening and tonight she would consult Madame Baudy on champagne. Nothing and no-one was going to stop her.

– TWENTY-FIVE –

ROBERT

With a sense of *déjà vu* Robert saw her before she saw him, so that, for a moment, she seemed like a stranger. Her dark head outlined by the sun, she was deep in conversation with Madame Baudy.

'Yes, but I should like your very best,' he heard her say as he approached.

He hesitated, curious to hear the reply.

'I believe we have some bottles of Dom Perignon and Veuve Clicquot in the cellar.' Angelina Baudy smiled at him. '*Bonsoir*, M'sieur Harrison.'

Judith turned her head and stared at him. He indicated he would wait for her at one of the terrace tables and she shrugged, and then resumed her conversation. He ordered a beer and lit a cigarette, watching her gesticulate with her hands, the slight tilt of her head as she listened to what the other woman was saying. He hoped she would decide to join him; he wanted to bring up the subject of Dorothy Young.

Earlier he had been surprised to catch sight of Judith leaving the woman's house. What on earth was she doing visiting someone like that? It was common knowledge in Giverny the woman was up to no good, that the locals mistrusted her. At least, that husband of hers had the sense to play further away from home. Robert had gone out to post a letter and, by chance, looked down the street just as Judith and Dorothy had emerged among the roses. He had hurried on, not wanting her to think he was spying. Then he paused to watch, as she seemed to hesitate before walking away in the opposite direction. The hushed, deserted air of the village, the sun beating down on the slight figure, seemed to create an aura of isolation about her. Probably she had become lonely and latched onto Dorothy, if it had not been the other way round. As he made his way to the tennis court, he was feeling guilty and played badly. He decided he would try to make it up with her at the first opportunity; she wasn't as much wayward as just impervious to her behaviour's effects on others.

He sipped his beer. If he were honest with himself, Harry had something to do with his change of heart. Robert was growing rather tired of his friend's jealous reaction if he so much as gave anyone else more than a few minutes' attention. There was a part of him that belonged to no-one, he had tried to explain, and Harry was being too possessive. The row over Robert's playing a singles with another artist had infuriated him.

'You don't own me, you know,' he had murmured. 'I'll do what I damn well like.' Then he'd called across to his partner to suggest another set.

He decided he had been unfair to Judith for wasn't that also her response when he had tried to interfere?

'Well, Robert, what's all this about?' Judith's voice broke into his thoughts. She had approached his table and stood looking down at him, hand on hip. 'I thought you weren't speaking to me, any more?'

He got to his feet. 'Oh Judith, can't we forget about all that? Be friends again?'

'Well, you were very nasty to me.'

'I'm sorry, I was only concerned that you… oh, never mind, do sit down and let me order you a cocktail.'

What a lovely creature she is, he thought again, exuding heat and light like a hothouse flower. Anyone who looked like Judith might be forgiven almost anything.

'Come on,' he urged. 'Champagne cocktail, that's your favourite, isn't it?'

She hesitated a moment longer but more for effect, it seemed, then sat down. 'It sure is,' she smiled.

The serving girl came and with a sense of celebration, he added some olives and other small dishes to his order.

'So what have you been doing with yourself these past days?' he enquired.

'Oh this and that.' With a spoon she fished out the rose petal and laid it on the table.

'I hear you've made a friend of Dorothy Young.'

She looked up. 'Who told you that?'

'Oh, you know how it is here. Nothing is a secret for very long.' He hesitated. 'Judith, you'll pardon me if I say something? I know you think I'm an interfering old fuddy duddy but really, I shouldn't have too much to do with her.'

Judith frowned. 'Robert…'

'I know you're young and fancy free,' he continued, 'and perhaps I have been too hard on you, trying to make you see things from my point of view but…'

'Robert,' she said again. 'It's okay, really it is. I have no intention of having much more to do with Dorothy, in fact, I probably won't visit again.'

'Ah.'

238

'She's, well…' There was a pause as if Judith sought to add something and decided against it, then she finished, 'Anyway, I have far more important things to do with my time.' She eyed his cigarette case. 'Might I have one?'

'Of course.'

He watched her smoke, gazing into the distance, a smile on her lips as if she were hugging some delicious secret to herself. In that moment, unconscious of herself, of the arrangement of her long limbs, still but poised for movement, she reminded him once more of a young animal.

'Do you want to know something, Robert?'

'If you feel you want to tell me.'

'Oh don't tease.'

'That was not my intention. Go on, I'm all ears.'

Judith stubbed out her cigarette in the ashtray. 'Very well. You know I visited Monet at Le Pressoir and we got on just fine? Well, I was invited back the other day and I spent a long time with him. He loves talking about Camille, that's his first wife, you know.'

Robert raised an eyebrow. 'Yes, I did know.'

'I remind him of her, you see. Well, anyway… afterwards Madame Blanche offered me an aperitif, which I naturally accepted.'

'Naturally.'

She pouted. 'Robert, you're making fun of me again. Now listen to this: she said I was having a good effect on her stepfather, raising his spirits etcetera, and – now this is the wonderful thing – would I become a regular visitor.'

'Holy smoke!'

'Is that all you can say?'

Robert was thrown by this news. He gazed at her, at once

impressed by her power to attract but also apprehensive of its seeming uncontrollable force, almost as if she were possessed.

'What do you think? Isn't that just the best thing you've ever heard?'

He sipped his beer, holding back the words that first came into his mind. Watch your step, you are entering a world you know nothing about. There is a history in that household, which does not concern you. Instead he said: 'I think you're a cunning little thing.'

'What do you mean?'

'The way you wheedle your way into men's hearts.'

'Is that what you think?'

'Oh Judith, you know you do. You can twist them round your little finger.'

'Not you, Robert, I'd never try to do that with you. I see you as a real pal, even a soul mate. I am so glad we are friends again.'

Robert patted her arm and ordered more drinks. He felt inordinately pleased they were talking again; he had missed her vitality and recklessness. An idea came into his mind; one that he thought would not only amuse her but also remove her from the somewhat claustrophobic atmosphere of this village and the likes of Dorothy. 'Say, why don't we go for a spin on Sunday?'

'In that lovely red automobile, oh yes, but where?'

'How about Rouen? Or maybe we could even go as far as Dieppe and have lunch in the port. They serve some wonderful fish there; I know a lovely little restaurant we could try. The only thing is we might not be able to get back until the next day.'

'You mean stay overnight, just you and me?'

240

'I am not planning to compromise you, Judith. You'll be quite safe with me.'

'Oh what a shame!' She laughed. 'I thought you were just the type.'

'Now you're teasing *me*, young lady.'

Judith leaned back in her chair and considered him. 'I can't make you out, Robert. You're a man, I'm a woman, you've been kind to me, friendly, but that's all. Don't you find me attractive?'

Robert felt himself recoil. 'Of course I do but... I'll tell you some day.'

'I'm intrigued. Anyway, I want to go to Rouen because of Flaubert.'

'What?'

'Gustave Flaubert, the writer, you must have read him. He set *Madame Bovary* there. She's one of my heroines: wonderful Emma Bovary who sacrificed all for love. She turned her back on convention and lived the way she wanted to live, even if it cost her her life.'

She shone with excitement and he was reminded of the image he had had when he first met her, of the flame burning brightly, too brightly.

'Nothing is worth that, Judith,' he said. 'Nothing.'

She sipped her cocktail. 'Oh, I'm not planning to die for quite some time.'

'I'm glad to hear it,' Robert said. 'So Rouen it is, we'll make an early start before it gets too hot.'

– TWENTY-SIX –

CLAUDE

It is the iris, which he contemplates today, drawn as always to the water garden where they line the serpentine path and randomly cluster near the edge of the pond. The design of the flower is perfect in his view, three large petals fold back from the stem and form the three points of a triangle, in the centre three smaller petals stand up, the shape of the fleur de lys. In the legends of flowers, purple iris were planted over the graves of Greek women and, among the duties of the Greek Goddess Iris, was that of leading their souls to the Elysian Fields.

There is always a tactile pleasure in painting them. He makes sinuous brush strokes to describe their tall stalks and whiplash foliage, lightly, lightly to suggest a breeze stirring the surrounding leaves and reeds. Then, using pure pigment, he swiftly dabs in the blossoms. As he looks at them now, he feels the urge to paint them yet again and smiles at himself. The old man is coming to life again, like a lizard feeling the sun, sloughing off the despondency of the last months. He feels eager to make up lost time.

Serene and silent this early morning, the air at the edge of the water is cool, damp and fragrant. Even while he breathes it in, there is a part of him wondering how to translate this from a sensuous to visual experience. What colours would one use?

He stands on the Japanese bridge and gazes at the light shimmering on the surface of the pond. The water mirrors clouds, which he would paint in delicate tints of pink, white and pale yellow. He gazes and gazes until he seems to move outside himself and become the thing he is gazing at, immersed in shifting water and light. It is then the idea flashes into his mind. It's not new, it comes and goes, but until now he has not given it much serious thought. Too ambitious at my age, he has mused, I'd need to develop new techniques and, anyway, where on earth would I paint anything so large? But this time it is different. The idea seems to drop like a stone into water, and the ripples it makes radiate out and out and out. He sees in his mind's eye, huge panels depicting those variations of light as a day progresses, subtle alterations shimmering on the water where the lilies float. Colour can translate the cool air, green reflections warming to sunset, water mirroring the clouds in an ever-changing facsimile of life. Then there are the willows, of course, they could form another panel: the willow trees with arching trunks, their leaf-laden branches drooping above the pond's rim, swayed by the suggestion of a gentle breeze.

Where would he show them? He imagines a circular room covered with paintings of water dotted with water lilies to the horizon, the calm and silence of the still waters reflecting the open blossoms with a dream like delicacy. But this would be more than sight or first impressions; this work would draw on memory and experience. Four panels, he decides, but all united in a flowing rhythm, a meditation on the spectacle of light, the floating world of water lilies.

243

Now he sees how he could work on them, mounted on wheeled dollies he could move around a room and interchange the sequence. That kind of painting could not be executed in the open air. He would transfer the fleeting effects he painted on site in the water garden onto giant canvasses. He'd need a new studio, of course, something much larger than he has ever had before, illuminated by northern light streaming through a glass ceiling. But that's not a problem, Claude, he tells himself. You've always devised something ingenious; if it wasn't exactly what you had in mind, you invented it, that is your forte. The only problem of course is his damned eyesight and getting the colours right, this business of relying on the labels of his paints, or relying on memory. Perhaps there are some other drops Cautela can prescribe, now that these ones seem to be failing him... anything but surgery. He has a morbid fear of it, wakes in the night sweating from a dream of having no eyes.

The pictures he would paint are crowding into his mind: *Morning, The Clouds, Irises by the Pond.* But I'm seventy-two, he scolds himself. How can I even think of embarking on such a project? Yet his brain continues to turn over the idea of these panels, of the huge brush strokes they would take, the layers of colour, and he thinks, seventy-two is nothing. Look at Michelangelo designing the dome of St Peter's when he was my age, or dearest Hokusai on his deathbed, asking for just five years more. If you're an artist you work until you can't hold a paintbrush any more

'Until you can't hold a paintbrush any more,' he addresses the little boat, which has appeared from beneath the willows.

'Excuse me, m'sieur?'

It is the excellent Michel, sponge in hand, wiping soot off the lily petals.

'Talking to myself young man, that's all. It's what you do when you're old like me.'

Michel gives him an uncomprehending look. This boy cannot believe he will ever get old, Claude tells himself. Others yes, but he will be the exception; we all think that. Look at that young man painting Camille in the wonderful green dress, falling in love with her. It never crossed my mind I shouldn't be twenty-five forever.

'Be good,' he tells Michel. 'Enjoy life. You know, wine, women and song.'

The boy blushes. Claude wonders what on earth has he said? He cannot imagine Michel Duval doing anything much more than working and a prim walking out with a servant; one of our servants, Blanche has told him, though making him promise not to let it go any further. Hardly *la douceur de vivre*.

'I've been looking at the irises,' he says. 'They're doing well as irises usually do, but I wonder if we might consider adding some other varieties, there are so many to choose from.'

'M'sieur Breuil…' Michel begins.

'To hell with M'sieur Breuil,' Claude raises his voice. 'Listen to me.'

He regrets this instantly, this cursed short temper of his. Michel has done nothing wrong.

'I will talk to Breuil,' he says. 'I will instruct him in what I require.' He feels expansive, needs to share these ideas, have them out in the open. 'I am about to embark on a great new project you see, young man, and the irises are important to it.'

245

'Very good, m'sieur.'

'More than good.' Claude spreads his arms to the sky. 'It will be my crowning touch, my swan song.'

– TWENTY-SEVEN –

CLAUDE

The morning in his studio passes swiftly. When work is going well, the time slips away. As he cleans his brush, his mind turns to food and the pleasant rhythm meals bring to daily life in the household. Alice would have been content that the kitchen garden flourishes and there is a plentiful supply of eggs from the fowl. Dear Georges is coming for luncheon today. When Blanche asked Claude what would please his old friend, he had said pike, yes that was it, pike gently simmered in a court bouillon and served with white butter sauce.

'How about chanterelles to start with?' she suggested.

Chanterelles. An image comes into his mind: autumn's palette of golden ochre, russet orange and vivid scarlet, a carpet of dead leaves beneath their feet as they walk, he and Alice through the woods. He is young again and a week ago, he painted Ernest in a group of hunters moving along this path. Now Alice's husband is away in Paris again and they are alone at Montgeron. The air is crisp with the now and then crack of a rifle shot but they are not hunting pheasants or rabbits, only chanterelles. She stops, she points, she takes his hand and hurries him along. And there they are, a group of them, fruiting yellow and bright orange among a litter of leaves. He stoops to pick one, sniffs it and holds it out for Alice to do the same. Suddenly they are kissing, as they knew they would from the moment Alice said, 'let's go looking for chanterelles.'

The kiss lets loose the stifled feelings, the hand touching, the glances of the past weeks as they passed each other or sat at dinner in the château. She pulls away. 'We shouldn't, Claude, we are both married.'

He turns her back to him and they kiss again and he wants her, wants to take her there and then, on the damp bed of leaves with the rifle shots fracturing the still air. Camille is dying and he is filled with a rage to live, spend his emotions. The apricot aroma of the chanterelles will always speak to him of lust, but also guilt.

Chanterelles! He realises for the first time since Alice's death, the pain of dwelling on her loss has eased; he has begun to have lovely memories of her.

'Chanterelles,' he repeats, 'in the weather we've been having? It's been so dry.'

But Blanche knows where she can lay her hands on some; she knows how much Georges likes them.

Bacon, lard and chanterelles with a clove of garlic and, of course, lots of black pepper, does Marie know the recipe?

The conversation at luncheon turns inevitably to his eyesight, what can you expect with a medically trained man as a guest?

'When did you first begin to notice something was wrong?' asks Georges, 'Can you remember?'

He casts his mind back to that trip to Venice, four years ago; he had no problem with colour then but there was a difficulty with space and distant objects. Afterwards, he had compared the Venetian work with paintings he had done in Antibes, some years before. The difference in detail had made him so angry he had destroyed the offending pictures.

'It is ironic,' Georges is saying, 'you who are so passionate about light and painting in the open air. These factors could be to blame for what has happened to your eyes.'

Then Claude remembers that time when he was commuting between his parents' house and Camille in Paris, about twenty-seven he must have been. There were problems with his eyes, even then.

'A doctor advised me not to spend so much time in the open air but of course I didn't listen.'

'Ah hah.'

'It did not affect my work. But now, I no longer perceive colour with the same intensity and I no longer paint light with the same accuracy. Reds appear muddy to me, pinks insipid, and the intermediate and lower tones escape me. It is a terrible anxiety.'

'Understandably. I wish you could combat this fear you have of an operation. As I've told you before, they are now fairly routine.'

'For ordinary people maybe, but my case is special. My goal in art is to portray the variation of light without interpretation. How can I accept an artificial correction of the sense I rely on to convey the truth and beauty of nature? I have to paint it as it looks, the exact colour and shape, until it gives one's naïve impression of the scene before you. My study is light, colour and illumination and for that I need my original colour vision to stay intact.'

'And there we have the impasse,' says Georges, taking the opportunity to help himself to more fish.

'Perhaps the cataracts will get no worse,' Blanche says soothingly.

'Oh they will, Blanche, without surgery they undoubtedly will.'

'Then he will just have to do the best he can with the sight he has,' she remarks, refilling the politician's glass. 'He is too old for an intervention.'

'I would not say so, not in the hands of someone like Cautela.'

Claude slams down his fork and asks them not to speak of him as if he is incapable of answering for himself, as if he is some kind of imbecile. 'They are my eyes and I am the one to make a decision about them, if you please! Apropos, I was talking to the young American girl who visits me sometimes. She is very perturbed about my loss of sight and tells me that in America, the operation is now commonplace. Perhaps I will speak to her again. She is an extraordinary girl, such flair and elegance. D'you know, Georges, she reminds me in some ways of my first wife, Camille.'

Blanche drops her knife with a clatter. 'Oh Papa, what an exaggeration, she is nothing like Camille. I still remember how beautiful she was, with such a fine character. Mademoiselle Judith is attractive but...'

Claude gulps some wine... a white Bordeaux, fresh, fruity and dry, to be sipped not gulped he knows, but he is annoyed.

'She is also well educated and informed,' he continues, ignoring Blanche. 'We have some lively conversations.'

'You should not listen to her, she is naïve,' Blanche breaks in. 'Too young and innocent of life, she has no idea of the risk. I speak for your own good, Papa.'

Claude gulps more wine. 'And you like me to be helpless and in your power because then you feel you have some function in life.'

He has gone too far, he realises that, but he has never been one to apologise. Blanche is staring at him with tears welling up in her eyes, then she turns away. Georges clears his throat and stares at his plate where his second helping of fish remains uneaten. Suppose I have been too pessimistic, Claude asks himself, suppose an operation could restore my sight? What joy that would be. Blanche is set in her ways; I'd do better to discuss this with Judith.

'I am beginning to think that perhaps Mademoiselle Judith's influence is not all for the good,' Blanche is saying. She turns to Georges. 'You know what these new young women are like? They think they know everything. In my day, you listened to your elders. Papa would be foolish not to heed his own feelings on this matter.'

'Yes Blanche.'

Poor Georges, Claude thinks, watching his friend's gaze shift from one to the other, wanting to please both of them.

'Eat,' commands Claude, indicating his plate. 'We are neglecting the pike. Come on, eat up and let's stop all this depressing talk, we'll change the subject. Tell me, what do you think about this Balkan League business? Will they go to war?'

As Georges launches onto his views of this alliance, of how Turkey has every reason to be nervous, Claude helps himself to another choice morsel of the pike and settles down to enjoy his meal.

– TWENTY-EIGHT –

BLANCHE

That luncheon marked a turning point at Le Pressoir, a shift from the light-hearted atmosphere of the past few weeks to a more sombre mood. The meal had proceeded from the magnificent pike to apple tart and cream, finished with coffee and calvados. Georges recovered his appetite and departed in a cheerful mood. Blanche, without another word to her stepfather, went up to her room. The afternoon felt sultry as if another storm might be brewing, there was a dull ache at the back of her head. For a while, she sat at her window, gazing down over the garden where Breuil and Michel could be seen working along the main path, which was now invaded by a blaze of brilliant nasturtiums. This calm scene did nothing to soothe her, instead she felt on edge and out of control. She realised that while she had often baulked against the uneventful routine of the household, the known rhythm of her daily life, she now viewed it with something like nostalgia. In a way, Papa had been right when he said his dependence gave some sense of purpose to her life, but now that status quo seemed to be shifting. He did not ask her to sort his paints and was irritable if she went to his studio but, more

252

disconcerting, she felt he was keeping something from her. Now that she came to examine this, there was an air of something similar about the young woman, Judith; it was as if they shared a secret, which excluded her.

I've only myself to blame, she thought, it was I who encouraged these visits, I who told her she was doing him good. He would never have met her in the first place if it hadn't been for me. I wonder now why I did it.

Blanche cast her mind back to that first encounter with Judith at Robert Harrison's birthday picnic. The girl had intrigued with her modern clothes and manner, her perception of the occasion, arousing in Blanche a mixture of envy and curiosity. She remembered how Judith had addressed Papa as an equal, been uncaring of how many strawberries she ate, laughed about the wine she had spilt on Mr Harrison's jacket. Blanche had an image of Judith and Monet, intent on each other, drawing away from the rest of the party, her father gesturing to the landscape, the girl's rapt expression. She recalled the compelling vitality about her, a sense of being utterly self-centred, fully aware of the picture she made in that pretty summer frock. How taken aback she had been, asking herself was this how American women behaved, seemingly uncaring of their effect on those around them.

The impression had faded and later she had chosen to ignore any misgivings she might have had; seeing Papa so much happier, she had only encouraged him to have more of her presence. Now, it began to seem, he preferred Judith's company to hers, he was even considering her advice about cataract operations! The phrase came to her, a cuckoo in the nest. Unable to sit still any longer, she went to stand at her easel to examine her half finished painting. Over the last few days, it had come on quite well. She had felt the return of her old command over colour and begun to paint with much more confidence, using the brush strokes Papa had taught her. She gazed at it critically, the mass of roses among leaves, a slice of blue sky, and now it seemed to her laboured. It hadn't the freshness, the lightness of touch, which had always been her forte. She felt she had failed to convey the image she saw onto the canvas. Was that true? Or was it these doubts creeping into her mind that made her see it that way? She hardly knew but certainly didn't feel like painting today, if she ever got round to finishing it. And if that was the case, did her life really have meaning?

Her wardrobe stood ajar, she went to close it and saw that some of her clothes had fallen off their hangers and lay on the floor. As she picked them up and laid them on the bed, she noticed a light summer gown of cream muslin scattered with blue flowers. It must have been pushed to the back of the wardrobe for she hadn't seen it for years. She remained holding it for a moment, remembering all those years ago, when the world had seemed to offer so much. It was a gown she had worn in those days with John Leslie.

1889

'He knows,' she said. 'Monet knows. Perhaps he's seen it all along, we've been together a long time.'

They were sitting by the river. When she had arrived at the Hotel Baudy and John Leslie had seen in her face something was wrong, he had seized her arm and hurried her here. The day was bright but there was a chilly wind that sent the clouds scudding across the sky. That morning as she had walked through the garden, she had noticed the blaze of autumn colour, scarlet and hot pink dahlias, smoky blue asters, the grass under the paulownia tree was scattered with leaves.

John Leslie said: 'He would have to have known at some time, perhaps its better now.'

Blanche thought, you didn't see the coldness in Monet's eyes, you didn't feel the rejection. But she couldn't blame John Leslie; no-one was to blame. What had happened had happened and it must be confronted. A flock of geese flew overhead. She looked upward to marvel at the perfect V of the birds' formation, envying their lack of conflict.

'It is going to be very difficult,' she said. 'Can you face the problems it will cause?'

He took her hands and gazed into her eyes. 'Of course.'

She felt the shadow of a division between them. He didn't really understand, how could he? He hadn't lived alongside a great painter for most of his life, not come under the influence of his work until her canvasses were sometimes indistinguishable from Monet's. Their lives had become so intermingled, had she the strength to unravel hers?

'All I know,' John Leslie was saying, 'is I want to be with you for the rest of my life.'

He was voicing the words she had longed to hear. Why then did she feel a sense of panic, of being torn apart?

'I need to think about all this, John Leslie.'

'Of course you do.'

'Will you give me a little time?' Let me try to work things out?'

He frowned. 'If that is what you want, darling, but please don't let anyone persuade you.'

Nothing was mentioned at Le Pressoir. Blanche resumed her day-to-day life, spending time with her mother and sisters, painting, joining in the family meals. Suzanne took her aside. She wanted to know how the romance was progressing.

255

'I don't know,' Blanche replied.

'You don't know! I thought you were madly in love with that American.'

'Please Suzanne, his name is John Leslie.'

'Of course, they just seem like a foreign species, so exotic.'

Blanche laughed. 'They are just like any other men with the same capacity for love and loyalty.'

'They are certainly fun,' her sister said thoughtfully. 'I wish I could fall in love with one of them. But I haven't met one I really like. Not yet, anyway.'

Blanche shook her head, 'I wouldn't advise it. It brings far too many complications.'

Her sister would have none of this. 'But that's all part of a fine romance, all resolved in the end.'

Blanche sighed, 'I've said this before, you are an incurable romantic.'

And I am not? She asked herself. Maybe I am too much of a realist and can see things as they are.

As the days passed, she found it increasingly difficult to imagine her existence anywhere else with John Leslie. Insidiously, life here was taking over and the task of escaping it seemed insurmountable. Then Monet asked her to come to his studio, that evening.

As she entered he was sketching but laid down his charcoal stick and stared at her unsmiling. 'Tell me, what has happened to you and me? We were happy together.'

She said nothing for a moment, looking back on their intertwined lives, the young girl enthralled by a real artist come among them, the realisation of her own talent under his eye and guidance.

'We were happy,' she said. 'At least most of the time.'

'Yes. We were happy until the Americans came along.'

American, she thought, John Leslie. Maybe I believed I was happy because I didn't know anything different. It was innocence. I was a child until I met him and then I realised I was also a woman and wanted the kind of love and joy that meant.

'We were happy,' Monet persisted. 'Yes, we were.' He reached for his cigarettes. 'And we can be happy again when all this is left behind.'

In that moment the uncertainty, the doubts she had been feeling over these past days left her and Blanche knew she wanted John Leslie with her heart and soul. He was where her true path lay.

'I can't leave it behind,' she cried out. 'I don't want to. He has made me come alive.'

'And you are willing to sacrifice all the time we have been together, worked together, how I have helped you develop into the artist you are today? Blanche, we have been constant companions, doesn't that mean anything to you?'

They gazed at one another and she saw how her life here had been jolted into self-awareness by the love of a man.

She said at last: 'I don't know how to live without him.'

Silence filled the room. A wind had got up and a branch tapped on the window.

'I don't want to let you go,' Monet said. 'I need you here, working with me.'

She took the gown to the mirror and held it against her, almost expecting to see the young woman who had worn it all those years ago, and was dismayed. Blanche folded it quickly and laid it aside. She would give it to Lilli, it was too pretty to be hidden away and should be worn again.

The room seemed stifling and she decided to take a turn

in the garden. As she came out onto the balcony, she heard the snip of secateurs and saw that Michel was pruning the Reine des Violettes; that last bloom had faded and died, two days ago.

'What are you doing?' she asked him. 'Don't be too harsh, I'm hoping it will bloom again in the autumn.'

'I hope so too, madame. I'm only following the instructions of M'sieur Breuil. You see, if you cut off tips of the new strong growth, you may force side shoots that can give more buds. It's worth a try.'

'I am so fond of that rose,' she said. 'It deserves special treatment.'

He turned to smile at her. 'It is certainly very beautiful, I too want it to bloom again.'

Gazing back at him, noting the dark eyes and smooth olive skin, she thought, yes, I can see why Lilli is so mad about him, but she is a little beauty, too. They make a handsome couple.

'I hear you are becoming a very good gardener,' she said. 'I know my father hopes you will stay with us.'

'Yes, madame.'

He seemed embarrassed and she wondered why. Papa had told her how enthusiastic he seemed about working in the gardens.

'I thought you seemed very happy here, especially…' She was going to say, especially now that you are walking out with Lilli, but changed her mind. '…as you seem to have a wonderful way with plants.'

'Thank you, madame.' He hesitated and in that pause she felt again the sense of concealment, of something unspoken. Papa, Judith and now this young man, it began to feel like a conspiracy.

258

'Don't let me keep you from your work, Michel.' She turned away.

While they were having supper, the storm broke. The dining room had become so dark they had had to light the lamps, although it was only a little after seven. There came a flash of lightning, which briefly illuminated the room, followed almost immediately by a deafening clap of thunder. Annette screamed. The tureen of vegetables she was carrying crashed to the floor.

'Oh I knew this would happen,' she wailed. 'My mother's cat was sitting with her back to the fire yesterday!' She crossed herself. 'Holy Immortal God have mercy on us. Amen.'

Blanche eyed her stepfather who had drained his glass and now sprang to his feet.

'Oh for heaven's sake, girl,' he shouted. 'It's only a storm. I'm more concerned for the vegetables. You had better fetch a bucket and cloth. Then go and ask Marie if there are any more, especially those beans.'

Blanche was pained by the sight of Annette clumping in and out with the bucket and awkwardly clearing the porcelain fragments. It was clear she was terrified of the storm, she bit her lower lip, obviously afraid to show it. Meanwhile the thunder growled overhead with intermittent flashes of lightning, which glinted on the glass and cutlery.

'You should not shout at Annette, Papa,' Blanche scolded when the girl had carried in more vegetables and left the room. 'You know how self-conscious she is.'

'Yes, yes, but she aggravates me so. You know how I cannot bear these local superstitions. A storm is a storm and we know how they come about.'

Even if Blanche agreed with him that such beliefs were

259

irrational, she had no intention of admitting it. 'They're such a poor family, be nice, Papa. I know how grateful to us they are for employing Annette with her... her disability. Imagine, it must be difficult to make sense of a world, which gives you a baby with a clubfoot. Perhaps putting the blame on superstition helps.'

He gave a deep sigh. 'Ah Blanche, always so comprehensive of other people's difficulties. You put me to shame.' He pushed a dish of tiny green beans towards her. 'Come on, take some of these, they are absolutely delicious, tender and sweet.'

She gazed at him, thinking how wonderful it must be to take such joy, such comfort in food. He was so at ease with the world of his senses, a quality she seemed to have lost. But then she had lost so much.

It began to rain, a dull and persistent sound. She imagined the garden inundated by this downpour, the world obliterated beyond the windows. It added to her sense of uncertainty, the feeling that everything was in flux. She was grateful when it was time to go to bed.

In the early hours she started up from a nightmare, soaked in sweat. The room was in total darkness and the night air came through her open window, sweet scented and silent after the rain. But the storm seemed to have entered her sleeping mind and she dreamt she was drowning in marshy ground, fighting to gain control but gradually being sucked under. Vividly she remembered the feel of the cold mud, the tug of it against her body drawing her down, the dreadful panic.

The sensation preyed on her mind so that it was the events of the following morning, which seemed unreal, as if she were one step removed from them. She heard voices in the garden and understood that plants had suffered in

260

the downpour. Her stepfather was saying something about the hollyhocks, grumbling to Breuil they had not been properly staked.

At luncheon he was morose and when she failed to answer some question, he barked at her: 'what's wrong with you, Blanche? You look as if you have seen a ghost.'

In the afternoon she made up her mind to try again with the painting, but could not concentrate and in the end she gave up and went to the kitchen. It was time to help Lilli with the laundry. As they settled to the task of sorting once again, Blanche found herself glancing at the girl who had scarcely said a word. After a while she asked her if she felt well.

'Yes thank you, madame.'

'You're very quiet today.'

'Am I madame? *Pardon.*'

Blanche eyed a food stain on one of her father's shirts. 'I was sorting some of my clothes, yesterday,' she remarked, 'and I came across such a charming summer frock. I thought you might like to wear it when you next walk out with Michel.'

Lilli raised her face to gaze at Blanche who was struck by the suffering in her expression.

'What is it?' she asked. 'What has happened, Lilli?'

'I don't understand,' the girl said. 'I don't understand, madame. He has become like a stranger. Everything was going so well but when we sheltered from the rain he seemed awkward and scarcely spoke to me.'

'Maybe he was just shy,' Blanche suggested.

'He wasn't before…' she began then paused. 'What have I done wrong, madame?'

'I can't imagine you have done anything wrong, Lilli.'

261

'I wasn't forward or anything like that.'

'I'm sure you weren't.'

They worked in silence for a while then Lilli paused.

'He has changed towards me, madame,' she said. 'When I think of how he behaved on the evening of the dance, so kind, so attentive, now he seems distant. Why?'

She grabbed hold of a pile of pillowcases and began to stuff them angrily back into the basket.

'I don't know what to say,' Blanche admitted. 'Let me think about it and then we'll talk again.'

1889

The weeks went by without seeing John Leslie. She stayed at Le Pressoir, hardly venturing beyond the garden. She painted, obsessively filling canvas after canvas, the only activity, which seemed in any way to anchor her. After a while, even that failed and she felt she was lost and adrift, shuffling through days that seemed to belong to someone else she didn't know or understand.

Early one morning in December, she went to find Monet in the garden. It was a beautiful day, a sprinkling of snow covered the ground and foliage and shone in the sunlight. All seemed still and sleepy.

It was difficult to believe that in a few months masses of daffodils and blue pansies would herald the spring again, Monet remarked. In coat and muffler, he stood with his feet planted square on the main path, looking perfectly happy in his own domain. He smiled at her.

'What brings you out here so early?'

'I want to ask you something,' she replied. 'It is very important.'

His expression changed and without a word he signalled they should return to the house. He led the way to his studio and closed the door. 'So?'

262

'I've tried to do as you asked me,' she replied. 'All these weeks I have tried.'

'And done very well. You are painting again, you have joined in family life.'

'But at a price,' she interrupted. 'You cannot imagine how I have felt inside and now...'

He was lighting a cigarette. 'And now?'

'Will you grant me a favour? Please. Will you talk to me about John Leslie? I want to try to make you realise what he means to me, what we mean to each other.'

Monet inhaled then blew out a smoke ring. 'I am sorry, Blanche, I will not discuss this any further. The subject is closed.'

The black painted stove glowed cheerfully in the dining room of Hotel Baudy; Blanche sat at one of the tables waiting for John Leslie. She had slept fitfully, dreaming, waking and dreaming again. In the morning she had dressed and, without breakfasting, hurried from the house. Madame Baudy had seemed surprised by this early visitor but, seeming to read Blanche's resolve, had invited her to be seated while she went to find him. The wood in the stove crackled and sent up a blue flame but she felt deathly cold. She tucked her hands under her cloak and waited, staring at but not really seeing the piano, the checked cloths, the cups and saucers and plates laid for the morning meal.

After what seemed an age, John Leslie came into the room. 'Blanche, I'm sorry to keep you waiting. I was still in bed.'

She gave him a small smile.

'You're cold. Shall I order some coffee?'

She shook her head.

He came to sit next to her. 'Oh darling, it's so wonderful to see you, after all this time. I've been thinking and thinking of you, wondering how you've got on. And now you've come back to me.'

She stared at him and this handsome, dark haired man seemed

263

to have nothing to do with her, at all. As always, he read her thoughts and held out his hand and she felt herself drawn to him though now it was with a sense of a knife going through her.

'It will have to end,' she said softly. 'I asked Monet to discuss you and me. I tried to persuade him to listen and understand, but he wouldn't. His mind is set against losing me. If I left and came with you, it would bring so much unhappiness and I don't have that courage, John Leslie. I can't do it.'

For a moment they stayed as they were, holding hands while the fire burned and gleamed on the nearest crockery. From a distance, voices could be heard in the kitchen.

Then John Leslie spoke. 'You never gave it a chance.'

She looked up to him then. 'There never really was a chance.'

It felt so right to be here, his hand in hers, his dear face so close; the idea of being without him seemed impossible. Tears ran down her face.

'Blanche, Blanche, oh my love.'

She felt she was being torn apart and went into his arms, laying her face against his shoulder, smelling the familiar scent of him. Just for a moment she thought that somehow there might still be hope, but then that passed.

'I have to go home,' she said.

'If that's what you want, I won't try to stop you.'

He was bitter and had a right to be. He turned away from her and there was nothing else to say or do but to leave. The tone of those last words rang in her mind as she hurried along the road, back to Le Pressoir, away from him.

That evening she stopped Monet on his way to the dining room. 'I saw John Leslie today. I told him I was going to stay here.'

She had thought he might thank her, even congratulate her good sense. But her tragic expression must have struck him and

264

he had the grace merely to nod. She moved past him towards the stairs and the sanctuary of her room.

Later she went into the garden to gather some flowers then walked up the road to the church. She stood and gazed at the cold marble, once again there were fresh posies laid there, people were still thinking of Maman. Blanche felt a pang of longing to speak to her, ask her advice. Her eyes filled with tears and she sank onto the marble surround still clutching her flowers. 'Tell me what to do, Maman,' she murmured. 'I feel anxious, as if I am losing control. Everything was going well in the household; we seemed to be turning a corner but now... I wanted so much to help Lilli find happiness but even there I feel I've failed.'

She went to sit in the church to pray to Saint Radegonde, but the air was oppressive and the dream of drowning had sapped her. After a while, she seemed to fall into a trance-like state. When she finally came to herself, she realised some time had gone by. Suddenly, she remembered Judith would be visiting Le Pressoir that day and she hadn't been there. What in heaven's name was the matter with her? For some reason she disliked the idea of the American girl alone in the house with her stepfather.

Panicking, Blanche rushed out of the church and hurried back along the street. She had almost reached the house when she saw something that brought her up short. Standing outside La Musardiere were Michel and Judith. They were talking and laughing, seemingly oblivious of their surroundings. She stepped back behind a convenient bush to watch them. There was something about their ease with each other, which suggested this wasn't the first time they had been together. What was more unsettling was that

265

they seemed not to be Judith, a wealthy young lady, speaking to Michel, the gardener, but just two young people revelling in each other's company. Then Judith said something about having to go and Michel laid a hand on her arm to detain her. She laughed and shook her head. Finally, they parted, each going in an opposite direction. Feeling mystified by the scene, Blanche hurried toward the house.

– TWENTY-NINE –

JUDITH

Judith had always got what she wanted. As far back as she could remember it had been so. In her nursery with its pretty rose sprigged wall paper, the cast iron bed dressed in flounces and ribbons, its silk sheets and plump pillows, there were always her favourite things for tea: white bread and peanut butter, honey cake and almond fingers. If ever she grew tired of these, Nanny would ring the bell and something else would be brought up. On her sixth birthday, she asked for a rocking horse and a magnificent piebald charger was delivered to the house in Madison Square. As she grew older, her list widened: frocks, outings, vacations, everything was granted to her. When Charlie came on the scene, he was added to the number of people intent on satisfying her desires. And of course, the European trip and this stay in Giverny had come about because her father could not refuse her. Now, she had hooked Michel.

Judith seated once again on the hotel terrace, gazed down at the tennis players with an unfamiliar sense of languor. For once, she was content to be alone, to think over the events of the past two weeks. She felt she had changed and discovered a part of herself she never knew she possessed.

It was hard to define, an urge to excite Michel, to push him further. She basked in the way he looked at her, quite blatantly now, his eyes running over her body, taking in her clothes, her hair, amazed when she smoked a cigarette on the terrace.

'Is that what women do in America?' he asked.

'The ones I know.'

'My mother would be shocked if she saw you.'

Judith had rocked her head from side to side in a mocking gesture. 'My, my, aren't I a naughty girl?'

He sighed 'It must be wonderful over there.'

'We sure have more freedom,' she admitted. 'If you're a good boy maybe I'll take you there some day.'

She dared not imagine what her parents would think if ever she did such a thing.

'And if I am not a good boy?'

She met his eyes, the pupils looked very large.

'And just what are you suggesting?'

'*Vilaine.*'

The thought of how her behaviour would infuriate Robert egged her on to blow smoke rings into the air, watching Michel through half closed eyes, to lean back in her chair with arms behind her head, exposing the shape of her body beneath the clinging silk; things she would never have dreamt of doing with Charlie. Michel followed her every movement with wondering eyes, wanted to see her every day though she sometimes pretended she had other things to do, recalling an overheard remark of her mother's: 'you have to keep these men on their toes.'

He seemed obsessed with her, wanting to keep her all for himself. 'What do you do when I'm not with you?'

'Oh this and that.'

'With the man, Robert?'

Judith waggled her finger at him. 'I told you, Michel, Robert is old.'

'Maybe he thinks not too old.'

'I don't mind what he thinks,' she reached over and patted his knee. 'I like young men, especially you.'

The night in the garden two days ago had altered everything. Her mind went to that early evening when she had gazed at herself in the mirror, satisfied by what she saw. She had spent a long time over her hair and make up, then gone to the cupboard to pick the green silk frock, low necked and clinging, the one she liked herself best in. The champagne had been ordered, there was nothing more to do but sit and wait for Michel to arrive, growing more on edge with every moment.

Her mind had turned to Dorothy and, although the woman had disappointed her, she mused on some of her advice about flirting with a man. She realised that she had never flirted with Charlie, never had to make any effort because he seemed to think there was nothing more interesting in the world than Judith. Their conversation was mainly about herself, it occurred to her; they never talked about his golfing, his friends or his work, they were just things he did when he wasn't with her. When she thought of him now, he seemed a shadowy, two-dimensional figure and, try as she might to recall him, all she could summon up was the smell of his hair and his very clean fingernails. Dorothy had said one should flatter a man, show interest in all he did and that is what she planned to do with Michel.

He needed little encouragement. They had had their cocktails then walked through the hotel out into the garden.

The night was perfectly still and shadowy. An intermittent moon sailed in and out of the wispy clouds.

'Michel, you haven't told me very much about yourself,' she began.

'Do you really want to know?'

'Yes, of course I do.' She tucked her hand under his arm and pulled him towards the upper terraces. She liked it here, hidden from the hotel, just the two of them, the feel of his sturdy body close to hers.

'Well, my mother is from Brittany and my father was born on the farm here in Normandy. Do you know, they have never even been to Paris? They are so dull, Judith, you have no idea, with eyes as blinkered as our old workhorse. They certainly do not like me working here at Le Pressoir.' He sighed. 'I get it every day: what's wrong with you, boy? The earth is for growing things to eat, not flowers. What use are flowers?'

Judith laughed. 'How boring they sound.'

'Very, very boring. What they would really like is for me to find a nice local girl, get married and inherit the farm.'

The honeysuckle was releasing its fragrance into the air, mingling with the roses, ethereal among their foliage. Judith leaned closer against him.

'Is that what you would like?'

'Certainly not. For one thing I am too young, for another I have escaped farming: all that mud and cows. I never want to go back.'

'So what's the problem?' asked Judith. 'no-one can force you to marry, can they?'

They descended the little flight of steps and arrived at the seat set in the rose bower. Here Judith sat and patted the space beside her.

'The thing is…' he began, 'the thing is there is someone who wants to marry me. Her name is Lilli and she works in the house. Oh she's pretty enough and nice enough,' he laughed. 'And mad about me.'

'How about you?'

'I enjoy her company, she is more intelligent than most of the girls around here. My mother says I would find it difficult to make a better match and I know she would accept if I asked her.'

Judith was becoming tired of this topic. She sighed. 'She sure sounds like a paragon of virtue.'

Michel turned to her; his eyes glittered in the dark. 'Are you jealous?'

She laughed. 'Why should I be?'

'There is no need. I don't want to marry a local girl and settle down in Giverny. I want to travel, see other places. The world is large.'

'It sure is.' She could smell the soap he used and that other scent about him that excited her.

Michel had not finished. Now that he had started, he seemed unable to stop as if all these thoughts had been tamped down in him and were now welling up. 'Then there is Le Pressoir and everyone saying what a good gardener I am. They tell me I have a lifetime job before me. no-one seems to understand me.'

Judith leaned over and touched his arm. 'I do, Michel, I understand all this very well. Father and Mother have my life all planned out.' She laughed. 'But I have other ideas they would not approve of.'

He laughed. *'Coquine!'*

'What me? Naughty! Whatever gave you that idea?'

They both laughed.

271

Michel said: 'you see, that is what I like about you: you are so full of life, not looking at me with those solemn eyes like my mother. Not telling me to be realistic like everyone else does. I am young, I want to enjoy myself, have some fun.'

'Oh dear, poor boy! Don't be sad.'

Judith jumped up and, humming the *Maple Leaf Rag* under her breath, began to dance the Turkey Trot.

Michel laughed and applauded. 'Bravo! Oh you look so funny, just like a bird!'

This was going well, Judith thought. She came over and took him by the hand. 'Now come on, let's open the champagne.'

As she had asked, it had been chilled and left on the table under the wisteria. Carrying the bottle and glasses, they wandered back to their hidden seat. Judith raised her glass to him, 'To enjoyment.' They drank, it was very good champagne. Michel poured again.

'Oh this is such fun!' Judith exclaimed, and then realised Michel had put down his glass and was gazing at her.

He murmured her name, then he took her glass and set both of them on the ground. He put his hands on her shoulders and continued to gaze at her. 'You are wonderful,' he said. He pulled her against him and started to kiss her. These were very different kisses from any she had had before, hard, savage kissing, which forced her lips open as Michel thrust his tongue into her mouth. He seemed so excited, his breath quickening as his hands slipped into her dress and found her breasts. She thought she should tell him to stop, maybe she had gone a little too far but as his fingers circled her nipples she gasped and pulled him closer and kissed him wildly. 'Oh, Michel!'

272

'Lie down,' he whispered, 'lie down.'

'My dress!' she protested.

Swiftly he slipped off his jacket and laid it on the ground. 'Lie.'

As if she had entered a dream she did as she was told. He knelt beside her, kissing her but now he was sliding his hand up her skirt, moving between her thighs to where her stocking tops ended in suspenders. He stroked the soft flesh there and she felt a thrill go through her.

'It pleases you?' he murmured. 'It pleases you?'

'Oh, yes.'

He paused and she realised he was pulling down her knickers. Again there was a part of her that knew she should protest but she lay still and let him do it. As Michel slid his fingers inside her and began gently to rub, she felt herself opening up to him, opening and opening, wanting him to continue to rub harder.

'How wet you are,' he grunted with satisfaction and she realised something was welling up inside her, spilling onto his hand. 'And again.'

She cried out this time.

'Shh!' he said. 'Shh, someone will hear.'

She laughed. 'I couldn't help it.'

'*Coquine*,' he said. '*Vilaine*. You like it, don't you?'

'Oh yes,' she laughed. 'Yes. It's wonderful.'

'Then I will stop.'

'No!' She sat up and clung to him. 'Don't stop, please.'

Suddenly he pulled away from her and was busy with his trousers. She watched him pull out a great erect penis, it seemed dark and huge and shining and she stared at it, fascinated.

'Lie down,' he said again, 'lie down.'

273

'No, Michel.'

'Come on,' he said and his voice was harsh, 'come on, Judith.'

'I'm frightened.'

'Shh no, I will be gentle… please.'

She let drop her hand and he knelt up above her, pushing this great thing inside her, slowly at first but then as he lost control, harder, much harder. She caught her breath on a stab of pain, heard his strange cry and then he fell against her, holding her breast and murmuring French words in her ears.

Judith lay with her eyes closed, smiling to herself. My God, I've done it, she told herself. She raised her head and they kissed, then she felt him stiffen.

'Shh, there's somebody coming.'

'No, it's just a bird or something.' She didn't want to move but continue to lie there and for him to kiss her again.

Now he was nervous. 'Come on, we'd better go.'

They dressed in silence and stealthily made their way down to the garden's lower level. Here Michel paused and put his hands on her shoulders so that she saw the gleam of his eyes.

'You were a virgin?'

She nodded.

'I'm sorry.'

'Don't worry,' she said. 'Don't worry at all.'

He held her close and she leaned her face against his shoulder. I've done it, she thought again.

'I'll see you tomorrow,' he said. 'And the next day and the next…'

She remembered something. 'Not Sunday.'

'Why not?'

'I am going to Rouen.'
'Who are you going with?'
'Oh Michel, are you jealous?'
'Of course I am jealous.'
'There's no need. It's just the old man.'

– THIRTY –

ROBERT

Madame Baudy asked Robert if she could have a quiet word with him. Her expression was solemn. Puzzled, he followed her into the dining room where the tables had already been cleared after breakfast.

She glanced around as if afraid of being overheard, then spoke in a low voice, 'I am sure it is all quite innocent, the young lady is educated and well behaved but...' she broke off, seeming embarrassed.

Robert felt a stab of apprehension. 'You're speaking of Mademoiselle Judith, I suppose?'

'Yes, M'sieur Harrison, the thing is this, she has fallen into the habit of entertaining a young man here at the hotel. They walk in the garden until sometimes quite late.' She clasped her hands. 'I understand what it is to be young, God knows I do and I am a broad minded woman but tell me, m'sieur, do you think it correct that a young lady should be alone in the garden with this young man? You see, the staff has begun to gossip. I would not want anything to mar our reputation. They say he works at Le Pressoir, as a gardener.' She shrugged. 'Not really the kind of companion for a young lady of her class, I would say.'

Damn, thought Robert, I knew I should have kept a closer eye on her, whatever Harry said. I warned her and she hasn't taken the slightest notice. Now it's all round the hotel. Soon the whole of Giverny will be talking about it. Silly little girl, can't she see what's she's doing?

He tried to make light of it. 'I'm certain you are right, Madame Baudy, that they are just enjoying each other's company. But as you say, you don't want gossip. I'll have a word with Mademoiselle Judith and explain you would rather they did not continue so.'

'Oh would you, m'sieur? It's very kind of you.'

Robert saw there was something else on her mind; a sly expression had crept into her eyes.

'I am sure you will not offend the young lady. She is a good customer, m'sieur, you understand? I have been serving her some of my finest champagne.'

Robert nodded. 'I understand, madame. I shall be diplomatic.'

'Good.' She rose. 'Can I offer you coffee?'

Robert shook his head, he needed to speak to Harry. He found him in the studio working on a canvas. It was a picture of the market in Vernon, full of gesticulating figures and the brilliance of a flower and fruit stall. Robert paused in the doorway and admired his friend's powerful shoulders, the curve of his neck. Sensing his presence, Harry sighed, laid down his brush and turned to him.

Robert smiled. 'I'm sorry to interrupt you but this is important. Listen, I know we discussed cancelling my trip to Rouen but something has happened which means I need to talk to Judith.'

'I thought you said you had had enough of that girl.'

'I'm anxious about her, not as much about her but the

277

effect she is having on people here. I want to persuade her to go back home.'

Harry grunted. 'If you can do that, I'm right behind you.'

'I think it is time she went. I really believe that if she stays in Giverny much longer she is going to do real damage.'

'Aren't you being a little over dramatic? She is only a silly, spoilt girl.'

But Robert was serious. From the moment he first saw her, he said, he had had this feeling she might stop at nothing to achieve what she wanted. It seemed he had been right. It wouldn't be long before the entire focus of Giverny would be upon her and, by extension, the other Americans at Hotel Baudy. 'We've had such a happy life here, I don't want it to change.'

'It already has,' remarked Harry. 'She's poisonous, in my opinion.'

'I don't think it's quite that. I sense something unknown about her, almost as if when she acts it is with a kind of blindness, as if something drives her. I don't know how to explain it.' He hesitated, trying to grasp what he meant to say. 'A kind of force, I suppose. Somehow you can't even blame her because I don't think she understands the effect of what she does.'

Harry gave a short laugh. 'Now you *are* letting your imagination run away with you. All she does is drink cocktails and wheedle her way in to seeing Monet. Annoying but hardly dangerous.'

He decided not to tell Harry about his conversation with Madame Baudy, his friend would immediately jump to conclusions. He had had enough of the judgements on his own life, criticism of the way he wished to live. He felt he

278

wanted to give the girl the opportunity of explaining herself. 'You must see I need to have this time with her away from Giverny.'

Harry was growing impatient; he kept glancing at his painting, obviously longing to get back to it. 'Okay, go, but get rid of her, that's all. I'm sick and tired of seeing her lounging about the place and of you wasting your time.'

'Harry, don't be angry.'

He had already turned back to the canvas. 'Go, I said. At least she'll be out of the way and I can do a good day's work.'

Robert left him and took out his annoyance on the De Dion-Bouton, cleaning and polishing his precious automobile until it glowed in the afternoon sunshine. Judith remarked on it when they came out of the hotel the following morning.

Robert paused for a moment to gaze about him. Weeks had passed since the day he had brought her here and she had exclaimed on the hollyhocks. Now they were going past their best, sagging a little on their tall stems. The roses bloomed on, but all too soon there would come the autumn flare of golds and scarlets, the dahlias and zinnias. Fallen leaves would mat the paths on country walks. The seasons moved inexorably from one to the next. He was struck by the brevity and fragility of his life in the face of nature and felt an irrational fear that, for some reason, he would have to leave this place he loved so much.

Judith, looking very young in her sailor blouse, was unconcernedly enjoying the morning. She held her face up to the sun and closed her eyes. 'What a heavenly day to go junketing in your beautiful car.'

They sped along the road and soon reached Vernon,

Judith humming a ragtime tune then breaking off to urge him to go faster. 'You're crawling along, Robert, everyone is passing you.'

'Okay, young lady, if you really want to see what my beauty can do.'

He put down his foot and they careered along the road, she laughing with delight. But soon Robert slowed down.

'That's enough.'

'Oh don't be a killjoy.'

'I'm not, I just want to get us to Rouen in one piece.'

By the time they arrived and found a place to park the car, it was eleven and Judith said she was hungry. They made their way to the Place du Vieux-Marché and sat outside at a pavement café table. Robert ordered.

Judith appeared ravenous, biting into her croissant and sipping her coffee.

'How good it tastes,' she exclaimed. 'So good. I don't think I've ever had such coffee or felt so happy.'

He wondered at the sheer exhilaration about her, she seemed to be hugging a delicious secret, gazing about her with a smile on her face. He saw through her eyes the play of the fountain, heard the cries from the market stalls and smelled the scent of roses, carnations and jasmine. It seemed heartless to broach the subject of her departure from Giverny. He would leave it until later, when they had visited the city.

'More of those wood-framed houses,' she commented, catching his eye. 'Aren't they cute?'

Cute? That gnarled wood, dark, rough-hewn, thick and heavy. Those houses were built to last for centuries. They seemed to symbolise continuity and permanence amid the impermanence of life until it struck one that their essence was the link between you, past generations, and generations to come. Man might be fragile but his creations left his footprint long after he had disappeared.

'Think of it,' Judith was saying. 'Emma Bovary saw these when she came to town to meet her lover. And these streets were the ones where she rode round and round with him in the carriage.'

Robert came out of his dream. Judith's perspective of Rouen was obviously different to his. 'You know the book very well.'

'Yes, I do. I have read it so many times.'

The plate of croissants was empty, their coffee finished. Judith suggested impatiently they paid the bill and moved on.

'I want to see all the places she went to.'

They walked under the great astrological clock and along the street named after it. They came to Cathedral Square where they stopped to gaze at the soaring building covered in lacy Gothic stonework, dominated by its three towers. Inside, the light streamed through the glass windows, carpeting the flagstones with their colours. A silver lamp burned in the choir and there was the sweet smell of incense in the air. They walked round the walls.

'This is where Leon waited for Emma,' Judith murmured.

'Who?'

'Leon, he was her lover. Oh look, there is the blue window with the boatmen carrying baskets. He was staring at that when she arrived. She had brought a letter for him, saying she couldn't carry on with the affair and then... oh yes, I see it over there, she went into that chapel and prayed.'

Robert, who had been inside the cathedral many times, thought that he had never had such a tour as this one.

Judith seemed to be finding her way around by memory or at least memory of the book she had read.

'So what did they do after that?' he asked.

'Well, a man came up to them, he was the beadle, and suggested he give them a tour of the church. Leon wanted to drag Emma away but she insisted on being shown round. It's a marvellous scene, he is bursting to get her on her own and she is trying to resist him.'

Robert glanced at his watch. Time was moving on and he was determined to speak to her before they left Rouen. They left the cathedral and continued along the cobbled streets. They visited the Musée des Beaux Arts and wandered happily among the paintings and sculptures. They moved through the fifteenth century, gazing at Perugino and then on to the sixteenth, where they admired Rubens, Velázquez and Poussin. Then it was the turn of the eighteenth century, a temple to art. Finally they came to an impressionist collection and there was Rouen cathedral, seen by Monet at all times of the day.

Robert still hadn't spoken to Judith. He glanced at his watch once more. 'Time for some lunch, I think.'

Over the sole, which they were told had come from Dieppe, Judith began to speak of Emma Bovary again.

'Once he had got her into that carriage, they made the driver go all over the city, all day. Can you guess what they were doing?' She laughed and took a gulp of cider. 'All day!'

Robert grunted. 'I bet that book was a scandal when it came out.'

'Oh, it was but then Flaubert led a very exotic life.'

The sole was delicious, it had arrived with prawns and mussels in a rich creamy sauce. He noticed that Judith was once again eating with appetite. There was something

282

different about her, he thought. She appeared less conscious of herself, more dreamy.

He helped himself to more potatoes and decided it was time to speak.

'Judith?'

She was sipping her cider and gazing around, again with that secret smile.

'There is something we have to talk about.'

'How serious you sound, Robert.'

'Well yes, this is rather serious, I'm afraid.' He sighed. 'There is no easy way of saying this so I'll be blunt. I think it is time for you to plan to go home.'

'What?' She set down her glass and stared at him.

'That is what I think.'

'But why? I am having such a wonderful time here. Why do you want to spoil it?'

'That is the problem,' he continued. 'You may be enjoying yourself but you're causing problems for the people here with your behaviour. Don't deny it, Judith, you have been seen entertaining a young man in the hotel garden. I've told you before, things like this are not done here, but you have taken no notice.'

She laughed at him then. 'Oh, always so prim, Robert, prim and proper. This is done, that is not done.'

'I am not prim and proper,' he protested. 'Far from it, but I do have some respect for the society I am living in. Here, young women of your class are chaperoned. It would bring shame on their families if they played fast and loose as you are doing.'

'Fast and loose!' Judith smiled. 'Is that what you think I am? Come *on*, Robert, you're a Yank, too. Everyone does it in the States.'

283

'Well this is not the States, Judith,' he insisted.

There was a pause. Judith took out her compact and inspected her face. He felt annoyance rising inside him.

'Have you always been middle-aged, Robert?' She closed the compact with a snap. 'I can't believe that. Surely there must have been a time when you went around with young ladies?'

'No, Judith.' The conversation had taken a different turn but he decided to continue on it.

'What?' her eyes widened. 'Never?'

'Never.' He drew a breath. 'I have never gone around, as you put it, with young ladies because… well, because I am the reverse side of the medal, you see.'

She doesn't understand, he thought. Mademoiselle Judith is not as worldly as she tries to make out.

'Queer,' he said. 'I am queer, Judith.'

A series of expressions passed over her face, not surprise as much as understanding, followed by slight amusement, and then slyness crept into her gaze. 'I see,' was all she said.

In that moment, Robert realised too late he had played into her hands. He who had held the power felt it shift. The longing to bring things out in the open, to say those words out loud had overwhelmed him. For that instant, it had felt such a wonderful release but now she had that knowledge, would she keep it to herself. 'This is between us, you understand?' he murmured.

'Well naturally, but I'm glad you told me. I have to say I did wonder. You and Harry seemed to be such good friends. Does anyone else know you're queer?'

'No,' Robert said quickly and again regretted it.

The sly look returned. 'Don't you fret. Your secret's safe with me.'

284

But was it? He asked himself as finally they made their way to the parked automobile. Would she find it irresistible to expose the secret he had kept all these years?

On the drive back, Judith asked if she could take the wheel and he refused.

'I can't have you knocking up my prized possession.'

'Don't be silly, Robert. I drive Charlie's motor all over New York. It's a piece of cake on this little road.'

He longed to be back in Giverny, away from her wheedling voice. She really believed she should have anything she wanted. 'I said no.'

Judith paused, then she said, 'You shouldn't be so nasty to me, Robert, you know.'

He was startled by the menace in her voice. With a sigh, he drew up by the side of the road, got out and they exchanged seats. She was a confident, able driver and for a while he settled back, even glanced out of the window. All of sudden, Judith accelerated and they shot forward, rushing along the road.

'Careful,' he cried out. 'Careful, Judith.'

'I am being careful,' she shouted back. 'I'm used to speed.'

'Slow down, do you hear what I say? Slow down.'

'Why should I?' she crowed.

'Because we're coming to several bends in the road and it's dangerous. Do you want to kill us both?'

At that she obeyed.

'I'll drive from now on.'

'Okay, okay.' With a flourish, she brought the car to a halt but remained for a moment sitting there, giving him a scornful smile. 'My, my, how you panic. What is it you're afraid of, Robert? Living?'

The remark was so perceptive, he was taken aback. This

young woman had got his number, all right. As he took the wheel and they covered the remaining miles to Giverny, he began to wonder what he would say when Harry asked how the day had gone.

He longed to be alone, to sit on the terrace, smoke a cigarette and absorb their conversation, the fact that he had told her he was queer. As they arrived in Giverny, Judith slid out of the car and paused,

'Thanks for the ride, Robert.' He gazed back at her, wanting her to be gone. Then he folded his arms over the wheel and rested his head. The sun burnt the back of his neck but he scarcely noticed.

Now he remembered that time with Scott. There he was standing in the doorway of the forge, watching his friend at work. He saw the pulse of white heat as Scott plucked the horseshoe from the fire. He heard the dull metallic ring as his friend pounded the shoe then carried it over to the waiting horse. The air was filled with an acrid smell, as the shoe was pressed against the horse's hoof and sizzled and smoked. He remembered his amazement that the horse never flinched.

'Hey, Bobbie,' Scott grinned at him. no-one else ever called him Bobbie, not even his mother. 'Escaped the office, have you?'

Robert saw the flame of Scott's hair as he bent over the anvil once more.

'It's Saturday, kid, I don't work on Saturdays, unlike you.'

Scott's arms were pale and freckled. 'Maybe but the difference is I enjoy what I do.'

His eyes were grey blue. They spent all their free time together wandering the countryside with Rusty, lying in the grass with a ham sandwich and bottle of lemonade. Talking always talking, setting the world to rights, as he could never do at home.

Robert heard himself try to be casual but it was difficult when he had to raise his voice above the sound of the hammer. 'Hey, I know you don't countenance my family much but it's my birthday next week and my mother is arranging a picnic.'

Scott was busy banging nails into the shoe and did not reply. Robert saw the fine muscled body, stripped to the waist, it gleamed with sweat. He wanted to plead though knew he shouldn't for it would sound childish. 'Please Scott, please come to the picnic. It won't be the same without you.'

– THIRTY-ONE –

JUDITH

Judith walked towards the hotel, surprised to find there were tears in her eyes. What a miserable ending to a day that had promised so well. She recalled his expression of a moment ago, the hardness of his gaze, his lips set in a thin line. He had glanced at her as though she were a stranger; no recognition of the pleasant hours they had spent together over these past weeks. All he wanted, it seemed, was to get rid of her, especially now, she thought, that I know his little secret. He's frightened I'll let it all out.

By the time she stepped into the cool entrance, paused at the reception desk to collect some notepaper and her key, she had recovered. She knew what she was going to do. In her room, she sat on the bed and began to write a letter.

Dearest Mother and Father,
It has been some time since I wrote to you, although I have been so happy to receive all your lovely letters.

Here she grimaced, picturing those shreds of paper that had filled the wastepaper basket.

I'm so glad you are both well and busy by the sound of things. Here in Giverny, I have passed some wonderful weeks in the company of painters, and my dream came true when I visited Monet and saw his beautiful house and garden. He is such a nice, kindly man and I believe we have become good friends. Can you imagine it, your daughter sitting with him in his studio, listening to stories of his life? I can scarcely believe it myself.

Judith paused and gazed around the room, seeing it once again with the freshness of her first sight, now seeming so long ago. She had grown to love this room with its simple rustic oak furniture, the red and blue tufted mat. With a stab of nostalgia, she remembered thinking, here I am in my very own room in Giverny and Monet only a few yards away. Everything had seemed set fair then: the prospect of a friendship with Robert, the anticipated visit to Le Pressoir, escape from all the expectations of her in New York. No, she was not going to contemplate failure. But how was she going to persuade them?

I have heard from Charlie, of course, and am happy to know that he is not moping around but going about town a bit. In fact, he seems to be getting along very well without me.

Again she paused, reread the last sentence and scored it out. Now she must come out with it:

The thing is, I want to ask you a big favour. Would you be darlings and allow me to stay on a little longer? I know you will say that there is the wedding to consider but surely it could be delayed for a month or two. It would certainly give you more time, Mother, to prepare for it all. In your last letter, I thought you sounded rather anxious. I really hope you will agree to this and I promise that when I do return I shall do everything to fulfil your wishes for me.

    With much love to you both,
        Judith

Yes, that would do. She waved the sheet of paper about to dry the ink, folded it carefully and slipped it into the matching envelope. It would go out by this afternoon's post.

Judith went to sit on the wide window ledge and gazed out at the garden. Her eye followed the small flight of steps that led upward towards the more secluded areas. She thought back to that night when she and Michel had lain on the ground and he had held his penis in his hands, huge and dark and shining. At the thought, she felt the strange stirring inside her, a welling up of moisture as when he had used his fingers in that feathery tantalising touch. She didn't know, of course, because they had never gone anything like so far, but she had a pretty good idea Charlie wasn't capable of giving her the same kind of pleasure as this man. When she thought about it, he was more like an adoring brother.

Judith moved back to stand by the window again. The last rays of the sun caught a tangle of white roses clambering over an arch, tingeing them with gold. They were supposed to meet again tomorrow but where would they go? Not the garden. It was obvious eyes were on them now and to be fair, she did not want to upset Madame Baudy whom she liked and admired. It would be madness to risk being thrown out of the hotel for something that had absolutely no future to it, whatever Michel seemed to think. Part of it was her own fault, she supposed, for leading him on.

As she opened the chest of drawers to take out clean underwear, her glance fell on the packet of sanitary towels nestled there. Next week Aunt Flo would pay a visit. This thought led her to another and it struck her Michel had not used anything when he came inside her. He had got so worked up, she couldn't have held him back if she'd tried. She remembered washing away the sticky stuff before she went to bed. Suppose he had made her pregnant? That would be an impossible situation to get in to, ruin all her plans. Maybe she'd got away with it this time but she couldn't risk it again, risk being cast off without a dollar. Anyway, she was getting tired of his ogling, his possessiveness, all she'd wanted was a bit of fun. It was time to cut it short though she knew he'd make a scene. What an awful bore.

Judith glanced at her travel clock. It was after seven and time to dress for dinner. Tonight she was going to make a special effort, let Robert see she was undaunted.

Taking out the Fortuny frock, marvelling again at its shimmering colours, she thought of her reaction when he had suddenly spoken out over that delicious lunch. It had seemed to her more a confirmation of things sensed and felt rather than known. She smiled at herself for ever imagining he might fall in love with her. But although she wanted to believe she was free thinking, she found she did not approve. It was only ever spoken about in hushed whispers at home. 'Serve him right if other people found out,' she murmured aloud. His smugness about living in Giverny! No wonder he had left America and equally, no wonder he didn't want to go back.

She heard her mother's voice talking about a friend's failed contraception, using the withdrawal method.

'Another one on the way,' she had told Father, 'and they can ill afford it. I don't know what's the matter with that husband of hers, selfish so and so.'

'How many is that now?' he had enquired. 'Four?'

'Four! This will be the sixth. She's ruined her figure forever.'

Judith remembered her mother smoothing her hands over her own very slender body, which her one daughter had left unchanged. 'Thank heavens for the diaphragm.'

'It's certainly been a good friend to you,' Father had remarked dryly.

– THIRTY-TWO –

CLAUDE

He wakes with a sense of approaching doom, of helplessness; he stares through the half-light trying to locate the reason, physical or mental. There is no bodily pain that might suggest sickness is about to strike, it is his mind that troubles him. Painting is a torture, thinking, thinking, always thinking, obsessed by the need to render what he experiences and praying he'll have a few more good years left to him.

He believed he had left them behind, those sensations of hopelessness and dismay that dogged him after Suzanne's and Alice's deaths, have dogged him at various periods of his life. Remember that time back in the sixties when he believed life was not worth living if he could not achieve what he had set out to do; how cold the dark waters of the Seine closing over his head? Remember when Camille died in his arms and he caught himself watching her tragic forehead, observing the sequence of changing colours that death was imposing on her rigid face. Blue, yellow, grey... in spite of himself he felt compelled to paint her, one last time. Never had he let his depression show in his art until that moment, always worked with joyous, sunlit colours. No, maybe for *The Magpie*, that frail bird perched on a gate like a staff of music in a world of white, grey and violet, maybe then it had come through, portraying his work's rejection.

This melancholy seems to have appeared from nowhere and for no obvious reason. He knows he is an esteemed painter, that ever since he realised nature was his muse he has achieved his ambition to create important work. Why only a week or so ago, he had felt such *joie de vivre*. Judith made him feel young again, she infected him with her carelessness, curbed this constant worry about his sight. This week he had started sketching for the Water Lilies series. What has happened? 'Time to get up, Claude,' he scolds himself yet lingers, for once loathe to begin the day.

He sits in his studio, smoking. A painting gazes down at him from the walls: sunny afternoon, vivid flowers and cool patches of shade. Camille's summer gown is caught by a breeze as she takes an after luncheon stroll, while his son plays with his blocks in the shadow cast by the table. This morning, he finds no pleasure in the memory of that long ago meal, those months of high summer in Argenteuil. He is seized by the old fear, irrational, as he knows it to be, that he will lose everything; his house and garden will vanish, his work written on water. He lights another cigarette, feeling himself drawn down into the black hole of despair. To have gone to all this trouble to get to this is just too stupid. Outside, there is brilliant sunshine but he doesn't feel up to looking at it. Instead he smokes while his mind returns to twenty years ago. He sees himself in Rouen's square, painting the cathedral. He moves from canvas to canvas, altering his view point but only slightly, fascinated by the play of light and atmosphere at different times of day and in shifting weather conditions. As always when painting in the open air, he is at the mercy of a fleeting cloud, a sudden ray of sunshine, or fog in the early morning. Each day is a fresh struggle with the obstinate coats of paint. At times he is exasperated and ready to give up the series. Those cathedral paintings haunted him and he had nightmares about them. They fell on top of him and seemed to be blue or pink or yellow. He has given himself a severe challenge, forsaken nature for the monochrome of ancient stone; there is no constantly changing water or moving foliage as a means of expressing the play of light. Yet somehow he induces harmonies of colour with the passing of time: pale and rosy at sunrise, purple at midday, glowing in the evening under the rays of the setting sun, scarcely visible in the mist. He transcends his task but glories in the struggle. He has come to detest the things in which he has success at the first attempt.

He opens his sketch book and glances through the drawings he has made over the past week: the whippy stems of iris, their fleur de lys crowned heads, willows bending to the water, agapanthus. Page after page he has covered, often working from memory for he knows the water garden off by heart. He lays it down with a sigh. All very well making sketches but isn't he crazy to think of embarking on such a grand project? How many years would it take? Would his sight endure that long? He lights another cigarette. If he could see Judith again, it might pull him out of these doldrums but since her last visit, Blanche has made excuses when he asks her when the young woman is coming again.

First she told him Judith had gone away for a few days, then she said he sounded as if he were in for a cold, better wait to see how it developed. Finally, 'Claude, why do you continue to waste your painting hours on a silly girl?'

Blanche has certainly done a volte-face. She had been all for these visits, the one to suggest them to him in the first place. When he thinks about it, this alteration stems from that luncheon with Georges and the discussion about his eyes. Memories of that splendid pike tickle his taste buds.

There had been one other visit. Blanche for some reason had gone out, apparently forgetting the appointment. It had been left to Annette to announce Judith's arrival. He smiles, remembering the conspiratorial glance they had exchanged, the tacit agreement they could now spend more time together without interruption.

'I'm taking a trip to Rouen,' she had told him. 'Robert, you remember, Mr Harrison, the one who gave the birthday picnic, is taking me in his splendid automobile.'

'Whatever you do, be sure to visit the cathedral, it is a splendid example of Gothic architecture.'

'It's at the top of my list. Emma Bovary met her lover there. Remember, in the book?'

'Ah, dear Flaubert, man after my own heart... utter perfectionist. Although, I have to say, I would never have had his patience. I met him once. Do you know what he said to me? Be regular and orderly in your life like a bourgeois, so that you may be violent and original in your work.'

'Oh my golly, you met Flaubert?'

'I did.'

'And he said that?'

'He did.'

'Regular and orderly, that sounds dull.'

'It is not if your alter ego does something entirely different.

296

His certainly did. He was lucky to escape prosecution, unlike poor Baudelaire.'

'I will never be great as Flaubert was great. I just have my life and I want that to be, maybe not violent, but certainly original. Do you think it will?'

She had leaned back in that familiar pose of hers, folded her arms and scowled.

He chuckled. 'Of course, *ma petite*, you are well on the way.'

She smiled then. 'Oh thank you. You're so nice and kind.'

'There are others who wouldn't say that.'

'Well, I think you are. Now come on what story are you going to tell me today?'

'Let's see. I know let's go back, way back to when I was even younger than you. Let's go back to when I was twenty.'

'Before you met Camille?' She sounded disappointed. 'I love hearing about Camille.'

'Several years before that but it was an important time in my life, I assure you.'

* * *

Autumn in Paris: the sky is a clear blue and the florists' buckets stacked with flowers, as if it were still summer. He has visited the Louvre where he watched painters copying the old masters. Instead he goes to sit at a window and paints what he sees. Now he walks along the Tuileries, scuffling the fallen leaves with his feet, breathing in the crisp air. He admires the Emperor's new garden with its beds of exotic plants and flowers, the statues, pauses by the orangerie where the citrus trees in their tubs have already been brought inside to over winter. He walks on, feeling he never wants to stop, cannot get enough of this city, which is now his home. This morning, he gazed down from his apartment window through the branches of the plane trees, telling himself he has arrived; he is a part of this centre of art and culture. He feels indomitable. As he nears the Place de la Concorde, a skinny boy in ragged clothes pleads for money. Claude drops a franc into the dirty hand. What on earth made me do that, he asks himself, I'm struggling myself on Papa's measly allowance. That franc would have bought me supper.

In November on his twentieth birthday, he stays late in the Brasserie des Martyrs with Pissarro and some other painters, getting drunk. The next morning a letter arrives. The lot has been drawn and he has a bad card. He is being called up. The only advantage is that, if he responds immediately, he can choose his posting. It takes very little time to make up his mind: Algeria. Delacroix is his motive, the master of colour, its explosion on canvas in scenes of dramatic violence. He has consumed them, *Death of Sardanapalus, Liberty Leading the People,* not for the subjects for he is not drawn to history or mythology, but for this consummate manipulation of colour. If his hero had been inspired by North Africa, might he not be similarly so? This fires his request to be posted to Algeria. There he can study the intense southern light, exotic subject matter and heightened colour.

In June of that year, 1861 he is drafted into the Zouave. If he is honest with himself, he has to admit he is also attracted by the uniform, the baggy trousers, the sashes and oriental headgear… all rather dashing. He learns to ride a horse, to handle a rifle and to march, all of which he finds tiresome. In the garrison, he amuses his companions by making caricatures of their seniors and of his friends. He knows his true *raison d'être*: he chose Algeria because of the sky. He finds it a splendid country with constant sunshine, hot seductive colours and this eternally blue sky accentuated by the greens of palms and exotic plants. Everywhere he looks he finds something new and, when he has time, he tries to render what he sees.

'I made a succession of small drawings of little Algerian scenes… fauna and flora, landscapes, countryside views, veiled women and young girls… everyday life. You cannot imagine how my vision developed, although I suppose I didn't quite realise it at the time, this impression of light and colour was the germ of my future work. And then I became ill. The first symptom I remember was feeling very tired, so tired I could hardly move. My head ached and my throat. I didn't want to eat and my temperature rose alarmingly. Typhoid, I developed typhoid, Judith, just at the moment when I had had enough of being a soldier.'

'So it was a blessing in disguise,' she remarks.

'You might say that. My aunt was very kind and bought me out. My father was not so delighted. He said he would cut me off without a franc if I did not go seriously to work.' He laughed. 'But I always went my own way.'

Judith makes a show of clapping her hands. 'Bravo, bravo!'

He inclines his head to her then changes the subject. 'Judith, would you look at something, please?'

He shows her one of his latest canvasses. 'I want you to tell me honestly, honestly please, how do the colours appear to you. Is there, for example, any dominant hue?'

She gazes. He can see her wondering what she is gazing at.

'Would you say there is a lot of red?'

She nods. 'Yes, there sure is.'

He sighs. 'The truth is I no longer see colours with the same intensity. The reds seem muddy to me, the pinks are insipid and the lower tones escape me completely.'

'You can't go on like this, can you? You must have these cataracts removed.'

'I am afraid.'

Judith shakes her head. 'Aren't you more afraid of going blind?'

'Blanche says it is risky.'

'If you'll pardon me for saying this, I don't think your stepdaughter is very good for you. She always seems to look on the gloomy side.'

'I suppose she thinks she's protecting me.'

The young woman rises from her seat and comes over to him. She takes his hands in hers.

'Protecting! Hey, that's the last thing either of us want, don't you think?'

They laugh and he feels the morning's melancholy drift away.

– THIRTY-THREE –

BLANCHE

Blanche, seated at her dressing table, gazed and gazed into the mirror until it seemed the face of a stranger looked back. As a child she had sometimes done this, frightening herself with the altered expression in her eyes until a maid servant had scolded her, saying she was inviting a devil in. Mirrors played tricks, she thought, they presented a mysterious other world, a sleight of hand which vanished the moment you turned round. Annette once told her she wouldn't sleep facing a mirror for fear of what she might see in it at night. Today these thoughts compounded her feelings of the house pervaded by something unspoken and secret and so she gazed, not seeing the bed and part of the wardrobe reflected behind her but only her watchful face.

She felt as if her mooring ropes had been cut and she was adrift, no longer her father's chief confidante but neither could she return to her painting. Yesterday, she had stood before her canvas, analysing the effect of the colours, noting how her reworking had gone too far; the roses looked too solid, she had not achieved the smudgy shades of pink, lilac, blue and deep magenta, the smoky effect she had chased. In exasperation she had snatched it up, almost ready to throw it on the floor and trample on it. Now it was stowed away together with her paints and heaven knew when she would get them out again. What was there left? Her life seemed without meaning; she was aware of getting older but still searching for who she was. Maybe she was wrong; the truth lay in the mirror, shown without emotion, an oval all-seeing eye. She was angry: all these years she had tried to please other people, gain their love. She had been the obedient daughter, then caring wife to Jean, while this mirror had reflected back a young girl then, inexorably with the passing of time, an elderly woman. All the while her true self, the artist, longed to emerge. Why had she not allowed this, even now sacrificing herself to a selfish, domineering old man?

The feeling had hung over her for days, ever since she had glimpsed Michel and Judith standing together outside La Musardiere. That scene preyed on her mind, their apparent ease in each other's company as if they were at very least friends, the girl's gesture of going, the boy putting his hand on her arm to detain her.

At the time, it had been just a fleeting impression. Now she returned to it, concentrating on the details, trying to find the meaning behind her sense they were equals, that there was an intimacy between them, something shared. Her mind turned to Judith's visits to Le Pressoir and of how they had been engineered. Why, one might almost imagine the motive of that birthday picnic had been to achieve this. She saw again the first meeting of her father and Judith, the girl moving heaven and earth to enchant him; she remembered her flattering remarks. No, she was letting her imagination run away with her and yet, when she came to think about it, was she? She recalled the low voices she had

302

strained to hear as she closed the door on Papa's studio, the burst of laughter as if she were the object of their amusement, the sense of complicity. Judith. Now as she continued to stare into the mirror she saw the young woman's face, pale skin, huge eyes and that knowing smile. She seemed to pervade the house, a subtle presence, and Blanche was sure of one thing: she did not want her coming here any more.

There came a light tap then the door opened and Lilli stood there, her arms full of clean linen. She looked startled to see Blanche.

'Oh beg pardon, madame. I didn't realise you were here. I'll come back when you're finished.'

'No,' said Blanche, 'no need, come in.'

'I'll just make the bed then, it won't take a moment.'

In the mirror, Blanche watched the accustomed movements of the girl as she stripped the bed and smoothed over the undersheet, neatly tucking in the corners. Then came the top sheet and the coverlet, all done, as she said, in a moment. Lilli straightened, sighed and then, drawn to the window it seemed, she went to stand there with folded arms, gazing out.

After another minute or so, Blanche turned from the mirror. 'What is it, Lilli?'

The other started out of her reverie. 'Oh beg pardon, madame.'

'You looked so thoughtful.'

Lilli sighed again and turned to face her.

'There is something troubling you, isn't there?' Blanche persisted.

'It's just all such a mystery and if there's one thing I hate it's a mystery.'

'You feel like that, too? As if there are things being kept secret?'

'Why yes, madame, that's it.'

Blanche patted the bedroom chair. 'Come and sit down for a moment.'

'Oh, but I've all the beds to do.'

'They can wait. Sit down and tell me what is on your mind.'

Lilli hesitated then did as she was told. 'It is Michel, madame. I met him by chance on my day off and I asked him what was wrong, why he had changed so and… oh, madame, I believe there might be someone else.'

The image of Judith and Michel returned, laughing and talking as if no-one else existed. 'Really?' was all Blanche could say.

'I can't understand it. Who can it be? I haven't seen him walking out with anyone and it could only be another domestic, couldn't it, madame?'

'One would suppose so,' agreed Blanche. 'I can't imagine who else it might be.' She remembered the sense she had had of two young people revelling in each other's company.

'There is something,' Lilli began and then hesitated. 'It's best I don't say anything.'

Blanche felt impatient, unable to take any more of these mists and mysteries.

'Out with it, Lilli, please,' she snapped, 'speak your mind.'

The laundry maid's eyes widened.

'*Pardon*, but I would hope that you, at least, might speak out and tell me what is happening.'

'Very well, it is like this: one day, a few weeks ago, Annette told me she had seen the young American lady talking to Michel in the garden. Annette said she thought they seemed intimate. I told her she must be mistaken, I mean, the young lady is of a different class.'

'That is true,' Blanche said. She was aware of Lilli hesitating again. 'And so?'

It's just it must have been after that he started to become so distant. Oh, madame, suppose it is she he loves, what shall I do?'

The pieces fell into place with an almost satisfying click; this was part of the secret. But how to answer Lilli? The girl was eyeing her anxiously.

Blanche rose from the stool. 'You do nothing, do and say nothing. You must just be patient.'

'But…'

Blanche held up her hand. 'If, and I am not convinced, but if it were the young American lady then there is certainly no future in that. She will be returning home shortly and I believe there is a fiancé.'

'Really?'

'Really.'

For the first time, Lilli smiled. 'She's been here rather a long time, hasn't she?'

'Too long,' said Blanche.

After the laundry maid had gone, she turned back to her dressing table, intending to tidy her hair but grew impatient of it. It seemed much less easy to manage these days, thinning somewhat and now she noticed a sprinkling of grey. She thought of how once it had been so thick and lustrous, let down and spread round her shoulders as she eyed herself in this same mirror after an evening with John Leslie. Young, she had been, attractive and desired, as she never would be again. Blanche laid down her brush and, covering her eyes with her hands, wept.

1890

As they entered another decade, life appeared to be settling back into its old ways. She and Monet ate breakfast together then loaded their gear into a wheelbarrow and made their way through the dewy countryside to watch the sunrise. They set up their easels side by side. The pattern of the days was restored; and yet not quite. It wasn't possible to eradicate the effect the Americans had had on Giverny, it was an altogether busier, noisier place.

'And there'll be more,' said Monet. 'Word is getting around and mark my words there'll be even more. The place will be inundated with them.'

* * *

The year progressed, punctuated by visits from friends, outings in the motorcar and painting, always painting. He had never mentioned John Leslie again, since that evening when she had told him it was over. But all the time, she tried to suppress the voice inside her that cried out for him.

Monet's earlier enthusiasm for the haystacks intensified and he began to talk of a more ambitious project.

'I feel it wouldn't be trivial to study a single image at different times of the day and of the year for that matter. To examine the effects of the light that form from moment to moment, the envelope of the atmosphere and the light shining through it.'

At first he tells her he believes he can accomplish this with two canvasses, one for sunny and one for overcast weather. Soon he comes to realise the transitory quality of the light how, in passing moments of the day and in various seasons, the haystacks absorb it from diverse parts of the colour spectrum. As a result, the residue is reflected off the haystacks and seen as ever changing, manifested in distinctive colouring.

He sighs and turns to Blanche: 'Go to the house, if you don't mind, and bring me another canvas.' This continues, 'And another canvas! Another!'

She sees what he means: how with mist the light is so diffused that hardly anything in the distance remains visible, or how the crisp transparency on a clear winter's day lets the light shine brilliantly on the side of a haystack. From one hour to the next, these effects of light modify so noticeably the appearance and colouring of the stacks. In *Grain Stack at Sunset* he used intense brick reds to give the shadowed side of the stack an incandescent core, vermilion and yellow for the light of the sunset that haloed the stack, the lit parts of the field scattered with particles of pink, orange, and mauve. Thus he painted canvas after canvas after canvas. He had employed this method before, of variations on a single theme, but there was something new here, a difference of emphasis. He was pursuing the very transience of light. Together they noted the elusiveness of certain effects. Monet attended to those canvasses no more than a few minutes a day. Further complicating matters, they realised that the light of successive sunrises could alter substantially, and required separate canvasses within the series. Sometimes they wrote the time of day on the back in order to return to the painting at the correct moment. Always beside him, ready to hand the required canvas at a nod or murmured 'four' or 'ten', Blanche understood he had so much to say about light and colour and atmosphere it would be impossible in one painting.

They started in September, rising before dawn to trundle the wheelbarrow filled with half-finished canvasses out into the fields. Throughout winter they worked solidly and by spring, Monet had painted an incomparable quantity of pictures distinguished only by light, weather, atmosphere and perspective.

Working alongside him was always infectious as they shared

307

and discussed ideas. Blanche painted her own version of the haystacks celebrating the autumn sunrise, showing the pink haze of dawn engulfing form so sun and sky, fields and haystack, near and far, were enveloped in a peculiar liquid atmosphere.

Monet was impressed. 'Excellent brushwork, you have handled colour very well. The landscape seems to be at once bursting into radiant life and dissolving before the eye.'

The following year, Monet showed fifteen of these paintings at a gallery in Paris. Uncertain of how they would be received, he was startled by the public reaction; wonderful reviews, critical acclaim. People were eager to buy the pictures, and it dawned on him that his public might finally have caught up with his vision.

'I have arrived, Alice, I really believe I have arrived,' he crowed at the dinner table. 'It must be downhill from now on.' He raised his champagne glass. 'Here's to the end of grubbing around for money. We can buy the house.'

For Blanche it came as an anti-climax after the intense activity of these past months. She distanced herself from the negotiations, the signing of deeds, Monet's plan to create a water lily pond. She had her own preoccupations, which had grown, even while apparently attending to Monet. She realised she could not live with her dismissal of the love of her life. Everything began to seem a waste of time, as if she had lived this life too long, seen this house, this garden too many times. She missed John Leslie. His presence haunted her. Once she thought she glimpsed the back of his head as she walked through the streets in Vernon. She quickened her pace to follow him and was bitterly disappointed when she saw the man's face and realised he was nothing at all like John Leslie. She thought about him as she helped in the house, collected the eggs or walked in Giverny and wondered if he thought of her. She wrote him letters, which she never sent.

Daffodils and blue violets crowded the garden again. She wandered its paths and tried to think back to that happy life she had spent with the family. Her mind moved further back to the chateau and her early childhood and then to how they had come here, Monet and Maman, and helped to create the garden. But however hard she tried she could not escape the feeling that life had only really started when she met John Leslie.

One morning her mother asked her to call on a woman in the village whose husband had recently died.

'Poor Madame Joubert, they never had any children so she must be feeling quite alone. Take her these flowers, would you dear, and give her my condolences and best wishes.'

The woman who answered the door wore black but her eyes lit up when she saw Blanche and the bouquet and she smiled.

'How kind, mademoiselle. Come in, won't you?'

'I don't want to intrude, madame.'

'You're not intruding at all. It's good to have some young company.'

Inside, the house was spotless and from the kitchen came the smell of baking cakes.

'You'll take coffee, won't you? And you must try a slice of my special galette.'

While Blanche sat in the little salon waiting, she heard the sound of Madame Joubert humming softly as she made the coffee. She didn't seem like someone recently bereaved at all.

'You're being very courageous, madame,' she commented as she finished the delicious cake and wiped her fingers.

'Courageous?' the other gave a short laugh. 'It is kind of you to say so but it doesn't apply in my case. Oh, I'm sorry for him that he died, he was a decent man and kindly but...' She paused.

Blanche had taken up her coffee cup but hesitated, not bringing it to her mouth. 'And now you are alone.'

'Oh yes. It comes to all of us, my dear,' she leaned forward, lowering her voice as if there were someone who might hear. 'But you know, he was always second best; I loved another. Oh how I loved him and he loved me.'

'Then why?'

'He was an adventurous young man. Didn't want to spend the rest of his life here. He wanted us to go to Paris, leave everything, families, friends and start a new life and I just wasn't brave enough.'

Silence in the room as Madame Joubert appeared to gaze along the path she hadn't dared to take. Then almost as if she understood, she looked across at Blanche and her expression sharpened.

If you were to ask my advice, young lady, I'd tell you not to make my mistake. Follow your heart.'

It was then Blanche sensed the pall of compromise and disappointment that hung over the room, the years of living with a man she did not adore, nostalgia for the one she did, which belied the woman's smiling face.

As she walked back to the house, his name clamoured in her head: John Leslie, John Leslie. She went to her room and wrote him a letter and this time she posted it. Two weeks later, when she called yet again at the Vernon Post Office, there was a letter waiting for her.

Your letter touched me. I agree, dear Blanche, we should not have parted like that. I was never convinced it should be so but respected your wishes. There are things left to be said. I am coming back to Giverny.

By seven o' clock that evening, she had recovered herself and was filled with stern resolve she was going to have it out with her stepfather. When she came into the dining

310

room he did not even glance up, seeming deep in thought. She took her place and the soup was brought, they took up their spoons and ate in silence. Duck came next in the usual peppercorn spiked sauce. To her surprise, he did not seem to eat with his usual appetite.

After a while, she asked: 'Is there anything wrong with the meal tonight, Papa?'

He stirred himself, seeming to come out of a reverie. 'It is quite good.'

For some reason this annoyed Blanche, not so much for herself she realised, but for Marie who had taken such pains to please.

'You think so? I find this well done.'

'Marie will never cook like Marguerite.'

Blanche sniffed and set down her knife and fork. 'You know what you must do? Stop this constant mourning for Marguerite. That time is over, Papa, gone and will never return. You will have to learn to accept, as we all have to accept, that the world is not arranged for our benefit.'

He gazed at her. 'You're angry.'

'No, I am not.'

'As you wish.'

He finished what was on his plate but did not help himself to more. Annette brought in the dessert; this evening, Marie had produced an authentic Poire belle Hélène down to the crispy almond biscuits stuck into ice cream.

'Oh, my goodness,' Blanche exclaimed. 'That does look so good. Please Annette, say thank you to Marie.'

'I helped with the biscuits, madame.'

'Well done.'

The girl grinned and clumped out of the room.

311

Blanche cleared her throat, 'and don't you dare say that this isn't a patch on Marguerite's.'

He shrugged.

'It is, in fact, excellent,' she persisted.

He ate the pear and some of the melted chocolate, and then pushed his plate away. He poured some wine. 'I am sorry but I have been feeling depressed today. I need cheering up. I'd like Judith to pay another visit, I so much enjoy her company.'

Blanche was spooning up the ice cream, a subtle taste of vanilla, and Marie had kept a light hand with the sugar; she was certainly coming on.

'I think we should discourage this Mademoiselle Judith,' she muttered.

'Whatever for?'

'She is an unsettling influence.'

'I don't see it like that.'

She took up an almond biscuit. 'Because you are an old fool.'

'Don't you speak to me like that. You are my stepdaughter and my daughter in law.'

'Yes and so I am doubly under your thumb and always have been, right from the time...'

'Don't bring all that up again. The past is the past.'

The pot calling the kettle black, she thought, what had he just said about Marguerite?

'So you are dissatisfied with your life?'

Blanche fetched the plum brandy and poured them both a glass. 'I didn't say that. What I am saying is that we had settled into a pleasant existence, quiet perhaps, but pleasant until this... this American arrived.'

'Ah well, I don't see it like that. She brings life and light to this place.'

312

'The trouble with you is you can't see what is in front of your eyes.'

There was a pause.

'That is true,' he said quietly.

'*Pardon*, but really it is I who sees what is going on in this household. All you are concerned with is your painting, nothing must disturb that but this young woman has created such disorder, you have no idea.'

He lit a cigarette. 'Maybe it is because she is young that you don't like her, Blanche.'

The remark echoed her earlier thoughts and it stung.

'That has nothing to do with it. She is not what you believe her to be, I have my reasons for saying that. I am telling you, Papa, I will not allow her to set foot in this house again. In fact, you can choose between her or me.'

He lifted his glass and finished the plum brandy. 'So be it, but you have become a very bitter woman.'

Five minutes later he had gone, back to his studio and she was left, gazing round the room. Yet again, she counted the chairs round the table and thought back to the time when there were voices and laughter. The Japanese prints gazed down, those young, lovely women in their kimonos seemed to taunt her. No wonder if she was bitter, any woman in her position surely had the right to be.

1891

That summer Le Pressoir bustled with activity as Monet set about his dream of creating the water garden. It was to be the ultimate source of his inspiration, he explained to Georges, when the politician joined the family for lunch.

'I visualise it as a cup garden, in the parlance of Japanese garden design, to inspire introspection. A mirror of water will

313

form the bottom of the cup and the plantings, wisteria, willows, bamboo, irises and so on will be its sides and cast their reflections. In the pond, I shall plant thousands of water lilies, all the colours that genius Latour-Marliac can offer me.'

'Sounds delightful,' Georges looked up from the coq au vin. 'The kind of place where we middle aged men can ponder our destinies.'

Monet wagged a finger. 'More than that, my friend, much more than that, I have plans. My water garden will provide the setting for a series on the theme of the pond and its lilies. I have an idea this will be my subject for a long time to come. However, the water lilies are far from being the whole scene. The essence of the motif should be the glass-like water, altering every moment, thanks to patches of reflected sky, which will give it light and movement.'

'Remarkable,' Georges refilled his glass. 'You must carry this out, Claude. Rely on me if you need any help.'

At the end of the existing garden and beyond the railway track, there was a marshy grazing area. His idea was to buy a piece of this land and then to divert a tributary of the River Epte, which served some mills downstream. Here he met with opposition. Local people, including a farmer called Louis Duval, held that the strange and exotic plants Monet grew would poison the water. Georges who was by now as enthusiastic of the project as his friend, used his influence to help push the permission through.

Blanche joined the family to watch the excavation. At first only a small pond was dug, which Monet soon pronounced not large enough for the studies he had in mind. It was enlarged and yet again. Then he took off in the car to Le Temple-sur-Lot to visit Latour-Marliac's nurseries and immersed himself in water lilies. This swiftly became an obsession as he bought and acclimatised many exotic varieties in extraordinary colours.

314

Alice began to complain. 'He thinks more of those wretched lilies than anything else, including me,' she grumbled to Blanche. 'And now he is going to construct a Japanese bridge. I only hope he doesn't plan to paint it red.'

'Of course it won't be red!' Monet snapped. 'What do you take me for? It's to be green, the same colour as the paintwork of the house.'

He spent hours on the site, consulting with Latour-Marliac, planning and supervising the plantings. Blanche welcomed this distraction. On the day of John Leslie's arrival, it was easy to slip away and meet him at Vernon station. She was there far too early, standing on the platform until she saw him alight from the train, his figure moving towards her, indistinct in the smoky atmosphere. He exclaimed as he realised it was she, Blanche, waiting for him, dropping his valise to the ground to take her in his arms.

'It's just so wonderful to see you.'

Tears ran down her face. 'I thought you were gone for ever.'

'But here I am, you see. Large as life and twice as natural.'

She laughed with happiness. 'Oh yes! Listen, shall we not go straight back to Giverny.'

He shrugged. 'Okay, let's go sit in that café.'

They held hands across the table, smiling at one another. He told her about the exhibition he had mounted in Boston, of the success he had had and she described how the haystacks series was enabling the building of the lily pond. Yes, he said, he had read of their success in the papers, it sounded a swell project. She took in his dark hair, the shape of his face, that remembered gaze and felt a simple joy but she knew she had to be strong.

'I had to see you again,' she said. 'It was too abrupt after all we'd had between us. I felt it wasn't finished properly.'

He frowned. 'Blanche, it isn't finished. I know what you said

315

and since then I've realised the tie between you and Monet is more powerful than I understood. But you are a woman, too, and have your life to lead as he has led his.'

She felt the familiar sense of conflict begin all over again.

'Let's see,' he urged. 'Please Blanche, let's see.'

They stepped out into the heat of the June day. The sky was pure blue, the air sweet after the grey, smoky station.

On the road to Giverny, John Leslie gazed about him as if seeing the landscape for the first time, the hedgerows, the lines of poplars. 'You know, I've dreamed of how beautiful it is here.'

The trap set them down outside Hotel Baudy, which was noisier than ever with the new influx of Americans. Reluctantly, Blanche told him she would have to return to the house in case she was missed.

'When shall I see you?' he asked. 'Tonight?'

'We will have to meet in the daytime when Monet is busy.' She sighed. 'There has been a new complication while you've been away. Last winter, Suzanne went skating and met Theodore Butler. Now they want to get married and my mother and Monet are doing their best to keep them apart. He has hardened even more so in his attitude towards you Americans. If he suspects that you and I are meeting also he will be furious and then heaven knows what will happen.'

'That's a blow.'

'I'm sorry,' she said.

'We'll find a way,' he replied.

It was as if they had gone back to the beginning of their courtship. Their meetings were chaste apart from a kiss or touch of hands when they could be alone. However, the separation had sharpened a hunger to talk to one another, a curiosity to satisfy the gaps of knowledge about the other's life, so that they told each stories of their pasts, their likes and dislikes... all those things their early passion had ignored. Blanche had the acute sense of passing time; she felt she wanted to cram in all the questions raised in her mind during his absence, know this man and his life as intensely as she possibly could. John Leslie persisted with Suzanne's belief that love always found a way.

Absorbed in his plans for the water garden, it was some time before it came to Monet's attention that John Leslie had returned.

'I hear that trouble maker is back,' he remarked at supper one evening. 'Painting, so they say.'

Maman met Blanche's eye. 'I believe he is,' she said.

Consideration of Theodore Butler as a possible husband for Suzanne was now underway; it appeared he had the wealth and position John Leslie lacked. Maman had softened towards Blanche and agreed there was no harm in she and John Leslie being painting companions.

Monet had grunted, 'I suppose I can't prevent him, as long as he doesn't come sniffing round here again.'

'I think you have made that perfectly plain.' Maman replied and changed the subject. 'This Japanese bridge you are planning: promise me you will not paint it red.'

'Of course not, you stupid woman,' Monet had replied.

* * *

They often painted in the garden of the Pink House, rented by another American artist, setting up their easels close together but seldom alone, thus satisfying Maman that they were chaperoned. Having initiated his water garden, Monet set off for Rouen where he planned another series, this time of the cathedral. But with the advent of Theodore Butler he wrote constantly to Alice asking for reports of what was going on in Giverny.

317

John Leslie appeared fascinated by the subject of the haystacks, urging Blanche for more details of Monet's technique, his expression of atmosphere and altering light.

'It is such a simple idea but what a breakthrough, to paint the same darn thing over and over. I wish I'd been in Paris to see the exhibition. The questions I would have asked.'

'I don't think you'll have the opportunity of asking them now,' Blanche said.

'Can't you show me how he did it? You were with him all the time.'

'I don't know if I can.'

'Why not?'

She shrugged. Love him as she did, she felt reluctant to share the work of those months, the vision that belonged to her and Monet. But there was more to it than that. She was afraid of what might happen if she showed him her painting of haystacks and explained how she had achieved it.

'I agree with you,' Suzanne said when she confided these thoughts to her sister. 'It's a subject best left alone. I have to say John Leslie is too curious for his own good. You'll never persuade Monet to accept him.'

Blanche clenched her fists. 'Why should it be any different for me than you? Just because you've always known how to get round him.'

Suzanne sniffed. 'Don't be so unkind, Blanche. You know it is difficult for me, too.'

At least I don't criticise Theodore.'

They stared at one another in silence for a moment.

'Oh Blanche, isn't it awful? I don't think it's fair the way he plays the stern father when he isn't even related to us. He did exactly what he wanted when he was young.'

'Yes and then he cheated on Camille.'

318

'You don't know that.'

'No, Suzanne, I don't, but I always felt there was something between Maman and he when we were all living in the chateau. You must remember how the atmosphere changed when Papa was away, those picnics, walking in the forest and singing?'

Suzanne smiled. 'He was a lot more fun then.'

They were calm now, they could never argue for long. They sat on the balcony to drink lemonade and discuss the situation.

'It's all this business over Papa dying,' Blanche said. 'Now the way is clear for Maman to marry Monet.' She refilled her glass. 'Make an honest woman of her. You know how she has always hoped for that. What with that and all this fuss over the lily pond no wonder he is so short tempered. I don't know what we can do.'

Suzanne was adamant. 'We shall go on seeing them, that's all. I refuse to allow him to destroy my happiness.'

If only it were as simple as that, Blanche thought, but perhaps it is where she is concerned. Whereas for me, this battle to capture a will o' the wisp, the goal to reach the essence of light that led one on but often seemed impossible to achieve, bound her to Monet in a way her sister could never fathom. There was always this conflict between art and life.

Nevertheless the knowledge that John Leslie was in Giverny, even if she could not always be with him, sweetened her mood.

'I don't know what I'd do without you,' her mother remarked. 'First it was all he was going through in painting the cathedral, those constant letters full of agony and despair. Now this water garden seems to have gone to Monet's head.'

It was true, mealtimes were dominated by his conversations with Latour-Marliac; how he had tried to prise the secret of hybridisation out of him but that it remained mysterious. He wondered at the nurseryman's palette that ranged from pale yellow to fuchsia and deep red.

319

'My God!' Alice exclaimed one day. 'Can you not speak of something else?'

He gazed at her in surprise. 'What else would you like to talk about, my dear? How the hens are laying? The price of a new hat?'

She threw up her arms in despair. 'Anything, Monet, anything else but those wretched water lilies.'

All the same, everyone had to agree, the new project was coming on splendidly; soon guests were arriving to be taken on a tour by the ecstatic creator.

Away from the house, Blanche continued to sit in the garden of the Pink House and paint alongside John Leslie, trying to live from day to day because she dare not think of the future.

'Don't be such a pessimist, Blanche,' he would tease her. 'You should take a leaf out of your sister's book. She's convinced of a happy outcome.'

In this way, the summer passed until at the beginning of October, John Leslie announced he was starting on a new project. He refused to tell her what it was and for three days she didn't see him.

'I have scarcely seen him myself,' Madame Baudy told her. 'Only for dinner when he devours a great deal and goes straight to bed.'

Blanche waited with a developing prescience that something was not right. A week later when she met him, this was confirmed.

'Ten of them,' John Leslie told her. 'Every day I set up my easel so as to paint exactly the same view in each of the series. Haystacks,' he smiled at her. 'My homage to the master.'

She saw a collection of small canvasses, each depicting three haystacks in an open field with farm buildings and the mass of a gentle ridge. They registered the passing of the hours as if of a

320

single day: a fleeting moment of dawn, the glow of sun edging over the horizon, effect of blinding light from the newly risen sun. Time appeared to pass before her gaze as it moved from canvas to canvas. The warm light of full morning was replaced by shortening shadows in his sixth painting. In the eighth, the still air of late afternoon was portrayed by flattened clouds in a calm, blue sky.

'What do you think of them?'

'They are very well done,' she replied.

So cleverly had he depicted the sense of passing time, that fleeting moment as the sun drops below the horizon, the moon risen over distant trees until in the last painting it hangs above the horizon at twilight. How short life is, she thought, how brief moments of joy and sun filled days.

'Very well done,' she repeated.

'Thank you, I'm pleased with them myself. They are probably my best work to date.'

What has he done? she asked herself and was filled with a sense of dismay. In spite of her trying to guard her unity with Monet, he had managed to intrude.

'I have a feeling when Monet sees these he may change his opinion of me,' John Leslie was saying. 'He told me one did not become an impressionist but I have. Perhaps now he will consider me a suitable beau for you.'

Blanche had returned to the paintings and was now examining them more closely, noting John Leslie's method of applying paint. Colours appeared bleached and muted in the third canvas. The forms of solid objects were so thinly painted that sketch lines could be seen through the pigment. The ninth canvas was dominated by the creeping shadows of dusk, rendered by a vibrating pattern of choppy brushstrokes to simulate the effect of transient light on surfaces. In his small, nervous but controlled

321

touches, she thought she recognised something other than impressionism's broken brushstrokes, pure colour and emphasis on purely visual experience. There was a sense of detachment that reminded her of experimental painters such as Seurat. This struck her as a direct challenge to Monet as if John Leslie were saying: 'Move over old man it's time for something new.' She was convinced that this was also how Monet would see it.

'They are too good,' she said.

John Leslie laughed. 'Not jealous, are you? I wouldn't want a painting to come between us.'

It did not, in the sense he meant but on a far wider scale, Blanche suddenly realised. If you were a painter or other kind of artist for that matter, you never wholly engaged with life or could be utterly faithful in your affections. There came that siren call to step aside, observe and try to recreate. But was it worth it in the end if it set up barriers, evoked rivalry, even hatred?

In that moment, looking back on her eleven-year-old self she wished her father had never invited Monet to the chateau, that she had never come under his influence and, most of all, that she had not been endowed with the gift to paint.

'Put them away,' she said. 'Don't let Monet see them.'

He started to protest but she held up her hand. 'Believe me, it is for the best.'

Monet did see them, of course. Somehow word had got out though from whom? Maybe it had been Robinson, in his naivety, who had spoken of them.

He arrived at the Hotel Baudy and found them, Suzanne, Theodore, John Leslie and Blanche in the middle of a game of tennis. He strode onto the court, pointing his finger at John Leslie.

'You! You young sir! I want you out of Giverny immediately.'

John Leslie threw a ball in the air and caught it. 'What have I done now?'

322

'What have you not done? Not content with continuing to court Blanche, you have had the audacity, the hubris to imagine you can emulate my work, steal my ideas. You are a scoundrel and a thief.'

Blanche met John Leslie's eye and shook her head sorrowfully. He nodded. She had tried to warn him but only now he understood.

'I'd escort you to the railway station this minute, if I had my way.'

'I'll go when I'm ready,' John Leslie retorted.

'And when will that be? I require an answer.'

John Leslie's face darkened. 'Who do you think you are, God? You believe you can control the universe but you won't control me. I wouldn't stay anywhere near you if you paid me. I shall leave, next week.'

'Very well,' said Monet. 'I'll leave you to your game.'

But the pleasure had gone out of the morning. They packed up their tennis racquets, collected the balls and walked back to the hotel. They sat on the terrace and soberly drank lemonade. Before they parted, John Leslie drew Blanche aside.

'I want to take off for a day before I leave,' he said. 'Will you come with me?'

Without hesitation, she answered: 'Yes.'

- THIRTY-FOUR -

ROBERT

'Oh here you are, I've been looking for you everywhere.'

Seated in the hotel garden, a cigarette smouldering between his fingers, Robert watched his friend's arrival with a feeling of dread.

' Aren't you coming for a drink, it's nearly seven?'

'In a minute,' said Robert.

Harry flopped down on the seat beside him. 'God, I'm worn out, I haven't stopped working all day.'

'How did it go?'

'Okay, I think, but it was one of those days when it didn't come easy.'

Robert remarked dryly that in his experience it hardly ever did.

Harry stretched out his long legs with a sigh. 'Ever the optimist, Robert. At least I know exactly where I am with it now, tomorrow it should be finished.'

'Good.'

In the silence, they listened to the melody of a blackbird, its soft tones fluting through the evening air. The notes were liquid and rounded, merging into one another, each phrase slightly different and often ending in a short series of higher pitched trills. Robert relished this peace after the difficult day; Rouen seemed like a bad dream. If only he could turn the clock back and never have launched on that unwise conversation.

'Robert?'

He realised Harry was speaking. 'Sorry?'

'You were miles away. I asked whether you'd got rid of Judith.'

'I think she'll be going soon.'

'You think? You don't know?'

'It wasn't easy, Harry,' he snapped. 'These things aren't.'

He dreaded Harry's reaction if he went on to tell him exactly what had occurred. It made him feel breathless to think about it.

'I did my best. I told her maybe she should consider her folks in America.'

Harry laughed. 'That's you all over, you can never come right out with something. You dance round a subject. Well, you'll just have to take a stronger line.'

Robert sighed. 'All right, all right, Harry.'

'Because I, for one, am sick and tired of seeing that stupid girl around the place. She's a parasite.'

And I am tired of everything and everybody tonight, Robert told himself, even you… no especially you. Love you as I do, there are times when you drive me mad.

'Oh Harry please, stop picking on me. You're not the only one who is tired.'

'Okay, okay.' Harry rose. 'Well, I am going to get that drink. See you at dinner,' he called over his shoulder.

'Maybe,' Robert murmured.

The evening passes, one by one the good-humoured

diners leave the table and make their way to bed. Lights are extinguished and the hotel settles to sleep but for Robert. Restless, he takes his place at the bedroom window and smokes. There is a full moon tonight, it steals silently over the garden, silvering the rose bushes and their blooms, lays a silver patina on the flights of steps, a wicker chair somebody has forgotten to bring in. He imagines the silvery roof of this building, its windows caught in moonbeams, while that scene plays and replays in his mind. Judith taunts him about being middle-aged, the terrible need arises to declare himself to the world, to express what he innately is. He sees again the sly expression creep into Judith's gaze, their mutual recognition that now she holds the cards. 'Your secret's safe with me,' she'd said. But is it? he asks himself yet again. Can she keep it to herself or will it be just too tempting not to spill? If this gets out, he will have to leave Giverny, his haven destroyed. He remembers his earlier thoughts on the frailty of life, its transience in the face of the ancient, wood framed buildings of Rouen. A premonition?

'One cannot help these things,' he speaks to an imaginary critic. 'It has nothing to do with morals or choice. I have committed no sin.' He thinks of how he had always known he was different, from quite a young age. When his friends started to talk about girls, he had tried to join in but it wasn't until he'd turned twenty-one that he understood where his preference lay.

The air was hot and dry and he felt slightly sick with the movement of the picnic wagon. There were about twenty in the party, the men in their ducks, the women with parasols and wide brimmed hats. Florence looked charming in a pale blue summer frock, she did not wear a hat but had

326

wound daisies through her hair. Scott sat up next to the driver and occasionally took the reins.

He saw the woodland his mother had chosen for the picnic, within reach of the river. White tablecloths were laid on the ground and there was a spirit lamp to make tea and coffee. Hammocks were slung between trees and the men carried out folding chairs. There was Scott suddenly next to him, throwing a careless arm round his shoulders, pulling him away from the group.

'Happy birthday, bubba. I wanted to give you this.'

It was the book his father wouldn't have in the house, the adventures of the boy who wanted freedom at all costs. He sniffed the unique scent of never before turned pages, of Mark Twain's latest, not long off the press.

He gave Scott a hug. 'Thank you, It's the best present I could possibly have but I'll have to read it in secret.'

'I thought we'd go up to the mill and read it together. no-one will see us there. Listen, you know I don't much like these affairs, as soon as you can let's slip off and go down to the river. We could maybe have a swim.'

Robert felt himself blush. 'I haven't brought my bathing things.'

Scott met his gaze. 'That's no problem,' he said. 'no-one's going to see us.'

'Oh here you are!' There was Florence, sun and shadow dappled, emerging from the trees. 'I wondered what you boys were getting up to. Hello, Scott.'

'Hello, princess.'

Robert remembered his annoyance at his sister's intrusion. 'I thought you were helping Mother.'

'Oh you know Mother, she thinks nothing is done properly unless she does it herself. Anyway I was bored.'

327

'Oh, we can't have that,' Scott said. 'It's not right for pretty young ladies to be bored now is it, Bobbie?'

'His name's Robert not Bobbie,' Florence pouted. 'You can't call him Bobbie now he's twenty-one years old.' She gave Scott a little push.

He pretended to stagger. 'Hey, hey, protect me, bubba.'

'He's not your brother, he's mine!' Florence pushed him again and Scott took hold of her hands, imprisoning her.

'Little monster.'

'Let me go, let me go!'

Robert saw the teasing expression on her face as she laughed up at him.

'It's not fair, you're so much stronger than I am.'

He thought: she knows what she wants and she will go all out to get it, whatever the cost. Scott was laughing too and he tried to join in, but it was impossible.

'Leave him alone, Florrie.'

He remembered the surge of another, quite unfamiliar emotion. It was jealousy followed by a feeling of helplessness and powerless as his sister continued to flirt with Scott and his friend took it all in his stride. The sun burned his neck and he understood why he wasn't interested in girls.

If Judith provokes Giverny gossip and he is forced to leave this village, which has been his haven for so many years, where would he go? America is out of the question. Morocco?

A cat appears from the dark bushes and slinks through the path of moonlight.

Morocco. They were two Yanks on holiday in Marrakech, striking up a conversation in a bar, extending the evening with dinner in the courtyard of a splendid old house with its potted palms, in the orange glow of lanterns. It started out as a light-hearted occasion but then, as they debated the pronunciation of tagine, their eyes met in an instant of recognition. For two wondrous weeks they had shared Morocco's history, its sublime night skies and fallen in love.

His mind sees the sand hills at sunset on the night they spent in the desert. Soft taupe moving through a spectrum of amber, sienna and gold, the long deep shadows. Then a row of men on camels came sailing across one of those dunes. Darkness, an absolute silence fell and crystal stars in their thousands spread across the sky. He and Harry came from their tent to gaze up at infinity, without words, almost without thought. In the morning, they climbed the seductive dunes but the powdery surface was difficult to walk on. Robert sat and lifted up a handful of sand to watch the fine grains run through his fingers. As he watched it slip from his grasp back into the countless other grains, he imagined infinity must feel like this; footprints in the desert, gone in an hour. It was a good place to contemplate mortality and the passage of time. There was nothing sad nor joyous here, it was just quiet and endless.

In the six years they have been together, they have talked sometimes of going back, but would Harry agree to this running away? He loves his painting life here, the inspiration Normandy offers. He would have to go alone, start all over again. Can he do this at his age?

A few days later, he was out walking when he caught sight of Dorothy Young and her parasol.

Before he could escape she called out to him: 'Why Mr Harrison, so nice to see you. I was saying to Paul only the other night that we hardly ever have that pleasure. You're

329

such a man for keeping himself to himself.' She showed her large teeth in a grin. 'How is your little friend?'

Robert felt his heart beat quicken. 'Friend?'

'Why, dear Judith, of course. Tell me I'm wrong but I have the feeling she is avoiding me.'

'I'm sure that isn't the case,' he replied, shifting his feet, preparing an excuse.

But the woman was having none of it. 'I hope it was nothing I said. I have so much enjoyed our girly chats. She's such a girl for having adventures. Why, the other day she told me such intimate details of Le Pressoir.'

He thought he detected a sly note in her voice but couldn't be sure. All right, so Judith had said she would not be seeing Dorothy again but could he trust her? And if she spoke about him to this chatterbox, it would be round Giverny like wild fire.

'I wouldn't believe everything that young lady says,' he replied. 'She has a romantic imagination.'

Dorothy gave her trilling laugh. 'Oh Mr Harrison, I sure don't think she imagined visiting Monet, nor hearing all his tales about his wife. In my opinion, she has a gift for reportage. She can repeat conversations she has heard verbatim.'

Robert said, dryly, 'I am sure it has been very entertaining. Personally, I think private conversations should be just that. Private.'

Dorothy twirled her parasol. 'I do declare, Mr Harrison, I never put you down as a prude. I can't wait to hear more of her escapades.'

He said he would pass on her invitation, bade her goodbye and went on his way with a heavy heart.

The following morning he breakfasted before Harry was

around. He had packed his easel and materials the night before. His plan was to go out into the countryside and paint. He knew he couldn't go on evading Harry forever; sooner or later he would have to relate that conversation he'd had with Judith and he dreaded his friend's angry reaction. But for the moment, he didn't know what else to do.

– THIRTY-FIVE –

JUDITH

Judith stood at the breakfast buffet table, helping herself to another croissant, aware as she did so that her hunger was not really physical. She felt uneasy with a sense of standing on shifting ground. Earlier, Harry had snubbed her and Robert appeared awkward, avoiding her eye or making banal conversation, as if he hardly knew her. They had soon left and she sat on in the empty dining room, wondering how she could fill the day before her meeting with Michel. She became aware that someone had come into the room and was silently watching her. Judith turned to face Madame Baudy who gazed at her for a moment with an expression of concern.

'A note, mademoiselle,' was all she said, holding out an envelope.

Judith took it, recognising the familiar stationery of Le Pressoir.

'Thank you,' She was about to add she would like some more coffee but Madame Baudy had already left the room.

The croissant forgotten, Judith tore open the envelope, aware her hands were shaking. The note was in Blanche's handwriting.

'Mademoiselle Goldstein: Will you please come to the house on Saturday morning, at ten o'clock. I wish to speak to you. Blanche Monet-Hoschedé.'

It was curt and to the point, without a shred of the former friendliness in its tone.

Judith gazed at the tables, the cast iron stove, the piano in the corner, remembering that first evening she had heard someone play as she sat by the window in her room, gazing out over the twilit garden. She saw herself seated among the painters, watching their faces flushed with wine as they argued over style and theory, compared one impressionist with another, laughed and ate. Oh, that sense of exhilaration, realising she had escaped, that anything now was possible. Now she felt nothing but loneliness.

Perhaps she could visit Dorothy; at least the woman was friendly and did not condemn her behaviour. She followed her own rules and understood Judith's desire to live. Perhaps she might do that. For the moment though, she felt as if she couldn't move, did not want to rise from the table and face the world outside. Time seemed to be running out and she didn't know how to halt it nor change its direction.

Her mood persisted throughout the seemingly endless day. She sat in her room and tried to read, she went out for a walk, which then seemed pointless so she turned back. In the end, she did not visit Dorothy but sat on the terrace with a book, gazing at the words without taking them in until it was time to go back to her room and change.

Half an hour before Michel was due to arrive at the hotel, she walked down the street in the direction he would come. Then she saw him sauntering towards her, stopping to gaze into someone's garden, obviously not wishing to arrive too early.

'Judith!' He seemed to sense her concern. 'What is going on?'

'Listen Michel, we can't meet at Hotel Baudy any more, we've been seen and people are gossiping about us, the garden is out of bounds.'

'Gossiping?'

'You know what it's like here, better than I do. If we're not careful, it will be all round Giverny.'

'Oh la, la! But what can we do? I have been impatient for this moment. I could not wait to see you again.' He seized her hands and pulling her against him, kissed her, daringly, she thought, considering they were in broad daylight.

'Cherie, mon amour.'

She tried to break away. 'Oh do be careful, someone might see us. There's nothing to be done, Michel, don't you see? This place is impossible, there are eyes everywhere.'

'No.' He clung to her. 'I want to be alone with you. I want to make love again. *Dieu*. It was so wonderful. Please, Judith,' he went on, 'Remember how you touched me, remember how you loved it when you got so wet and I came inside you? How did it feel?' As he spoke he was stroking her breast, 'I want you,' he murmured.

She sighed. He was going to be difficult.

'Please, Judith.'

'Listen Michel, I want to talk to you, just talk, do you understand?'

'Very well we will talk.' He smiled at her. 'Then maybe you will change your mind.'

She shrugged. 'But I don't know where.'

'Near the river? There are those trees and bushes. no-one would see us there.'

'Okay, let's go.'

He hurried her down the street, away from Hotel Baudy, past la Musardiere and the door to Le Pressoir, they crossed the road. They plunged into a thicket of trees, shadowy now as the day died.

'Here,' he said.

'No, a little further.'

They pushed through some undergrowth and arrived in a clearing, silent but for the sleepy chirping of birds.

'Here will do,' Michel said. He turned to her. 'Oh Judith, *cherie*, I love you. I haven't stopped thinking about you since that night. You are magnificent.'

His eyes shone with excitement and she realised she was losing control. She spoke sharply. 'I said I wanted to talk to you.'

'Yes, yes, we will talk,' he muttered, 'later, later, first we make love.'

'Michel!'

If she had expected the kisses, the tender caresses of the time before, she was to be disillusioned. Michel seemed to have no time for anything like that. He held her tightly and pushed his hand into her dress, pumping at her breasts, his fingers squeezing hard on her nipples, making her cry out, which only seemed to excite him more. He moaned and pushed her by the shoulders to the ground. She could hear his quick breathing as he pulled down her knickers, roughly rubbing his fingers over her clitoris, all in silence, in an awful hurry with none of the words he had used before. In spite of herself, she felt the moisture welling up as he pushed his fingers further inside her.

335

Then he spoke. 'You are ready?'

'No Michel, I don't like it, not like this. You should use a condom, you really should. It's not safe!' She tried to shield herself with her hand but he pushed it away.

'Yes, yes, ready. You are ready for me.'

She made to raise herself but before she could, he had unbuttoned his trousers and pushed his great penis inside her almost savagely.

'Good,' he grunted. 'So good.'

Nothing mattered to him it seemed but to get inside her and thrust, thrust, thrust before he cried out and collapsed on top of her.

She lay still until he rolled away and when finally she sat up, he was sitting a little distance away, smoking a cigarette.

'Can I have one?' she asked.

He handed her the packet.

Judith pulled at the cigarette angrily.

'What's the matter, Judith?' he asked, at last.

She threw the cigarette away and standing up, arranged her clothes. 'I must go.'

'Oh no, not yet, please.'

'Yes Michel, I must. And that's the end of it, no more of this.'

'The end?'

'Surely you understood?'

'Understood what?"

'That it couldn't go on.'

'But why not? We love each other. I have spoken to my parents and they would like to meet you.'

At the thought of entering the Duval's farmhouse, Judith smiled. 'How could you have ever imagined I would meet your parents? Your family belongs to a completely different world to mine.'

His face clouded over.

'You said you would take me to America. We would drive in a limousine on Fifth Avenue.'

'Oh Michel, I said a lot of things but you must have realised I was only teasing you.'

In the twilight, she saw the gleam of his eyes staring at her. She began to get annoyed. Why couldn't he understand?

'It was just a bit of summer fun.'

'What? What are you saying? Judith, please.'

She didn't know what to add so started to walk back towards the road and he followed. Here she paused for a moment.

'Understood?'

He shook his head. 'Why did you make love to me if you didn't feel anything? Why did you treat me like a dog?'

His words hit home and for a moment there was silence. When she spoke, her tone had changed and was filled with regret.

'Michel, I tell you it is not possible. It is not that I do not like you, you are very nice but I could never take you home and present you to my family as a fiancé. They expect me to marry into another local family, someone of my own class.'

'The same as mine.'

'In a way yes, I with money, you without but whatever, we don't mix.'

He gave a great sigh then said, 'Very well, Judith, but you should remember something in all this, you're not a virgin, any more. I wonder how that would go down with your smart friends, with Madame Blanche, the old man.'

'What do you mean?'

'Maybe I'll spread that news around.'

'If you do that, then you are truly a son of a bitch.'

'You've treated me like one, why shouldn't I behave like one?'

'I am sorry,' she said again and walked away.

– THIRTY-SIX –

BLANCHE

On Saturday morning at precisely ten o'clock, Blanche opened the door and found Judith waiting there. She thought the young woman looked paler than usual and was quite plainly dressed, apprehensive, one might say. Then she dismissed the idea because it had no bearing on this encounter.

'Good morning, madame.' Judith's voice also sounded subdued.

'Good morning, mademoiselle, if you would please follow me.'

She led the way into the dining room, it was far enough away from the studio to prevent Monet from overhearing. She had ordered coffee to be served in half an hour, believing this gave her enough time to say what she had to say. They sat on two of the chairs that ranged round the room and Blanche caught Judith give a swift glance to the Japanese geisha girls, as if seeking their support.

'What a beautiful morning,' she began. 'As I walked along the road, I couldn't believe how blue the sky was and I saw the most gorgeous deep red rose.'

Certainly,' agreed Blanche. 'But we are not here to talk about the weather.'

Judith widened her eyes. 'Ah, and what are we here for, madame?'

Self-possessed as always, this young woman, Blanche thought. We'll see about that. She pulled down the cuffs of her blouse feeling she was preparing for a fight.

'I will come straight to the point. You are no longer welcome as a visitor to the house and certainly not to see my stepfather.' Her words hung on the air, unremarked by the geisha girls, bent on continuing their secret, inner lives.

'Why?' asked Judith.

'I don't think there is need to go into reasons.'

'Oh isn't there?' Judith glared at her. 'You can't just summon me here, dismiss me without telling me why.'

Oh dear, thought Blanche, I knew it wasn't going to be easy, not with someone like Judith, unaccustomed to people denying her anything.

'I think you'll find I can,' she replied. 'You have been admitted here as a special favour and now, I am sorry to say, that favour has to be withdrawn.'

Judith seemed unable to sit still any longer. She rose and walked about the room. 'Because you are jealous of me, madame, that is what it is, isn't it?'

Yes, of course I am, Blanche said silently. Jealous of her young strength and power, the way she looks, her expectations of life. Why not admit it? I am jealous.

She gave a short laugh. 'How do you come to that conclusion?'

'Monet needs me. Since I have been coming here, he has regained his enthusiasm for life. You told me yourself how much he enjoys my company. He is working well and I make him laugh, I encourage him to do something about his eyes. Whereas you, madame, make him fearful.'

I who have dedicated my life to him, then and now, taking on the role of assistant, house keeper and almost surrogate wife! Blanche was angry now. 'Oh I see, little Joan of Arc come to save us from ourselves. You are a romantic, mademoiselle, and you know what happens to romantics? They are doomed.'

Now it was she who rose and gesticulated with her arms.

'It is time you woke up and saw yourself as you really are. You have no idea of this culture neither do you belong here. You are just a parasite, a nouveau riche. You lie, you have told both my stepfather and me a pack of lies, pretending you were a painter, that you admired my work. I don't know why you came here, not for any artistic reason that's for sure. What you have succeeded in doing is upset people.' She paused to take breath.

Judith moved to gather up her bag. 'How dare you speak to me like this, you provincial, old woman. I'm not staying here to be insulted.'

Blanche shook her head. 'I haven't finished with you yet. There is something I wish to know: have you been consorting with the young under gardener, with Michel?'

'What?'

'You heard what I said. Have you?'

Judith had closed her eyes for a moment, now she opened them and glared at Blanche. 'An under gardener! What on earth would I be doing with someone like that?'

This threw Blanche for a moment. Was the girl telling the truth or was she a good actress?

'It has been known,' she continued, 'young ladies leading innocent young men on. My laundry maid believes you have been seen with him.'

'And you're going to take the word of a servant against mine?'

Blanche remembered Lilli's anxiety, her own sudden conviction it was true. 'She is more than a servant, mademoiselle. She is a beautiful, young woman who was walking out with Michel until something happened, a short while ago. I do not intend anyone to ruin that for her.'

Judith's smile mocked her. 'Well, that's just dandy,' she said. 'Condolences to them both for a life of struggle ahead and bringing all those God damn children into this world.'

There came a knock on the door and Annette stumped in with a tray. 'Coffee, madame.'

'No coffee for me,' Judith said.

Blanche smiled at Annette. 'I don't think we'll be needing it after all, thank you, Annette.'

As the door closed, she spoke with a fresh vehemence.

'You are not welcome in this house, mademoiselle. I shall instruct the servants not to admit you.'

Judith rose. 'The only person you'll be hurting is your stepfather.' She moved towards the door. 'But at least, you'll have him back in your power, which I can imagine is your intention.'

How am I going to break it to him? Blanche thought.

'He doesn't want you to come again. He has told me you are a disturbing influence,' she lied.

– THIRTY-SEVEN –

CLAUDE

August and the garden burns with colour. There is a fine show of dahlias: the vibrant vermilion of Bishop of Llandaff, exquisite Clair de Lune with its lemon yellow outer petals and paler inner segments, and the pastel baby pom pom, which always touches his heart. One of his favourite asters is out, a mass of lavender blue; it makes a cool contrast to the hotter shades. Claude walks down the main path, stepping over the carpet of nasturtiums, yellow, red and orange. They sprawl, they creep, invade space wherever they can, clamber over other plants, but he loves their good-natured growing. It is impossible to feel down hearted on a morning such as this, full of activity, demanding his attention.

'Lovely aren't they, m'sieur?' Breuil has come to stand beside him and together the two men share this vision, explosion of colour, array of varieties.

'No sign of any aphids,' Claude remarks with satisfaction. 'Remember last year, the trouble we had. It broke my heart to see the damage those little beasts did.'

'Ah, you can thank young Michel for that.'

'Michel? Didn't know he was an expert on pest control.'

'You'd be surprised. He's come up with a wonderful solution, something his father uses on the farm.'

Claude thinks back to the last conversation he had with the young man. Gardening seemed to be the last thing on his mind, boy wanted to travel, he'd said.

'Saponaria,' Breuil is saying. 'Natural and most effective.'

'The highly invasive rock plant, hmm.'

'Yes, but that's the beauty of it. You always have a plentiful supply. What you do is mix up the leaves, or roots for that matter, with water. Sieve to obtain the liquid and then spray it on the plants.'

'And it works?'

'You can see for yourself. Not an aphid in sight, the soapy water kills them.'

Claude beams at the unblemished pompom, its bright cherry red centre, and thinks of Michel with new respect.

'So you're pleased with him, are you?'

'It's like this: he was eager at the start, interested to learn and he picked things up quickly. I told you myself how promising he was.'

'And you don't say those things lightly,' Claude smiles.

'I have my standards, m'sieur.' As if to demonstrate, he leans over and nips off a couple of fading flowers.

'I know you do and very admirable they are.'

'Thank you. As I say, he promised well but then, some weeks ago, he began to appear distracted, forgetful. I had to pull him up on several things left undone. I was beginning to think…' he shrugs. 'Ah well, as it turns out…'

'He seems to have come to his senses?' Claude suggests.

'Exactly that.'

'Good, I like the young man. He has had the strength to rebel against his family's wishes.' Claude remembers the

344

brush he had with Michel's father when he had the first small pond dug: all that nonsense about his 'strange plants' and how they might poison the water. 'Old man Duval is something of a tyrant. It can't have been easy for him.'

A breeze stirs the cosmos and sets them aquiver like pale pink and white butterflies.

'I think he has the makings of a good gardener. Encourage him all you can, Breuil. We'll none of us be around forever.'

How impossible it seems, to leave all this beauty and step into the void, he has no time for religious hopes of a life hereafter. Nature in all its variety uplifts his soul, astonishes so that the mind is entirely filled with the experience and is the experience. This is the nearest he comes to worship.

That time on Belle Isle as he watched the mountainous waves rise and fall, dash themselves furiously against steep cliffs, toss the spray high into the air, what ecstasy to see that sea in fury. Desolation when it calmed too quickly. He sees himself dressed in oilskins, the wind trying to snatch his palette and brushes from his hand, sea soaked, tempest battered in the grip of the sublime. Terror on the edge of beauty.

It is foolish to allow himself to think of extinction when he has work to do, important work. Probably my crowning achievement, he tells himself sternly as he leaves Breuil and goes in search of Michel.

He enters the water garden and goes to stand on the Japanese bridge, gazing down into the water where clouds are reflected, so that above and below, sky and water commingle. Near the edge of the pond, the light is dim and the muted surface of the water reflects the dense curtain of foliage that shades its rim. His mind shifts and meditates on

345

the changing light and colour, how he will capture it, how he will present his concept of water without horizon or bank.

'M'sieur?'

He shakes his head as if to clear it of the mist of his thoughts. A young man is standing on the far side of the pond with a box of something in his arms. It is Michel.

'Well then, what have you got there?'

'The iris, m'sieur, ready for planting.'

'I'll be right with you.'

Breuil has made it perfectly plain he thinks there are sufficient iris in these gardens, but Claude knows better. The rhizomes bring a smile to his face, irresistibly they remind him of turds, the dark, rather skinny turds the kitchen cat sometimes leaves in the garden. He thinks it is amazing what will spring from them. There will be one variety that is dark as printer's ink with a hint of maroon in the ebony black tints. Another will produce deep purple falls and a white standard. A third will yield an apricot fall edged with white and tipped with tangerine beards.

'Nice and moist,' he murmurs. 'Feel them, Michel, just as they should be. They should never be allowed to dry out.'

'Yes, m'sieur.'

'Now I suppose you have never planted iris before, true? This is how you do it: the iris rhizome needs to be planted so the top surface of each bulb is exposed to air and sunlight. My method is to make a depression in the soil and fashion a little mound in the centre. I set the iris bulb on the mound, spread out the roots and use my hands to pull soil up around the sides of each bulb, leaving the surface so I can see it. Have a go.'

The boy is quick to understand and Claude watches, nodding his approval as the second rhizome is put into place.

346

'And how about you, Michel?' Claude remembers Breuil's remark about distraction. 'Have you managed to convince those parents of yours that you are doing a serious job?'

Michel looks impatient as if he would like to be allowed to finish this job. 'They are resigned, m'sieur. At least I bring in a wage. It has been difficult to persuade them but I think they realise I like this work.'

'So you have decided to settle down?'

The young man sighs. 'Yes m'sieur, I suppose I have.'

'No more wanderlust?'

'That is for the wealthy, I have realised that.'

'You need a companion, it can be a lonely job if you are on your own.'

Michel frowns.

'You don't want to be living with your parents for the rest of your life.'

'Oh la la, never that.'

'Find yourself a good wife, that's my advice. Have some children, they give you roots.'

Here am I handing out advice I never thought I'd take myself, he muses. 'You'll have someone to look after you in your old age.' As I have poor old Blanche, he thinks. 'But of course, your turn will come before that.'

Michel shrugs. 'My sisters will do that job.'

Thank God for women, Claude tells himself. And thank God, I wasn't born one. I'd never have done what I have, otherwise.

He leaves Michel to his work and turns back to the house. His eye is caught by the brilliant scarlet of a group of field poppies, which he happily allows to mingle with his cultivated varieties. Beautiful, delicate poppies that only last a few days before their silky petals scatter. He thinks of the old wives' tale: place a poppy petal in the palm of your hand and strike it with the fist. If it produces a snapping sound then the loved one is faithful. Poppies were Alice's favourite flower, there was no need to test for faithfulness in her, nor all those other women in his life: Aunt Marie-Jeanne, Camille and Blanche, especially Blanche: angels, all of them, supporting his moods, watching over his inspiration. But what of Judith, where does she come in all this? Seductive Judith enticing him out of his old age to make him believe new things are possible; he cannot put her out of his mind, whatever Blanche might say.

– THIRTY-EIGHT –

JUDITH

Rain fell throughout the night in a persistent drizzle. Each time Judith awoke, she lay and listened to the gentle, steady downpour. When she finally got out of bed, it had slackened and, as she sat at her bedroom window, the sun broke through and across the sky arched a rainbow. She gazed and gazed at the colour spectrum and was sorry when it faded and the rain stopped. She dressed quickly, glanced at the opened letter lying on the bedside table and decided against breakfast. As she stepped out of the hotel into the street, she saw the sun's growing heat had already drawn moisture from the surface of the road and the air smelled sweet. She had only gone a few yards when she saw, ahead of her, Dorothy's bobbing parasol and hurried to catch up with her.

Dorothy gave her a wry smile. 'Oh my, look who's here.'

'How are you, Dorothy?'

'Fine and dandy, thank you, but where have you been hiding yourself?'

Judith apologised. She felt absurdly relieved to be speaking to someone, anyone, but Dorothy was still eyeing her quizzically.

'I thought I might have upset you,' she said at last. 'I did send a message by Mr Harrison, inviting you for tea but I never heard anything back.'

Judith shook her head. 'He never told me.' She felt tears welling up and tried to blink them away. 'I wish he had.'

Dorothy patted Judith's arm. 'Honey, what is it?'

She couldn't speak, the events of these past days flooding over her: Robert, Michel, Blanche and now the letter. It was just too much. The tears ran down her face and she sniffed and fumbled in her bag for a handkerchief.

'Here, have mine.'

A lacy one was thrust into her hand, it smelled quite strongly of Dorothy's perfume. She dabbed her face and blew her nose, but the tears kept coming. 'It's all just too awful,' she muttered.

Dorothy took her arm. 'Oh dearie, come along. We'll go back to the house and have some coffee. You can tell me all about it.'

Judith allowed herself to be led along the street. They were in the picture hung parlour once more. As the door closed behind them, she felt she had stepped into a haven. She gazed around her, seeming to see the room with a fresh eye. The somewhat worn and threadbare carpet, the cheap material of the flowery upholstery were homely and welcoming. She sank into one of the rosewood chairs, catching the scent of lilies in a vase nearby. Nothing awful, she felt, might happen to her here, no cruel words or rejection, only the sense of being safe and protected.

'Lord knows what's happened but you sure do look washed out.' Dorothy stood over her, an anxious expression on her face. 'Slip your shoes off, honey, and rest your feet on this little stool.'

350

Judith obeyed and lay back in the chair, feet propped up while Dorothy fussed about her, drawing up a little side table.

'Coffee will be ready in just one moment, then we can have a nice little talk.'

Soon there came the rich scent of good coffee and a plate of almond biscuits was set on the table beside her. Judith sipped and felt her body relax. She didn't want to talk but just be, after all these days of tension and striving, but Dorothy was curious.

'Aren't you going to tell me what's been going on?' she asked. 'The last time I saw you, I'd say everything was hunky dory.'

'It was,' Judith set down her cup. 'Absolutely.'

'Then what happened?'

She sighed. 'It just did.'

'So tell me about it.'

'I really don't know where to begin.' The almond biscuits were nutty and sweet, they tasted like those long ago favourites of her childhood.

'Shall we start with your beau? Your young gardener?'

'Michel.' Judith dabbed the handkerchief to her eyes as fresh tears threatened. She saw in her mind's eye his intent gaze, the gleam of dark hair in the sunlight. She heard his whispered words as he made love to her, *'mon amour.'* 'Oh Dorothy, I did what you said, I flirted, I led him on.'

'How do you mean?' Dorothy took yet another almond biscuit. 'How far did you go? Was it just a bit of spooning or...?'

'More than that. Much more.'

There came a silence in the room and Judith wondered again if she could possibly be pregnant. Aunt Flo had not arrived but that was not unusual, especially if she were anxious.

'So, you had fun?' Dorothy rose and refilled their cups.

'Well, yes, at first, but then he got so serious. He thought I'd take him to America.'

Dorothy frowned. 'Oh, Judith, honey.'

'I just got carried away. Of course, I didn't mean it but he thought I did. He talked about introducing me to his parents.'

'You, to his parents?'

'I know and I tried to explain.'

'You should never have let it go that far,' Dorothy patted Judith's cheek. 'But I forget, you're so young, so inexperienced.' She sighed, 'Maybe I shouldn't have encouraged you.'

Surprised by her reaction, Judith shook her head. 'No, I was foolish, that's all. Foolish and cruel and I used him. I just hope he goes back to that girl of his and forgets all about me.'

Dorothy sighed. 'Lordy, lordy! Tell you something, I don't do it often but I think this calls for a cigarette. I'll just creep into Paul's studio and steal his.'

They drank coffee and smoked. Judith spoke and Dorothy listened. She told of the meetings at Hotel Baudy, 'so romantic, he said I was his little love.'

'But then he became so possessive, questioning my every movement, ogling me all the time. I couldn't stand it any longer so I just told him, plain and simple, it had to end.'

'Poor, misguided young man,' Dorothy murmured.

'Don't say that.'

'Why not?' Dorothy set her cup back on the tray. 'Seems like he had really fallen for you and believed love could conquer all.'

352

At that moment, Judith had the sensation of awakening from a dream, as if only now was she seeing things as they really were.

'It was my fault,' she said. 'I led him on. I offered him champagne and talked about travel and America. I flirted. He's never been outside Normandy. It must have seemed very glamorous, so different from his everyday life. But I never dreamed he'd imagine we had a future together.'

She saw herself wearing the slinky frock with the low neck, urging Michel to have another cocktail, walk in the garden, alone with her. She remembered how awkward he had looked on the evening he first arrived at the hotel, dressed in the ill-fitting suit. They came from two different worlds, how could he have ever imagined it could be more than a fling?

'Well, you did what was probably best,' Dorothy put in. 'No good feeling guilty about it, honey.' She held out the box of cigarettes. 'Go on, take another, Paul won't mind.'

Judith took up the lighter.

'It's not only that, as if it wasn't bad enough, then there has been Robert. Almost as soon as I came here, he was going on and on at me about returning to America. I thought he was being so unfair, considering he does as he pleases.'

Dorothy blew a perfect circle of smoke into the air and regarded it proudly. 'That old queen,' she said.

There was a pause while Judith took this in. 'So you know?'

'Of course I know. Him and that Adonis blond, all muscle and no brain.'

'Robert told me no-one knew here.'

Dorothy laughed. 'Not the locals, maybe, but I didn't live

in Paris for nothing, except that they carry it off a damn sight better there. Robert! Jumpy as a Mexican bean, always afraid someone is going to find out, and yet he has the cheek to disapprove of me. Oh, I know he does, looking down that long nose of his. At least I'm normal.'

'You surprise me.'

'Little Judith, there is a lot that would surprise you once you'd been here as long as I have. It is amazing what people get up to, the tricks they can play. That's what I meant when I said a vacation is fine but it doesn't do to live here. Things get messy and life isn't such fun, any more.'

Judith realised she was paying attention as never before, listening intently to what Dorothy said.

'I know you thought I was a spoil sport.' She bit on an almond biscuit, 'or even jealous because you are young and pretty.' She paused. 'Isn't that what you thought?'

Judith examined her nails. 'Maybe,' she said.

'I suppose I was just trying to save you heartache. But I guess in the end, one can't pass on experience, we all have to go through it for ourselves.'

Another hour passed while they talked. Judith produced the letter she had received the day before, from America.

'They want me to go home. Mother says they have indulged me enough and it is time I knuckled under.'

'She means marry your fiancé, what was his name… Charlie? Is that such a bad thing? He sounds like a nice young man.'

'Oh he is, very nice, but I'm not at all sure I love him.'

Dorothy stretched out her arms and laughed. 'Oh, love! Look where it's got me: looking for amusement because I am often so bored. Soon I'll lose my looks and who's going to be interested in me then? America's waiting for you,

354

you'll have a good life there and, as I keep on saying, it's more important the man loves you. Judith, you've had these beautiful months in Giverny, short but sweet I know, but it really is best you keep it that way.'

She felt Dorothy might be right but she had had such dreams.

'I know, honey, and it's hard to accept things don't turn out the way we'd like them to. But I promise you, you'll be fine.'

It was early afternoon by the time Judith left Dorothy. She stepped out into the sun, almost surprised to find herself there. During the last few hours, her world had shifted and decisions had been made. She hesitated, at a loss of what to do, then started to walk towards the river. Here she sat, staring at the perfect mirror image of poplar trees in the water, as if they inhabited that second, watery world. Then a small row boat appeared with a man at the oars and the water quivered and fragmented the reflection. Judith thought back over the past weeks. It had been a magical time when everything seemed to contrive for her happiness, as if fate were truly on her side. And now, seeing it in retrospect, she thought how foolish she had been, ignoring everything that was said to her. Voices came into her mind, words that reasoned but were also hostile. There had been Robert on the day they had gone into the countryside to paint. 'It is called being accountable for your actions, Judith, of being aware of their repercussion on others. That is why you would never fit in.'

He had tried to warn her that her behaviour was causing problems, that such things were not 'done here'.

Then Dorothy: 'Live here for some time and the attraction wanes. You realise the differences in culture, the fact that the locals don't accept you, will never accept you.'

Michel had asked: 'why did you make love to me if you didn't feel anything? Why did you treat me like a dog? You're not a virgin anymore. I wonder how that would go down with your smart friends, with Madame Blanche, the old man.'

That stepdaughter of Monet's, Blanche, had been the most outspoken.

'It is time you woke up and saw yourself as you really are. You have no idea of this culture, you don't belong here. You are just a parasite, a nouveau riche. You lie, you have told both my stepfather and me a pack of lies, pretending you were a painter, that you admired my work. I don't know why you came here, not for any artistic reason that's for sure. What you have succeeded in doing is upset people.'

She realised that all of them had sent the same message, telling her she could never realise her dream. There was nothing left but to go home but, before she did, she would try to make amends.

In her room, she wrote a letter to Blanche and gave it to the boy to take to Le Pressoir. Now the person she had to see was Robert.

– THIRTY-NINE –

BLANCHE

Blanche was dismayed to notice a long tear on the right sleeve of her favourite blouse. She had been wearing it when she picked roses for the house, yesterday, but did not remember snagging it on the thorns. As she went to the window to examine it, she caught sight of Michel and Lilli in the early morning garden and lingered, watching them. They seemed to be in serious conversation and there was a moment when the young gardener took Lilli's hand. Then they parted, he down the garden, she presumably back into the house. What was all that about? Blanche was intrigued.

The dining room was empty. Papa had obviously breakfasted and gone to his studio. She sat and waited, thinking yet again that the room was decidedly too yellow, until Annette stomped in with the coffee pot. She appeared to be in a bad mood, dumping a basket of bread and dishes of butter and jam onto the table.

Blanche smiled at her. 'Just eggs, this morning please, Annette, I am not very hungry.'

'Yes, madame.' Annette's expression was grim.

After rather a long pause, the girl returned with a tray on which were a plate of fried eggs and also a letter.

'Come just now, madame,' she muttered.

There was only one person who wrote to her on Hotel Baudy stationery. She slit the envelope and drew out a sheet of notepaper. In the now familiar calligraphy, Judith wrote:

Dear Madame Blanche,

Please accept my sincere apologies for any problems I may have caused you or M. Monet during my stay in Giverny. Since our conversation, I have been thinking over all you said and I realise I had not understood the French way of life, nor your position in the household. You must believe that I did not come here with the intention of harming anyone. I suppose all I wanted was to be happy, but that should not have meant at the expense of other people's happiness. I have now decided it is best that I return to America and I have written to my parents to arrange a passage on the *Mauritania*. You have been very generous towards me, madame. Please would you grant me one last favour? Would you allow me to say goodbye to M. Monet?

Yours sincerely,

Judith Goldstein

Blanche laid the letter down and stared at the cooling eggs. She buttered bread and sipped some coffee, scarcely noticing what she did. Judith's words sounded sincere and it was a well-crafted letter over which she had evidently given thought. Perhaps Lilli had been wrong in suspecting an involvement with Michel. The question was, what should she do about it? On the one hand, the young woman was going away so what harm could there be in granting such a simple request but... Blanche wished she could be more decisive. She was always able to see the other person's point of view.

Throughout the morning, she went about her tasks with Judith's words murmuring in her head. While she discussed the day's menus with Marie and tried to concentrate on household accounts, her mind was busy elsewhere. Had she been wrong in her judgement of the situation, taking out on Judith what was truly within herself? Had she just become a bitter, middle-aged spinster, jealous of youth, terrified of losing any power she had?

Trout with almonds for luncheon with some very good spinach and pommes frites; her stepfather ate heartily, she with little appetite. She enquired, without really caring, whether he had had a fruitful morning and he replied that he had.

Over dessert, a pear tart with a slightly too sweet frangipane base, he suddenly said, 'I am thinking of paying a visit to Paris to see another specialist.'

He glanced expectantly at Blanche and she thought, I am not going to lose my temper, nor try to warn him off. I am sick and tired of taking responsibility. 'Very well, Papa,' was all she said. 'You must do as you think best.'

'I want to ask his opinion of the success rate with cataract operations in America,' he continued, pouring extra cream over his tart. 'Mademoiselle Judith has been most encouraging. She told me of several experiences of her father's friends.'

Judith. She thought of the letter again but said nothing.

'I find it strange there has been no word from the girl.'

Blanche rose to fetch the plum brandy.

'She's young, Papa. You know what the young are like. Perhaps she is amusing herself elsewhere.'

359

He grunted. 'She gave the impression that she enjoyed my company and I certainly enjoyed hers. Make some enquiries, Blanche. I would like to see her again.'

In the afternoon, Blanche checked the little cupboards for their store of eggs and decided to collect some more. She left the house and stopped briefly at the foot of the steps to gaze at the white frilled skirts of fuchsia blossoms, contrasting beautifully with their red sepals – like a host of little dancers. How simple the natural world, she thought, and how complicated the lives of human beings. This garden was content to grow, to bloom and then to die, to accept the changing seasons without regret for the past or fear of the future. The loud crowing of the rooster broke into her thoughts and she crossed to the hen run, discreet under a big fig tree.

As she opened the wire door and stepped inside, she entered a peaceful, feathered world. Hens strutted across the floor but many of the fat brown birds were sitting, quiet apart from a little chirping or clucking, others were eating or drinking. Clean and calm, they turned their inquisitive eyes to stare at her without fear. She was known to them as they were to her. They were her special task and she had come to understand them as thinking, feeling creatures who showed love and care for their young. They enjoyed dust bathing, nest building and seemed to form friendships. Each one of them had a name and now Genevieve came clucking towards her. As she sat on a stone slab, Eloise climbed into her lap. Blanche closed her eyes and sniffed the warm scent of the birds. She felt soothed and comforted, listening to the soft cluck cluck, the occasional cry of the rooster.

'Oh madame, here you are.' It was Lilli.

Blanche gave a start and immediately felt embarrassed to be discovered here, mistress of the house, with a chicken sitting in her lap.

'What is it, Lilli?' She spoke sharply and saw the girl flinch.

'I wondered if I might have a word, madame.'

Blanche sighed and, lifting the chicken off her lap, came out through the door, shutting it carefully behind her.

'Beg pardon, but I only wanted to tell you that Michel has apologised to me. He would like us to walk out together again.'

'Isn't that what you wanted?'

Lilli shook her head. 'I am not sure, madame. He behaved very badly towards me. Do you think I should accept his apology?'

'I cannot tell you what to do, Lilli,' she replied. 'You must listen to your heart and follow it.'

'Yes madame, beg pardon for troubling you.'

'I am sorry, I didn't mean to sound harsh,' said Blanche. 'I just seem to have lost confidence in my ability to advise anyone about anything. I tried to encourage you but I didn't know what kind of young man he was. I feel I am of no help to anyone.'

Lilli was immediately all sympathy. 'But you have been to me, I'll never forget all you've done, madame. I just wish you could be happy, too.'

That's all any of us wants, Blanche thought, not money or success when it comes down to it, but to be happy.

As usual, she decided to go to the church with some flowers to lay on her mother's grave. 'You always seemed to know what to do,' she told her. 'When we were children, the time Marthe had that accident you sprang into action.

361

You nursed Suzanne but you became so angry with the doctors because they hadn't diagnosed her complaint. You never stood any nonsense.'

Blanche thought of the rumours that her mother had destroyed all letters and paintings of Camille. She could certainly be very jealous. Then there was her anger over the painting of Suzanne with a parasol, 'using my daughter to conjure the ghost of Camille.' In Blanche's eyes the pose might be similar, but there lacked the presence of the dead wife.

Maman saw things in black and white. She would have said, 'get rid of this American girl, she has caused you enough trouble, let her go.' But as she undressed for bed, Blanche was still undecided as to what to do about the letter.

– FORTY –

ROBERT

'I can't believe it. She is actually leaving this place.' Harry set down his beer glass and leaned back in his chair with a sigh. 'Maybe we can get back to how things used to be.'

'Yes,' said Robert. But can we? He asked himself. The effect of Judith's presence in Giverny would take a long time to fade. Even if other people forgot her, he never would. She had encouraged him with her quest to affront her destiny at whatever cost, she had helped him understand that his own actions had been not to run away from life but to embrace it in his own fashion. She had envied and applauded him before she knew his reasons why, and he regretted he had spoken and perhaps disillusioned her. Judith was a romantic. Her problem had been that she could not see the repercussions of attempting to live a fictional life... until last night, he reminded himself. She had not meant to do harm. Robert stared down at the deserted tennis courts, trying to understand his emotions.

'Well, I think this calls for a celebration,' Harry was saying. 'Let's have another beer.'

'Not for me, thanks.' Robert lit a cigarette.

'No? Well I'm having one.'

He rose from his chair. Robert, watching him as if he were a stranger, saw a tall, fine muscled man, tanned skin, hair bleached by the sun. A man with the assurance of youth, far more like Judith than he would wish to believe. Harry waved at the serving girl, indicating his empty glass. She was busy with customers at another table and paid him no attention.

'Hey,' he called. 'Over here.'

'One moment, m'sieur.'

Harry sat down again. 'Damn the girl.'

Again Robert was reminded of Judith, how she too wore self-esteem with the same flair as she did her clothes. 'The world doesn't revolve round you, Harry,' he said quietly.

Harry laughed. 'Someone's in a bad mood. What's up?'

'Believe it or not, I am quite upset over this question of Judith. When she told me she was leaving, she was so emotional and repentant for anything she thought she might have done wrong. To be honest, I felt sorry for her.' He remembered those dark eyes filled with tears, the regret in her voice.

'Oh my God!' Harry struck the table with his fist. 'What is the matter with you, Robert? I thought you agreed with me that the girl was a damn nuisance, that she didn't belong here and now you say you feel sorry for her.'

'Life is not all black and white, Harry. When you're my age, you'll discover how many in betweens there are.'

Harry acknowledged the second glass of beer with a curt nod. 'Listen to the wise old man talking,' he sneered. 'You sound like you're eighty not fifty.' He reached over and took a cigarette from Robert's pack, flicked the lighter, exhaled a stream of smoke. He picked up his glass and, turning his body away, nodded to a group of painters at another table.

Something about these actions infuriated Robert. 'You know what you are?' he demanded. 'Completely self-centred. Nothing must disturb your life and if it does, you can't, or rather won't take it. Sometimes I wonder if there is any room in it for me.'

Without looking at him, Harry remarked that that was nonsense.

But Robert was adamant. 'It's not nonsense.' He rose and walked away. He heard Harry call after him, but he did not turn back.

He went towards the river, a route that Judith took. He knew because she had told him, and of the bench where she'd said she went when she wanted to think. He walked until he found it, sat down and held his face to the sun, closing his eyes. Silence and stillness, when he looked again, he saw the mirror image of poplars in the green water. A pair of ducks skidded onto the surface and the reflection splintered for a moment, then came together again.

His mind returned to yesterday evening, the dining room noisy with voices and laughter as the evening meal began. He saw the gleaming faces of artists, some of them far more talented than he, but known at Hotel Baudy as David, Gustave and Richard; jugs of wine and baskets of bread were set on the red checked tablecloths. He had just raised his glass when he caught sight of Judith in the doorway. As she came into the room, he thought he had never seen her look more beautiful. However much she had sheltered from the sun, it had warmed the extreme paleness of her skin so that it gleamed like old ivory; the lamplight burnished her hair, bringing out its auburn tints.

She was wearing the gauzy Fortuny gown, it sheathed her body and rippled with those shimmery shades that had reminded him once of an exotic moth. How long ago that seemed. And yet, as she approached the table and sat among them, time seemed to fold up and she was once again the young woman without a care in the world, delighted when he admired her clothes. She was charming and flirted a little. She sipped wine and asked him about his day. Painting, or had he just been playing tennis? She winked and he could not help comparing her humour with the severity of Harry.

When the chicken chasseur arrived and everyone was delving among the mushrooms and shallots, fishing for a choice piece of chicken, a discussion began, turning again to impressionism and its genesis.

Richard spoke of the developments in colour theory, the painters' search for its exact analysis and light in nature. 'An impressionist painter depicting an orange, for example, might break up the shadow with dashes of complementary blue.'

Photography came into it, added Gustave. 'Remember, back in those days it was still naïve: all that cropping to improve the composition, those shapes and forms at the edge of the image? If you look at *Four Dancers*, you'll see how Degas used precisely that technique.'

David broke in to suggest the influence of Japanese prints was probably the most important, particularly where Monet was concerned. 'Those compositions of the Ukiyo-e masters.'

'Ukiyo-e, yes,' Judith exclaimed. 'Now I know what you are talking about: pictures of the floating world, moments in people's lives, the change of the seasons.'

366

Moments in people's lives, Robert thought, ah yes, and how fleeting.

Judith was gesticulating, aware she had the others' attention. 'When I visited Monet, he told me all about them. His favourites are... hmm, let me think, yes, Hokusi, Hiroshige and... and Utamaro.'

The girl has a photographic memory, Robert marvelled. He was taken by her rapt expression.

She drained her glass and leaned towards her audience.

'Now listen to this; Monet told me a wonderful story. He once found a marvellous collection of those prints in a shop in Amsterdam. He was bargaining over some china, Delft, I think, when all of a sudden he spotted them, piled in a dish. The salesman didn't seem to understand their value and let him have them with the china jar. There! What do you think of that?'

They were impressed, Robert could see that. His usually boisterous companions were quiet, digesting this.

Then David spoke: 'That sure is a swell story, miss. And Monet told you himself?'

'He certainly did.'

'Darn me, don't know how you do it. None of us has ever got that near to the miserable old so and so.'

'Well, let's face it,' Gustave retorted. 'You're not twenty-five and pretty as a picture like our young lady here.'

There was a roar of laughter and someone refilled Judith's glass. She rose to her feet, the wonderful dress shifting colour with every movement she made. She held her glass to the light so that the red glowed within, her eyes glittered. He had to hand it to her, Robert thought, the girl had a perfect dramatic sense.

'A toast. A toast to Monet!'

'To Monet.'

They drank and went back to their absorption with the satisfying chasseur.

David leaned across the table. 'So tell us what else Monet told you?'

'Where do I start?' replied Judith.

She was off, describing the visits she had made, the stories he had told her of his early life and how he had finally achieved success. 'I have sat with the great man in his studio, I have walked with him in his beautiful gardens, he has made sketches of me. Once he said he would like to paint me.'

The words rang with nostalgia, though Robert wondered who would notice except he who knew her so well.

As the dessert plates were taken away and the cheese brought in, Richard rose and carried his glass over to the piano and lifted the lid. Once again, Robert listened to *Silvery Moon* and watched Judith sing along with him. After a while, the pianist stopped playing and said something to her.

'I can't,' Robert heard her protest, 'I can't, not in this dress.'

And as the tune changed to the *Maple Leaf Rag*, she returned to the table. Everyone was talking and, under cover of the noise, Judith turned to him.

'Robert, there is something important I need to say to you. Can we go outside in the garden?'

It was as if all evening she had been wearing a mask; now it was stripped away and he was startled by the agonised expression on her face.

'Are you cold?' he asked as they stepped outside. It was cooler on this early September evening, the first hint that summer was coming to an end.

'A little, I guess.'

'Here, take my jacket.' He draped it round her shoulders.

'Always fussing, Robert,' she sighed, but her tone was wistful.

'Someone has to look after you,' he replied. As he said the words, he felt a shock of recognition. It was as if, at some subliminal level, he had known what would happen all along and had tried to protect her from it, as once he had tried to protect his sister. Scenes came into his mind: that first impression at Vernon railroad station, of a flame burning too brightly, Judith's earnest expression as she defended romanticism. 'All the heroines in the books I read die young.' The extraordinary intensity about her, the sense he'd had that she would stop at nothing to get what she wanted. And now, there was something she had to tell him, something that was obviously tearing her apart.

With this sense of *déjà vu*, he led the way up the flight of steps that led to the second level of the garden, where the garden's scents were ghostly on the night air. As before, the lights still burned in the dining room and Richard played on and sang. They arrived at the seat under the rose bower.

'So what is this all about?' he asked.

She was silent, staring ahead of her, though what she saw in this gloom he couldn't tell.

'Judith?'

She turned her face to him and he made out her exquisite features. Was she most beautiful when she smiled or was serious, he wondered.

'Tell me.'

She turned away. 'I am going back to America. I can't see what else I can do.'

'I see.'

'I didn't do anything wrong,' she went on. 'I just wanted to live like the books I read. I wanted all this…' she spread her hands, 'colour and sights and life.'

'You have done,' he told her. 'I don't know many other young ladies who have been entertained by Claude Monet.'

She considered this. 'Well I guess there is that.'

'And you've had nearly four months in Giverny, more than you planned.'

'Uh huh, but…'

'You want to stay here, live the bohemian life. You told me, remember? If I could do it, so could you.'

'Yes, but I know now I was wrong and you were right. I don't fit.'

Faintly the sound of the piano came to them and Richard's pleasant voice. He sang: 'I dreamt that I dwelt in marble halls.' They paused to listen to the words.

'Sounds like a sad tune,' she said.

'Yes it is, *The Bohemian Girl*, I once saw the opera, in Bologna I believe it was. Arline sings this song, she's a gypsy who is discovered to be the daughter of a noble man but she always remembers the gypsy boy she loved.' Robert realised the poignancy in this and broke off.

They listened while Richard finished the song, '…that you loved me. That you… you love me still the same.'

Judith sniffed. 'But I didn't, you see, I didn't. He believed I loved him and all I did was hurt him.'

'So that's what it's all about.'

'Michel was a part of everything that didn't come right, but what I am really sad about is that girl I was, the one who danced the Turkey Trot on Vernon station.'

'You will again,' Robert said. 'You'll be the belle of the ball at New York dances.'

She shrugged.

'We can't go back,' he added. 'This is it.'

'Yes, I know.' Her eyes shone in the dusky light. 'I want to say how very sorry I am, Robert. You have been so kind and good to me and I have just been horrible. I pushed you to arrange that picnic so that I could meet Monet, I wheedled my way into his house. I tried to take his daughter's place in his affections and I flirted with a gardener. What more is there?'

'I should think that was quite enough,' Robert smiled.

'Don't laugh at me, Robert. I have been so stupid and you tried to advise me and I took no notice,' she reached for her handkerchief. 'No notice at all.'

She sounded so forlorn, he wanted to tell her: stop, stop, it hurt him to hear her remorse.

'Anyway, you were right. And my parents want me to go, so I am going. I have to face up to who I really am and, I guess, come down to earth.'

He was startled to find how much this affected him. It was as if she spoke of himself, of all the disillusionment life brought about.

'I only meant to help,' he said.

'I know. I had so many dreams but I guess that's all they were, stupid fantasies.' She turned and put her arms round his neck as a child might do.

'Think of me sometimes.'

He felt a lump in his throat. 'I surely will.'

A cloud had hidden the sun and the surface of the river was dark. The afternoon had passed and Robert rose, buttoning his jacket. As he had told Harry, he would miss Judith but he had to accept it was for the best. Now he went in search of her.

'Listen, I want to get away from folks here for a couple of days. How about you and I make a trip to Deauville? We'll have a swell weekend.'

She gasped. 'Oh thank you, Robert, you're a darling.'

– FORTY-ONE –

JUDITH

Passage booked *Mauritania* September 17. All our love Mother and Father. Judith read the telegram once again. It took just two words to spell her defeat, the end of her dream. Passage booked.

Since its arrival the day before, delivered by a boy on a bicycle, she would have found it difficult to describe her feelings to anyone else, let alone herself. There was a kind of comfort, a letting go in her acceptance of her fate. At times, she even found herself thinking of her return to New York; a picture would come into her mind of the busy streets, the streetcars and stores. What new exhibitions would be on show at the Met, would Macy's have their winter stock in? She imagined the excitement in the house on Madison Avenue, Mother engaged in long telephone calls with Charlie's mother. Together they would accelerate the machinery, moving inexorably towards the wedding. What was Charlie feeling as it drew near? She had had no recent word from him.

As she walked through Giverny, she felt like a ghost, as if all that had happened was beginning to seem like a dream, or a story she might hear herself recount in the future. 'I sat in Monet's studio and talked to him of his Japanese prints. He told me about his life with Camille. He sketched me, Monet sketched me.'

If only she could see him once more and say a proper goodbye, she would have some sense of conclusion, but there had been no word from Blanche.

FORTY-TWO

ROBERT

There was a sense of ritual about his preparation of the automobile in readiness for the trip to Deauville. It seemed to Robert as if they were about to enact some rite of passage, complete the sequence that had begun on that June day at Vernon station. He remembered the cloudless sky, Judith dancing the Turkey Trot, her pleasure in the bright hollyhocks, the roses in their summer glory. It seemed appropriate she was leaving as everything began to fade.

As he washed the chassis of the De Dion-Bouton and polished her metal work until it was shiny bright, he was in melancholy mood. He felt stale and rather hopeless, wondering what lay ahead of him, as if Judith had infected him with her zest for life and without her, he would lapse back into the so-so painter who knew he would never go much further with his work.

'I want to make my life a work of art,' she had told him once. She did and wherever she went she would take that luminosity with her, the magnetism that made everyone look at her when she walked into a room, whereas he...

The sun caught the windscreen of the automobile and

he turned to gaze at it. If there was one thing to gladden his heart it was this. What a piece of superb engineering: how she ran like clockwork, obedient to his touch, the sheer beauty of her. His mind turned to the account he had read of the marquis' conception, how it had all began with a fascination with toys, albeit scientific ones. It read like a fairy story: a titled, wealthy man walking in Paris takes a turning off the rue de la Chapelle into little Passage de Léon. He sees a shop with a toy locomotive in the window and is intrigued. The two shopkeepers are engineers who have made a starvation living so far, but have dreams of building a steam car. They are delighted when the Marquis de Dion asks them to build another miniature. Eventually, the company is formed, De Dion-Bouton, and becomes the largest in the world, producing such vehicles as this little darling, renowned for their quality and reliability.

Robert gave the gleaming door handles a final wipe and stood back to admire his work. Perfect! She was a fitting carriage for this jaunt together. He was determined to show Judith everything, treat her like a princess; it would be such a thrill to be at the side of such an elegant, young woman. He could see them walking along the promenade, cheering on their horse at the races, then she in the Fortuny dress, stacking the chips in the casino. Of course, they would win. He would ask the manager of the Normandy Barrière whether the young lady might have a little tour. He had heard so much about the recently completed hotel with its half-timbered turrets and gables, making it resemble a grand English country house. He imagined her expression as they walked through those stately rooms and finished with a cocktail in the garden. He wanted her to have a weekend she would always remember.

FORTY-THREE

CLAUDE

Pre-dawn light slinks into his bedroom, enlivening the paintings on the wall. Their titles are a mantra in his mind: *Haystacks, Gate onto Flowering Cherry Tree, Camille on her Death Bed.* He heaves himself out of bed and pads to the window to watch as another day dawns, the garden gives itself a shake and reasserts its presence. A red stain spreads across the sky. Oh dear, rain on the way.

He dresses, choosing something suited to the city, a dark grey tweed, loosely woven, one of his favourites. A cravat? No. He opens the door of Alice's bedroom but this morning it is not to say good morning to the empty bed but to take a chair and sit beside it. He has things he wants to tell her.

'Listen, *cherie*, and tell me what you think of this. I am going to Paris today to see that nice specialist you always thought so much of. The old Panhard is coming out of hibernation and Silvain will drive me there.'

He stares at the white bedcover with its broderie anglaise edging. The room seems preternaturally silent and he yearns to hear her voice once more, reminding him of how she fell in love with that first Panhard and throve on speed.

'Remember the 937-YZ? All of us muffled up in those

377

fur cloaks I brought back from Norway, gloved to the elbows, and those goggles? What a sight we must have looked. Those picnics!'

He sees the enormous wicker basket stuffed with enough food to feed a siege. 'Remember the terrible roar of that wall of water, rolling in across the mouth of the Seine; the equinoctial tide we went to see? And, oh Alice, remember that journey through Spain to stand before *Las Meninas*, that brushwork, the harmony of colour, shapes and individuals?'

How long has he sat here, lost in the past? Claude pauses by Alice's photograph, brings it to his lips with a kiss. 'How I wish you would be there beside me today, my love,' he murmurs and leaves the room.

– FORTY-FOUR –

BLANCHE

With a shiver, Blanche moved from shadow into sunlight and stood with her arms hugged across her chest. It was beginning to be fresh in the early mornings. So he had gone off to Paris; in spite of all her advice, he had decided to take no notice. When you think about it, why not? Isn't that what he has always done, right from the time he was a child who neglected his homework and filled his notebooks with caricatures? He had told her often enough, and of the day he had packed up his paintings and left home to board the train for Paris. She imagines him, a disorganised youth, spending too much time in the beer hall, but set on the uncertain path of his own choosing. Women saved him, of course, Aunt Marie-Jeanne buying him out of the army, then Camille, his muse and lover. Blanche remembers Camille's wonderful eyes and the unconscious way she took a pose. She finds it difficult even now to accept her father began an affair with Maman before his wife's death. Wilful, always wilful, and she made to feel it was her duty to look after him, that was until the arrival of Judith.

In spite of herself, she had been affected by the young

woman's lack of guilt, that New World culture, which seemed to pay scant attention to duty. Judith. Had she been too hard on the girl? Was there something in her last, cruel words, accusing Blanche of being middle aged and clinging to any remnants of power? She wondered when she would depart on her journey back to America. There was still time to allow her to come to the house, one last time. Maybe, if she had told her father about the letter, he might have stayed, instead of dashing off to Paris. Was she paying him back for his treatment of John Leslie?

There was no doubt, Judith's influence had not been entirely bad, had given him back his courage. Again she had this sense of indifference, why should she care so much?

As she entered the house, there came a tremendous crash from the kitchen, an exclamation. Blanche hurried in that direction and found Annette staring down to where a tray of cutlery lay, strewn over the floor.

'Well really Annette, what is all this?' she began, then realised the girl was unduly upset.

She screwed her fists into her eyes and moaned, rocking her body backward and forward.

'What is it? Blanche cried. 'What is it?'

Annette continued to rock and Blanche took her arm and led her gently to a chair. 'Sit down for a moment and tell me what this is about?'

'Lilli,' the girl stuttered. 'Lilli.'

'What about her?'

Annette gazed at her and Blanche noticed what beautiful eyes she had, hazel with a touch of green and docile as a baby animal.

'She's taken to ordering me about, madame, getting me to carry things for her,' she laughed shortly. 'Anything that's too heavy for her precious arms. A madame, she has become.'

'I haven't heard about any of this,' Blanche remarked, thinking that it was some time since she had had any real conversation with Lilli. 'Why should she be behaving so?'

Annette dug in her apron pocket and brought out a large checked handkerchief, that looked like a man's. She blew her nose loudly.

'Fancies herself, she does. Now there's an engagement in the offing, she thinks she's the cat's whiskers.'

An engagement! So she had decided to forgive Michel, forgiven him and never said a word to Blanche.

Annette was quietly sobbing again, muffled by the checked handkerchief. 'It will never happen for me,' she wept. 'Not with my foot, I'll die an old maid.'

'Oh little one.' Blanche laid her hand on the other's shoulder. 'Who knows in this life? Your knight may still come along and sweep you off your feet.' Oh dear, she thought, perhaps not the best phrase to use.

'It's not what my mother says,' muttered Annette. 'She says she will have me at home all her life; that it is her punishment for something she did when she was a girl.'

Blanche patted Annette's shoulder before moving away. The thought of Lilli moving serenely towards marriage reminded her of Suzanne and her own reaction when her sister was making wedding plans. She understood exactly how Annette was feeling now, disadvantaged, lacking in some vital respect. Oh, the inferiority of the unmarried state.

– FORTY-FIVE –

ROBERT

Pale early morning light, ground mist rising from the road, trunks of trees ghostly in the forest. A warming of the atmosphere, sun filtering through the mist, pink on the bark of a silver birch, orange across a farmhouse roof top; glimpses of river like polished silver, moving cloud patches the meadows, extinguishing, illuminating a field of scarlet poppies. A road among trees, shaft of light through leaves, dapple of sun and shadow on the road ahead.

Mist, piercing light, enchanted, magic, dreamlike. Road empty, dashing along. Autumn, roots, branches; sky, bright, beautiful... clutch glides beneath the hand, taking wing. Impressions. Impressionism. Optical mixing, putting touches of pure colour, side by side, the brain blends the colours to obtain the effect.

The girl's flowery presence, carnation, iris, vanilla, speaking, singing:

> 'Oh go 'way man I can hypnotise dis nation,
> I can shake de earth's foundation wid de
> Maple Leaf Rag
> Oh go 'way man just hold you breath a minit,

For there's not a stunt that's in it with the
Maple Leaf Rag.'

Laughing.

Forest again. Gloomy, trees pressed close together,
undergrowth, mysterious, monochrome; light, rushing
towards the light, dazzle.

'Robert!' Horror.

Robert opened his eyes and found himself lying on the
side of the road, his face pressed into a mound of leaves. He
did not know how he had got there, remembering only a
thump then nothing after that. Raising his head, he saw a
tractor skewed to the left and two men climbing out of it.
He heard their voices, watched them running towards his
overturned car.

Judith? He pushed himself up to a sitting position and
then, when it appeared he was uninjured, managed to get
to his feet. Giddiness for a moment, but he closed his eyes
and took deep breaths. What about Judith?

The men were standing by the car and he hurried across
to join them. Gazing down at the huddled figure, Robert
noticed marks on the pale beige fabric, recognised it as the
same two piece she had worn on her arrival at Vernon
Station.

He knelt down beside her and took her hand, turning it
over to feel her pulse. Thank God! She was alive.

'Shall we help move her out of the road?' One of the men,
the older asked.

'No, it's better she stays here until we can get help. If she's
broken anything, it will only make it worse.' Robert realised
he must take command. 'You…' pointing to the younger
man, who he now saw was scarcely more than a boy, 'can run

for help, a doctor and alert the hospital while you, m'sieur, can flag down traffic, while I stay with the young lady.'

He fetched the tartan car rug, scarcely taking in the ugly dent in his beloved's bonnet, the caved in metalwork. While he covered Judith, he gazed at her face, shocked by its ghastly colour. There was a flask in the car but he pondered the wisdom of giving her brandy. He didn't know what to do, that was what was so awful. He had never been in a situation like this before and felt useless. If only help would come quickly. She still showed no sign of regaining consciousness so he sat there, chafing her hands between his own. After what seemed an age, Judith opened her eyes. He saw her pupils widen, her gaze flicker about fearfully, then up to his face.

'What happened?'

'Shh, it's okay.'

'But where am I?'

She was struggling to sit up but he held her down.

'Just stay where you are, help is on the way.'

With a sigh, she let her body subside and he took her hands again. 'It was a stupid old accident,' he told her. But we've survived, he thought. Thank God, we've both survived.

'A tractor,' she muttered, 'now I remember, it was coming towards us.'

Robert saw that moment again, as his eyes adjusted to the light and the tractor had seemed to appear out of nowhere, too late for him to turn the wheel, take the automobile out of its path. Judith was trying to shift her body.

'Try to keep still,' Robert urged. 'Just for a little while.'

'Robert, I must. My legs seem to have gone to sleep.'

* * *

384

Although Robert protested he felt fine, the doctor insisted he stay in hospital overnight and he was put unwillingly to bed.

'You've had a bad shock, M'sieur Harrison,' the nurse who brought him supper insisted. 'If we let you go home, we couldn't be sure you were resting.'

Robert eyed the sausage cassoulet. 'I don't think I can cope with that.'

'Then eat as much as you can. It's good food and shouldn't be wasted.'

The nurse had a rosy countrywoman's face and small, dark eyes. Her apron crackled as she moved. She bustled round him, propping his pillows and setting a table across his knees.

'How is the young lady?' Robert asked 'Mademoiselle Goldstein. She was in the accident, too.'

The nurse straightened up and looked at him. 'I don't know, M'sieur Harrison. The doctor is going to examine her again shortly, I believe.'

'Her legs,' he persisted, 'There is nothing wrong with her legs, I trust.'

As he spoke, he noticed a change in the other's expression, her gaze shied away from meeting his.

'Too early to say, m'sieur.'

He slept badly. The ward was noisy and there was activity throughout the night, it seemed. Sometimes, he glanced across to the lamp lit night table and saw the nurse seated there, reading. Somewhere in this hospital, Judith also lay. Was she awake too, thinking as he was of where they should be, what they would be doing? For a moment he fantasised, creating an alternative scenario, the drive ending as the automobile entered the town, stopping outside the hotel he

385

had chosen, their stroll along the promenade, the sun sparkling on the sea. He imagined her arm through his, her voice, 'Gosh, Robert, isn't this swell?' Staring into the darkness, it seemed to him the accident was a dream from which he would awake.

'Nurse, nurse!' A call from the other end of the ward and footsteps passing his bed brought him back to reality.

The following morning, when he was up and dressed, he asked to see Judith. The nurse had gone off duty, replaced by a younger, prettier one.

'I'll have to ask Dr Brown,' she said. 'She didn't have a very good night.'

Dr Brown, also quite young and wearing spectacles, invited Robert into his office. He appeared ill at ease, taking off the spectacles only to put them on again.

'It's early days,' he began.

'So everybody keeps telling me. Can you explain?'

'Mademoiselle Goldstein is under observation. There appears to be injury to her legs. Now whether this is temporary trauma or something more sinister...'

Robert felt his heart race. 'What do you mean? What are you telling me?'

Dr Brown brought out a folded handkerchief and began to polish his spectacles. 'I am sorry, M'sieur Harrison, at the moment, the muscles in the young lady's legs appear affected, it is what we call flaccidity.' His eyes without the spectacles were blue and candid. 'There could have been some damage to the lower motor neurones which, in turn, could lead to paralysis.'

No. It couldn't be true, not Judith, lovely, lively Judith who seemed to be in motion even when she was sitting still. He had a mental picture of her, arms flapping in a birdy

386

movement, hopping from foot to foot on Vernon Station. He cleared his throat. 'When will you know?'

'We are calling in a specialist from Paris.'

'So it isn't confirmed yet? Not a hundred percent?'

The young man shrugged. 'Not a hundred percent.' He drew a sheet of paper towards him and uncapped a fountain pen.' I understand Mademoiselle Goldstein is American. Do you have any contact details for her family?'

'Why no, but the Hotel Baudy will surely have her address. She was due to sail for New York in a couple of weeks to be married, I believe.'

'So how long has she been on vacation in Normandy?'

'Nearly four months.'

Dr Brown raised an eyebrow. 'Four months! This young lady must have wealth.'

Robert sniffed. 'What is the good of money if you are reduced to this?'

'Exactly. Poor young lady.'

In silence they both considered this.

Robert asked: 'Have you told her?'

The doctor put the cap back on his pen. 'Not yet, we don't want to alarm her until we know for certain.'

Judith's bed was in a side bay. The nurse drew the curtain and stood back to allow Robert to step in. 'Someone to see you,' she spoke softly, as if to a child.

'Hello Judith,' Robert said brightly.

There were dark smudges under her eyes but otherwise she looked her old self. She had put on lipstick and her hair was combed. She gave him a rueful grin. It was impossible to believe that she couldn't swing her legs off the bed and say 'Come on then, what are we waiting for?'

'How are you feeling?' he asked.

'Okay, just a few bruises.' She held up her arm and Robert saw the purpling mark spread over her forearm. 'A bit of a headache, the doctor told me it was slight concussion, nothing to worry about.' She looked puzzled. 'It's just my legs, the muscles feel so weak, see I can't lift them. And they won't let me get out of bed.'

He stared at the blanket-covered mound in the bed. He remembered her silk stockings, those long legs swung so effortlessly from his car, strong legs made for movement, for dancing. The image returned to his mind again, the movement of her legs as she hopped from foot to foot. He said nothing.

'Robert?'

'It's because of the accident, Judith,' he replied. 'Your body's had a trauma and is reacting like this. It's to be expected.' He met her eyes.

'So it's normal,' she said.

'Yes.'

'I'll be able to take my passage.'

'Of course you will.'

Judith sighed. 'That's good. After all this, I'm ready to go.'

Robert felt tears coming into his eyes. He closed them momentarily, trying to blink them away. He thought: take me back these few hours, play that scene again, let me slow down when I see that bright light at the end of the forest, let it be a few minutes later when the tractor has passed by. Don't let this be true.

'Hey, Robert,' Judith had reached over to pat his arm. 'It's okay. We didn't die, did we?'

'No.' He swallowed and pulled out his handkerchief. 'We didn't die.'

'Then don't cry. There's nothing to cry about.'

But there was: the fragility of human beings, our petty misunderstandings of each other. Blind destiny. Being born is a fate, but knowing how to live is a choice. Maybe he wasn't good at making choices.

'You were right about what you said, Judith, I am afraid of living.'

– FORTY-SIX –

BLANCHE

It turned out that Lilli was related to the nurse who was looking after Judith in Vernon hospital.

'Louise is a true chatterbox, madame,' she told Blanche. 'She couldn't wait to tell me all about the accident.'

Blanche, who was folding some of her father's newly ironed shirts, froze. 'Accident?'

'The day before yesterday, madame, I thought you knew, that young American lady and a gentleman, also, Louise says.'

Blanche closed her eyes for a moment and took a deep breath. 'And where was this?'

Lilli shrugged. 'I don't know exactly, somewhere on the road to Honfleur, I believe.'

What was Judith doing there? And who was the man? Robert Harrison! An image came into her mind of that birthday picnic when he had introduced her to Judith. They had seemed very friendly so it could have been him.

'And they survived, thank God.'

'Well, yes, madame. Oh, it's created quite a stir in the hospital, I can tell you: to have such a wealthy young lady on the wards. The rumour is going about she is an heiress.

Louise said she'd never seen underwear like it, pale peach silk and such expensive lace. As for her outer clothes, the last word in chic, Louise saw a Chanel label. Such a pity about those oil marks though, she says they'll be ever so difficult to get off. I suggested hartshorn but she was afraid to try it on such an expensive outfit. I know what she meant, it sometimes leaves a mark. Then I said what about...'

'Lilli, please tell me the nature of their injuries,' Blanche could not help interrupting. 'Are they serious?'

'As far as Louise could tell me, the gentleman escaped almost without hurt. But the young lady,' a sly expression crept into her eyes. 'Well, that's a different kettle of fish.'

Blanche felt her heart skip a beat. She abandoned any pretence of folding the linen and sank into a chair. 'What do you mean, Lilli? Please be more precise.'

It was obvious Lilli was relishing this moment, basking in the withheld information perhaps or, Blanche guessed, triumphant that her perceived rival was defeated. Slowly, the girl folded and refolded a tablecloth, smiling to herself. Blanche swallowed, she felt sick. Lilli took up another tablecloth and began to fold it.

Blanche's voice was stern. 'Tell me at once, please.'

The expression on the other's face became solemn. 'It's very sad, madame, I'm sorry to say. The doctor called a specialist from Paris, at the expense of Mademoiselle Goldstein, of course. There've been dozens of telegrams from America, from her parents to say that money is no object. So they called the very best doctor they could find.'

'And?' Blanche prompted. 'And?'

Now Lilli appeared genuinely upset. 'He said her legs were paralysed. It is not likely she'll walk again. Ever so

391

brave she was, Louise said. People like us would have been screaming the house down. I suppose that's breeding for you. It seems she cried for a bit and then she said, 'well, Charlie won't want me now.' no-one knows who Charlie is, but there are rumours he is her fiancé.'

'That's right,' said Blanche. 'She told me she had a fiancé waiting in America.' Oh my God, she thought, dearest God, forgive me for whatever I said to her. How unkind I was, this is too much.

'Which brings me to my news, madame,' Lilli was speaking. 'Michel has proposed and I have accepted. We are betrothed.'

She continued to describe her parents' delight, the plans for the wedding, of how, in spite of earlier difficulties, everything was ending 'like a fairy tale.'

Blanche scarcely listened. Into her mind came the image of that letter, of Judith's familiar hand apologising, asking to be forgiven and her request for a last visit before she left. I should have replied, she told herself, I should have allowed her to say goodbye to Papa. What harm could there have been in that? I was wrong. Then she thought, maybe if I had, things would have been different. She might have stayed in Giverny and this wouldn't have happened.

'Madame?' Lilli was gazing at her expectantly, 'If you would, I should be so grateful.'

Blanche could sit still no longer. She rose and crossed to the window, stood gazing over the garden. She noticed how, almost over night it seemed, the colours had changed to richer tones: dahlias, asters and rudbeckia, heralding the change of the season.

'What is it you want, Lilli?' she asked

'You were so kind with your help when I first walked out

with Michel. You dressed my hair and lent me your shawl. Would you please advise and help me to choose my wedding dress? My mother has no idea of style and would have me wear her old dress. But I want this to be the most important day of my life and I want to look as beautiful as I can for it.' Lilli stopped. It was clear Blanche was not listening.

'Mademoiselle Judith Goldstein,' Robert had introduced and the young woman had proffered her hand in such a gracious way, murmuring, '*enchanté.*' Bobbed hair, model dress the epitome of summer with its simple collar, the blue and white birds eye spot silk cravat. Every eye had been drawn to this freshness, this youthfulness... to beauty, Blanche told herself. No doubt about that with her skin, those eyes, the whole essence of Judith. Now she was crippled. What good would her looks do her now? I did not answer her letter, she told herself, I didn't allow her to say goodbye. She was young and had the capacity for happiness. I was jealous of her. I denied her because Monet took my happiness away.

1891

The train ran through lush rolling country as they travelled north; Normandy's pastoral, peaceful landscape with its fields and hedgerows. It was like gazing out over a living painting, Blanche thought, recalling Monet's remark that the source of his inspiration was always nature.

'I've never done anything like this before,' she said.

'Neither have I,' John Leslie replied.

We mean not you and I together and soon to be parted, she thought. They smiled at one another, knowing this was a journey they would always remember.

When they stepped out of the station at Dieppe the air was different, fresh and breezy, filled with the cry of gulls.

Blanche seized his hand. 'Let's go and look at the sea.'

People strolled along the promenade, children bowled their hoops and nursemaids pushed prams. The atmosphere was clear and luminous, impressionist light. Blanche took a deep breath and closed her eyes, intoxicated by the tangy air. The tide was on the turn and they scrunched over the pinkish grey pebbles, down towards a strip of glittering sand. Once, Blanche glanced back to see the imprint of their shoes and thought how soon the returning sea would wash them away. Tomorrow they would have been here and gone away. Enjoy every moment, every smallest detail. The gentle splash of waves breaking on the shore was a background to her thoughts. Remember when this day is over and it is time to say goodbye, always remember this. She met his gaze.

'I know,' he said.

They stopped still and remained looking at each other, conscious of the time remaining to them.

'Let's explore the town,' she said.

'Okay. First stop coffee at the Café des Tribunaux.'

He seemed to know the way and she followed him through the streets to a picturesque junction. A well stood in front of a half timbered building where John Leslie pointed out its small belfry. Inside the café's cavernous depths, they were met by the buzz of voices, French but also English, and saw that many of the tables were occupied. As they found a vacant one and took their seats, they caught snatches of conversation and realised they were in the company of writers and artists.

'Think of it, Renoir drank here, Pissarro, Flaubert and Maupassant,' John Leslie murmured.

Neither of them mentioned Monet although they knew he too had been there.

They talked. They spoke again of small things about themselves and of the past before they had met and more recently, of moments they had shared. They seemed to be completing their story before they each took another path. They didn't mention the future.

Later they climbed up onto the old fortress and walked round its ramparts, then stood to gaze out over the view of town and sea. He put his arm around her shoulders and turned her to face him, gazing into her eyes.

'Oh, Blanche.'

She thought, I can't bear this, I can't.

They ate lunch on the old quay, surrounded by families and to the cry of the fish vendor. There was sole cooked à la Dieppoise with mushrooms and cream, and with it they drank cider. Blanche was surprised at how hungry she was, that she could relish the food so much. The Calvados took the edge off things.

'And now?' she asked. 'Where shall we go? I don't want to be among all these people, any more, I want to be alone with you.'

He nodded. 'I know what we'll do, go to the old fishing quarter, le Pollet.'

It was a perfect choice with its silent winding lanes, narrow flights of steps, walking between brick and flint fishermen's cottages, silent now like children who don't want the day to end. She knew she would remember every step of that walk forever, the terracotta of the brick, the grey of flint. They struck upward and came to a little chapel perched on the cliffs and pushed open the door. The silence within was tangible, dust motes floating in a beam of light that came through the altar window. They peered into its side chapels and admired models of small boats that decorated the walls. Blanche read some of the marble slabs.

'It is a memorial for those who died at sea, all those fishermen who never returned.' She thought of rough seas and storms, of

395

boats lost beneath the waves and these men's souls that had finally come to haven here.

'How peaceful it would be to end your days here,' John Leslie said, as always reading her thoughts. 'I wish we could stay.' He moved closer and took her hands. 'Never go back.'

I can't bear it, she thought again. How can this be happening?

The afternoon was ending, with a last look around the chapel they went out. A wind had got up and battered them as they stood for a moment gazing down to the harbour, then began the walk to the railway station.

The pain was so sharp now; they still clasped hands, but life beyond this place was prising them apart. The current of the journey took them up and rushed them along. At Vernon, the platform was crowded; they walked to the other end. They would part here and return to Giverny separately. Tomorrow he was leaving and she would never see him again. For a long moment they clung to one another then moved apart.

There were tears in John Leslie's eyes. 'Remember I love you, remember all we have said and done together and keep it in your heart.'

Blanche nodded. 'I will.'

She sat in the trap, blinking back tears. She asked the driver to set her down a little distance from the house and completed the rest on foot. When she arrived, she paused for a moment to gaze at the closed door before she opened it and went inside. For a moment it seemed as if the house were empty, then from the dining room she heard voices and laughter. She hesitated, wondering if she would go straight to her room, then with determination turned towards the dining room. As she entered, the family fell silent and all eyes turned onto her. Blanche saw their gaze was uncertain as if they didn't know what to expect of her.

She heard her mother's voice, 'Here she is, safe and sound.'

But it was only Monet she could look at now. His gaze was fixed on her as if he were trying to decide what she had done.

Then Maman rose and held out her arms to her, 'Blanche.'

She leant her face against her mother's shoulder and closed her eyes, feeling her long familiar form. 'Here I am, Maman.'

She heard her say: 'We've been waiting for you, darling.'

Monet rose and held her chair out for her to sit, then everyone followed suit, offering her this plate and that, filling her glass. Marthe gave her a swift kiss on the cheek. The circle was complete again.

She noticed that only Suzanne remained apart from the reunion, as if she did not want to be infected by this defeat. As she met her sister's eye, Blanche understood that while she had lost, Suzanne would win.

She turned back to the kitchen, to Lilli, who now looked anxious. It wasn't the girl's fault. Why should she begrudge her some happiness?

'Of course I'll help you, Lilli. You shall be the most beautiful bride.'

Blanche roamed the garden, she felt she could not keep still. She came upon Michel near the greenhouses with trays of plants, loading them onto his wheelbarrow.

'I hear I must congratulate you, Michel.'

He looked at her shyly. 'Thank you, madame.'

'I hope you will be very happy.'

'Thank you.'

She did not know what else to say so made to move on, but he stopped her. 'A moment, madame. It is said that Mademoiselle Goldstein has been injured, is that true?'

Blanche found herself reading the same guilt in his eyes as she had felt on hearing the news.

'It is true.'

'I am sorry.'

'So am I, Michel, so am I. Listen, I shall visit Mademoiselle Goldstein tomorrow. Can you prepare a pretty bouquet for me to take her?'

Judith scarcely looked at the flowers, a magnificent selection including a few late roses. 'Thank you,' she said, sniffed them then called a nurse to put them into water.

Blanche had found her sitting up in bed in a charming bed jacket. She wore scarlet lipstick. She had been reading a fashion magazine and seemed her usual self, but Blanche could not help glancing at the blanket-covered legs.

'Yes that's me,' Judith remarked, catching her glance. 'Kaput. No more Turkey Trot, that's for sure.'

'You mustn't say that.' Blanche found she was trembling.

'Why not? It's the truth.'

'You're young, medical science is making advances all the time. Who knows, there may be something they can do.'

Judith gave a scornful laugh. 'Know something? I keep on remembering that conversation you and I had once, when you accused me of being a romantic. "You know what happens to romantics?" you said. How right you were.'

'I didn't mean this.' Blanche felt herself on the verge of tears. 'I'm sorry, so sorry. If there is anything I can do?'

Judith was silent for a moment, then she said: 'there is one thing you can do for me. Don't tell Monet you have seen me like this. I want him to remember me how I was, the day he sketched me and told me I reminded him of Camille.'

'Very well, and what about your return to America?'

'Ah, Father and Mother have taken complete control of all that. I'm to have a nurse accompany me and first class travel all the way. My every whim satisfied.' She grimaced. 'But I don't expect to find Charlie waiting on the quay.'

'Why not? He loves you.'

For the first time, Judith met Blanche's gaze. 'Oh madame, our worlds are so very different, more different than perhaps even you know. You were right when you told me that people here take care of each other, they have a sense of duty and strong family ties. It's dog eat dog in New York. Charlie's family would never agree to his being saddled with a cripple. It wouldn't do at all. There's the difference. It has taken this to make me understand.'

- FORTY-SEVEN -

ROBERT

'I couldn't be the one to tell her, how could I when I didn't believe it myself, that she wouldn't walk or dance again? And anyway, it wasn't confirmed then, there was still hope.'

It seemed to Robert, someone else was speaking in a voice that gasped for breath, as if the words choked him.

'So what exactly happened?' Harry urged. He had gone in search of Robert and found him in his room, where he had stayed all day. 'You went to the hospital…'

Robert stared out of the window, down into the garden where a cat lay sunning itself. It surprised him how the world could continue, unconcerned while tragedy occurred.

Icarus and Daedalus, Judith and he, the one reckless, the other fearful. Daedalus made fragile wings of feathers, glued together with wax. They would not withstand the heat of the sun. But the joy of flight, the ecstasy of floating through another element was too powerful for young Icarus and he forgot his father's warnings. Soaring higher and higher still, the wax melted, the feathers fell away and he dropped like a stone into the sea.

'I went to the hospital and gave my name. I said I was a friend of Mademoiselle Goldstein and wanted to visit. The woman on duty gave me an odd look, which made me nervous. Then she said: "I don't believe Mademoiselle Goldstein wishes to see you." Had she taken a turn for the worse? I asked. "No, she is doing well in spite of everything, but I am afraid you cannot see her."'

Robert turned to face his friend. He recalled his puzzlement, his raised voice, and then suddenly Dr Brown was there. The young man appeared more than ever ill at ease.

He drew Robert down the corridor, saying softly, '*Pardon*, M'sieur Harrison, but the young lady will not see you because she says you lied to her. You told her she would walk again. I know,' he continued, 'I know what we agreed, but I believe she needs to put blame on someone.'

'The doctor thinks she needs to blame someone for all this and she's right, Harry. We are all to blame.'

Harry sighed. 'How do you make that out? Come on Robert, don't take on so.'

'She may have looked so confident and she certainly seemed to be able to take care of herself.' Robert stared at his friend. 'But she's so young, Harry, and naïve in many ways. Until she came here, she'd been pampered and petted all her life. Suddenly she's pitched into another world where the mores are so different. She carried on in the only way she knew how, but in the end she couldn't cope. And I...' he broke off, shaking his head from side to side.'I want to tell her I'm sorry and I can't, if she refuses to see me. I want to comfort her. Soon she'll be going back to America and I have to live with all this.'

'Now listen here.' Harry rose from the bed and crossed

the room to lay his hand on Robert's shoulder. 'You cannot take all the blame for this, you'll drive yourself mad if you do. You're right, she is a young lady used to having everything her way. You can't take responsibility for that.'

Robert had a momentary vision of Florence, flushed and excited, dancing to the black fiddler's reel. 'She could be difficult.'

'Difficult! She was downright impossible, she...' Harry paused. 'Hey, there's been enough trouble between us over the past few months. Isn't it time we stopped quarrelling?'

'Yes,' Robert nodded, 'you're right.' He smiled. 'Truce?'

'Truce. Now come down and have some dinner. Starving yourself is not going to help her.'

The following morning, Robert sought out Harry and found him, painting in the studio. He hesitated in the doorway until the other looked round. His night had been spent sleeping fitfully with thoughts of Judith, lonely and helpless in that hospital bed, coming and going in his mind. At times, he seemed to hear his mother's voice: 'take good care of her, Robert.'

Harry said, 'What's wrong? You look as if you've seen a ghost.'

Robert had started up in his bed, pressing his hands to the sides of his head as the images of the two young women seemed to unite, while he heard his parents' sad tone: 'now you're not to blame yourself, son.'

'Harry, I've been thinking. I don't believe I can stay in Giverny. How can I? Life here will never be the same again.'

Harry laid down his brush. 'Shall we go for a walk?'

They went a short distance along by the river until they came to the bench.

'Judith's bench,' said Robert. 'She told me she sat here

when she wanted to work things out. Oh God, when I think about it, she was trying to work things out by herself and no-one gave her any help, we just criticised. I always thought she was really an innocent, too immature to realise her effect on other people. Right from the start, Harry, I had this awful premonition she was in some way doomed. She had so much energy, too much, as if it would consume her.' He turned to his friend, 'I don't know what I'm saying, it's just a feeling I've had all along and now it's come true. I needed to save her from herself and I failed.'

Harry's expression was grave. After a long pause, he spoke. 'Robert I'm sorry. I suppose I didn't understand how much all this… she meant to you. All I saw was a young and rather foolish girl. But it was more than that, wasn't it? Far more where you were concerned?'

He was down by the creek again, Rusty and Florence were with him. It was the time of the slack tide, an hour before it started running He saw himself take a flying leap into the water and felt the initial chill that soon passed. Rusty bobbed beside him. He trod water, calling to Florence to join him. She stood on the bank in her bathing suit with the sailor collar. Then she, too, ran into the water. They swam in circles, laughing and flicking water at each other. He swam further out and she followed him. She was a strong swimmer. He remembered how they swam all through summer, walking along the path from the house on sunny afternoons, carrying their towels and a bottle of lemonade.

'Watch for currents,' his mother said. 'And don't let Florrie swim too far out.'

He couldn't stop her, she did what she wanted and laughed at him if he said it might be dangerous. Over and over again he warned her but she took no notice.

He saw that the leaves were beginning to fall, the grass was browning. The fields were being ploughed and the longer, wider views were beginning to reappear. It was near to the autumn equinox and the tides would be high.

His mother's face appeared to him, disfigured by anguish. 'The silly child, how could she have been so foolish? She knew about the tides, we've told her often enough.'

'I warned her never to go in the water without me. Whenever we went to the creek, I always told her.'

'It wasn't your fault, son.' He had never seen his father cry before. 'I know you did your best but she was so headstrong, so full of life.'

'Oh, she was.'

Robert watched his parents cling to each other. He felt isolated in the thoughts he couldn't voice. Scott, that morning he'd been with Scott.

'Now you're not to blame yourself, son,' they told him.

But the guilt grew and never left him: 'If I'd been there and not lying in the fields with him.'

He could never tell his parents what he truly was. He would leave this town and America, go to Paris and learn to paint.

'You're right, Harry, a whole lot more. From the moment I first saw her, she seemed to embody everything I wish I'd been: her recklessness, her desire to experience life at whatever the cost, her courage, if you like.' He broke off, gazing at the grey surface of the river, for the sun had gone in and the wind was chilly, ruffling its surface. 'Watch for currents,' came his mother's voice in his head. 'Don't let her swim out too far.'

Robert turned back to Harry. 'And what a price she paid,' he said, sadly.

They rose, and in silence walked back towards the hotel.

'You're going to have to deal with it,' Harry said.

'I know, but I can't do that here.'

'Then what shall you do?'

'Go somewhere else. Not America, I won't go back there. Paris, maybe.' He thought of the busy streets, the artistic life. Maybe he would take some more classes, throw himself into his work. Perhaps in time he could forgive himself. 'Yes, Paris, I think.'

'Then I will come with you,' said Harry. 'Yes, Robert, you'd be no good on your own.'

There came a burst of laughter from the terrace where a group sat with their drinks. It all seemed unreal to Robert, like a dream.

'I know what you think of me, sometimes,' Harry continued. 'That I am vain and too full of myself but, for what it's worth, I love you.'

He looked so young and earnest that Robert had to smile. This is my life, he told himself, this is what I have created, this love is what I have. It's not perfect, but it will do.

– FORTY-EIGHT –

BLANCHE

'The days are drawing in,' said Claude, walking back towards the house.

'We're almost at the autumn equinox,' said Breuil. 'Soon it will be too dark to see after four.'

'There is a fine apple harvest this year. We shall have pork with apples and cream, and bourdelots, of course,' said Blanche.

'The fires are laid and ready, madame,' said Annette.

One by one, the fires were lit throughout the house. Rich scents filled the kitchen, of roasting meat and spicy casseroles. The shutters were closed. The last flames of colour burnt in the gardens before they settled down for winter. In the greenhouses, orchids bloomed and exotic ferns thrived, serene in their cosseted climate.

The mist that lingers in the Seine valley hung over the water garden. Each hour was different, from vaporous, foggy mornings to bright, sunny afternoons, and brought its special light onto the pond. The surrounding trees turned scarlet, orange and yellow and dipped their images into the water. The sumac flamed. Every now and then, some leaves dropped, danced momentarily in space, then

406

drifted onto the pond among the lily pads, creating a brocade of scarlet, gold, green and blue. The boat awaited Michel who would come with his net to skim the pond and remove the dry leaves floating on its surface; Michel who was now a married man and an expectant father.

Then the rain fell and the wind rose, extinguishing this ephemeral fire.

So with all the shutters closed, the moon gone behind a cloud and rain drumming on the roof, darkness settled. That year would come to seem to the inhabitants of Giverny the death of a golden era, and for Claude, the advent of Judith, a sunset touch. The nights now were full of wind and destruction; news came of uprisings, of cities besieged, a bloody series of conflicts, names took on new significance, Albania, Thrace and Macedonia.

The trees plunged and bent and their leaves flew helter skelter until the lawn under the paulownia tree was plastered with them. News came of persistent rumours circulated in Novgorod: the anti-Christ was born and the world was about to end; of the 'miraculous' recovery of the young haemophiliac, Alexei. It appeared Russia was ruled by a ménage à trois, Nicholas, Alexandra and Rasputin. The Czar's mother announced, 'I see that we are going by great steps toward some kind of catastrophe.'

Blanche ceased to feel guilty about Judith's letter. There was no use crying over spilt milk and anyway the state of Europe, not to mention Papa's eyesight, were enough to worry about. She kept her word and never told him of Judith's injuries and was relieved when, after a while, he resigned himself she was gone forever.

In front of Claude's studio, roses decided to flower that December. Fragile and valiant they faced the cold nights, there was even one in bud, which asked only a little more warmth to bloom. On Christmas Eve, Blanche prayed to Saint Radegonde for the recovery of Judith. There had been no word. Once more, the sun began its climb into the sky. Crab apple and Japanese cherry offered their blossom to the breeze, like flakes of pink snow. The surface of the lily pond was absolutely still. Standing on the Japanese bridge, gazing at the reflection of the willows, one lost any notion of self and merged into the waterscape. The wisteria bloomed, filling the air with its jasmine like scent. As the lavender toned flowers faded, a second white wisteria took its place. And the lilies, those lovers of warm water and sun, opened in the early morning and closed in late afternoon. The pale lilies charted their random course, clustering together into single rafts of leaves and blossoms, then spreading off in different directions at the whim of the moving water. Some of them changed colour during the life of the bloom. Their luminous effect varied continuously with a cloud that passed over, a freshening breeze, and a heavy shower, which threatened and fell.

The fatal summer had begun. The roses were exceptional that year. They bloomed everywhere, clambering trellises, on fences and trees, on the façade of the house, or among peonies and sweet rocket in the mixed borders. All kinds of colours might be seen, pale cream, pure white, soft yellow, varying pinks, red and orange; light and delight, a golden summer. At this season, among all the peace and loveliness, there was something out of harmony. Shots rang out in Sarajevo. At night, cannon fire could be heard all the way from Bavois. How could one turn a deaf ear, continue, as one moved about the house, or walked in the garden to believe in beauty? The family scattered, only Monet and

Blanche remained to wait the war out, then Georges was invited for luncheon.

At Blanche's request, he arrived an hour earlier, meeting her at the gate to the water garden. They stepped inside and walked along the curving paths, rather overgrown now with the lack of gardeners; only Breuil and Michel remained, the one too old to fight, the other discovered to be too short sighted.

'So, how is he?' asked Georges.

'Very despondent, he worries about everybody, his son Michel, my brother, friends' boys, they are all in the army. He lives in daily anticipation of the post.'

'At the rate these young men are dying, he has a right to be anxious. Apart from the shellfire and the snipers, disease is taking a heavy toll.'

'I know. Jean Pierre has written to us about the men going down with trench fever, it sounds like a very nasty disease. And only the other day, we had news that Renoir's son had been wounded. His mother was so shocked, she collapsed and died.'

Georges paused to admire the petals of a pale blue agapanthus, its round head rising above slender leaves. 'It is an awful, senseless and degrading war. Every time I tour the front line, the stench is appalling: rotting carcases, overflowing latrines, the pervading odour of dried sweat from men who haven't bathed for weeks, sometimes months. Add to that the smell of cordite, a lingering whiff of gas, stagnant mud, cigarette smoke and cooking food… imagine to be forced to live with that, day in, day out.'

They had arrived by the pond. Blanche watched the water boatmen skidding across its glassy surface. 'He follows the armies' movements on a map. He sits in the salon and says he will never leave this place, and if the savages insist on killing him, they will have to do it in the middle of his paintings. To be honest, Georges, all this talk of death is getting me down. We don't see another soul here, it isn't very cheerful.'

For a moment they were silent, gazing on the water lilies, serenely content to dwell in this watery world that was focused on mirroring their beauty.

'What's happened to his water garden project?'

Blanche sighed. 'He says he is unable to concentrate on painting. He feels ashamed to devote himself to pursuing art while so many of our people are suffering and dying for us. At other times, he says he is just too old to contemplate such a huge subject.'

Georges grunted. 'He is the same age as I, and I'm running France, faced with this lack of movement and stalemate. I wish I could turn my back on it.'

They turned and began to make their way back towards the gate.

'He must do it,' Georges said. 'It's even more important now than ever. How can we have any hope for a better future if we bow to death and destruction? We must keep the torch burning.'

As they neared the house, they could see Monet sitting on the balcony, smoking.

'I will try to convince him at luncheon.'

'Thank you, Georges.'

'No, the thanks are due to you. Where would he be without his blue angel?'

'If you can persuade him, you know I'll always be at his side.'

'With a subject on such a huge scale, he will need both your moral and physical support, Blanche.'

410

'I know.'

The Battle of Mons. Stories appeared in the press of a divine intercession, allegedly observed by many soldiers, during the opening action. 'Looking over the barrier, the astonished British saw four or five wonderful beings much bigger than men, between themselves and the halted Germans. They were white robed and bareheaded, and seemed rather to float than stand. Their backs were towards the British, and they faced the enemy with outstretched arm and hand as if to say: "Stop. Thus far and no further." The sun was shining quite brightly at the time. Next thing the British knew was that the Germans were retreating in great disorder.'

Blanche couldn't stop thinking about it. She imagined the instant of shocked silence as the shining figures appeared. 'God is on our side,' she told her stepfather. 'Isn't that a sure sign we shall win this war?'

Monet sighed. 'The British have always had a predisposition to believe in ghosts and spirits. There were heavenly sightings at Culloden and two, I believe, on a battlefield called Souter Fell. It seems to me that this Angel of Mons business is just the most recent manifestation of a long legacy of apparitions on the battlefields of British armies.'

'It has raised morale so much. Surely anything that brings hope and courage…'

'I am with you there. They need all the help they can obtain, poor devils, with this bloodbath going on.'

He continued to follow the battles on his map. In the village, a house that had once belonged to an American painter was requisitioned and turned into a hospital. An endless cortege of stretchers passed by Le Pressoir, bringing the wounded back from the front line.

411

At the height of the war, work was begun on the third and largest of the studios. Many of Giverny's men had been conscripted; it was a hard task to recruit enough to create the lofty building with its huge north-south skylight. Somehow, Blanche assembled a crew of labourers who were either physically or mentally unfit to go into battle. As the construction took shape, she felt heartened by the returning enthusiasm of her stepfather. One morning, he urged her from her breakfast to come and see his latest scheme.

'But Papa…'

'You can have your coffee later. You must see this.'

She eyed the system of awnings while he demonstrated how they could be drawn either partially or wholly across the skylight.

'You see? They allow me to filter and control the flow of light so as to create the natural luminosity of the pond.'

She smiled, happy to hear the strength returned to his voice. 'Ah, Papa, this must be the first time in your life you have actually been able to control light, before it has always controlled you.'

Not long before the studio's inauguration, Georges was again invited to lunch. He looked tired, his shoulders bent as if from the weight of responsibility. He spoke of the armies' exhaustion, the accumulative effect of snatching sleep between trench duties. 'There comes a time when nothing, not food or cleanliness, is as important as closing your eyes. You know you shouldn't. You know, if you are on duty, it will result in court marshal but it is irresistible.'

He brightened at the pop of champagne corks and held up his glass to the construction. 'Magnificent! A splendid achievement.'

Blanche glanced at her stepfather. He was frowning.

412

'You think so?' he demanded. 'It is far too big, I would say. Frankly, Georges, I am ashamed at having allowed that ignoble thing to be put up.'

'Oh come now, Papa, after all this work!'

'I who have always been the first to oppose construction projects likely to disfigure the site.'

Blanche caught Georges' eye and raised her eyebrows.

'What is done is done, my friend,' the politician said. 'You cannot undo it so you might just as well get on with your work.'

At luncheon, Monet had recovered enough to talk about how he would approach the subject. 'I don't intend to work on it piecemeal. I'm ready to try to represent the pond as a whole,' he said over the roast fowl and a salad, laced with so much peppercorn it brought tears to Blanche's eyes. 'Imagine a circular room, covered with paintings of water, dotted with water lilies, to the very horizon, walls of a transparency, alternately green and mauve, the calm and silence of the still waters reflecting the open blossoms. The tones are vague, deliciously nuanced with a dreamlike delicacy.'

'Impressive,' said Georges, pushing some lettuce to the side of his plate. 'What a saga! You created the lily pond so that you could paint it and now you want to have a unique space created to show the paintings.'

'I have to finish them first,' Monet remarked, dryly. 'I often wonder whether I have enough time left.'

Blanche and Georges exchanged a glance. Was he descending into one of his dark moods?

'Don't talk nonsense, my friend, You're a little child in comparison with the likes of Frans Hals.'

'That's a foolish comparison, I have nothing like his talent.'

Oh dear, Blanche thought, it sounds as if I am in for a few days of cheering him up.

Nevertheless, the work progressed and Blanche was drawn into this dreamy world of tranquil beauty. The green and mauve that Monet had envisioned were present, but woven into a complex range of yellows, pinks, whites, deep blues, and ochre. She prepared his canvasses, which were mounted on dollies. At his instruction, it was she, the physical presence Georges had predicted, who wheeled them about the studio, arranging and rearranging the sequence of the paintings.

She was aware he was calling upon all his experience and a lifetime of observation to tackle something so immense. The gigantic size of the canvasses demanded a different approach. Working with a large brush, he would introduce the dominant colour of the motif while drawing in the principal form of the composition.

'These underlying rhythms are important,' he told her. 'They animate and unify the different canvasses within a sequence.'

As she had expected, there were days when he despaired and these usually coincided with weariness.

'I'm too old,' he moaned. 'Today I worked until I could no longer hold the brush and what have I achieved? They can say what they like, I am not a great artist.'

'That's ridiculous, Papa, it will be a *tour de force.*'

'They are so large, too large for me to cope with. I cannot reach to the lower areas near the floor.' He patted his stomach. 'This will not allow.'

'Well, you must admit you have always enjoyed your food.'

'I know, and this is the result. It was all very well when I

414

roamed the fields and painted in the open air. Now a walk to the water garden is about all I can manage.'

They were sitting on the balcony in one of their moments of *détente* when there was nothing but friendship between them. Blanche had carried out some freshly made mille-feuille to eat with their tea.

'You can't abandon it, Papa. Can you imagine Georges' reaction? We are all setting such store by it.'

He shrugged. 'What can I say? The spirit is willing but the flesh is weak.'

She gazed at the hand he had laid on the table, dry, horny skin, it represented a lifetime working with paint, long hours outside in the sun and the wind. He was moving towards eighty, of course he was finding this a strain, not only that, this war was weighing on him. And they had said it would be over by Christmas!

'Then I will help you, in any way I can. At very least, I can do the backgrounds. I can still get down on my hands and knees, thank God. Just show me what you want me to do.'

He met her eyes, his own bloodshot and weary. 'Oh Blanchefleur, would you? I've taught you well enough, haven't I? I'm sure we can do it together.'

It was as if the intervening years had disappeared; they were back together, working side by side. She crouched near the floor, painting in the backgrounds. It was hard work but she was enjoying it. The light was gentle, filtered through the awning; time seemed suspended as they painted hour after hour, while beyond on the battlefields of France men died.

'Remember what you said to me once, Papa? That we shouldn't work together as I would become too influenced by you? Well now, it's paid off. I challenge anyone to tell the difference.'

'*Vilaine!* If you think you're so good why don't you paint the whole thing? Then I can take a little rest.'

'There is only one Claude Monet, Papa.'

They joked and bickered while they painted but there was an intensity about their work together, engaged in this massive project, a feverish desire to recreate an expanse of water without boundaries, realm of the water lilies' floating world. As Georges had said, it was a riposte to the savagery beyond Giverny, the wasteland of the battlefields, and the slaughter of youth.

Blanche was also delighted by the deepening of friendship between the two men. About once a fortnight, Georges would travel to the house, to discuss progress with the panels, view the work, then stay for as long as he could. It was a great joy to her to organise these rendezvous and listen to their long, friendly discussions. However hard Georges was working, he always found the energy to urge her stepfather on.

'You know sometimes I think all this is beyond me,' she heard him confide. 'It's an impossible task.'

Georges clapped him on the shoulder. 'Courage, my old friend, paint the impossible.'

The following morning before he left, he came to find her sitting on the grass, under the paulownia tree. She was reading to little Michel but broke off when she saw him.

'Don't let me disturb you.'

'Not at all. Michel, say hello to Mr Clemenceau. He is a very important gentleman.'

Shyly, the little boy held out his hand, which Georges took, looking questioningly at Blanche.

416

'He is Lilli's child,' she explained. 'Lilli was once my laundry maid in the house and their father is one of our gardeners. Michel here is my godchild. Yes, you may go and play,' she continued. 'But remember, Maman will be here in a little while.'

They watched the child, engrossed in bumping the little wooden train over the grass.

'She must have been a very special laundry maid,' he remarked, 'for you to take so much interest in the child.'

'She was – is – pretty, intelligent and sweet natured, she deserves the happiness she's found.'

'And you, dear friend? Have you found happiness? There was a young man once, I remember, before you married Jean.'

'John Leslie, yes, I loved him very much. We might have been married if...'

'If Claude had not prevented it, there was a great fuss at the time, I recall.'

Blanche smiled. 'It was a long while ago.'

'If you had married him, do you think you would have had children?'

She considered this. 'I've often wondered but I really don't know. We were both painters, you see. There was always this conflict between life and art. You might say we were even rivals. Children could have got in the way.'

Georges nodded. 'From what I've seen, it's not easy to be an artist and lead a life that's not affected by it. I think of poor Van Gogh, Verlaine, Rimbaud.'

'It's difficult to find a balance. I can remember being absolutely unable to concentrate on painting for thinking of him. It was one of the things that angered Papa about John Leslie. He couldn't support another man having that kind of influence over me.'

417

'But you're painting now,' Georges commented.

She darted him a suspicious look. 'What do you mean?'

'You're helping Claude with his panels, aren't you?'

Blanche turned her face away to watch the child. 'No I'm not. I wouldn't dream of making a brush stroke, it would be a sacrilege.'

There was a pause then Georges said, 'I am glad I don't paint but I, too, would like to create something. Yes, I have the children but I want something more. When we have smashed Germany, I shall retire to somewhere wild and deserted and make a garden.'

Blanche and Monet were in the studio from dawn until dusk and the panels grew in number. Their effect was remarkable: the cropping of the lily pads and flowers at every edge, made this aquatic world appear to extend beyond the frame and even beyond the scope of the viewer's sight. Where the water lilies were most thickly painted, they appeared to float on the reflections and on the open spaces, their swirled lines created by a loaded brush.

With the second battle of the Marne, the war had reached a turning point and Georges was in an optimistic mood, crowing that the Allies were trouncing Germany.

'And then, if I have anything to do with it, we'll make the Bosch repay all they have destroyed.'

Monet told him he wanted to make a gift of the series to France, it was the only way he could think of to contribute to the victory.

'I've come to a decision. I certainly don't want the paintings in the Jeu de Paume but I agree to their being installed in the Orangerie. I like the idea, especially as I used to stroll through the Tuileries Garden when I was a young man. And it's near my beloved Seine.'

He unfolded a sheet of paper to demonstrate his detailed plan. 'Not one circular room any more, I have changed my mind about that. I shall require two oval spaces with an entirely glazed roof, which means the whole thing must be designed by an architect and rebuilt.'

Georges examined the plan in silence. 'I see what you mean, you are painting the pictures from a particular point of view, which can only have their final impact if they are displayed, as you suggest, and point up the effects of light and depth.'

'Exactly. I am inviting the viewer to take a tour of my water garden, thus it is important to consider the height from which the eye will fall on the water lilies.'

'You are going to a great deal of trouble,' Blanche told Georges as they strolled in the garden.

'And so are you, dear friend. It cannot be easy to live with his moods.'

'It is his failing sight that upsets him so much.'

'Yes, I've noticed, particularly lately, it is affecting his work to a much greater degree.'

'And he will keep on retouching. I tell him to stop but he is obsessive about it. He won't realise he is in danger of spoiling them all.'

'I continue to think he should have those cataracts operated on, you know.'

Blanche sighed. 'I don't think you'll ever persuade him to undergo that. He's so terrified something will go wrong.'

Autumn was approaching once more; the nasturtiums had practically taken over the central path. In spite of Breuil's and Michel's efforts, the reduction in gardeners made it hard to keep on top of the work. In the distance, they could see Michel struggling to control a rambling rose.

They walked on until they came to the patch of lawn and sat down.

'Apropos the cataracts, there's something I've often wanted to ask you. A few years ago, I came for luncheon, one day. We talked of Claude's eyesight and he spoke of an American girl. The two of you seemed to be at loggerheads over her.'

'Judith,' said Blanche. It felt odd to say her name, though she still thought of her, sometimes. 'Judith Goldstein, yes.'

'She seemed to have quite an influence on him.'

'Yes, she did, for a while.'

'And you didn't approve.'

'Oh well, one over reacts sometimes.'

'Knowing you as I do, it didn't seem like over reacting. What was the problem?'

Blanche found it difficult to conjure up the powerful emotions she had felt, the anger the young woman had provoked in her. It all seemed so long ago and, with the current state of the world, rather pointless.

'She was so different,' she said. 'She came from another culture where women are much freer. She enchanted Papa, that is certain. I think she enchanted most of the people she encountered while she was here.'

'Except for you.'

'For a while, I was fascinated by her way of seeing the world. She aroused questions, made me reflect on my life and how I had lived it. She gave me doubts at a time when I was feeling so unsure of myself.' Now that she had begun, Blanche recalled her resentment of Judith, of her seeming ability to choose her destiny without consideration of others' feelings nor with any sense of responsibility.

'And now?' Georges prompted.

Now? What did she feel? Contentment, conviction of

where her true path lay. Judith had been partly responsible for that. She had revealed to Blanche the strength of the tie to her stepfather when it had risked being usurped. She wondered what had happened to the young woman on her return to America. There had been no word from her in all this time.

'Now, I wish her well. She was very young and the young can be reckless. I hope that, in some way, her life has worked out for her.' She realised she meant what she said.

– FORTY-NINE –

BLANCHE

October and November brought rain, strong winds, and even sleet and snow. In spite of these setbacks, the Allied advance was sufficient to ensure the signing of the armistice in that railway carriage in the chilly, drizzly Compiègne Forest, to come into effect at the eleventh hour on the eleventh day of November 1918. And as high pressure settled over the continent, in the following days the sun came out. At Le Pressoir, Blanche was alarmed when Monet had a fainting fit brought on by the cold. By his birthday, however, he had recovered well enough to celebrate the glorious victory with Georges who had abandoned his desk to come to see him.

Eight months later, on Bastille Day, they abandoned the studio and travelled to Paris to attend the Victory Parade. With hindsight, Blanche almost wished she had not gone but Papa had been so eager. She had anticipated the pageantry and music, the hordes of infantrymen, and glittering breastplates of the cavalry. She marvelled at the foreign legionnaires in their white kepis, turbaned Moroccans, the immense Senegalese and Algerian and Indo-China riflemen. She tapped her foot to the battle hymns as the Allies filed past and *Over There* was succeeded by *Tipperary*. Then the hero of Verdun appeared, the pale, austere figure of Marshal Pétain on his white horse, majestic in dress uniform. Behind him, marched men from all of France's 21 army corps, their bands playing *Sambre-et Meuse* and *La Marche Lorraine*. But while the crowd broke into a frenzy of joy and thanks, of cheering and flag waving, spontaneous dancing and singing, her mind returned again and again to those men who had led the parade, they had been almost unable to do so. The worst wounded, lacking eyes and limbs, shuffled along with canes or in wheelchairs. Many of them were covered in bandages from ghastly head wounds, or were still green from gas. At their sight there were gasps and tears. It started as a victory celebration but, for Blanche, the sight of those wretched men turned the whole thing into the gloom of mourning. While these living soldiers filed through the Arc de Triomphe, one could tell that in many people's minds, the army of the dead marched above them. How many people in that crowd had lost a loved one, she wondered, and how many still retained the hope of his survival? When you considered so many had no known grave, wasn't there the possibility that some might be still alive?

There came the clanking of tanks, spewing noise and exhaust as they passed under the Arc. In spite of their success in battle and importance to the war, they brought up the rear of this great parade. Were they no longer important to Europe's generals and politicians? Was it true, as she overheard an onlooker remark, 'A sight like this will never be seen again because there will never again be a war.'

She turned and met her stepfather's eyes. His expression was incredibly sad.

423

Not long after, Georges came to stay for the weekend. He looked grey with exhaustion but nevertheless, he suggested a tour of the water garden, 'to see peace and tranquillity once more.'

The three of them paused on the Japanese bridge, gazing down at the green reflections of the weeping willows.

'The war may be over but France has so much to mourn,' her stepfather remarked. 'The soil has been ravaged, railways torn up, roads destroyed... it will take a long time to recover.'

Georges sighed. 'Those war wounded are not the only burden facing us. Think of all those men returned from the trenches, blaming us for four years of destruction without cause. We are exhausted and don't know how to answer them. And where are those with youth and energy to take our place? They're either lying dead in the wasteland of Verdun, or among those terrible war wounded we saw in the parade. I'll tell you something, Claude, there is only one thing for it, Germany must be made to pay for the war.'

Although Blanche tried to dissuade him, Papa wanted to see for himself what had happened to his beloved countryside. The following day, they drove to Verdun, in Georges' powerful automobile. She was sickened by what she saw. Where once there had been a landscape of peaceful fields, farms and village, now all was laid to waste as if it belonged to an alien world. There seemed to her no sign of humanity, woods and roads wiped out and the ghostly marks where village stone walls had tumbled together.

'Nature has been murdered,' her stepfather wept.

Georges said he wanted them to drive on to see something else. 'Ypres. It is quite far, but if I put my foot down on the accelerator, it shouldn't take too long.'

424

He parked the vehicle at the foot of a path that sloped gently upward. In silence they walked to the little flat plateau of a hill. Here they paused and gazed downward.

'Oh, how beautiful!' Blanche cried.

The field lay spread out before them and, clustered among the disturbed earth of burials, were poppies, their delicate, vibrant red flowers fluttering in the breeze. They spread out towards the horizon like a scarlet sea.

'Poppy seeds can lie dormant in the ground for a long time,' Georges said quietly. 'I spoke to a local farmer and he told me that. Remember those warm months we had in the spring and summer of the war years? The ground was disturbed by the fighting and the seeds began to germinate, and *voila*, all these poppies.'

'Papaver rhoeas,' murmured Claude. 'The corn poppy, flower of remembrance.'

Into Blanche's mind came the lines of the poem she had read a short time ago.

> *We are the Dead. Short days ago*
> *We lived, felt dawn, saw sunset glow,*
> *Loved and were loved, and now we lie*
> *In Flanders fields.*

Remember, Blanche told herself, these sleeping heroes, and remember that I have loved and been loved.

Over the next few days, as she worked in the studio, though continued to stress to Georges, she was only preparing the canvasses, this sense of peace and reconciliation grew. Calmly, she looked back to that last day with John Leslie, recalling it down to the smallest detail. She saw them walking on the beach at Dieppe, how she

425

had looked back at the imprint of their shoes on the strip of sand, committing it to her memory for when the time would come to say goodbye. She remembered the noisy café but how, in the midst of all those other people, they had seemed to be alone in their own secret world. They had talked as if they were completing their story before they went their separate ways. She saw again the shape of his face as they stood on the ramparts and he gazed into her eyes. The lunch they had with the splendid sole and her surprising hunger, the walk in the fishermen's quarter; those Pollet cottages, the terracotta of the brick, the grey of flint. They stood in the little chapel, and she felt again the moment they had both sensed the peace of souls at rest and wished they could stay there, too. Perhaps they had, she thought, perhaps a part of them remained safe in that cliff-top haven.

'Remember I love you, remember all we have said to each other and keep it in your heart,' he had said as they parted. She recalled the joy and the pain that had followed, now both had faded. It had happened and nothing could ever take it from her.

There had been such a sense of homecoming, that night when she rejoined the family. Now as she stood in the kitchen, she seemed to be revisiting it, a kindness, a warmth like her mother's arms around her. Blanche felt a wave of affection for her stepfather. There had never really been a choice because she could not cut away that half of herself, which painted and belonged to Monet. She wandered round the house, into the library, the salon, opened the little pantry cupboards to peep inside, familiarity wrapping itself around her. She arrived in the dining room, for once untroubled by the yellow paint. Soon they would sit down to supper and bicker over painting then laugh, or eat in companionable silence. Tomorrow, they would work together again and continue to work until the panels were finished.

Blanche looked round the room, at the empty chairs, the table set for two; she met the veiled gaze of the geisha women on the walls. This was her home.

ACKNOWLEDGEMENTS

My heartfelt thanks go to

Clare Christian who has shared with me the journey of writing Monet's Angels and given me her generous support, advice and encouragement. A truly wise book guru.

Jan Huntley who opened my eyes to the life and times of Claude Monet and gave me a unique viewing of his house and garden.

Andrew Kidd who has safely navigated us not only to Giverny but on many other journeys.

Sheba my beloved black cat – my constant writing companion and perfect stress buster.

ABOUT JENNIFER PULLING

Jennifer Pulling is a writer, playwright and journalist who has worked for many national newspapers including the *Guardian* and *Telegraph* and magazines ranging from glossy to tabloid. Her travel features have been published widely in the UK and abroad. Her most recent plays include *End of Story*, which examines the relationship of Harold and Primrose Shipman and her latest, *Swallow*. Previously published books include *Feasting and Fasting, The Caring Trap* and *The Best of Taormina*. Her next non-fiction book tells the story of her work with the stray cats of Italy and will be published in 2015. To find out more about Jennifer Pulling please visit www.jenniferpulling.co.uk.